THE CLANSMAN

STUART LINDSAY

The Clansman

By Stuart Lindsay

Dedication:

To Tee, for the bacon sandwiches and cups of tea.

To the men and women in HM Submarine service.

To my Dad, for that time we tried to work out how far the Roman Empire would have got had they won at Carrhae.

To my wee brother Ross, even though you aren't so wee anymore. I'm still better at FIFA than you.

To Bruce the cat; my XO on Elite: Dangerous, co-author on this, choice maker on Mass Effect 3, assistant manager on Football Manager and lover of gammon steak. Miss you, wee man.

This is for you.

Acknowledgement:

This book, none of my books, would be possible without the help of a lot of people to shout at me along the way.

My thanks, as always, go to the men and women of my current boat who got really excited, or at least pretended to, when I said I was writing a sequel.

To the UCs who cut the bio and the TS's that track it and brought these characters to life with their dits.

As always, to my Dad for teaching me to read and write as well as remember that just because somebody says you probably can't do it, doesn't mean you shouldn't try. Second year English teachers can be wrong.

Table of Contents

Map

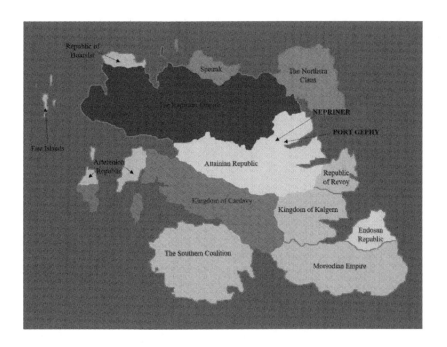

Prologue

Nepriner was nothing more than a shadow in the distance, a black shape of hate and broken dreams amongst the windswept plains. A pall of smoke still hung over the city like a black shroud where the armies of Rupinia and her cohorts had tried to burn out the Cardavian legions and Attainian regiments. All their bombardments and sacrifice had seemed to serve was to construct nothing more than a close quarters urban nightmare.

The snow had settled like a thick, white blanket over the plains that provided no comfort to the seventy thousand survivors of two Imperial armies. He hawked and spat onto the ground, wrapping the tartan plaids around his large frame to try and bring some more warmth to his cold body. His thoughts were dark. The flower of the Empire had been broken upon those walls, the men dashing themselves against them like a vessel with no steerage does against rocks. Quittle had watched it all like a cuckold husband, unable to affect the outcome and unable to voice his concerns.

He turned back in the saddle and looked south again at the column, the detritus of baggage and other non-essential kit littering the road to either side of it. There were also, nearly everywhere he looked, the lumps and bumps in the ground which signified where men had simply sat down and froze to death. He could, if he squinted, just about make out the shape of the rear-guard who were desperately trying to fight off the harassing probes of Cardavian and Attainian cavalry. They were no longer the soldierly body they had been in the summer when they had come sweeping south with the fire and sword, their trumpets blowing and standards streaming behind them. Now they were a collection of men held together only by flimsy oaths of loyalty who happened to be travelling in the same direction at the same time. If the Coalition really wanted to then they could wipe out the entire army on the march and encounter little resistance.

How had it come to this? How had an army, an Empire, that had never known defeat suddenly find themselves completely and utterly outclassed? They had victory within their grasp! They had finally breached the walls, had wiped out the greater part of the Coalitions manpower, had killed three of their leaders and isolated the civilian leadership with tales of treachery. They had only needed to take the damned citadel! How had General Beran Corus and his men held out against them when everything in military science had pointed to the siege being another easy victory for the men of the Empire?

He turned about again and looked forward, placed as he was in the middle of the column of defeated men. The Empire hadn't known a setback like this, hadn't known to be rebuffed as badly after they had invested so much time and effort into gaining something. Nepriner had been besieged for five months and had seen two full Imperial armies camped before its walls and fighting within its streets. He glanced at the figure of Field Marshal Neard, once again surrounded by his Staff Officers and ensconced within their own little world. He cursed the man having had such high hopes for him.

The Field Marshal was a man who loudly proclaimed his own knowledge and lofty ideals, would loudly proclaim that he didn't like sycophants and toadies. He would go on in great detail about his service to the Empire in times past when the Republic was still a threat. How then, Quittle thought, did he bollocks this operation up so much? Granted, he had managed a lightning march through the north eastern territory of the Outer Republic, but his subsequent operation outside Nepriner had been amateurish at best. He had only attacked on one side for weeks on end, throwing his men at the wall as if they were a child's toy. He had refused, point blank, to use native Rupinians with their heavy armour and consistently used the lighter Clansmen when assaulting the wall. He used cavalry, willingly, in a city and was then surprised when they were next to useless in the close confines but continued to use them anyway. Every setback he received, rather than doing something about it or going back to the planning stage and starting anew whilst time was on their side, would see him surrounded by the self-same sycophants he was enveloped in now who would reassure him that next time the plan would work.

Quittle was a herald of His Imperial Majesties diplomatic and as such wasn't in a position to affect military strategy. However, he was also a clansman. The youngest boys within the clan, as well as being given lessons in maths and language, were taught their histories and military strategy at an early age. They were taught how to use weapons as if they were extensions of themselves during their play fights and other physical activities. They were raised by the Clan for the Clan, and it was the same for all the clans of the north. They were bred for war, had grown up with the training and knew it by sheer instinct. Military strategy and theory came naturally to a Clansman, particularly one as well educated as he had been.

He remembered the day when they had finally launched the siege towers at the wall. He remembered with an alarming alacrity when the Clansmen had been packed into them and sent onwards as nothing more than a diversion. He remembered as the hulking monoliths were slowly brought up to the walls and used as target practice by the defenders of the city like it was a nightmare he couldn't stop. He would always picture in his mind seeing men of his country and even his clan come screaming out of the burning wooden shelters, their skin blackened and their plaid on fire, as they sought a puddle in the ground to try and douse the flames that licked at them. He remembered the images, and he knew for as long as he lived he would continue to do so.

The most galling thing about this sacrifice, this waste of manpower and life, was the fact that it was merely a diversion. It wasn't meant to succeed, and even if it did then it would only be by happy chance as a secondary objective. They were going to be used to simply divert attention away from the battering rams and the sacks of black powder that the men of Speirak had brought with them. The sacrifice of so many young men and friends had bought them a large hole in the wall, something that they didn't even exploit fully. In short, it seemed, they had died for nothing.

He growled under his breath as he shifted his seat on the saddle trying to find a comfier section and get some feeling back into his numbed arse, cursing inwardly as his leg touched a piece of leather which was freezing cold. He cast his glance towards the men of Speirak, taking a sadistic delight in seeing the men suffer underneath their light, brightly coloured tunics. They were more suited for their warmer climates in their deserts and jungles back home, not at all suited for this winter terrain that was more like the climes of the peninsula that the Clans hailed from.

"You look lost in thought, Bear." Quittle turned in the saddle at the use of his nickname and saw his friend Tortag pulling up alongside. The man had the appearance of a badger these days due to the silver streaking the formerly coal black beard, something that was only emphasised by the streaks of ice and snow that coated it.

"I am sick and tired of this, Tor." The man nodded and looked along the column, seeing his own unit of infantry trudging along in the snow. There were no complaints from the clansmen other than the fact they couldn't play their pipes, the powers that be believing that it would only serve to demoralise the Rupinians and the Speirakians within the force. There had been grumblings at that, darker complaints than those that usually accompanied an order which wasn't entirely popular with soldiers, and that had taken Tortag by surprise.

"At least the lads brought their gaiters and winter gear with them, unlike those stupid Speirakian bastards. That lot couldn't organise a piss up in a brewery, and they were about as much use in the siege as a glass hammer!" Quittle nodded, a small smile beginning to tug at the edges of his mouth but a thunderous expression still around the eyes.

"You look as if you're about to explode and kill someone if they so much as look at you in the wrong way." Tortag guided his horse around the upturned remnants of a cart, anything useful and salvageable from it having been looted long beforehand. He wondered whether it was a cart that once belonged to the Imperial army or whether it had been one belonging to a refugee who couldn't make it to Nepriner on time. "Now, talk to your friend Tortag and tell me what's wrong?"

"Tortag the Clansman or Tortag the Imperial Officer?" Quittle heard himself say, cursing his mouth as he did so. As a diplomat he should have known better than to voice his frustrations and show what was in his thoughts. He turned about in his saddle and saw the dark look crossing his friends face. "I apologise. That was out of order."

"Apology accepted." The man said, taking a deep breath to calm the feeling of anger rising in his chest. He exhaled slowly and watched the warm air flow like a thin mist out of his mouth.

"For what it's worth, speak to Tortag the Clansman."

Quittle looked at him, almost struggling to find the appropriate words. He realised what he was about to say wasn't appropriate at all, no matter which he phrased it. What he was about to say, if he were to say it to anyone else, would be considered sedition and, especially given the circumstances, would probably see him given a drumhead trial and hung at the nearest tree as a warning to all would be rebels.

"Do you remember when your lads were pulled back from Port Gephy and forced to go onto the siege towers?" He watched his friends face as the expression changed from a more neutral one to one of consternation.

"Aye. I remember. I barely escaped with my life, and most of the lads over there were lucky enough to come out of this disaster with the skins left on their back." In fairness, Quittle thought, the clansmen had done particularly well in coming out of the siege with most of their original stores. They had been jealously guarded, particularly when the first onset of winter had come on. The knowledge that warm clothing and other supplies were going to be a rare commodity had proven a massive incentive to protecting their kit.

"Do you remember the meeting of the chiefs?" There was a sharp look at that from Tortag. After the catastrophe that was the siege towers, Quittle had asked for the chiefs of the clans' regiments to meet him in the heart of the highlanders' side of the camp. They had gathered in the tent unsure of what business was to be conducted, only to hear from a man who was supposed to be the voice of the Emperor himself that it was time to strike out and head for home. He wanted them to throw aside the cloak of allegiance that they wore and declare independence for themselves. There was outrage amongst some, calculated silence from others, and support from one or two. There was no sense of unification amongst the clan chiefs gathered there, but then that was an age old problem when it came to the men of the north.

"I remember. I also remember telling you, Bear, to not even think about such things. It wasn't the time then, and it isn't the time now. Right now

I'm more concerned with getting my lads back home to their loved ones rather than declaring ourselves outlaws." He paused, wishing for a second that he had a warm drink. "By the Gods, Bear, have you thought what would happen to our families if we did that? The Rupinians have outposts throughout our lands, we're damn well occupied for all intents and purposes! A rebellion would die on its arse quicker than you would like."

"But you've thought about it?" Quittle asked, a small flame of hope beginning to burn in his chest. He would need manpower, not a lot though, to begin fanning the flames of rebellion until the metaphorical brush caught and the entire thing became a conflagration whereby the Empire would have to cut ties with its unruly northern lands.

"Yes, I've thought about it." Tortag was silent for a few moments, running it through his head, as he thought over the problem. "Look, let's just get ourselves home first and then we'll work out what we can do. You realise if you mention this to the wrong Chief, and bear in bloody mind you've mentioned it to all of them during that gathering, that you'll be hung, drawn and quartered for a treasonous rebel?"

"Some things are worth dying for, Tor. Look at us. We're the finest soldiers they have. You remember your history as well. We threw ourselves in with the Empire when it became obvious that the Attainians were just using us as fodder, as a meat shield to protect their own bloody soldiers. We were told that would never happen again, we were told that we would be valued and that our history and traditions would be respected." He looked to his north and saw the remains of a village, the broken beams and charred remains of buildings now coated in snow.

"Are you telling me we should sacrifice our men and our friends for shiny baubles and little treats? Are we men of the north to live like dogs forever begging for scraps from our masters table?!"

"I'd advise you to keep your voice down, Bear." Tortag looked at his friend with concern in his eyes. He had seen him passionate before, and what man of the north couldn't claim to be passionate, but he had never seen him wear his heart on his sleeve like this. Quittle was always a man who took the calculated risk and one who had weighed up all the options and understood the options available; he wasn't one to suddenly sign his own death warrant on a whim or a passing fancy.

"How long have you been thinking about this?" Tor asked.

"Since we began the march south and Field Marshal Neard decided to take no prisoners. We aren't murderers, Tor, we're not meant to make war on women and children." He remembered the columns of refugees that had been overtaken and slaughtered to the last person by the Speirakian light cavalry, the bodies surrounded by their worldly goods and things that they thought they would need in their new lives in the south. He remembered especially the young woman who had died shielding her infant children, one of whom still clutched a doll in her hands even as her brains slowly slid down a burnt farm wall. "The siege towers and the conduct of the siege was the final straw."

"You won't feel any differently when you get home?"

"I have no idea, but I do know that something needs to be done."

Chapter One - **Triumph**

A triumphal procession was something he had never taken part in before, and it was something he never hoped he had to replicate again. It was good to savour the glory, and it was fantastic to be back in Silveroak alive and whole in body, but the depleted Legions behind him were testament to the hardships that the Cardavians had had to live with for the last five months. There was a lot fewer here than should have been on parade. A Cardavian legion should muster some five thousand men apiece and, therefore, there should have been twenty thousand men here in their best kit having put blood, sweat and tears into making sure that anything that was supposed to be shiny was as reflective as a mirror. Cloaks were to have been brushed and shields were thickened with enough paint to add several new layers of protection to the hard wood and leather combination. Instead, he was lucky if there were some six thousand men with him now.

The legionaries behind him marched in unison, grins on their faces as they waved to the public and handed out tokens or favours. A few of the bawdier whores and prostitutes were offering their own versions of favours as well and were met with ribald jests and songs. Tavern owners would come out with mugs of ale and watered wine, thrusting them into the passing soldiers' hands who were only more than happy to take it off them and enjoy the hospitality. Beran was mounted at the head of the column just behind the massed bands of the four legions with Velawin as head of the Kings Own, Grimfar as head of the Eagles and his brother Dunwal as head of the Marshal legion. Each man wore his cloak bearing the colours and insignia particular to their own legion.

The Standards bearing the emblems of the four legions were held aloft in front of all, the same colours that men had fought and died for when they were in Nepriner. He hadn't saw fit nor right to replace them and therefore they were still bleached from the sun, carrying blood stains and smoke damage. He wanted the public to see them, and more importantly the politicians who were gathered at their final destination, to know what the Cardavians had been through. It wouldn't make an ounce of difference to them, he knew, but it was the principal of the matter. Perhaps it would make them think twice before sending legions in piecemeal fashion to an environment that needed saturated with soldiers, perhaps it would make them think about the Islanders and Highland legions which were currently deployed in Nepriner waiting to repulse the next Imperial attack come the Spring or early Summer; or perhaps it would serve no other bloody purpose than to put someone's nose out of joint within the higher echelons of command.

Beran waved and grinned at a passing tavern owner, someone who he was pretty sure either Aleill or he actually owed money to. The man in turn simply smiled and waved back until a flash of recognition crossed his expression. Velawin caught the look that the landlord had on his face and turned around in his saddle, his hands resting on the reins of his horse as he cocked an eyebrow at him as he caught on as well. Beran just simply grinned and winked, determined finally to enjoy the moment and live in the here and now.

"I reckon Aleill will have to settle his debt with that bloke soon enough!" Beran shouted at Vel with a grin fixed onto his face.

"That's if he'll ever talk to you again! I think the silly bugger thought he was going to be up front here with us." Beran turned in his saddle and looked down the route of march and saw Aleill and the hulking figure of Erallac riding on horseback in front of the Grey Wolves legion. The Wolves had taken pride of place, marching at the front of the column, and the two men could be seen even from here bickering away quite happily.

"I reckon if he doesn't keep his mouth quiet for another thirty seconds then Erallac will make sure he never speaks to many people ever again!" Dunwal said, eliciting a laugh from the three other men present. The senior officers present who had managed to survive the siege had grown extremely close during the course of it and knew enough about one another to write a large novel on the strengths and foibles of each other's character. There were people who should have been here, Beran knew. Men like Trent who had fallen by the eastern gate when the Imperials had finally undermined it and damn near wiped out the Attainian Sentinel regiment. Trent had held it long enough for the defences to be stabilised and for the men to regroup in other areas that needed to be shored up. There was also Lord Ironside who had been instrumental in bringing the defences of Nepriner up to scratch. All Beran felt he had done, and it was in this he recognised his own sense of self-deprecation, was simply hold the men together. It was a point he had brought up with Talice when he had first received notification that the King had commanded there to be a triumph and that Parliament had duly followed it through with a very quick vote. Beran had claimed that there were others more deserving of the honour, whilst Talice had told him to 'Shut up and enjoy the glory'. He grinned at the memory, knowing that she would be sat with the King and the Queen now at the base of the Royal Palace with pride etched all across her face. He would see her soon enough for that is where they marched.

"How are things with you and the wife?" Vel asked, almost as if he were reading his thoughts.

"Going well! She's getting used to living in Silveroak and I'm currently getting used to being in the city without necessarily going to a tavern every other night." He smiled when he remembered a slight disagreement they had when he had said to her that it would be expected of him to go drinking with people every other week, she had responded by saying that if that was his intention then she may as well stay in Nepriner. There were teething problems, but then when wasn't there when two people were adjusting to entirely new settings? A month previously their sole goal in life was to stay alive for the duration of a day. Being under siege with the nigh constant threat of death or disfigurement tended to put a different shine on things.

"Tell you what as well, it's nice actually having a house even if it is still living in barracks." As the commanding officer of a legion he was entitled to his own private house within the barracks, something that he had never actually taken before but now found prudent. It allowed them to save for a proper house of their own as well without having to worry about paying for repair and maintenance costs, a bill that Beran made sure was picked up by the treasury.

"Any chance at children yet, brother?" Dunwal said, waving to a young lad who had dressed up as a soldier for the occasion.

"Not for want of trying!" Beran said with a grin, eliciting a loud laugh from Grimfar. Grim was the newest one to become involved with the small cadre of senior officers having served with the Eagles right from the start of the war.

He was a Section Officer, risen up from the ranks and had taken part in the bloody last stand that had occurred in the Attainian village of Turgundeon. He had taken command of the remnants of the Eagles legion when the entirety of its command had been wiped out in the battle and, with help from his friend Nekstar, had managed to guide the survivors and several hundred refugees who had been left behind to the safety of Port Gephy. He was a quiet man, initially thought of as one given to introspective thought, but it was evident that once he got to know someone that he was more than happy to give voice to his thinking. Beran liked him, which said a lot.

"How you finding being in the capital, Grim?" Beran asked the man as they rode on. They were within sight of the main Temple areas now where priests were calling down blessings on their heads. It made a pleasant change, Beran felt, for the pious idiots were normally asking for peace throughout the continent and generally decrying men who took part in his trade regardless of why they were doing what they were doing. They were dressed in their finery now, all in white with their large domed hats carrying their staffs of gold inlaid with emeralds and all manner of precious stones.

He wasn't a religious man by any stretch of the imagination, indeed he tended to have a strong dislike for organised religion in its entirety, but he realised it would do some of the men good. Others, and he knew there were

16

people like him within his ranks, would see it as just another part of the triumphal ceremony to get past.

"It's bigger than I imagined. I've never been here before, always been based out of Nights Wood."

"That's out east, isn't it, near the border?" Beran asked, Grim nodded. "Been there, had a couple of friends that were based there once so I went down to visit them. Good area for drinking."

"Nek and I were planning on getting beastly drunk tonight, as it happens, but I think the King has sunk those plans." Grim wondered, and it happened to worry him when he noticed it, that he had adopted some of the nautical slang his friend Nekstar had picked up during the course of their stay within Port Gephy. The sea battle that they had borne witness to when the Republican fleet smashed the Imperial blockade was perhaps one of the only things that Nek hadn't complained about during the duration of their campaigning in Attainia. Grim had to chuckle as he remembered that Nek had even found reason to complain during the march home when the supplies they had received from Ardwyn hadn't turned out to be fresh oysters and larks tongue or whatever it was he had been expecting.

"If it's any consolation," Vel began, "I don't think any of us are looking forward to it. Beran might, he's used to hob-nobbing with royalty."

"Never met the King in my life, or any royalty for that matter, not even when I gained command of the Wolves. I don't think you've met him either have you, Dunwal?" Dunwal shook his head to the negative even as he continued to look forward. The road they were travelling down was long and broad and was lined on either side by well-wishers and families. The people around here weren't as earthy as they had previously seen, coming now to the religious districts and the main areas for business and commerce. A large temple was blocking the road off at the end of their march with the marble steps glistening after a recent downpour of rain. They would turn right and join onto the main thoroughfare where the crowds would be at their thickest. The Kings Road would lead them past the parliamentary buildings and then straight onward to the palace.

"I don't suppose you know what the form is, sir, do you?" Grim asked.

"No, your best bet is to ask Aleill when we are finished here." Beran answered as the standard bearers began to wheel about to the right. There was a loud cheer from the waiting crowd as they saw the first of the military round the corner. "He's minor nobility through his father and will certainly have a better idea of how to conduct oneself in front of royalty. I'm guessing that scratching your arse mid-meal and belching the national anthem will probably not be welcome."

The massed military bands of the four legions began to thump out the marching songs of the four different Legions in accordance with the order of march, the massed trumpets and drums raising the atmosphere within the streets to a fever pitch as they rounded the corner.

"Right gentlemen, backs straight and ride with a purpose. We've got people to impress now, and every bloody eye will be on us," Beran said, a fixed grin on his face as the four horsemen rounded the corner themselves. The view from the bottom of the Kings Road was spectacular with a straight view all the way to the palace with all the important buildings in between. Beran was reminded, somewhat, of Nepriner and how it had the Republican way leading from the Citadel and the keep there all the way to the north. He knew from his history, and his own reading, that Attainian culture had done a lot to influence the cultures of the kingdoms and empires that dotted the continent, but it wasn't until now that he could truly appreciate it.

The barracks of the Kings Guard was a squat looking series of granite buildings at the bottom of the road and nearest the turning. Beran thought it was completely at odds with the rest of the buildings hereabouts, the rest tending to be ostentatious in the extreme as embassies vied with each other for grandeur and design. A lot of the buildings, barring those that were extremely tall, however, were hidden from view by the temporary seating that an army of workers must have set up during the course of the night. There was no traffic on the Kings Road, something rare in one of the main arteries of the city and the kingdom itself, and the only ones who were on it were the legions. They had pride of place today, and by the Gods they had earned that pride!

The band was beginning to pass the main parliamentary assembly, a building made of red sandstone that had darkened considerably over the years giving it a deep burgundy colour. It was six stories in height with six pillars supporting the peristyle on the exterior of the building. The roof of the building was topped, first and foremost, by a large domed copula at the top of which was a golden weather vane carved into the shape of a bull; the heraldic symbol of the Royal family. The roof also held bronze statues of famous statesmen and women of the past, notably those who had either done something in the name of science or expanded the borders without losing an entire army in the process; most had turned green with age. Beran had only been in there twice; once to accept his commission making him a loyal friend of the King and a trusted officer, and the second to accept the command of the Wolves. He turned left in the saddle and faced the building as he was going past and threw a salute at the royal standard which flew at the mast. A loud cheer from the crowd greeted the gesture and Beran found himself smiling along.

His eyes focussed on the distance, seeing the original wall which surrounded the palace of the King. Silveroak was originally one of many tribal settlements in the area, a small gathering of farms and villages that eventually developed into the greatest kingdom on this side of the continent through the judicial use of diplomacy and violence in equal measure. The city needed to defend itself and, at least initially, the castle where the Warlord sat was the greatest treasure that the land held. Now, of course, royalty had ideas and the title of Warlord was now King and Cardavy didn't go storming throughout the lands trying to grab as much of it as it could for itself. Everything had become a lot more civilised. Beran often wondered whether it was easier and simpler in those days, particularly when political interference would be at a minimum, but figured that legionary commanders of old probably had their own problems to contend with.

The wall surrounding the palace was built from large blocks of tuff that had been expelled by an old extinct volcano a dozen or so miles east of the capital. The man hours, the sheer amount of man power and labour that had to go into building the old fortresses wall, must have been tremendous and never failed to amaze Beran. He had never been inside, however, and this was to be an entirely new experience for him. The castle that the wall protected loomed over all, much modified over the years from a purely functional building into the palace it now was. It still held some defensive purpose, thought Beran as he viewed it with a military eye, but he wouldn't like to try and attempt to hold it like he did the citadel of Nepriner.

"I take it that's the bloody Kings Guard legion then?" Grim quipped. There was a long standing rivalry between the legions and those that were in the Guards. The Guards were seen as an easy draft, little or no duties outside the city and were generally only employed for ceremonial function. Their billets were said to be the best quality and, more importantly, the rations they enjoyed were second to none. "No wonder their cloaks are so bloody white, they never get the damned things dirty."

"Don't let Erallac hear you say that, he was proud of his time in the Guards. I still think it's the only reason the Wolves know how to march in a straight line; better than the bloody Marshals anyway." Beran said with a wink and a grin towards Dunwal. He merely smiled back as they began the slight climb up the slope that led to the drawbridge which was extended over the moat separating the palace complex from the main city.

"I don't think he's biting, Ban." Vel said with a smile, referring to the nickname that Aleill had overhead Talice calling Beran when he had regained consciousness after having been wounded by the blast of an explosion from the black powder bags that the men of Speirak used to blow up the northern gatehouse.

"I can't believe you lot are still calling me that."

"Now that's a bite!" Dunwal said with a grin. The massed bands of the legions came to a crashing halt and began to split off to either side of the drawbridge. The standard bearers waited at the entrance to the gatehouse, the colours of the four legions fluttering in the mid-afternoon breeze with the sun catching the golden emblems atop the staffs. The four officers pushed on. The legions wouldn't be able to squeeze into the palatial complex and certainly wouldn't manage to get across the drawbridge without raising a few concerns that the wooden structure would collapse, therefore it was up to the standard bearers and the four commanding officers to take the thanks of the King and the gratitude of his court. They rode underneath the large gateway and Beran couldn't help but remember when he had ridden out from the relative safety of Nepriner to meet the herald of the Imperial forces and discuss terms. It was entirely separate circumstances, and yet there was a degree of similarity to it that he found surprising. Then he felt as if he were a rabbit waiting for the sharp talons of an eagle to pierce his back, such was his sense of isolation, and now he felt the same given that he was in an entirely new set of circumstances that he wasn't used to.

The entire complex seemed to be thronged by the white cloaked Guards with every man standing statue still in the same pose of attention. They were within sight of the palace now and could see the large gathering on the stairs. Beran wondered, for the briefest of seconds, whether he was expected to ride his horse up the stairs or dismount at the bottom. He began to seriously wish he had listened to the master of ceremonies and actually took in what he said rather than treat his words with a degree of flippancy. They reached the bottom of the steps and Beran took the decision to dismount from his horse. He slid off the back with a degree of ease, but the old shoulder wound he had sustained during the siege caused him to have a sharp intake of breath. It still niggled at him occasionally, particularly during the colder weather. Winter had, so far, been mercifully kind to Cardavy.

He looked up the marble staircase and saw the great and good of the realm gathered there. He saw the King in front of the throne, his young Queen at his side. He instinctively felt himself about to run his hands down his uniform to make sure everything was straight before stopping himself. He heard the men dismount around him and waited a few seconds before ascending the steps. He couldn't see Talice, not yet, but he knew she would be watching him from the top of the stairs. For him, time had slowed to a crawl and the sound of silence within the area was almost deafening. He was aware of the brightness of the sky underneath the afternoon winter sun, he was more than aware of a flock of pigeons that had decided to settle at the top of the palaces roof, and he wondered what he should be thinking about at that particular time.

When he was a young officer he remembered they had spent an entire morning on the drill square learning how to climb a set of steps in the official manner, shortly before the pass out parade. It struck him as a ridiculous farce now, and he hoped he thought it was a ridiculous farce at the time, but it suddenly began to niggle at him whether he had done it in the correct manner this time. Was there a Guards officer likely to be hiding behind a statue, ready to jump out and decry him as a fraud simply because he didn't keep his arms locked to his side whilst he ascended the steps and because he didn't take the first step with his left foot? It was a preposterous thought. He reckoned that he should now be thinking of the glories and the laurels he had won, the medals of bravery and honour and all the other sundry awards that would ordinarily make most people happy. However, what he wanted to do now, more than anything else, was to crawl into the ground and get this entire charade over with.

Yes, they had beaten the better part of two Imperial armies, but they could have done so in a better fashion. They had lost the entire city! The only reason he was here now as part of a triumph rather than as a man who was being ransomed and coming with terms on behalf of the Emperor Rhagan I was the fact the relief, no matter how bloody late it happened, had actually appeared. It had been a damn close thing, and he couldn't help but think that as he ascended the last few steps. It had been a damn close thing in a city which would probably have been better off if they hadn't actually been there in the first place, but then where would the line be drawn?

The Empire, or at least the Rupinian driving force behind the Empire, wouldn't be happy until the last of Outer Attainia had finally been brought to heel and the Republic itself becoming nothing more than a puppet state. Nepriner was a symbol for both sides; for the Republicans it was where their glory had started and for the Imperials it was their birth right.

Cardavy had to be there, otherwise the Attainians would have collapsed. It was, therefore, a philosophically minded Beran that bent the knee to his King. He heard the words to stand and looked directly into the eyes of the man who controlled the lives and destinies of millions of men, women and children. He found himself at a loss of words for once, not overwhelmed by the situation but certainly wondering whether it would be prudent or not to say that it was nice that the weather had held out. He was rather given to understand that it was royalty that broke the ice; surely that was one of their main tasks these days?

"General Beran Corus of the Grey Wolves legion," the King spoke eloquently, "Your country salutes you and your men. You have defied an Empire and saved a Republic. You fought odds which few men had even contemplated fighting and managed to do something rarer than that; you managed to win. How do you feel?"

"Bit out of place if I'm being honest, sire." It was honestly said, a little too honestly judging by the looks a couple of the senior politicians nearby threw at him, but the King smiled with genuine humour at the blunt speaking soldier.

"Prefer to be out on the field, eh? I remember my short time with the legions, when my father was King. We know you'd rather be out in Silveroak just now with your men. Tell me," the King asked with a curious expression on his face, "how did you feel when you thought that you would have to make your final stand in the citadel?"

"I…well, to be quite honest, sire, I don't know how I felt. I was a little scared, I grant you, but I was more worried for my wife. I am a soldier, sire, and therefore have come to terms with death and wounding. I'd rather avoid it," that raised a chuckle from a few around him after the King laughed, "but my wife was there, and it would have been a rubbish honeymoon for her if I were to fall at the last. It would have made a more interesting story though, certainly goes against convention!"

"Surely, sir, you deserve a happy ending?" The Queen asked him with a quirk of a perfectly styled eyebrow. He had never really looked at her before, had never obviously seen her in person, but he was struck by the elegance with which she carried herself. She was slender and fair, but not frail and, having lived within the political circles and inner sanctum of courtly ritual that surrounded the King in Silveroak, Beran assumed she was astute and intelligent.

"I got mine, ma'am, but I lost friends in the process and a lot of good men. Whilst it was a happy ending, it was bittersweet."

"You didn't answer the question, General, how did you feel?" The King steered the conversation back to the original question. Beran didn't know how he was expected to answer, certainly not without offending someone who was gathered there, and he wondered why the King was so curious to know. He decided to be honest, to be anything else would be to go against his character.

"I was angry, Sire. We had fought long and hard for the city and a lot of lives had been lost up until that point. We had been promised relief, we had been promised that the city wouldn't have to be held for any longer than three months. In short, sire, we were lied to. I had to justify to my men why we were doing what we were doing. I had to tell them, and our allies, that their sacrifice was worthwhile. I had to order them, when abandoning sections of the city to the enemy, to desert their wounded comrades and friends."

"Very frankly said, General." The King sounded impressed, which was a good thing, but judging by the looks of the higher echelons of the military gathered hereabouts he knew he had stepped on too many toes. "No," the

King finally said, "I am glad you answered honestly. Your reputation precedes you of course, General, your wife did say that you were the equivalent of a hammer when a small chisel will do when it comes to diplomacy."

Beran decided not to push his luck anymore, not with so many present. Candid honesty between friends was one thing, but between subject and ruler it was entirely different; once or twice could be refreshing whilst the third time doing it would be impudent. He smiled at the King instead and bowed his head slightly, noticing Talice watching him from the shadows for the first time. She wore a smile on her face, but the eyes were warning him not to push it any further. She was within the crowd of officers who had gathered at the top of the stairs and therefore she was, without doubt, in a better position to judge the crowd than Beran was.

"Well, General, it is time to receive your reward," as if on cue a steward brought forth a velvet pillow upon which sat a golden torque. A second man was standing behind him bearing four new sets of colours for the four legions that had been assembled all with the legend "Nepriner" inscribed upon them. "For services rendered to the Kingdom and our allies, we are delighted to award you with this golden torque as a symbol of our appreciation. It has been well earned in the most dangerous of circumstances and your men have done you proud. For that service, we have awarded the legions within the campaign a new battle honour to be worn on their standards.

"They can be proud of what they have achieved, and they will be an example to all our legions in the forthcoming campaigns against the Empire." Beran didn't see so much as felt Velawin stiffen next to him. They knew that they would be possibly going back to Outer Attainia, but nobody had expected it to be this soon. "We trust you will be coming to the feast later on, General Corus?"

"Of course, sire, I wouldn't miss it for the World." The King smiled and beckoned Dunwal to step forward to receive his reward, followed by the rest of the officers. Once the awards had been handed out with the men sounding duly grateful they were turned about to display their prizes to the crowd which had followed them across the drawbridge and stood at the bottom of the steps. They held their prizes aloft whilst the King looked on like a doting and proud father. The ceremony and the triumph were over, but now the political and social quagmire that was the feast loomed fast in the minds of the four officers.

"Will Aleill be there?" Talice asked as she adjusted the necklace that she wore in a mirror. She wore the same dress that she had been wearing when she was finally reunited with Beran in Nepriner. It was still a source of constant delight to her that everything had developed as well as it had, especially when it seemed as if everything they had done and sacrificed had, at one point, seemed to be in vain. The necklace she wore was another simple one, for she was never one for flamboyant displays of wealth, and was a three tier apple cut design upon a slender platinum chain. It was a rich piece and she admired it with quiet pride in the mirror before adjusting her long red hair. She noticed that Beran hadn't been paying attention to her words, instead seeming to be lost in thought as he watched her dress her hair. "Well?"

"I hope so. I told him all the senior officers of the legion had been invited, and you know what he's like when it comes to the social scene and rubbing shoulders with the greatest of the realm. It would take a pack of wild horses to drag him off in the opposite direction," Beran gave a chuckle as he stood up from the couch and walked over to the small trestle table and poured a glass of red wine for each of them. He passed one to her and she smiled her thanks as he kissed her cheek, running his hand across her bare shoulder and feeling the softness of her skin. "Anyway, Aleill would never skip the opportunity to have a free meal because he's massively cheap. He'll probably try to launch a political career tonight as well."

She chuckled at the thought. Aleill and her had not enjoyed a lot of time together during the course of the siege, the two having various duties to attend to. Whilst Aleill had been fighting the Imperials and trying to deny them the wall, and then eventually streets, she had been busy organising first aid parties and the medical facilities within the town. It had been a stressful time for her given the amount of death and maiming she had come across, but she felt that as the daughter of a Senator of the Republic that it was only right she try to do her bit. She wouldn't fight on the wall, for that was not where her strength lay, but she would give assistance wherever she could and providing medical care was the best she could do.

Aleill and her had become friendly during the march south, however, and she found him to be a witty and charming companion when he had a mind to be. He was obviously in the legions for a short amount of time, but his natural abilities and leadership qualities had seen him rise to the point where he was able to command the archers attached to the Wolves. A thought struck her, "How will Erallac cope?"

"That's half the bloody reason I want to go!" Beran said with a grin as he settled himself back onto the couch. He knew he would have to get dressed soon and looked at his parade uniform with a degree of loathing. No soldier liked to get into parade dress more than once a year, however, he did enjoy the fact that after his recent deployment it seemed to fit him better than it had in a few years. It was often quite funny, during ceremonial divisions, to see soldiers who hadn't been keeping up their physical standards quite as stringently as they should when their parade dress was skin tight. He remembered innumerable times seeing men having to get their friends to help them out of under vests or having to loosen the straps that secured their innumerable buckles.

"What do you mean?" Talice asked with a smile, enjoying seeing Beran relax and be in good spirits. She had worried about him initially when they had come back, for it would be the first time that they lived together without constant Imperial bombardment or fighting off hordes of Clansman and Speirakians. However, married life had come naturally to them. It helped that they had been seeing each other for four years prior to her disappearing to her family estates for a year, but the two just naturally felt comfortable in each other's company. Her main worry was that he would quickly become bored without the stresses of command and leadership to contend with every day, but thus far her fears had proven unfounded.

"Erallac doesn't do civilised," he said with a smile, "He pretends to do it, and he can carry it off for a little while well enough, but eventually he will turn round and tell someone that they are talking shit or being a pompous arsehole. He's brutally honest, especially with a drink in him."

"Sounds a bit like you, Ban," she said with a knowing smile, putting an earring on her left ear and catching the sparkle in the candle light.

"It probably explains why we've been in trouble so many times!" She chuckled with good humour as she fitted the last earring before finally taking a sip from the wine.

"You need to start getting ready, Ban, otherwise you'll be late. I'm given to understand it doesn't do well to keep royalty waiting," she said standing. She herself had barely got started and was about to start putting on her make-up on. She watched him with the mirror as he drained the last of his wine and stood up, his hands resting on his knees as if he were propelling himself up. She saw him approach the parade uniform with an almost hostile expression on his face. "You look good in it, Ban, it suits you."

"A soldier who is fit for parade…"

"Isn't fit for a battle, I know. Believe it or not, Ban, but I do listen to you when you keep going on and on." He grinned at her and walked over, his arms encircling her waist as he crouched onto his haunches. He nestled his head into her neck and gave it a kiss, "And this isn't the time. You need to stop procrastinating."

"You are worse than some bloody drill instructors, you know that?" He said standing up as he moved off again to the uniform. He picked up the grey tunic and slid it over his head, making sure it the fitting was correct before he put on the well-polished parade armour. He looked to the other armour that was nearby, placed on an old tailors dummy with a wooden cross piece going through it.

"You'd love to have me as a drill instructor."

"I'll grant you that they've never looked as good as you. They tend to be bullish men who are rather thick about the neck and even thicker when it comes to intellect."

"Do you think that you spoke perhaps too freely to the King earlier on?" She asked realising that the question had been niggling at her since the parade. She had been proud, prouder than she thought herself capable, when she saw the column marching up the Kings Road. When the four standard bearers and four horsemen had come through the gate, she thought her heart would burst. However, when the King asked Beran how he felt when the citadel of Nepriner became the last line of defence before the slaughter, she had felt the icy finger of dread slowly slide down her spine. She knew her husband, she knew fine well that the man could be diplomatic when he wanted to be, but she also knew that he liked to annoy people. His answers to the King weren't necessarily designed, she felt, for the Kings ears but rather the men around about him. Beran wanted them to know that he blamed those in power for their bad handling of the relief and everything that it entailed.

"I don't think the King thought that way, and that's the main thing, Tal. The King wanted an answer, an honest one at that, and he already knows of my reputation. I have enough allies within the higher echelons of command to know that I won't lose my command over this, if that's what it is worrying you."

"It is and it isn't. What about life after the Legions, Ban? You cannot be a soldier for the rest of your life."

"Toady up to them?" The parade dress was nothing like the normal armour that he wore, and he wouldn't trust the kit he wore now to stop an infant with a pointy stick let alone a Rupinian with several inches of cold steel and a grievance. The breast plate he wore was emblazoned with the sign of a wolfs head in mid howl, the cloak a dark grey with fur lining around the neck. The trousers he wore were a dark woollen material, rounding it off with a pair of brown leather calf high boots with a golden belt looped round his waist where his scabbard would normally hang. He decided the entire ensemble could do with more chainmail for added protection, but then he was likely to face a battle of words and wits in the Kings hall rather than one of swords.

"What do you think?" He said turning around to Talice.

"You look as if you're ready for a fight rather than a meal," she said, running a critical eye over his uniform. She slid behind him and picked up the grey cloak and placed it over his shoulders, fastening it in place with a golden chain. She held up the heavy helmet, noticing that the nose guard modification Beran had made to it during the siege was still there. She quirked an eyebrow at him but he merely shrugged his shoulders when he took the offered helmet from her.

"That helmet saved my life more times than I would have liked during the siege," he looked at himself once more in the mirror and moved over to the couch, surprised at the mobility of the uniform as he was able to sit down on the couch. "Anyway," he said as he thought back to her question, "I haven't thought about life after the legion. I know what I would like to do, but I'm not sacrificing my principles just to have an easier time of it, Tal, wouldn't be right."

She nodded as she made the final preparations to her own dress. She knew that he wouldn't; he wouldn't be the man she married if he did, but she did sometimes think that he deliberately made life difficult for himself. He didn't like to play the part of the martyr, nor would he particularly suit it if he did, but she did think that he could sometimes make it easier for himself. She turned around and looked at him, seeing him watching her as she smoothed down her dress and making final adjustments.

"You make a man tempted to disobey orders from his King, Talice."

"I'm from a Republic, Ban, I'm meant to," she said with a grin, as he slowly stood up. His arms encircled her waist as he kissed her on the mouth, her tongue darting out in a teasing manner before she skilfully pulled herself. "Enough of that. We have to go."

Chapter Two – **Hungover**

Grimfar woke with a hangover and a curse, his face stuck to the pillow of his bed as he tried to instantly recollect what had been done and said the previous night. A moment of fear struck him as he tried to remember whether he had said anything rude or insulting to the First Lord, or Gods forbid the King or the Queen, but he assumed that given his door wasn't being knocked down that he had managed to avoid a major incident.

He dared to raise his head from the comfort of the pillow and immediately cursed, his voice coming out as a hoarse croak as light streamed in through the open window. Sounds of the street instantly filtered in as if on cue and he turned about on his back with a great effort.

It was only then he realised he had no idea where he was.

He sat up with the impending hangover suddenly abating, but not fast enough to suggest that it had gone for good. He looked around his surroundings and saw that the room he was in was reasonably kept and that the bed linen he currently lay under was clean and tidy. This, in his mind, was all for the good. He had woken up in too many places too many times not to appreciate clean linen and a lack of smell.

He quickly scanned the room for his discarded uniform and saw that it had been neatly piled up, which suggested to him that somebody else had done so. He knew how he acted when he was drunk and he knew he wasn't the tidiest of people, the clothing would have been discarded in a large pile on the floor for himself to worry about in the morning. The door began to creak open and he instinctively felt the need to jump under the covers or dive for the open window, half expecting an angry husband or father to jump through brandishing a club.

"So you're alive then. I'm surprised after the skinful you had last night!" She was a pretty lady with dark hair that was almost black. It seemed to shimmer in the light of the morning sun. She had a half smile on her face and a glint to her eye and he noticed that they were a deep brown colour. He realised he had absolutely no recollection of her. His bewilderment must have reflected on his face for the lady cocked her head and sat down on a stool next to a dresser, "You can't remember a bloody thing, can you?"

"Not really. I was in some state, apparently," he said realising that honesty would probably pay out best for him here. He could blag like the rest of them, and what man of the legions couldn't blag when it came to reporting something that had quite obviously gone wrong, but he figured the woman before him was too shrewd to be taken in with light words and an easy smile. Nekstar was better at that sort of thing anyway.

"How much do you remember of The Imperial?"

"The what?" He asked, completely oblivious to what she was asking. He looked again at her properly and wondered if she was some sort of spy, lest why would she be asking about some bloody Imp?

"The Imperial; it's a tavern." She saw the complete lack of understanding emblazoned across his face. "Okay, we're off to a good start," she said with an exasperated sigh. He noticed she had brought two steaming mugs of tisane with her and she passed one to him even as she took a sip from her own. "Do you remember who I am?"

"At this point in time, miss, I'm finding it hard enough to remember who I am!" He tried to say it with a winning smile, but expected it came out as more of a grimace. She wasn't impressed either way and his blatant attempt at going on a charm offensive had backfired. "I am really sorry. I haven't had much opportunity to drink lately."

"Yes; you said at great length last night. Shall we start anew?" He was at a disadvantage to dictate terms so he merely smiled and nodded, "I am Katrin, and I was enjoying a quiet evening with some friends when you and your friend stumbled through the door of the Imps demanding 'drink, song and a decent laugh' or something. Anyway," she said with a smile playing upon her lips showing pearl white teeth, "you seemed in high spirits and funny so we invited you and Nek to sit with us and you decided to stay for the rest of the night."

He looked at her for a few more moments as mental images of the evening blurred through his mind, fragmented images and half-truths combining to form a semi-decent picture of the nights' adventures. It was true enough that he hadn't had a drink in ages, at least not before the events of Turgundeon, and therefore his tolerance of alcohol was obviously a lot lower than he previously remembered.

"I didn't insult anyone, did I?"

"Apart from not remembering who I was?"

"I did say I was sorry."

"I know," she said with a small smile again, flicking a stray hair away from her eyes. "No, you were in good spirits last night and good company. You kept on going on about some meal with the King and how you had told the gathered Lords and Ladies that, and I quote, 'their dits were shit' and that you were off to find some fun." She saw him going white as she spoke to the point where she couldn't help but play along and keep the wind-up going; he had, after all, forgotten her name. Nekstar had explained that his friend had, instead of standing on the table and shouting it like he made out that he had done, had more or less mumbled it into a wine glass and then sauntered off after the main toasts had been finished.

"So you know who I am then?" Grimfar asked cautiously, wondering how deep in the shit he currently was. At this point in time he was still the acting officer in charge of The Eagles, but he knew fine well that it was just a temporary measure and that he was due on draft anyway alongside Nek. He wondered if he would have to throw himself in the glasshouse for impertinence and, indeed, how long such a sentence would be for saying that the Kings ministers and friends couldn't tell a decent story. Was it technically treason or would he have to punish himself under the catchall charge of 'bringing the legion into disrepute'? His hangover was also beginning to come back with a vengeance to add to his woes and he felt utterly miserable, his stomach beginning to rebel at the sweet tisane and his head beginning to feel as if a column of infantry had decided to march through it with a marching band.

"Oh yes, you were vocal on that one as well, but you did get confused about your rank quite a lot and ended up going into quite intricate detail as to how your entire career had progressed thus far. You said you only chased your commission because you were fed up with 'posh boys farting about and getting folk killed', and then how the officers of your legion had 'managed to get themselves killed in some damn fool action' that didn't need to be fought," she chuckled and he couldn't help but smile as she mimicked his voice and his mannerisms as she quoted him.

"After you went through all of that, Nek and you ended up jumping onto the tables and began singing songs from your Legion and, when a couple of the Kings Guards started complaining, you called them 'a bunch of inboard wankers who wouldn't know the pointy end of a sword from the other without a manual'. I actually have no idea what that meant, but it certainly seemed to annoy them and you went and had a fight before getting us all chucked out the Imps.

"After that, Nek and you decided that we should go to another tavern and we ended up taking you to the Black Bull where you spoke at great length on how Nekstar was your best friend and that he was a 'decent bloke really'. Then, when you had your fill, I brought you back here and put you to bed," He looked at her with an eyebrow raised before she suddenly cut his ego down to size, "before you even start, we didn't do anything because you weren't in a position to actually do anything; though that didn't stop you from trying. I'll give you that, you were very trying. It was quite endearing actually," she said with a chuckle and another flick of her hair, this time placing the rogue hair behind her ear and then fixing it in place with a wooden hairband.

"Well, you can't blame a man for trying. I owe you a great deal of thanks then, Katrin, you probably saved me from making an even greater tit of myself than I already did," a thought occurred to him as he looked at the bruised knuckles where he had obviously landed a decent couple of punches on one of the Guards, "where is Nekstar anyway?"

"He's sleeping off his hangover in the spare bedroom. He woke up briefly, asked how you were, made a suggestive comment about us and then passed back out again."

He was at a loss to what to say, not necessarily being used to waking up in the rooms of attractive women these days. He had had his fair share of success prior to marching north before the actions at Turgundeon and then Port Gephy, but since then he hadn't actually lived much of a life. If anything, last night was the first night in a long time where he didn't have to report to anyone or look after the welfare of hundreds or thousands of people. It was good to let loose sometimes and have a drinking bout or two if only to blow away the cob webs and remember that there is more to life than just the bloody legions and its problems.

She watched him for a few more seconds before giggling, "I was only joking, by the way, Nekstar reassured me that you only mumbled into your cups that the Kings Ministers couldn't tell a decent story and that you were quite well behaved throughout the entire night…at least, that is until you met my friends and I." She didn't actually begrudge him it, if anything it had made the night a lot more interesting than it previously had been. She thought it was like looking after a large and friendly bear who simply needed fed and watered to be kept happy.

There was something strangely attractive about the man in her bed as well, she found. He wasn't classically handsome, and certainly there wouldn't be a queue of poets or artists trying to capture his likeness for the likes of posterity, but there was something charmingly amiable about him. There was a power to his eyes, a quiet confidence in them, and he was a charming person even when deep in his cups. His features were soft, but also had a certain hardness to them that came with years of service with the legion. He was a juxtaposition. Whilst his manners and gestures suggested he was an officer, the way he fought against the Guards was testament to his abilities in a fight and his time in the ranks. She couldn't help but notice when she stripped him for bed the sheer number of scars that the man carried on the front of his body, with very few on his back. It was evident that he was a man that faced his troubles head on. She was interested, but she wouldn't let him know that for now.

"So have you any plans for today then?" He asked her, fumbling for a conversation that didn't involve a tale of his drunken antics. She smiled at his obvious discomfort.

"No, it's my day off today and I was planning on just reading a book and taking some time to myself," she said reaching to place the now empty mug on the dresser.

"What is it you do?" He knew the conversation was stilted, but he had very little else to go on at the moment. He was, for all intents and purposes, in a room with a stranger whom he assumed he had shared a bed with but had found himself unable to perform due to sheer amount of drink. The ice breakers, the conversations that they would have had last night, had been lost to the muggy fog of the hangover.

"I'm a doctor at the Royal Hospital," she nodded towards the uniform that was hung up in the open wardrobe. He hadn't even noticed it, however, he was becoming decidedly sore and stiff underneath the blankets. He had never been one for being able to lie in a bed whilst not asleep for long periods at a time without needing to move or walk about, his back would sometimes stiffen up or he would just generally feel uncomfortable. He knew he was naked underneath, but having considered it was probably her that got him safely home, undressed and put to bed then it was probably nothing that she had not seen before.

"I don't know if I could do that for a career," he said as he braced himself to stand up.

"You look as if you want to get out of bed. Would you like me to leave?" She said with a degree of astuteness that took him by surprise, though he took care not to show it.

"It's not as if it's anything you haven't seen before, is it?" He noticed a slight flush to her cheeks and assumed it was embarrassment though hoped there was a degree of excitement there; the Gods love a trier after all. He gave a wry smile as he pushed back the quilt and stood, swinging his legs outward and sitting up. He rubbed at the back of his head and felt his mind adjust for a few seconds as it tried to cope with moving up into a semi-vertical position. He was getting too old for this pissing up, even if he was only thirty-two. He knew fine well he probably wouldn't feel completely human again for another day, at least, and whenever Nek decided to surface from his pit he was sure to get a ribbing for being a lightweight.

She watched him as he stood, noticing the muscles work on his arms as he found his trousers and socks amongst the neatly folded pile of clothing. She knew her friends would be gossiping, for when was Silveroak not full of gossip? By the time she made it to the hospital tomorrow she also knew that most of her colleagues would be quite happily discussing her promiscuity; a young female doctor taking two soldiers home? Gods forbid! She could almost hear the rumour mill now and what it would be saying, but she didn't give a fig for the opinions of the majority within those walls and therefore considered it water off a ducks back.

"I still owe you a proper thank you though," he said sitting down on the bed to pull on his boots. "How about I treat you to breakfast?" He stood again and moved over to the pile and picked up the short sleeved shirt bearing the colours of the Eagles legion and pulled it over his head.

"I believe it's fashionable to call this time of day lunch," a thought struck her, "I take it you have the time off and you aren't absconding or whatever it is the legions call it? I won't harbour criminals, no matter how charming they are."

"Get a lot of soldiers passing through, eh?" He said with a grin causing another flush to the cheeks. He wondered, briefly, if he had overstepped the conversational boundary until he looked into her brown eyes and saw the humour there.

"You'll never know, and for that little comment you can take me to my choice of restaurant."

Silveroak was a maze, a warren of streets and side streets with a plethora of alleys and closes peeling off from them. The noise was astounding, the chaos of a battle in full swing being the only thing Grim could liken it to. There were, within minutes of leaving the apartment that Katrin rented and called home, a dozen different languages that Grimfar could only just identify even if he couldn't understand a word of what was said. What struck him most of all was the amount of diversity within the capital as they walked down one of the more affluent streets. There were representatives from every major country or Empire on this side of the World, and a few that he didn't recognise. He wasn't particularly well travelled, generally going where the legion and the powers that be decided he needed to go, and therefore he was quite struck by the different colours and clothing that the people wore.

He found it surprising, most of all, to see men from the Kingdom of Speirak walking down the street talking to other people who could possibly come from the likes of Attainia. He knew the war was still on going and therefore found it surprising that two opposing sides could quite happily meet in the capital city of one side of the allied coalition, but then, he reflected, money speaks a different language and has no borders.

Nekstar had briefly woken when they had gone through to the living room and asked the same general enquiries as he had done, but Grim was pleased to see that his friend seemed to be suffering the effects of the hangover a lot more than he. They had invited him to come along, but at the mention of food he had turned a tinge of green and rolled over to quell his rebelling stomach. It was, therefore, with a slight spring in his step at the suffering of his friend that he walked down a street with, what seemed like, a dozen different types of eatery that catered for every taste.

The sun shone high in the afternoon sky bathing the city in it's warm glow, the fluffy white clouds above calming the rays so that the temperature was slightly cooler and therefore breathable. The rains of the previous night had done a lot to dampen down the dust within the air that carts and the footsteps of hundreds of thousands of people cast up. It was, considered Grim, a very pleasant day. What topped it off was the intriguing woman who even now held onto his arm, laughing at some pass-remarkable comment he had made about a group of people they had just past.

She intrigued him, and not just for her looks, but for her sheer vivacity. Granted, they had only known each other for a short while and the majority of that time he had known her he couldn't quite remember in any significant detail, but the way she laughed and the way she thought struck him as unique. There was an intelligence to her, and certainly doctors had to be intelligent, but there was also a deep grounding of common sense that was sometimes found lacking in those who had lived in the library too long studying from books. He reckoned, though he obviously wasn't completely sure, that she had an interest in him. Why an intelligent and attractive woman should have an interest in him he hadn't quite worked out, but he had dispelled easily the idea that she was a spy or some sort of trap out to ensnare him and release state secrets because, if she had been, then she wouldn't be a very good one. He was, after all, only the local acting commander of a legion and therefore didn't know the movements or the logistical supplies and such like that came with the posting. His job over the last few months had simply been to fight, to march, to fight some more and try and get as many people home in one piece as he could.

The sky darkened as a flight of pigeons obscured the sun and he felt himself instinctively mutter a quick prayer that they wouldn't decide to shit all over him. Some people may believe that getting shat on by a bird was a sign of future good luck, but for Grim it was a sign that he needed to wash and polish his uniform and kit prior to it getting stained or rusted.

"You look as if you've never been to Silveroak before," Katrin said as she viewed him looking at the buildings. They were on the pavements, the road running through the street being filled with traffic of all sorts. Palanquins carrying the richer members of society contended with merchant carts that were filled with goods being taken to and from warehouses where they would later fill up their shops and stalls with stock. Carriages carrying revellers who had started drinking early in the day were trying to work their way through without making the occupants sick. The city had a carnival-like atmosphere as people carried on the celebrations of the triumph; Cardavian arms triumphing always brought the crowds into the streets.

They had walked past several taverns that were standing room only and had decidedly stayed away from them, even though at this time Grim was of the opinion that another ale or two would be a decent equaliser and set him up for the rest of the day's events. He hadn't anything planned, however, and he was content to allow her to lead the way.

"I haven't. Once I won my commission and passed out I was ill and wasn't able to make it to the city in order to receive it from the Parliament. I got it through the mail service instead via a courier when I was in Nights Wood," the couple had to stop and allow a group of visitors past as they went into one of the taverns. He was becoming decidedly hungry now and wondered where they were going for they had walked past a half dozen places that looked good enough.

"I've never been there, what is it like?" He noticed that her eyes had alighted on a suitable location and they crossed the street, suddenly moving with a purpose rather than walking at a bimble-like pace. They had to stop in the centre of the road as carriages of the richer sort from the northern gate made an appearance. The general appearance of them, and the direction from which they travelled, led Grim to assume that they came from the Arterenion Republic.

The Arterenion were an interesting people, they being a former colony of the Attainians as well. They enjoyed close relations with the mother state, but were for all intents and purposes just allies. What made their appearance more interesting was the memory it sparked within the deeper recesses of Grim's mind, remembering hearing a couple of politicians discuss with the First Lord last night about the proposed political union that may happen between Cardavy and the Arterenion people. It was interesting times they lived in, but Grim couldn't help but feel that events had gathered a momentum of their own ever since the Cardavians had got themselves involved in the defence of Attainia and her provinces. He realised that she had asked him a question, but couldn't for the life of him remember what it was.

"I'm sorry, I wasn't paying attention," he said as the mounted escort for the delegates began to make their way through after the carriages. There was a mixture of members of the Kings Guards as well as some cavalry that belonged to the Arterenions wearing full plate and plumed helmets. They cut a figure, he would grant them that, but a pretty uniform a soldier does not make.

"I said," he presumed she was used to dealing with patients that had minor brain damage for she said it with a greater degree of patience than he could have mustered, "I've never been to Nights Wood, what's it like?" They eventually crossed the road once the convoy of delegates and cavalry had eventually made their way further down the street, though they had to carefully step around the shit that had spattered onto the cobbled road by a horse who obviously couldn't hold it in anymore.

"It's nice enough and quiet in its way; a fairly large town that still has that small town mindset if you know what I mean? The Eagles, when we were based there, got on with the natives well enough and we were generally welcome in most of the taverns and shops because we didn't create much in the way of bother. Otherwise, it's just like every other farming community within the Kingdom," He wondered if there was anything else he could add onto about the town but decided there wasn't. It was a fairly settled place where things very rarely happened, most outrages being perpetrated by the river that ran through the entire town and often flooded out certain parts of the town. Whilst Grim had every sympathy for people who were flooded out of their homes and businesses, he did sometimes think they brought it upon themselves when they started buying property in the middle of flood plains or next to rivers because the property was cheaper.

"Will you be heading back there soon?" She asked, full of questions and curious. He held open the door for her to the place where they were evidently going to eat and she thanked him with a smile and a nod. He saw again the deep brown eyes, almost hazel in colour, and couldn't help but smile back. He liked this sort of easy life, particularly given that it didn't happen very often.

"I don't know. I expect within the next day or so they will assign a new commanding officer to the Eagles, as well as pretty much the entire hierarchy. They won't want me kicking about, nor Nek, just in case we lead a mutiny or something," They sat at a table that was empty nearest the window allowing them a perfect view out onto the street, "I was due on draft anyway, so was Nek, so we'll probably end up coming here and staying in one of the transit barracks until they find a new posting for us. To be honest with you, after nine years in the same legion I'm looking forward to actually kicking back and relaxing."

"You won't find it boring?"

"No!" He said with a laugh, "I long for boring, Katrin! I haven't had boring in so bloody long I've forgotten what it feels like. Anyway," he said as he sat further back into the wooden seat, hearing the creak of wood as it adjusted to supporting his full weight. He felt his back click into place and the tension flowing out of his shoulders thereafter, "I'm not all that interesting. Tell me about you, you don't have a Silveroak accent…sounds more like it comes from the west coast."

"I'm originally from Raventhorne Keep," a waiter came over and gave them a pair of menus. He was asked for a bottle of white wine and two glasses and thanked with a smile as he moved off, "It's a royal burgh in the south west, decent sized with good links to the sea that helps bring in money. There's some industry and farming, the usual stuff that goes with towns really, but it wasn't the place for me. Too many familiar faces, a bit like your Nights Wood actually. Everybody knew everyone and therefore felt they had a right to know their business. I left as soon as I was old enough to study at university here in Silveroak and haven't looked back since."

"Do you still have family there?" He asked as the waiter brought a wooden bucket over inside of which was a tin container which held ice and the bottle itself. The waiter poured Grim a small glass at first and looked expectantly at him, which was met with an expectant look back, "I'll need slightly more than that, friend, if I'm to appreciate it."

"Does sir not want to try it first?" The waiter was almost aghast at the prospect of someone having wine without trying it first, as if the entire idea was an anathema to him and one which would possibly see the collapse of civilisation itself.

"Does it taste like wine?" Grim asked, the waiter nodded, "Then crack on and fill the glass, I'm sure it'll be fine." The waiter looked across to Katrin for help, judging her to be more respectable than the grizzled veteran. He may wear the uniform of an officer, but the man was no gentleman. He saw no hope of alliance or agreement with the young woman, however, who was too busy chuckling away as quietly as she could whilst the exchange between two cultures continued. The wine was poured and the waiter moved off to discuss the barbarians who sat by the window; he would almost dread asking them what they wanted to order for a meal, presuming it to be something ordered out of a trough with too much gravy and salt.

"I do," she said taking a sip from the wine which had a crisp and sweet taste, "my parents still live there, as well as my brother. I sometimes go to visit, but not all that often." Grim nodded as he took a sip himself and looked to the other patrons within the establishment, seeing, of all things, a man of the Northern Clans in full plaid chatting to a woman with a broad grin splitting his bearded face. The last time he saw a clansman the man had been busy trying to split his own face in two with a small hand axe and it was hard to reconcile the two sides of people. He wondered, briefly, if the man was at Gephy or Nepriner or even had any relatives that had served there. He wondered if the man even cared for the battles that had been fought hundreds of miles away from this city.

"So what made you become a doctor?" Grim asked as he turned about again, taking another sip from his glass and feeling his headache begin to diminish already. He had been worried initially when he saw the wine that his stomach would rebel completely and he would have to rush off to the toilets, but so far it had held out.

"I'm too stroppy to be a barmaid, I don't have a great deal of patience when it comes to teaching children and dealing with pretentious parents, and I am too belligerent to be a housewife spitting out brats for a man who isn't there all the time or there too much. Medicine was the only thing that was left open to me after all those other options had been discounted!" She said with a smile. The waiter came over carrying a piece of paper as if it were a shield to prevent him from being infected by the savagery that the two of them offered. They made their orders and he went on his way again breathing a sigh of relief, noting that the man hadn't asked for a plate of raw pork as had been expected.

"You do yourself a disservice. I daresay you had to have the patience to teach me how to go to bed last night!" She chuckled happily and Grim found himself smiling along with her again, enjoying seeing the small dimples of her cheeks and the way her eyes lit up whenever she found something funny. He wondered, very briefly, if there was a future for them and dismissed the thought from his mind. He would live in the here and now, he decided, and anything that happened or developed from that would be left to the fates.

"You were alright, really, once I managed to persuade you that you didn't actually need another drink. As I said, you spent more time singing with Nek than anything else and the only person to whom you were a menace was whoever happened to be selling food at that time of night. You had quite the appetite."

"I've found from previous occasions that if there's a chance of food then you may as well eat it, because the Gods alone know when you're going to get some next!"

The banter between the two of them was easy, back and forth conversation that never seemed to stutter or develop into an awkward silence. The sun began to set in the west casting warm colours across the darkening sky and reflecting beautifully off the clouds that he could see from the window seating, and still they sat and chatted. He saw the way the sun caught her olive-skin complexion which only seemed to enhance her face. He hoped he was decidedly fresher looking than he had been earlier on in the day, but he left that up to the Gods to decide.

Eventually the waiter lit a small candle at their table and they realised how much time had passed since they had first entered the restaurant. Even though the sun set naturally early this year because of the winter, it was still a good three or four hours. They stood up and Grim paid for the meal and the drinks, refusing to even entertain the idea of Katrin paying for it, and they walked out into the early evening. There was a touch of wind and a chill in the air, the sky being generally cloudless. The stars sparkled like diamonds in the sky, twinkling and hanging there as they framed the moon. The light pollution from Silveroak was minimal, but even now he could see workers lighting the street lamps with their long wicks and poles.

"So, General, what do you want to do now?"

"Well, the night is young Katrin so I'm leaving it entirely in your capable hands. I am merely a visitor to your city so I'm out of suggestions, and I doubt I have an open invitation to the palace."

"Do you like music?" She asked with a slight cock to her head and an involuntary shudder. He realised she was cold and unfastened the golden chain that allowed the heavy red cloak to hang at his shoulders. Taking it off, he offered it to her and fastened it up, brushing her hair back so it wasn't caught up in the folds of the cloak. She looked at him anew then, a different sort of expression that he hadn't seen on her face before.

"I must admit, when it comes to music I'm more used to the band of the legion. They aren't exactly known for putting on popular music that doesn't involve us march to some Gods forsaken place." He could still hear in his head during the quiet moments in the dark when he was alone the song they had marched to when they had entered Turgundeon. He didn't think he would ever forget that song and who he had sang it with, try as he might.

"Well, I'll take you to a proper opera house. The theatre should be opening at this time of night, and if it isn't then we can always have a couple of drinks in the tavern across from it until it does. How about that?"

"It sounds like a plan," he said with a grin, holding out his arm as she linked hers through his. He felt her hand reach lower and hold his hand, their fingers clasping together.

"You know, Grim, I think I quite like you," and they walked down the cobbled streets with Grim feeling as if he was floating on air. Love, he thought to himself quietly, was often found in the unlikeliest of places and when you were least looking for it.

Chapter Three – **Queen of the South**

The city of Vitrossy, capital of the kingdom Molenbeek in the Southern Coalition, was one of towering spires and majestic buildings. The city was host to a magnificent pantheon where thousands could worship to the Gods, the shape of the building allowing the songs coming from a thousand throats to reach up to the heavens. There were columns depicting military victories against enemies and sometimes allies in the major squares where markets would set up to carry out their trading. The major guilds had their headquarters within the heart of the city and helped to provide the city with riches through tax and trade, the monies gathered from such helping to build new roads through the countryside linking the capital to the smaller towns and villages acting as the hub for a small, yet powerful, country.

The city burned now from a thousand fires, the mountain range behind it acting like some sort of hellish backdrop as clouds gathered above them. The rain lashed down upon the broken remnants of the army as it sought to escape from the destruction. The Ufwalan army who weren't involved in the siege stood in the pouring rain in rank and file and watched as their light cavalry darted in and out of the mass of fleeing soldiery and slaughtered at will. Lightning flashed through the sky and Morro counted a full two seconds before he heard the rumble of thunder. He couldn't tear his eyes from the scene as the trebuchets continued to pound the city into smithereens, broken spires falling into the once beautiful squares and other buildings.

It was enough to make a grown man weep, but then such was war.

He flicked his glance to his left and saw his Queen sat astride her white horse, the animal a pale colour now as the rain continued to fall. Wellisa looked resplendent in the uniform of a light cavalryman; a black woollen jacket that came in at the hips accentuating her figure with golden braid at the front in decorative patterns with bronze studs for buttons. She wore a circular fur hat on her head, the heraldic symbol of her house, a lion rampant, on the front cast out of solid gold topped off with a white and black plume trailing down her back. She sat without a seeming care in the world, the four men of her cavalry escort carrying an awning so that the rain didn't bother her.

Morro shuddered as he looked at her. His devotion to Wellisa was total and he still considered her to be the daughter he had never had, but she had changed over the last few months. The civil war that the rebellion had become was put down with an ease that made those who sought conspiracies think that the entire episode had been engineered by the Queen. Then the wars of blood and conquest had begun, Wellisa seeking to bring the rest of the Southern Coalition under the heel of Ufwala.

Thus, Vitrossy burned.

There was another loud explosion as the main clock tower of the university finally collapsed after having sustained a continuous bombardment. The castle of Vitrossy stood alone, carved into the mountains themselves, and unable to affect the destruction of the city around it. Morro knew it would be a matter of time before the King decided to surrender, knowing that the longer he attempted to hold out then the more of his people would be killed. He would be a man with a hollow throne, the King who had led his people to slaughter because he couldn't bring himself to bend the knee to the Queen.

The fields around about had once been resplendent with wheat, the area a golden colour during high summer and pleasant to ride through. There used to be apple orchards hereabouts as well, he remembered, where the locals made a fine drink that was fit to put hairs on a man's chest. The only colours in the fields now where the black and yellow uniforms of the fallen defenders, speared through as they ran or punched with arrows as they tried to offer defiance.

He had watched the battle, seen the bands and then the regiments of infantry and cavalry come out as the bombardment carried on into its ninth day without any attempt on the wall. The defenders of Vitrossy couldn't take it anymore, knowing that they had to show some sort of defiance, but then they weren't to know that Wellisa had promised the officer commanding the garrison a rich a reward should he betray the city. He had jumped at the offer, much to the surprise of Morro, and thus the entire army had marched out with standards flying in a desperate display of defiance. Wellisa hadn't even bothered to order her catapults and trebuchets to begin firing at the mass of men that was advancing on their position and, instead, ordered them to continue firing on the wall of the city and the city itself. There were already three sizeable breeches in the wall itself and all that was left to do was order a general assault.

The men of Vitrossy had adopted their formations with a practised ease, comfortable in the knowledge that their long spears would be able to keep the Ufwalan cavalry at bay. They had thrown up large stakes around the four distinct circular formations and secured them with hawsers and rope they had taken from the docks and jetties that were littered along the river, the merchant guilds generously deciding to aid the defence of the city in their own way with materials and money. Their archers had taken up position between the massed spears and their cavalry on the flanks.

Morro had watched with a detached fascination that only a military man could have as the Ufwalans made their own dispositions to counter that of the Molenbeekians; they may have paid off the garrison commander, but there were still loyal and true officers amongst their ranks. He had offered his advice to the Queen but she had simply tapped him on the shoulder as he came up and thanked him, saying that the plan was hers and that it would work. She had said it with a smile, the self-same smile that he had once thought of as innocent and sweet. Aye, she was a canny one.

The Ufwalan cavalry were placed on the flanks; heavier cavalry on the left flank and lighter cavalry on the right. The infantry was formed up into a solid shield wall of eight ranks, the five thousand men in the blue and white uniforms split into different divisions and companies based upon the Cardavian model. Their round shields were painted in their own peculiar colours of swirling patterns and heraldic symbols belonging to their lords and other feudal masters, their banners flying in the afternoon sun. The order was passed down the line and the men were told to stand firm until ordered to move forward. The archers were the last, each carrying a longbow made of yew that would send shafts of death pouring into the waiting formations. It had a greater range, especially given the weight of the bow, than those that were carried by the Molenbeekians.

The Ufwalan cavalry were the first to engage, sent screaming down the flanks to counter the Molenbeekians who, in turn, simply ran away. Morro couldn't believe it as he watched. He knew that a bribe hadn't been paid to either divisional commander, but he couldn't find any explanation as to why the cavalry felt the need to retire from the field. Surely they must have understood that by leaving the field that they had left the infantry to their fate, that the shield formations couldn't now break up and redeploy without being destroyed in a piecemeal fashion over the broken ground. The Ufwalan archers moved forward until they were within extreme bowshot range of the formations and began peppering them, taking their time to destroy them in a piecemeal fashion and only stopping to allow the cavalry to break through the centre of the formations and destroy the archers in between. It wasn't even a battle; it was more like a slaughter.

It had lasted for all of an hour and the longbow men of Ufwala only stopped when the rain that continued to pound their heads had started. By that time the damage had been done, the spear formations breaking apart as men sought the safety of the walls and disappeared in all directions only to be picked apart by the light cavalry of Wellisa. The infantry hadn't even needed to engage, had stood witness as the slaughter took place.

"I don't think I've ever seen an action like that, my friend, and I don't think I ever want to see one like it again," Garren, the Cardavian diplomat, had moved his chestnut horse up to Morro as they watched the infantry begin to slowly advance across the quagmire that had once been a field. They marched in solid ranks, no resistance or shows of defiance coming from the walls. Why would there be, anyway? The defenders who could have offered resistance now littered the empty plain before them, mute testimony to the greed of their garrison commander and the killing power of the Ufwalan longbow and cavalry.

"No, I agree with you. You've got to give the Queen credit though, she engineered this victory," he said holding out his gloved right hand as he beckoned to the field. He could hear the crows above them now and other scavengers, even the distinct call of the seagulls, but he couldn't see them for the downpour of rain that continued to plunge around them.

"Aye, woe betide anyone who gets on the wrong side of her."

"I think they already do, Garren," Morro didn't know how he was supposed to feel as he looked down upon the field of death. He had been in the army, albeit in the intelligence, and he knew that the information that he had once provided the royal court of Ufwala and the old King had led directly to the deaths of men in the clandestine warfare that sometimes took place on the Cardavy-Coalition border. This, he felt, was wholly different.

"Is this the last bastion of the rebellion, or does the civil war still rumble on?" Morro looked at the diplomat and rubbed at his sodden grey beard. The Cardavian diplomat had been an ever present figure in the court of Wellisa ever since he had been introduced. It seemed like years ago now, but was likely to be only six or seven months. When he had first been introduced it had been at the crowning of Wellisa after she had inherited the throne from her father, being the only legitimate child of the King and the first Queen. It had been quite the occasion, Morro remembered, as the Imperials and the allied Cardavians and Attainians had argued their own specific cases as he each side tried to woo the Queen of the South. Ufwala, even then, was a strong power and likely to be the first and last court of appeal for a friendly ear in the south. To set up a rival power would cost too much money and, potentially, go horribly wrong for those that sought to play their political games. Wellisa knew this, had sussed it out quicker than most would have thought, and had used every weapon within her power to woo the Imperials and the Allies in turn. She did not care for their wars, had absolutely no reason nor any perceived gain to side with any of them.

The Imperials were far away and offered nothing in terms of support or manpower, but were willing to offer money and the hand of their Emperor Rhagan I if Wellisa were to accept their terms of alliance. They tried to promise that they wouldn't expect the Southerners to get involved in their continuing war with Attainia and Cardavy, but given that Ufwala and her neighbours in the Southern Coalition shared a land border with Cardavy then it was unlikely that their neutrality would be sustained or respected for long; that and a union of the crowns was sure to see the legions of Cardavy come marching south.

The Cardavians had, in decades and centuries past, been a major factor in their being no true southern kingdom. The Coalition had stayed fragmented, their only bonds being a common tongue and the same Gods; in all other things the vast majority couldn't stand each other and went at it like bickering children, occasionally falling out and making up again to unify against somebody else before repeating the entire process over and over again. Cardavy had sought this, encouraged it, and would often back one kingdom against the other whilst offering a third a greater hand in the region. However, the wars in the north against the Empire of Rupinia had distracted the Cardavian gaze away from the lands of the south. This had meant that the Kingdom of Ufwala had begun to rise, to ascend from the chaos and become a power broker within the Coalition. Morro had to give the Cardavians credit; they realised reality and didn't seek to change it. All they wanted from an alliance was an open borders policy, free trade deals and neutrality in any war with the Empire. It had been that simple and they were easy enough terms to fulfil.

Wellisa had played them off against each other deftly enough, far more experienced in matters of state at the young age of twenty-four than some statesman could ever hope to be in their entire lifetime. She had won trading concessions from the Cardavians as well as the right to buy their armour and weapons, from the Imperials she had won herself a small trading fleet where she was able to expand her economy and send the exports of Ufwala and her lands across the globe.

Then that bastard Clansman, thought Morro, had gone and fucked it all up. The surly looking idiot had decided to take it upon himself to provoke a war by assaulting the Cardavian ambassador. The man had been lucky to escape with his life for he wore no armour and carried little or no weaponry, and why would he when he had been at an audience with the Queen? He was near murdered outside the gates to the castle, and the Cardavians had responded in kind. A flurry of diplomatic activity ensued between Morro, in his capacity then, and the Cardavian parliament as both sides sought to avoid a war that neither wanted to fight. There would be no profit in it and, at any rate, both sides knew that Cardavy would win it and would simply destroy their developing southern neighbour and deprive themselves of trades and the monies that it brought.

The cancer went deeper than just a surly Imperial diplomat. The Imperial delegation, in their arrogance and stupidity, had carelessly tried to recruit people of the court to their cause. They spread information and rumour suggesting that Cardavy was eyeing the Southern Coalition with a keen interest, beginning to think of developing it into a protectorate and therefore a province in all but name. The then Chancellor had demanded that Wellisa throw her hand in with the Imperials listing the promises that they had made as if they were sacrosanct stating, with a naivety that Morro had found alarming, that they would be provided with manpower, ships and other materials of war to defend their fledgling Kingdom and even take the fight to Cardavy.

Utter rubbish!

The Queen had seen through the lies and cast the rebellious party out from the Ufwalan capital. A brief and bloody skirmish had been fought between the Queens Guards and the rebellious group resulting in their rout, but not their surrender. Garren, once he had recovered, had been summoned to court and taken to task by both the Queen and Morro about Cardavian intentions. The frankness of the man, the honesty and lack of deceit, had persuaded the two that the Cardavians had absolutely no intention of ruining anything or trying to take over.

"You look lost in thought, Morro, are you alright?" Garren wore a worried expression on his face and opened a pouch in a saddlebag, taking out a leather flask and offering it up to the Chancellor. Morro took it with a nod of thanks and pulled the stopper out before taking a drink, wiping his mouth afterwards as the wine began to warm his throat and insides.

"Still drinking my wine, Garren?"

"Only if it's still relatively cheap and decent, Morro, anything else would flag up in expenses and our treasury is on a tight budget these days," Morro grinned a rare grin at that and replaced the stopper after taking another swig and passed the leather canteen back to the Cardavian. "So is this the end of the rebellion or is Wellisa going to take over the rest of the Coalition one Kingdom or Princedom at a time?"

"She has four Kingdoms under her belt now, and an alliance with three others, that only leaves five that we can't be sure of." He paused as he watched the first of the soldiers beginning to filter through the breach in the wall of Vitrossy and enter the city, briefly wondering how many of the people within the city would still be left alive come the next morning. The rain hadn't ceased either causing his mood to darken even further. "If they were to all band against us then we'd be in trouble, especially if we were to receive a setback in which case our two erstwhile allies might decide to jump ship and join them. I'd recommend to her just now to consolidate her power, not seek to make the others join with us, at least not through military might at any rate."

The two men heard the order from one of the artillery officers to cease fire and the sound of silence from the lack of catapults or the rumblings of bombardment was perhaps more unnerving than anything else. They could now clearly hear the fat raindrops hit metal armour with a sharp clink, they could hear the seagulls as they cried out for food or the distant caw of crows as they fought each other for a morsel of dead flesh, the stamp of a horses hoof as it squelched into the soft ley or the harsher sound as the hoof struck the cobbled road. Morro looked at the city again and then at his Queen and wondered what she was thinking.

"Out of interest," Morro said as a thought struck him, "Cardavy hasn't said anything about this, have they?" Garren looked at him and quirked an eyebrow, considering his answer.

"No, not officially anyway. They are slightly concerned that their formerly peaceable neighbour in the south has suddenly developed an apparent blood-lust and is seeking to unite the south through fire and blood, but no, officially they aren't going to be doing anything. They may or may not send a delegation, but I'm not sure."

"Who would be part of that delegation?" Morro asked. He looked towards the dark mountain ranges, the clouds circling over the spires of the castle that was embedded into the range. Morro had to wonder at the mind of the architect who first thought of it for he considered the man a genius. He would have to be a tyrant, or the foreman would have to be a tyrant, in order to carve a castle out of sheer cliff face, but the place was virtually impregnable. The only thing that let the defences down was the city, for the soldiers who resided within would have family and friends and loved ones stuck within it. Why should they hold out and continue to offer resistance against the inevitable when their loved ones were being raped and slaughtered? He thought then of Nepriner and the stories he had of heard the resistance that was offered there and a disturbing thought struck him that he didn't want to contemplate let alone give voice to.

"I have no idea, maybe a few of the Kings ministers. I know he won't send the First Lord, not whilst the war in the north continues and the possibility of a political union with the Artenonians." In truth, Garren was worried about the developments within the coalition. Wellisa, at first, appeared to be a reasonable Queen who was willing to listen to her councillors, but, with each passing success, she seemed to be more sure of her power. Why shouldn't she be? She was one of the most powerful women on this side of the continent, loved by her people within her own lands for her humanitarian interests and her fierce pride in her nation. On the other hand, she was feared by her enemies for her sharp wit and sharper swords. Garren was a little in love with her, he had to admit. He had fallen under her spell at their second meeting when she held a feast and a dance for the assembled delegates. The evening had gone well and Garren had spent the majority of it with the Attainian diplomat Roac, a man whom he couldn't stand at the time but had terribly misjudged. The Queen had come up and asked for a dance, thinking him bored or depressed as he sat nursing his wine and the rest was history for him.

Wellisa was almost impossible to define. She was of average height, but her personality made her seem larger than life. She was beautiful in her own right with blonde hair and a body that would send some men into raptures of poetry and others into thoughts of lust. She exuded confidence. Her smile could entrance an entire room, the nod of her head could send supplicants into raptures of ecstasy, and she had a tenderness to her spirit that very few would ever actually see. It was clearly evident for those that knew her, for why else would she invest so much of her time and energy into reforming the educational and health systems in her land. She had set about planning to build hospitals and given incentives into recruiting nurses and providing them with free education. She had also raised the literacy and numeracy skills in her Kingdom within her short reign already. There were, like anywhere, cynics ready to suggest that the groundwork had already been set up by her father, but Garren was of the opinion that it was her strength of character that had seen the much needed reforms through.

The Southern Coalition had had Queens before in its various different states, but more often than not they would play the typical damsel in distress ready to be wooed by whatever nation took their fancy at the time. They would deliberately use their sex to make them appear less of a threat and therefore go unnoticed, but not so Wellisa. Garren knew she used her sex as a weapon, often taking chauvinistic politicians and Generals completely by surprise with her depth and breadth of knowledge. She was willing to play the stereotypical woman insofar as it helped her achieve her aim, wooing one person or nation in order for them to carry out a deed that she needed doing.

She was no-one's fool.

Garren looked at her now as she shared a joke with one of her officers causing the man to throw his head back in laughter. He narrowed his eyes and wondered if the man was being sycophantic, as some were want to do, but it appeared he was laughing out of genuine good humour. She turned around and caught him looking at her, giving him a wave and a smile in the same movement. The mannerisms, her relaxed nature and good humour was completely at odds with the scenes of devastation and death which she had been the designer of, and, he knew, it was that quality that made her a dangerous opponent.

Cardavy wouldn't involve themselves in a war in the south to change the leadership of Ufwala, these things often sorted themselves out as far as he was concerned, but Cardavy was beginning to take notice. What he said to Morro wasn't a lie, rather it was a half-truth. Officially Cardavy wasn't concerned, but, amongst the corridors of power in Silveroak, Garren knew from his sources that there were those who were beginning to sit up and take notice.

It was felt amongst many that the Coalition was a thing of the past, but once the Queen had done with her domestic enemies then where would she turn next? She was like most rulers, never mind women thought Garren, unpredictable. She was sensible enough to know that she would need a period of consolidation, to seek to hold onto her gains and win over the population that a few weeks or months or indeed years before had been enemies, but after that?

If the Queen was to unite the coalition under the banner of Ufwala then she would have a pool of manpower that could rival most nations on the continent, with most of the people hereabouts being used to war and the privations that it would bring. She would have undisputed access to gold, iron and coal in abundance. If the sinews of war are infinite money, then the Queen would have the most powerful army in the World. Would she look to the north, at Cardavy, who had long kept her people broken up and odds with each other? Or would she seek to create her own private lake by launching an amphibious assault on the Marsodian Empire and thus securing the Drirc sea?

"You look lost in thought, Garren," she said softly as she broke into his thoughts. He looked at her, not realising that she had moved her horse quite so quietly to sit alongside him. He had been so fixated on the mountain range in the distance, on the city that, even now, was finding that to offer resistance was futile, that he had been unaware of his surroundings. "Congratulations on your victory, Highness. The Queen of the South rises again. Your plan was well executed and the city lies at your mercy," she watched him critically for a few seconds as she weighed up his words. She liked Garren both as a person and a professional, but his words, like all those who used and crafted words for a living, could often have an undertone. She glanced away and looked at the city, still and silent now saving for the blue and white uniforms of her men moving through the breeches. She couldn't see, but she knew they would be forming up in their companies and making ready to march on the castle of Vitrossy.

"Woe to the vanquished, Garren. How would you treat those within the city?" He looked at the city again and then back to her.

"I would offer those who seek clemency exactly that, I would safeguard the women and children and implement measures to defend men who offer no forms of resistance. I'd probably isolate their former leadership from their support and secure the goodwill of the people by sorting out emergency accommodation for those that have been made homeless, supplying food and medical supplies as well beginning to rebuild as soon as possible," she nodded after he had concluded, watching the city as the light began to slowly pierce through the clouds. The castle in the mountain range was illuminated by a bright ray, almost as if the Gods themselves were showing the error of their discussion. She looked to the mast that hung at the top and could still a flag flying from the mast, but what colours they were she didn't know.

"And if the castle still holds for the King, what then? How do you suggest I go about reducing the castle?"

"Don't do what the Imperials did at Nepriner, ma'am. You've done better than them already. You effected a breach within a week of being here and forced the garrison out. The city is yours. The question really is the mountain range," he had only spent a year in the Cardavian legions and was by no means an expert, but he liked to think he was an enthusiastic amateur historian and had a decent grasp on tactics and strategy, "If the Molenbeekians have tunnels in those ranges, which I'd suggest they do given that they've had a castle there for bloody centuries, then they'll probably have a large cache of stores and maybe even a route in or out where they can be supplied from. That would make your life a lot harder."

"Naturally, so what do we do?" She already had a plan formulated in her head, but she liked the Cardavian diplomat. The man had an honest face and even Wellisa recognised that a lot of her courtiers and ministers, with the exception of Morro, were only too happy to agree with her readily enough and see to her whims. Such things were good every now and then, but such favours and ready agreement could, if not would, lead to abuses of power. If that happened then she would be little better than a tyrant, she knew, and therefore everything she had done thus far would be for naught.

"Well you've only got the one option as far as I see it, ma'am. Unless they strike their colours then begin bombardment of the castle and render it indefensible and force them into any holes that they have."

She nodded and looked towards the city once more, becoming bored with viewing it from a distance. She had a company of bodyguards with her and paid them well, did she not? She smiled as she looked across to Morro and saw the look on his face, recognising that he knew exactly what she was thinking. He shook his head once, a slow smile beginning to spread across his grey bearded face, and he nudged his horse towards her.

"Are you thinking, Highness, of doing what I think you are planning on doing?" He had known her for as long as she had been alive. He had seen her within a few minutes of her birth and brought up to be a polite young girl who was sometimes given to impulsive thought. He had watched as she developed into a teenager and rebelled against her father in very subtle ways as she honed her personality. Now she was a young woman who had an impish grin to her face when she was about to do something that was probably not very wise but would set her pulse racing. She was a woman that craved adventure, not courtly ritual of nicety and false smiles.

"Coming for a ride, Morro?" She took the reins in her gloved hands and flicked them once, the pale horse moving forward at the trot. She pressed her stirrups in very slightly and the horse responded by going to the canter. The bodyguard, taken completely by surprise, scrambled to follow behind her as men set off at the gallop to catch up; Garren saw one or two being over-rough with their mounts causing them to rear and send them crashing to the ground. They stood up dazed and confused as the remaining infantry cried themselves hoarse with laughter. Morro merely shrugged his shoulders and chased after his Queen, revelling in the feeling of the wind whipping past him.

She looked behind her, the white plume on her fur hat flying in the breeze and saw that a decent amount of her bodyguard had finally managed to catch up. She leant lower into the saddle and whispered into the horses' ear urging her to go faster, giving another soft kick with the heels to hasten it. The horse responded magnificently as she thundered along the road.

She saw the battlefield in clearer detail now as she sped towards the city, seeing the shapes of black crows flying into the air as the thundering of hooves from her and her bodyguard approached. The Molenbeekians had fallen in their droves, she could see now as she approached the site. The men had fallen in their tight circular formations, the stakes they had driven into the ground and secured together with rope standing in places as mute testimony to the futility of resistance. She had to harden her heart at the scene, but she didn't affect to look away. She owed it to the men who had fallen, even though they had offered defiance and violence against her in equal measure, to actually look at the destruction she had wrought. She justified it to herself by saying that it was not she who had betrayed them, she had merely facilitated the destruction of their army by finding the weak link in their chain. They had been poorly led by weak officers, and she held to the old maxim that she would rather face a thousand lions led by a sheep than vice versa.

The rain was beginning to ease now, but she knew she was drenched wet through even though she couldn't feel it as yet. Her heart hammered in time with the pounding of the horses' hooves and she felt more alive than she had done in recent months. However, with the lessening of the rain came new sounds from the battlefield and she could make out the occasional cry from men who were wounded and dying. The medics and those who knew first aid would be amongst them soon enough, but she had seen enough battlefields of late to know that the looters would be congregating around the wounded like vultures soon enough. It was better to die a quick death, she thought, rather than to suffer the agonising wounds that many of the men around her would be suffering now. When the looters came they wouldn't care what uniform the man wore, and would swiftly divest of him it at any rate anyway, as well as any jewellery or other precious materials whether the person they were stealing from was alive or dead. She had seen bodies before when she had walked a battlefield where men had their fingers severed and teeth removed so people could get stuck rings or gold false teeth, and she could only pray to whatever Gods were listening that the men had been dead before they underwent such humiliation and torture.

The wall loomed above her, the mountain ranges impressive and vast in the backdrop with their snow topped peaks. She knew west of her were one of the three passes that the Cardavians held, one legion encamped in a permanent fortress in each pass so as to prevent war bands from the south coming into the Kingdom with loot and pillage on their mind. The conquest of Vitrossy and the country as a whole would see the border under the direct control of Ufwala. Perhaps the Cardavians would reduce their military commitment in the south, perhaps as a loyal ally she could take control of those passes for herself and give them reassurances of friendship. She could, if she proved a leal and honest friend, perhaps take those cities back that the Cardavians had once won through conquest. She shook her head at the thought knowing that that way madness lay. If she were to make an enemy of Cardavy, or become too presumptuous, then she would lose everything she had won so far. She was not that powerful, not yet.

"Are you sure you want to do this, Highness?" Morro had caught up with her, but the mount he rode was sweating freely and he had obviously ridden her hard just to catch up. She slowed down to a canter instead of the gallop and looked towards the gate, noticing for the first time the murals above the gate depicting the Vitrossy coat of arms and various scenes from their past. The gates were raised and the massive doors were wide open, two companies of her soldiers waiting by the gate for the expected artillery train that would soon begin to roll through the city and set up position to bombard the castle.

"You always taught me to show no fear in the face of adversity, my friend, why should I should fear now in the moment of triumph?" She countered with a smile, seeing the marks where stray boulders had smashed into the walls and caused some of the facings to become loose and expose the red brick underneath.

"It is sometimes the moments of triumph when we are at our weakest. Remember your history lessons, Wellisa," he said using her name, something very few in the court were allowed to do. "Remember more recent times! The Empire thought they had won at Nepriner when they had everyone bottled up within the old citadel."

"I don't see a relief allied army coming from the south any time soon,

Morro," she said with a chuckle, stilled almost when she saw the thunderous expression on her ministers' face.

"Wellisa, you are being facetious. You know fine well that you have no heir and that if you get struck by a peasant, even, throwing a tile from a roof then your Kingdom will fracture itself into civil war," He looked at her levelly, knowing he was speaking out of turn and, moreover, that he was gambling on the Queen having some sort of affection for him. "I don't chastise you, I know why you need to do it, but let me deliver the terms and you can stay out of harm's way."

She made her way through the shadow of the gate and came out the other side, seeing the scene of destruction that the artillery crews had wrought on the city. Those buildings that were nearest the wall were either demolished or in danger of falling over from the amount of damage they sustained; various localised floods had taken effect where boulders had smashed into fountains that would have decorated the area and, perhaps more worrying in the long term, other less sanitary floods had developed where the sewage system had been blocked by the amount of debris being taken down the drains.

The two companies of infantry formed up on either side of her, the cavalry bodyguard taking up position to the front and rear thus boxing her in. Morro moved his mount closer and stayed in the centre, alongside his Queen whom he believed was being far too headstrong in this matter.

"Morro, I know, but this needs to be done." Wellisa wanted to chastise him further, decry him for questioning her in front of others, but then Morro had done it quietly himself and any such reaction from her would be sure to start the men around to gossiping. If any story, any rumour, could get blown out of proportion then it could be done by a soldier; and this was true of any Kingdom or Republic or Empire. People may say that someone can gossip like a fishwife, but a soldier can make a story fly around the World faster than many thought humanly possible.

"So be it, my Queen, but if this all goes wrong then don't blame me," he said, conceding defeat as gracefully as he could with a smile.

King Jaca had always considered himself lucky. He was born the second son but had managed to inherit the Kingdom when his brother, contrary to all good reasoning in the mind of Jaca, decided to become a temple priest and devote his life to the Gods. Jaca had also inherited Vitrossy, one of the premier cities of the Southern Coalition that had large iron and coal deposits in the mountain range from which his castle and his main strength had been carved. He instituted reforms that took away the powers of sections of the clergy and the nobility and given it to the people and become instantly the more popular for it, even giving them their own assembly so that they could discuss issues and petition him. His army had never known defeat and Molenbeek was recognised as one of the more benevolent powers within the Southern Coalition to the point where even the Cardavians left him alone! He had been beloved of the Gods, up until he had thrown his hand away by siding with the rebels during their abortive coup against Queen Wellisa of Ufwala.

Queen of the South! Gods; he hated that bloody name. He spat out over the battlements and watched the glob of spittle and mucus fly out and hit the dusty courtyard below where he could see the Ufwalan infantry massing. The rain had cleared, he considered, and it was a rare piece of luck that it should clear when his incendiaries had become soaked and the torsion gear on his ballistae had become wrecked because some damn fool engineer hadn't had the foresight to cover them until the deluge had been going on for fifteen minutes. He cursed the man inwardly and looked out properly over his beloved city.

He could see the blue and white uniforms of the Ufwalans everywhere he looked, the town hall already flying their colours, and the black and yellow jackets of his men lying festooned all around the place where men had either ditched their kit or fallen in the limited street fighting. He cursed again the garrison commander who had, effectively, opened the gates of the city to Wellisa; even now he hung from a gibbet, the last kicks of life having left him some ten minutes ago. Jaca hoped when it came to his own death he could die well, either with a sword in his hand or preferably in the bed of a buxom wench and not shitting himself like the commander did.

"I'd say we've fucked it," he said to the sergeant who stood next to him. The man merely nodded with a grunt and looked out over the once vibrant city, seeing the merchants quarter being ransacked by both civilians and Ufwalan soldiers alike in a rare display of unity.

"We've got the castle, sire, and the tunnels in the mountain range."

"Would you want to fight in those tunnels, sergeant? Better to fight out in the open, methinks, where a man can actually see the sky and have fresh air on his face. At any rate," he said with a grim chuckle, "it's too bloody dark in here to see what you'd be stabbing at." The man grinned, the dust and grim covered face splitting apart and showing remarkably white teeth. "Aye, there is that, sire. Why do you think Valcha betrayed us?" Jaca shrugged his shoulders, the unaccustomed weight of the armour beginning to chafe at him slightly.

"Greed, it always boils down to greed. Wellisa is good, she knows how to find the weaknesses of men. Gods, she's taken the bloody north of the Coalition without so much as even breaking a sweat so reducing the likes of Valcha to a quivering mess of anticipation probably wouldn't be that hard. You know old Mera the whore?" The sergeant nodded surprised that his King did; when he had joined the army many years previously he had to conduct a joining routine which saw him going around various different offices and speaking to bored clerks to get a chit stamped. That night, after he had handed in the chit and managed to wrangle some extended leave, he and the lads had gone into the town and he had found out that Mera was the unofficial final stamp in the joining routine.

"Aye, I know old Mera. Why, sire?"

"Well, if she can still set the likes of Valcha shaking then he was obviously a man who wasn't in full control of all his faculties. Weakness for women, and Wellisa with her blonde hair and hour glass figure and fair tongue knows how to play on it. She's good," he said with a chuckle, "she's very good."

"You respect her, sire?" The sergeant wasn't necessarily surprised at the admiration his King had for the Queen of the South, as the men had started calling her, but he was surprised at how open he was about it.

"Aye, I do, and what isn't there to admire? She combines beauty and intellect with a rare ease, and she's got the manpower and the resources behind her now to back her threats."

"So why did you go against her then, sire?" The sergeant realised he was probably speaking out of turn, but then it was his section of the wall and they were likely to die anyway so he wasn't necessarily too bothered about protocol. If they did manage to get out of this, he thought as well, then the younger lads around them would recount the story of how he questioned the King as well. It wouldn't do his reputation any harm, at any rate.

"Moment of madness, sergeant. Nobody expected her to crush the rebellion as quickly as she had," he was going to go on but saw some activity taking place in the open space between the castle wall and the town proper.

"Looks like we've got guests, sire."

"Right royal guests at that, sergeant. I wonder what she wants," he could see she was talking to a stocky grey haired man and he figured him to be Morro, the old soldier become politician who had proved as astute in politics as he had in the Ufwalan intelligence. He had met the man only once when he had paid a visit to the old King, back when the Molenbeekians and Ufwalans called each other friend rather than every other name under the sun.

"They'll send the grey haired one out," a young soldier said from somewhere down the line, which was met with a murmur of agreement. There wasn't, other than the occasional muffled conversation, any other noise coming from the castle. Jaca knew fine well there would be plenty of noise coming from the city, and it seemed to him that only moments before he could hear everything, but all was now still and silent as he watched the feminine figure on horseback analyse the castle and the mountain range. He felt as if he were on inspection, even stood a little straighter, and could've sworn that she looked straight at him for a few seconds.

"Your helmet, sire?" He had been lost in thought when he felt the nudge on the back of his arm as the sergeant passed his helmet, a steel domed affair that had a golden crown welded into it. It wasn't ostentatious or grand, but practical and served the purpose of protecting his head and differentiating him from the rank and file if he were ever captured; at least he could expect to be spared death, if he were captured, if only because of the ransom. He took the offered helmet and placed it on his head, the added weight causing him to curse silently.

"Movement, sire!" The cry was taken up along the wall as men made ready their bowstrings. Jaca held up his closed fist and roared at them to hold his arrows. He watched as the figure of the Queen nudged her horse gently forward and away from the bodyguard that accompanied her, standing still as statues. All eyes were upon her now, but she showed no fear, riding proud with her back straight and her eyes fixed on him; she looked like a victorious General on a triumphal procession or a parade ground, which she in fact was he thought. The sound of her horse striking the flagstones with its hooves echoed throughout, the steady drop becoming mesmerising.

"She is within range now, sire." The sergeant was the only man within the entire castle, it seemed to himself, who still had the presence of mind to seize control of the situation that was developing before the walls. Everyone else seemed to be falling under her spell and, he had to hand it to her, she was making a right good entrance. Jaca held up a gauntlet fist, his index finger held aloft as he motioned for silence, his other hand gripping onto the battlements as if for life itself.

The horse stopped. Jaca could see her eyes sweeping the walls as she examined the last few defenders, those who had managed to either escape the slaughter out on the field before Vitrossy or those who had simply not been summoned to fight with the rest of the garrison. Finally satisfied after her inspection, she focussed her eyes on Jaca.

"King Jaca!" Her voice was strong and commanding, a voice used to being obeyed. "I bring you greetings from Ufwala!"

"I'm afraid, ma'am, that we are in no state to receive you at the moment. If you wouldn't mind going home and coming back in a few years then we'll be properly ready!" He saw her chuckle and brush a stray blonde hair from her face.

"I come to offer you terms, Jaca. Surrender the fortress and the city, give homage to me as your overlord and you may keep your life and your throne." An outbreak of muttering spread along the wall as men discussed the new option that was suddenly delivered to them, none of them expecting to be able to see out the day let alone the rest of their lives. Wellisa watched them, surprised at herself. She had expected to take the advice of Garren earlier, something that roughly conformed with what she had been originally planning at any rate, but now she had her sights set on a much greater prize. The homage delivered to her would make her High Queen, her erstwhile two allied Kingdoms would follow suit, and it would make the transference of power much easier. She would receive manpower, or payment in lieu of such, without necessarily having to worry about administering her new province.

"A pretty offer, Wellisa, and almost as pretty as you if I may say so! What assurances do I have that you speak true, what's to stop you from butchering the garrison like you did with their friends and comrades earlier on?"

"I hadn't offered them terms, Jaca, I offer them now to you. You know I can take this fortress easily enough, I have the ladders and other siege equipment to render your wall useless. My men can pour through the breaches in your defences like water rushing into a sinking ship. Your gesture of defiance, of resistance, would be futile. You would die at any rate and condemn the men alongside you to die as well. You would make widows of wives, and orphans of children. Have your people, Jaca, not suffered enough for your vainglorious attempts at triumph?

"You didn't need to back those nobles within my Kingdom who decided to rebel against me, their liege lord! Yet, here we are," she said opening up her arms, an eloquent gesture as she signed at the broken city which lay around them. "On the other hand, you can join with Ufwala and swear homage to me. You will find me a good Queen, for I will leave the administration in your hands. There will be no regime change and you will still be their leader."

"What's the catch?"

"No catch," she said with a smile, "You will render to me manpower or payment as tribute, but these deals can be thrashed out by our Ministers in the comfort of meeting halls. Now, I'm done talking. What do you say?"

From his vantage point on the wall he could see the trebuchets being dismantled, the same artillery that had made the wall of Vitrossy seem like a stone dyke seen on a farm. He could see the massed ranks of infantry and cavalry threading their way through his city, the civic buildings already flying the flag of Ufwala. Would it be better to bend the knee? He had buggered up once, he knew, and enough men had already died for that mistake. He looked along the wall and saw his men, covered in dust as they were and sweat streaked from their exertions in the fighting and falling back to the fortress.

"What do you think, sergeant?"

"Sire?"

"What do you think of her offer; would you take it if you were me?"

"The Queen of the South is victorious again, sire, and if we accept her offer then we are the border. I'd take her offer, it's either that or die in the tunnels."

He looked down at the Queen and knew he had been completely outplayed, even if he were to throw some defiant words at her then one of two things would happen: she would storm the walls and raze the fortress and Vitrossy to the ground and a build a colony here for her veterans, or he would be killed by his own men and they would open the gates to her. He chuckled drily for either option promised him death.

"Open the gates and strike the colours!" He bellowed out to the men around him. He fixed Wellisa with a stare, she having the good grace not to smile during the moment of her triumph. "You have my surrender, ma'am, under your terms."

Garren watched from the group of bodyguards as the Queen laid out her terms. He was astounded at her gall, but there was a degree of unease to the entire process. He had just watched Wellisa as she laid out the terms for her new Kingdom, seen the creation of a new power block that Cardavy would have to seriously consider from now on. She was the border, this Queen of the South, and the one great broker of power in the Coalition now.

He knew, as he would communicate to the Parliament as soon as decently possible, that the only option available now to keep the Coalition from forming a significant threat would be to somehow band the rest of the South against her. He remembered the words of Morro earlier on, detailing how the Queen held the lion's share of the land now and the resources to go with it. Even if Cardavy was to play politics and unite the rest of them and give aid, what were the chances that they wouldn't have to deal with a new Wellisa in the shape of someone else?

Aye, he thought remembering the first time he had met her in the hall of her capital, the great game would make for interesting times.

Chapter Four – **The Clansman**

He could smell the musty scent of damp clothing, the almost sour-milk like scent of dry sweat and the occasional whiff of shit and piss. He could hear the grunts and weapons checks around him as men looked through their weapons and made sure that they were secure or within easy access, it was too late now to make sure that they were sharp enough. He could hear one man, maybe two, muttering to whatever Gods it was they prayed to. He could hear the arrows thudding off the wooden door and the crash of pottery as they smashed against the sides. There was a new scent to the air and his heartbeat began to quicken in anticipation, for the smell was oil. He knew now what the enemy were planning, he knew now that they were being slowly pushed towards their deaths. He knew that there was nothing that he could do about it, crushed together in the mass of fighting men and humanity as he was.

The tower shook as a large boulder smashed into one of the lower supports and he could hear the cries and curses of the wounded and the living trapped within the tight confines and unable to move. He wanted to scream, but as a Chief he knew he couldn't show any weakness so he swore instead. He swore loudly again causing the man to his right to chuckle grimly, all eyes focussed on the wooden ramp.

Shafts of daylight were beginning to break through as the lead shot from slings and heavier rocks and bolts from the ballistae smashed into it. He was glad it wasn't raining, but then if it had been then that damn fool Neard wouldn't have thrown most of the clansmen attached to his army at Nepriner in these wagons of death. If the rain had actually stayed on for a bit longer then the ground would still have been too sodden for the towers to move and he would have been able to spend a day in camp without having to worry about death.

The tower stopped and the ramp began to slowly creak open.

"Gain the wall today, boys, and the city is ours!" He roared, though he didn't know who he was trying to convince. His eyes were fixed forwards, focussed on the ramp and the shafts of light that were getting brighter. "We are Clansmen, and there's a reason why the Rupinians need us to take this wall. Show them how real men from the north fight, lads!" Dozens of clansmen roared their approval at his words and he felt the better for it.

He flexed his fingers on the leather grip of his sword, his palm sweaty, and began to feel an intolerable itch on his leg. He flexed his fingers that held his shield and felt the blood flow back into them, the feeling of warmth rushing into the previously numb fingers.

The ramp came down with a crash onto the wall and he could just see over the head of the man in front of him. There was a solitary soldier there, an older man wearing the uniform of a Cardavian general with a close cropped red beard. He was carrying a pot and a brand, his weaponry by his side. Tortag tried to roar out a warning and the order to charge at the same time, knowing that the enemy in front of them intended to burn them and the tower. It came out as a strangled cry, nowhere near loud enough to alert the men to the danger they were in.

He saw it in slow motion as the older man threw the pot underhand as one would bowl a ball. The brand was dipped into a burning iron brazier in the same movement and swiftly followed. The older man drew a short stabbing sword and reached down, calmly, and picked up the large tower shield that was indicative of all Cardavian soldiers. Tortag watched it all in slow motion, everything happening before his eyes as if it were taking place underwater. The man, and he could only assume it to be Lord Ironside given the colour of the shield and the description of him that Quittle had provided, slammed the shield once and then twice with the sword as he challenged the Clansmen to come on.

The pot smashed into the ground at the feet of the man just in front of Tor. He looked down at it, and though Tor couldn't see his face, he knew it would be non-plussed. He knew when he saw the burning brand that the dawn of comprehension would spread across his face to be slowly replaced by fear. He wouldn't be surprised if the oil that was, even now, beginning to pool and drip through the wooden slats, wasn't added to with a steady stream of urine.

The clansmen began to charge, but the brand smashed into the deck of the assault platform. The gasses kicked up by the oil were the first to explode throwing men backwards in a confusion of burnt remains and blackened bodies. The oil soaked sides and wood quickly caught on and all was confusion.

He charged through the flames, knowing that to step back was death, except this time he didn't fight with Lord Ironside to the death. This time the ramp went back up and the tower was slowly dragged away from the wall, all exits secured and bolted down as the clansmen were cooked alive. He screamed, but it was just another voice added to the multitude.

He woke up.

They were within sight of the mountains of home, the snow topped peaks looking like something out a child's storybook. He could see through the open tent flap a solitary Eagle flying high in the air circling over a patch of gorse somewhere in the distance evidently looking for some prey. The sun was beginning to rise, the cloudless sky being cast in colours of red and oranges. It would have been an ideal winters morning had he not been surrounded by the four hundred survivors of his command, all that was left of the two thousand clansmen that had come from the Black Moon clan. He was lathered in cold sweat, regardless of the heat of his tent or the poor excuse for bedding that he had. He had expected to make this journey home in triumph, to be welcomed as the hero who had finally put paid to the Attainians and their ambitions that they had launched from Nepriner in decades' past. He was supposed to be feted and lauded, and returning with the vast majority of his men and friends. Instead he was returning home like a beaten dog, his tail tucked between his legs, and the vast majority of his men and friends dead on the fields outside the defiant walls and within the streets.

His back ached like the devils, his neck stiff and unyielding as he sat up. He was getting too old for this shit, he knew, but always he would promise himself that it would be his final campaigning season. He promised his wife a score of times, but she would look at him with that knowing smile and, with a little sadness in her eyes, nod. He would carry out his promise with good intentions, locking his shield and armour away in an oak chest which would then be kept outside in one of the outhouses on the farm he lived. He would hang his sword up above the fire and he would talk to the younger farmhands that he employed about days spent around the fire with friends out in the field, remembering the glory of the battle and the rush of excitement when shield wall smashed into shield wall, and remembering the better times around fires afterwards when they had won the day.

Aye, he would recount those stories and then get the itch again. He would stalk around the barn like a bear with a sore head and his wife would know the campaigning season would be coming soon again. He would take to drink, forgetting the bad times in campaign where he had pissed himself in fear knowing that he could be killed or seeing hale and healthy friends being killed or, even worse, crippled. He would revel in his reputation in the taverns of the local village or the larger towns and would talk with other old soldiers.

Then some bastard Rupinian would come with a commission from the Emperor asking for all healthy and able bodied men to take up the sword once more. He would leave the village and walk back to his farm. He would see his wife and hold her for a while and promise that it would be his last campaign. She would smile that knowing smile with a little sadness in her eyes and the entire cycle would repeat itself.

Well a pox on it, he thought. This time it would be his bloody last.

He had led his friends and clansmen into that bloody fiasco that was Nepriner. He had seen his men burnt alive and treated like shit because they couldn't take a wall that couldn't be taken anyway with only bloody ladders. He had taken part in the hell that had been the fighting in the

Industrial district, as buildings and massive chimney stacks collapsed under the continuous bombardment regardless of the friendly casualties. He could still remember barely escaping with his life as a squad of Attainian soldiers who had been making a break for the north east and the isolated Wolves had cut the section he was with to pieces during a ferocious and quick night fight, himself surviving after he had been knocked unconscious into deep shadows with a nasty leg wound.

He swore swiftly, rubbing at the back of his neck with his left hand trying to loosen off the stiff muscles and feel something other than pain for a change. His stomach flared up reminding him of hunger, and it was another feeling he could do without. He wondered what his wife, Elyn, was doing at this point, possibly waking up herself and toasting some bread over the fire for her breakfast or seeing to the animals in the field. He pictured her now in his head and smiled at the image. She was his beauty, and damned to the rest of them. She was the only woman he had ever truly felt for, had ever truly understood him and had actually managed to deal with the fact that he was a bit of a bastard. He would dream of her when he was away on deployment. He would think of her constantly when the clan allowed or when the bastard Imperials allowed. He thought of her especially in those quiet moments when there was no real call on his time, when he could actually take time to himself to digest mentally what had happened throughout the day and make sense of it all. His only rock, his only real beacon of hope, he knew, in his life was through that woman.

Aye, he pictured her then with her warm smile and her love for him. He remembered the day when they had first met, at some celebration commemorating something or other. He had cursed her sister's husband good naturedly for being in the wrong clan and had been invited to a drink for it, though he had only eyes for her. Next day he tried asking her to step out with him, to go to a tavern to see the hangover condemned with a fresh pint or two. He gave a rueful smile, remembering the scene even as he finally became fully awake; she had turned him down. She had said something along the line of having a good night, but never wanting to see him again. Well, he had cut off all ties for two weeks until he got wrapped up into some damned exercise he couldn't get out of. Decrying everybody who had ever heard of Rupinia, he decided to visit her again just to give it one last chance. Fifteen years later they were still together, still happy regardless of what the needs of the Empire threw at them, and looking forward to future days.

"You awake, chief?" He heard the call from outside and cursed it, evidently noisier than he hoped to be when he had stood up.

"Aye, I'm awake. Come in, Kiegal, you got something new to tell?"

"The usual, chief, nothing else apart from that. Lads are happier being in home soil now than they were on the march back," he said as he entered the tent, ducking his head as he did so. "At least it's good weather, fucking freezing though."

"It's the north, what did you expect?"

"I was hoping to spend it in Nepriner, in all honesty, everyone knows it's bloody sunny down there all the time."

Tortag grunted and stretched his legs, hearing and feeling a grinding in his knee caps. He was more shocked these days when he didn't click or crack whenever he stood up, "Is there anything decent for breakfast?"

"Oatmeal again, chief."

"If I see porridge or oatmeal or any mixture of warmed up shit when I get back home then I swear to the Gods I will murder someone," Tor said with a passion rarely felt by anyone about oatmeal, "All I want is one bloody sausage, just the bloody one!"

"You've woken up in a fine mood."

"Fuck yourself," he said, a grin spreading across his face as he chucked the canteen of water towards his second. Kiegal was a veteran, and probably the only man in the clan that he could truly depend on it when came to a fight and had the scars to prove it. He wore an eyepatch over his left eye after having had a spear rip down his face during one of the innumerable clan skirmishes that often took place, half his right ear was missing from another fight and his knuckles seemed to have permanently broken and scarred skin over them. Yet, for all the physical characteristics of a thug and a soldier, Kiegal was probably one of the most genuine and intelligent people that Tor knew.

The man had left clan country when he had reached his majority and went off to study in Rupinia; studying, of all things, criminal law and philosophy. He had set himself up well and had passed the majority of his exams with flying colours, coming top of his class on average and even thinking of taking it further and conducting further studies so he could become a lecturer himself or move into politics. It was then that the impetuosity that was both a curse and a blessing of all clansmen infected the man and he left the university and went back to the Black Moon clan.

"So what's the plan today then, chief?"

"Usual. Keep bloody walking until we're back in town, do a final head count and then get our back pay from the Empire. We'll need to check on records as well for next of kin details for those that died if we didn't know them, we had a lot of new boys with us this time."

"Too much new blood if you ask me, Tor. Empire is starting to stretch our ranks too thin."

Tor had been looking at the chart he had hung up on a wooden cross piece but now turned around and looked at his second in a steady manner. He had flashbacks to his last meeting with Quittle on the long and bloody retreat back to the Empire.

The snow had been up to their knees by that point and Nepriner was nothing more than an ugly nightmare, far away in the distance and unseen. Ahead of them lay open country, hills that rolled gently into plains and glens that once would have had farms and country houses dotted about in abundance. Now all was empty and still, a void landscape that had been burnt out and destroyed during the lightning offensive conducted by the Imperial army in the early Spring and Summer. It felt like a different lifetime when they had marched south with nothing but triumph and victories behind them, when an Attainian couldn't so much as break wind without worrying that he would find an Imperial sword at his throat.

Quittle hadn't said much to him after that occasion when he had put forward the idea of seeking independence for the clans. Tortag had thought about it, but he had dismissed such thoughts as a childish fantasy. Every boy or girl within the clans thought about breaking the chains of dependence the Empire held when they were growing up, raised on nationalist rhetoric that always focussed on the glorious parts of military victories and paid little attention to the bloody defeats and hardships that led their forefathers to signing the act of union with Rupinia in the first place.

The herald had been quiet, far more quiet than was thought normal, and his face had grown darker with each passing day. Every casualty, particularly those taken by the clans, was felt almost to be a personal injury to the man. It had raised some concerns with even a few of the Rupinian officers asking him what was wrong, but he rebuffed all attempts at talk and instead had become more insular. He refused, point blank, to speak to the Speirakians.

It was on the final night that Quittle had finally approached him, coming up to the fire wrapped in the tartan cloak of the Red River clan from which he originally hailed. Black Moon and Red River had always historically got on, sharing the same origins and the same part of the peninsula. He had Quittle round at his farm a few times as friends just to have a few drinks and talk about life, but he could see on the face of his friend then that it would be no easy home coming or no easy banter between the pair. The men around the camp fire could see it as well and moved away to other find other warm places to sit, keen to be away from the brooding tall man and the chief.

"Have you thought about what I said?" Quittle led off the conversation as soon as he sat on the dead, wooden trunk.

"No," Tor had lied easily enough, "Weather is starting to improve though so the going will get it easier."

"This isn't the time to piss about!"

"This isn't the time to start pissing into the wind either, Bear!" He hissed, his temper flashing as he looked at the man suddenly. Quittle looked as if he were about to launch himself over the fire, reach for one of the many knives he had on him these days and attempt to slice his throat. "Look," Tor said trying to calm the situation before it developed, "we'll get back, like we always do, and forget this shit. We've suffered a reverse and, aye, a lot of good men have died because other men made the wrong decisions. If we go against the Empire now then you can be damned sure the Speirakians and Rupinians would be calling for our destruction, we aren't in the position to fight bloody sleep right now let alone the Imperial army."

"But it's worth trying for…better than this damned servitude surely?"

"Look, Bear, I don't know what the fuck has got into your head lately, but you've seriously got to think things through. You're an intelligent man!" He took a drink from the wineskin and cursed at the bitter and vinegary-like taste. "Why do you suddenly hate the Empire anyway? You weren't fighting in that city."

"I saw enough of it, Tor. Did you meet any of the Cardavians or Attainians we were fighting against?"

"Only when they were busy trying to kill me or the boys, why?" Quittle actually offered a small smile at that and took out his own wineskin, taking a deep drink before rubbing off the spillage on his upper lip with his left arm.

"I met a few of them. Their commanding officer was Beran Corus, a Cardavian, he was in charge of the Grey Wolves that held out in the north east of the city when we had them surrounded. Stern bastard with little give in him. Seemed well liked though. There was another called Takol," he racked his brains for a few seconds, "I can't remember his surname just now. Anyway, he was one of the last Attainian high ranking officers towards the end, got himself killed in the fighting at the arena. I offered him the chance to surrender and you know what he said?" Tortag shook his head, "He said that they didn't have the facilities to handle us so they couldn't accept our surrender! I liked him. I liked most of them. Ironside was a good man as well, he was there with the Kings Own. He held the wall when we launched our towers."

"Older man with a red beard?" Quittle nodded, "Aye, I know him. He was the bastard that burned half my men to death. Brave bastard, but a damned butcher." There was a break in the cloud and moonlight bathed the snow covered clearing, the trees suddenly seeming to tower over them as they were illuminated. Tor could just about make out a winter hare sniffing at the air before it scampered off again into the woods, unsure why so many men were camped near it. "Why are you telling me this, Quittle? You aren't one for running your mouth."

"I don't know. I suppose what I'm trying to say is that there are good men on either side of this damned war, and that the further we advance into Attainia then the more we lose sight of what we originally set out to do." He paused for a few seconds and tried to find the right words, "Attainia is like having a dog. The dog did a shit in the middle of the house. You smack it on the snout and tell it not to do it again. The dog learns. You don't rub the dogs nose into the shit and keep going on about it. We've done what we need to do, the rest of it is just greed and it's bleeding the clans dry of money and people."

"You're suggesting a bid for independence again?"

"Of course."

"Forget about it. Even if we secede from the Empire, the clans have never united under a proper leader in hundreds of years."

"Neither had the Southern Coalition and my sources say they've found a Queen."

"And are you going to be our King?" There was a warning glint to his eye then and Tortag saw the fervent self-belief of a fanatic within them. He shook his head and looked into the fire once more, his thoughts colliding together before looking back at his friend, "You're a bloody Imperial herald, Bear, you've never led men into battle and there's few who look on you as an actual clansman. What hope have you got to lead anyone?"

"You'll see," he promised, "when you get home and receive their demands again, you'll see. I'm splitting off with the Rupinians tomorrow and heading to the capital to report to the Emperor. I'll be back in clan lands by the Spring, and you'll have started the rebellion by then."

He had stalked off then without even a by-your-leave or any sign of farewell, just the vague word of prophecy hanging in the air that left Tortag with an uneasy feeling in his stomach. He stood now within his tent, the mountains of home looming in the distance, and saw Kiegal staring at him. Nobody within the higher echelons of the clans were young and idealistic fools, not headstrong enough to think they could take on an entire Empire by themselves with no financial or military support. Aye, there was romantics amongst them and even a few who were cynical born from the need to protect their old idealistic inner-selves, but out and out idealists there was none.

"Have you been talking to Quittle?"

"Bear the herald?" Tortag nodded his head, "No, *I* haven't." He said pointedly.

"But?"

"Well there's rumours, Tor. The lads are talking about a gathering of the clan chiefs, of back pay getting denied and another pop at the Attainians.

They are even talking about Rupinian colonists taking some of the lands in clan country." Tortag stared at him, disbelief etched over his face.

"See when I asked if there's anything new? You remember that?"

"Aye."

"That's the sort of shit I was on about," he gave an exasperated sigh and knew that the rumours would gather momentum and men would begin to question each other and expand on the details. It would get worse when they got home, he thought, for then they'd all get drunk and talk about it in even greater overblown detail. That would be before they came across those that had been left behind by those that had fallen, the families that would be seeking blood payment in order to survive. The Imperial treasury would have to pay them quickly or would ferment a rebellion, and if the Imperials did ask for a single man before the clans had received their payment in full then someone somewhere would do something bloody stupid.

"We don't even have a name for our country."

"Say again, chief?"

"We always call it clan country, or the areas after whoever happens to control it at the time. It's not like you see the Cardavians calling themselves 'Square Shield land' or whatever. Its primitive bollocks is what it is."

"We used to have a name, before it was taken from us."

"Taken from us? You sound a lot more convinced than you are letting on, my friend," he saw the look on the face of Kiegal and knew that the old warrior was being deadly serious, that something of those rumours had touched the soul of the grizzled man and lit a spark. "So what was the name of our Kingdom of clans?"

"Traemwen...I don't suppose you want a history lesson do you?" Tortag rubbed at his face suddenly wearing the palms of his hand and looked at his friend, shaking his head as he did so.

"No, go tell the men to get their kit ready and to start making a move. It's time to go home."

The town of Cafeld was quiet and yet filled with people, it was as if an order had been given for there to be absolutely no audible sign of human life there in a dull mockery of the chaos that had been Nepriner. It was as if they had marched into their own funeral and caught everyone in the act of dividing up their possessions.

The clansmen walked in on sore feet, battered and bruised, their blisters having developed blisters a long time since. Their tartans were faded and bleached under the sun, the only darkness to the pattern being those areas where snow had settled and eventually formed a damp spot. Their weapons were clean, but they were hidden in mud and half broken scabbards or sheaths. Some of the men carried wounds, bandages hastily tied around their foreheads or their arms or any other exposed section. Many didn't even carry a bergen any more for their kit, trusting instead to the hastily salvaged sacks they had found in some barn to carrying their possessions. There were no bands, no fanfares and no welcoming dignitaries to see them back in. There was no landlord standing at the local tavern thrusting his daughters and pints of foaming ale onto grateful soldiers. No happy milkmaids handing out cheese and favours for later, and certainly no damned Imperial waiting there with kegs of alcohol from his Imperial highness and heavy chests filled with months of back pay to be paid in gold.

"Well this is quite the welcome party," Tortag said as if to no-one as they walked through, his sword hanging limp by his side. He could see people who he knew well and each and every one of them had the same look of concern on their face as they scanned the returning warriors for loved ones. The thin, keening cry was taken up in the southern section of the town where they had walked in from and was gradually taken up all along the line as they slowly filed past.

They reached the town square where people would often gather for fairs and celebrations, the Imperial representative for the area standing on the dais with his hands clasped behind his back. The clansmen walked up in some semblance of military order in rank and file, but their sorry and dejected appearance did little to raise the military ardour or fighting spirit around them. He was flanked by two Rupinian guardsmen, tall men and broad shouldered with not a speck of rust on their black and purple armour. Their white horse hair crests were perfectly combed, unblemished, and erect as the winter sun shone brightly onto the bright spear tips.

They approached the dais and stood still before it, Tortag and Kiegal at the head of the survivors of fighting men. The memory of different times came to him almost like a flash when he had been about to march on Nepriner and the southlands that awaited, the looks of joy and excitement on the faces of the men behind and before him. He remembered the cheering crowds and all the signals of victory that had been foretold, the town priests had come out and poured their blessings on them in a variety of different ways each peculiar to their own Gods, and then they had been sent forth with a stirring speech on how the clansmen of the Black Moon would right the historical wrongs that had been inflicted on them and take their revenge on the very city that spawned the Attainian empire.

Aye, it was a different time. The sun shone still as brightly, but he felt no warmth from the winter rays. A cold wind blew in from the west and there was a gathering of dark clouds following behind that signalled the rain to come. Strangely, he started to automatically think of the list of jobs he would have when he finally got home; odd jobs dotted around the farm as well as those that needed to take place on a daily basis. There would be no rest, he knew, and he would end up picking up the sword as he always did after the fields had been sewn and the lambing season over.

"What happened in the south, Chief Tortag Mane? The Rupinian spoke with the lazy rolling accent that was native to all of his kind, the type of accent that irritated Tortag in the extreme. It spoke of condescension, brash and arrogant in its tone. Tortag looked up and instinctively felt his shoulders shrug, the streak of belligerence innate in all clansmen coming to the fore.

"Shit orders from shit leaders that led a lot of my men being killed," there was angry muttering in the crowd but Tor only had eyes for the Rupinian on the dais. "Enquiries and self-justification can wait for later. My men are cold, hungry and tired. They have walked all the way to Nepriner, fought a battle over a period of several months and walked all the way back again. They need to go home and get their heads straight. I trust you have their back pay?"

"Taxes have been difficult this season, clansman, therefore the back pay will continue to be in arrears until all taxes have been collected." There was a low muttering amongst the ranks, a dam of emotion that was steadfastly trying to hold back the wave of anger that was threatening to topple the men from the dais. It would be easy to do, Tor thought, and the damned Rupinian was playing into the hands of the likes of Quittle when he said that there would be no wages. Kiegal knew as well, saw the look on his chiefs' face, and bellowed at the men to remain quiet.

"You mean to tell me, sir, that we will fight your wars and battles for you and when…when we finally get home that you expect us to work the land and then pay for the pleasure of having done all that for you? I'm sorry, Rupinian, but I don't see the reward there."

"Nevertheless, clansman, that is the way things are. The Emperor demanded victory and instead he received two broken armies, a damaged reputation and a land that hasn't been tilled or mines worked. He cannot afford to pay for his armies if he doesn't get the bounty from receiving cities into his benevolent fold."

"You mean until he has looted and pillaged his way across the bloody south, like you now seek to pillage our lands!" His anger spilled out, he wasn't one for smooth words and silver tongues, and the official before him was merely the figurehead for the system that was now trying to put them over a barrel.

"I'd hold your tongue, Chief Tortag Mane. You hold your title on the sufferance of his Imperial Majesty Rhagan the First. You can be replaced."

"You say strong words for a man that only has two guardsmen with him. Your own fort is close at hand, but I think I can reach out and kill you three times over before your men are even aware that something has arisen." He was going to go on further, might have even acted, had he not felt a hand on his arm as Kiegal pulled at him to take a step back both mentally and verbally. Tor turned and looked at his friend and saw the warning look in his eye and knew within an instant that he had said too much, that, whilst being the clan chief he held power over the clan, he had no actual power when it came to the Rupinians within his land.

The Rupinian, in turn, stared down from the dais with nothing but contempt in his expression. He knew he wasn't in a position to do anything at the moment, but there would be a reckoning. He hadn't asked for this draft to the arsehole of nowhere. The weather was, for the most part, foul and the natives were ambivalent at the best of time. He looked up at the turf and wood stockade that marked the boundary of the wooden fort and longed to be within the warm confines of the building, the cold western wind sending a chill through his bones. He glanced back to the assembled clansman and felt a sneer coming to his face before quickly wiping it off. He knew it wouldn't pay to antagonise them further, that the men of the north were a sensitive and proud people who could hold a grievance for a long time. They had held once against the Attainians for centuries from expanding north, and he was sure that they held a grudge because the Rupinians were there now. He had long suggested, when he was in the safe confines of the capital and far away from this place, that they needed a bigger occupying force within the lands. His superiors had argued that there would be no profit in it, that the north would just be an open abscess if that were to happen where money and treasure would pour in and little come out.

He looked down upon the assembled mass then and wished he had a full regiment with him, enough to keep the natives down and reinforce the Emperors orders, but all he had were three hundred men. Of those three hundred he wasn't even sure how many he could depend on when it came to a fight, for surely these were the self-same men that had managed to avoid most forms of active service in the south and instead had taken the easier billet of what was, effectively, a policing force?

"Chief Mane, dismiss the assembly and your men. I expect a full report on the actions of the clan warriors' tomorrow morning."

Chapter Five – **Training Days**

Velawin ran through the city park, his breathing in time with the pounding of his feet. Every four steps would see an inhalation or exhalation of breath as he kept his rhythm going, making sure to not break his stride and suddenly lose his concentration. This, of course, did not prevent him from looking around and seeing the couples walk arm in arm by the ornamental lake or children running through the trees playing their games, but for the most part his attention was focussed on the path in front of him and not smashing into anyone. It was a nice day and cool, the only mist hereabouts being created by the steam coming off his body.

He was sweating freely; the droplets of sweat running off his forehead and staining his training shirt even further. His back was on fire with the strain of the rocks within his bergen, extra weight to make the running experience that little bit harder and a little bit more challenging. He swore now through his gasps of breath, cursing his lack of foresight knowing that he had weighed the bag too heavily prior to going out running. His shoulders were damn near rubbed raw and the back of his neck felt as if it had taken a pounding. He would be stiff and sore later on he knew, and that was before he even considered the state of his legs.

He pushed on and moved off the path to allow a man walking his dog the right of way. His right knee cap was feeling loose, but the left felt tight and tugged every time he started off the run. It was beginning to flare up again, the pain running down his calf and into his ankle. He had considered seeing one of the medics to see if they could recommend any type of stretches, but decided against it given they would order him to stop running for a period of time. He decided that when he made it back to barracks that he would go for a cold bath, something to loosen the muscles and take away the burning feeling within his muscles.

He was approaching one of the hills within the park, but the title of hill was giving the slight slope too much of a compliment. He still braced himself mentally and felt himself automatically shortening his stride as he began the slight ascent. His breathing became more laboured as his legs pumped, but he kept his chest out and his feet close to the ground. He kept his count going in his head, the consistency helping him to concentrate and not focus on the physical pain that was screaming at him to stop and take a breather. He knew fine well that if he were to stop then he would probably struggle to start again, or, if he did start again, then he wouldn't be able to have a consistent run without stopping and starting.

He reached the peak of the slope where it levelled off and ploughed on once more, shaking his hands to loosen the wrists and the shoulders as they hung limply by his side. He allowed himself a minute or so of a light jog to loosen off his legs properly before he picked up speed and started to make for the southern exit of the park. The faint trill of bird song was like music to his ears, interrupting his thought process for a few seconds as he listened to the melody. He knew through discussions with Aleill that the majority of bird song was just them trying to find a mate and shouting out warnings to would be predators, but there was something about it that spoke to him on an instinctive level. The sun was beginning to set, the few clouds in the sky being cast into pink colours and slowly darkening to purple.

He was glad to have escaped the confines of the barracks with everything that it entailed, the feel of his feet pounding against the hard road was almost as relaxing as it was sore after a while. He had finished handing over the Kings Own to some staff officer, a jovial enough man but instantly forgettable in appearance and name. He had grown attached to the Kings as only a commanding officer can for they were, for all intents and purposes, his men and his first command. He had led them into battle and, more importantly, led them out of battle again. It was a comradeship born out of necessity but matured through mutual respect and admiration, something he was surprised to find that he had fostered in the short time he had been with them. However, he was glad to be back with the Wolves, a legion which he considered home.

He had first broached the subject with Beran once the man had managed to escape both the legion and his wife for more than five minutes. They had found themselves in a tavern they used to frequent when they had been living in the barracks by the eastern gate during the days before Nepriner. They had settled themselves into their old spot at their old table as if nothing had changed, though Beran got the drinks in this time which was possibly a first as far as either could remember.

"I'm not being funny, Ban," he said still using the nickname that was sure to get a flash out of Beran one of these days, "but there's too much bloody paperwork in running a legion. I never wanted command, not yet anyway."

"Well why not?" Beran asked as he took a sip from the tankard, "I mean, you're well suited to it, Vel, and none better. When I was knocked out, wounded, isolated or whatever then it was you the men looked to take command of the situation. You held Nepriner when I wasn't able to. You deserve your command."

"There's a difference though; that's in the middle of the battlefield. Look, you've got three types of officers the way I see it," Vel replied whilst sitting further back into the leather chair, "the first lot are the usual who rise to the top because they know how to fill out the write paperwork and kiss the right arse. You've got the second lot that could fight an action with his eyes shut and probably get the vast majority of his boys out alive providing the situation allows but not a lot else and, unfortunately, are completely unsuited to peace time duties. Then you've got the last lot, the rarest lot, who can do both.

"Now you, you my friend can do both. I, on the other hand, can't stand bloody paperwork and would sooner be, as Erallac put its it; 'hiding in the bushes somewhere playing grab arse'. He's not wrong," Vel took a sip from his drink and watched a few of the soapy suds cling to the brim of the glass tankard before slowly drifting down again. "As I said, it's not that I don't want it eventually, just not now."

"So what do you want now then?" Beran waved at a group who had walked in and gave a cheer when they saw the two officers from the triumph, other people occasionally looking over to see what the commotion was before settling back to their drinks and throwing glances back at them. It was one thing to be well known, Beran thought to himself privately, but it was a pain in the arse when it came to just wanting to enjoy a quiet drink or have a nice meal with the wife. He missed those days when you could do that without being expected to regale the entire place with stories they weren't entirely interested in anyway.

"I want to come back to the Wolves, if you'll have me. I know you haven't found a light infantry leader to replace me yet, I looked at the drafting order chit when I was at headquarters when I was putting in for the transfer and trying to find out who my relief was."

"I don't have to do some joining interview bollocks with you, do I?" Beran said with a grin, "It'll be good to have you back, Vel."

He had been back in the Wolves for a week now and things hadn't changed, not to the point where he didn't recognise where he was at any rate. There were, like Beran had said during the triumph, a lot of men who should have been there. Nepriner had cost the legion dear in terms of blood and sacrifice and there was now pressure on the Wolves to recruit new men into the legion on a daily basis. It had been one of the first debates he had seen when he had entered the mess when he had moved back into the barracks. It was decided to send Erallac and a few of the junior officers to the old hill overlooking the city where the legions, in times gone by, would conduct their muster before going off to take another hill fort or another city state. More of the men, those who were on light duties because of wounds that weren't too ghastly to look at and were on the right side of 'glorious', were often sent into the streets to try and stir up support. It was, however, universally decided that the last person who should be sent out was Aleill.

For all that, there was a new lease of life around the legion and there was rumour abound that they were due to being going south instead of north to relieve round the Stags, a legion based in the south of the Kingdom in the western pass that marked the boundary between Cardavy and the Southern

Coalition. It would be a peaceful billet and give the men enough time to rest and regain their strength, as well as time for Velawin to train the newest light infantry recruits in how to run around a mountain range.

He felt the first spit of rain hit his face and looked up, cursing inwardly through gritted teeth as black clouds raced across the sky carried by an ever increasing wind. He had another mile to run and, even in the early morning, the streets were beginning to fill with various bakeries throwing open their doors for the first of the early risers. He skipped off the pavement and watched out for the deep guttering, not wanting to get an injury through a snapped or twisted ankle, and started to run on the inside of the road.

The rain began to fall more heavily and he spurred on, determined to make it back to the barracks in time before he was drowned out or ended up catching the cold or the flu. He had run this track many times now and knew he would be home, and dry, within three minutes.

He peeled off the road and went down one of the innumerable streets of Silveroak, his internal sense of direction taking over. The city was still a rabbit warren to him, full of street signs and everyone bustling about as if they had no other business to attend to other than choking up the streets, but he knew where the important things in his life were located.

Running alongside the large tufa wall that separated the barracks and the training ground from civilian life, he could just about make out the sight of the wrought iron gates that was the primary entrance into the barracks itself. The original fort, he had learnt from his own reading, had been designed to take some pressure off the hill fort which was now the Kings Palace. By having an outlying fort the enemy would have to take care of it prior to pressing on with the siege proper of the fledgling capital. Now, like most other cities Velawin had went to, the original purpose had been subsumed within the mass of humanity and it was now incorporated into the new wall which encircled the Cardavian capital.

He slowed down to a walk spotting a commotion outside the iron gates, a member of the guard staff interviewing a tall man wearing the uniform of a Cardavian officer. He wore the black cloak of the Leviathan legion, normally stationed in the south western corner of Cardavy to support the marines if there was ever the need for a force to be embarked at sea. It was strange, therefore, to find one of them demanding entry at the gate of the Wolves. It was even stranger when one considered that there was an inter-legion rivalry that existed between the Wolves and Leviathans for some reason which everyone had forgotten but fully understood was a matter of life and death.

"Is there a problem here?" Velawin asked, the rain starting to dissipate and calm down. He was still far too warm and the steam was rising off him in clouds, something made worse when he took off the bergen full of rocks and put them on the ground. The relief in his back was instant and he was able to roll out his shoulders properly and stretch.

"You are General Velawin Celadan, sir?" The man was dressed well, the armour new and the rank badges denoting his rank still shiny with little wear or scratches on them. He had an open and honest face, someone ill-mannered may have called it round, but he didn't seem the sort that would necessarily go out their way to be a pain in the arse for the guardsman at the gate of a barracks.

"Not anymore, I am simply a Commander now. I have control over the light infantry of this legion. You are?"

"Aglon Miliner, formerly of the Leviathans and their heavy infantry. Recently promoted," Velawin nodded as the man handed over a collection of papers with the broken seal of the Cardavian parliament, presumably some sort of joining instructions and letter of promotion.

"You are a long way from home, Aglon." The man nodded, a grimace crossing his features as he looked around the city as if it were going to grab him and beat him about the head.

"I prefer being near the sea, sir. Leviathans have been based out of Noriandie on the south west coast with the fleet for the last ten years, we've set down roots and the locals know us. This, being up north here, is entirely new to me."

"Not your draft preference then?" Vel asked, the beginnings of a smile tugging at his lips. He knew the answer before it was even out of the man's mouth and handed him back the documents, satisfied that he wasn't some sort of Imperial spy or someone likely to do harm about the camp.

"Since when do the legions ever go for any of that? That would be conducive to good morale!"

"You haven't served under Beran before have you, or maybe even with him?" The man shook his head, "No? Sounds something like he'd say. So what was the problem here then?"

"My cloak of all things! Not the right colour or something like that, and the, and I quote, 'giant squid on the back looking like a runny shit' in no way looks like a wolf. I think the duty officer has been summoned as well."

"Brilliant," Velawin turned to the guardsman and his good humour was rapidly starting to disappear. He needed some food to stop the faint cramps he could feel beginning in his calf muscles, and he knew that he would have to show the man to the mess given that he was the only officer present at this point in time. It would hardly be a decent greeting to the legion if Aglon were to be literally abandoned on the doorstep in the middle of the street. "Who is the duty officer today?"

"Commander Lexand, sir," the guardsman answered causing Velawin to grimace. Erallac wouldn't be a bad introduction to the legion, but given that he was drinking last night then he was liable to be worse than a bear with a sore head and wouldn't be entirely sociable.

"Inform him that I've taken charge and can vouch for our new friend. Have the mess steward come down and collect his kit and take it to his new billet," he beckoned the man forward and picked up his bergen of rocks once again, grunting under the weight. "Welcome to your new home, Aglon. Welcome to the Wolves."

"Have you actually sat there all day on your fat arse doing nothing?" Aleill said with a grin, bringing over two glasses of fresh orange juice to where Velawin sat next to the fire place. Vel looked up from his book and gave a grin, folding the uppermost corner of the page over so as to mark his place before shutting it and putting the novel on the table. It was an interesting read and certainly diverted attention away to the humdrum of modern life, but he felt that the plot line was a little too predictable at times. The fire crackled reassuringly behind him and it was only now that he was aware what hour it was, the sun having set a long time since and the bright light of the sun being replaced by the orange glow of candles. He stretched out his legs, hearing the click of his knees as if they were sliding back into place.

"I'll have you know I've done three things today, which is probably three things more than you've done all week. I've went for my run, I've had a nice bath and a meal afterwards." Aleill took a drink from his orange and nodded.

"Well, I'll have you know that I've done two things today, and one of them involved dealing with some civic dignitary."

"I'm sure you enjoyed that."

"The man was a buffoon, almost as great an ox as Erallac. Where is he anyway, I thought he was duty?"

"I've only seen him once today and that was down the parade ground where he was safely ensconced within his office having given strict instructions for nobody to disturb him. I think he's been sleeping off a hangover."

"He owes me a pint after last night." Aleill tried to maintain an indignant expression on his face, his blue eyes in sharp contrast to the mop of dark hair that he had on his head. "That man, who has no class I should add, managed to step on my dress cloak and rip it in two."

"I heard; the steward told me when I asked him what had gone on last night given that he was still cleaning the place up. He also told me that you were doing your damndest to annoy him and had challenged him to count to twenty without taking off his boots." Aleill grinned, his chin going at an angle as he gave the look that he claimed would launch his political career and endear him to the masses. It was wide and toothy and Velawin couldn't help but grin along.

"Ah well, it was worth it. He still owes me a drink. That was a good cloak."

"Why not just sew it back together, or, if you can't face the manual labour, get someone else to do it?"

"Because I'd look like a bloody peasant, Velawin. I'll buy a new one down Saegar Avenue tomorrow."

"Saegar Avenue?" He had never been a big one for street names, tending to deal more in geographical features or landmarks. It was the curse of growing up in a small town and one which city dwellers, like Aleill, found irritating to the extreme.

"It's been a month since we got here, and at least three weeks since the triumph, and you still haven't learnt the street names? What do you do during your bloody runs? It isn't to look at women anyway!" Velawin was very particular when it came to choosing a woman, something that he had taken no great pains to hide either, but it was something the men that he loved best found hard to believe. It was generally accepted standard for a legionary, no matter what rank or position of authority, to be a lover of women no matter how old, standard of beauty, age or anything like that. Indeed, as Velawin had learned when he was in the ranks in what seemed like a bygone era, it had been actively encouraged to go after the most "rats" girl around. To say someone was rats was to say they were beyond all redemption, a not particularly nice thing to say, but such was the way of the legions. Therefore, as Vel had learnt, the more rats a woman was then the better the dit and the more 'legendary' the person. For some legionaries, and Vel didn't count himself amongst them, reputation was everything.

"It doesn't sound like the type of place that I would necessarily go to, in all honesty," Vel looked at his orange juice and wished it was something stronger and decided to order two glasses of white. Aleill quirked an eyebrow but was happy to go along with the idea, never having been known to be one that would turn down a free drink when it was offered. Aleill, therefore, in turn decided to take a more complimentary tone as if he were returning the favour.

"It's an upmarket shopping area, full of idiots in all fairness, but they sell a decent cut of cloth. If the rumours are right, then I'm going to get a proper cloak with some water proofing."

Velawin quirked an eyebrow, tasting the wine as he did so and revelling in the fresh taste of it. There was a fruity flavour, but that was all he could identify believing that most self-proclaimed wine connoisseurs were just making their trade up.

"Why, what have you heard?" The pair looked up as Aglon sat down in the spare seat, well broken in and comfortable. A dark looked passed over the face of Aleill, one who normally would at least keep a civilised expression on his face if only to keep in with the idea that he was a man of the gentry and therefore above such petty things as arguments or dark thoughts. Velawin wondered at it for a second before realising the seat, though it belonged to the mess, actually belonged to the deceased Trent as his favoured place.

It was a tricky situation for the man wasn't to know, and Aleill wasn't the type of person to go off at the deep end and suddenly explain the errors of his way, but Velawin didn't want the man to suddenly develop a complex as Aleill directed barbed comment after comment in his direction. In, what was for Aleill, a rare act of tact he merely looked at Vel. It was a directed look with some meaning that, by the likes of Aglon, would simply question whether it was sensible to discuss movements of the legion in the mess whereas Vel understood it to be about the seat. Velawin, in turn, held out his palm subtly and motioned for him to keep quiet. Such things like mess protocol could wait and, if Vel was to be honest, the death of Trent was sad but it had occurred over three months ago and time couldn't stand still for any man.

"Rumours, Aglon, are what makes this legion work. Was it the same with the Leviathans?" It was the first time had seen the man out his uniform. He was completely bald, a vanity Vel guessed, and was liable to be a man who shaved his entire head nigh on a daily basis. He had an amiable face like he thought earlier, open and honest, and there was a humorous glint to his eye which hid a humour and wit that even the likes of Aleill would find hard to break down. He was tall, taller than Velawin at any rate but shorter than Erallac, but he was, as a polite man would describe, liable to run to the rotund if he were to miss out on any physical training sessions.

"Of course; the fleet were worse you know. Good men in the Navy, even if they have been shat on by Parliament." The Navy had been recently cut back, the Cardavian parliament deciding to trust more to her allies within Attainia to conduct patrols. Since the Attainians had broken the blockade around Port Gephy their Navy had received a large influx of income and, more importantly, it was thought that their sailors and their natural experience was to be superior to the Cardavians. It was not a feeling that was felt amongst the Cardavian fleet. "It was said that if you ever wanted to know where your next positing or deployment was to be then all you needed to do was talk to the landlords of the taverns."

"Yes, well, anyway," Aleill said as he interjected before Aglon demonstrated his breadth and knowledge of all things naval, "I've heard from a good source in Parliament that we are due to be going south to relieve around one of the legions in the passes on the border with the coalition." Aleill took a drink and looked towards the fire, deciding not to afford the newcomer to the legion an easy reception. "Your neck of the woods, I suppose, anyway."

"Anyway," carried on Velawin before the ill feeling could go any further, "Aleill has the rights of it. We may, or may not depending on rumour, be marching towards the south."

"But I thought we were heavily under manned?" Aglon asked.

"Aye," Velawin was inclined to agree before Aleill could interject, "but we are just relieving around."

"So when would we find out?" Aglon asked, glancing over at Aleill. He realised that there was atmosphere between them, but he didn't know what it was concerning or why an atmosphere should even exist when this was his first few words to the man. It wasn't even like they were talking about anything controversial, rather they were doing what all soldiers do everywhere and talking about where they may or may not be sent to next. He knew about Aleill, of course. He was a gentleman, minor gentry through his father, and had generally been seen as a bit of a fop, according to his messmates, prior to going into Nepriner. There the man's character had flourished and he was never seen without his bow or a knife in his hands waiting to receive the Imperials.

"Whenever we get our orders. I don't know what it was like in the south, but, contrary to popular opinion, the closer you get to the centre of power the less likely you are to know what's going on." Aglon smiled, knowing it was exactly the same with the Leviathans and the fleet. He took another glance at Aleill and frowned beginning to become a little offended. He wasn't one for necessarily hoping that everybody liked him, but he did wish to know that someone had justifiable reasons for being pissed off with him other than being the new man on the scene. It wasn't likely the man was threatened either, or indeed even felt threatened, for Aleill already had his reputation and was of the same rank. As a heavy infantryman he would have very little to do with the leader of the Wolves archers. He flicked a glance to Velawin and nodded in the direction of Aleill. Vel nodded and held out his palms lowly gesturing for him to keep quiet for just now.

"Nope, exactly the same in the south west and Noriandie I'm afraid," said Aglon catching onto the hint. "Will General Corus be joining us at any point?"

"You haven't seen him already?" Velawin asked, surprised.

"No, I did call at his office, but I was turned away by one of the secretaries.

Apparently he was busy with some inspection," Aglon replied.

"You're in for a treat when you do meet him," Aleill said, finally coming out of whatever self-imposed exile he had taken from the conversation.

"How do you mean?"

"You'll see when you meet him. I don't think he'll be in the mess tonight, but you can live in hope. He's generally with his wife most nights now. His house is in the middle of the camp near the parade ground," Aglon nodded as if he knew where it was, but the tour by Velawin had been short and brisk. He had been asked if he wanted a longer one, but given that Vel had already went to some trouble by sorting out the guard staff and getting his kit taken care of whilst still in his running rig, Aglon had thanked him and declined the enquiry.

"Anyway," Aleill carried on, "Ban will probably be in tomorrow."

"Ban?"

"Don't ask, and don't call him that," Velawin said as he flashed a look towards Aleill. "Our master of archers over here is trying to get you on a bite. It's an old joke between a few of us, but it's best not to invite you into it until he gets to know you a little better. No offence intended."

"None taken," Aglon said honestly as he finished off the last of his wine, seeing that the two men had things to discuss that were better off left said in private. "Anyway, I've had a busy day and need to get my head down. Velawin, many thanks for your help earlier. Aleill, a pleasure to meet you."

He stood up and picked up the glass once again, nodding to the two men in final farewell as he walked away to return the glass to the bar for a refill. Velawin watched the man depart and join another group of officers before he turned around to Aleill, staring sullenly once more into the fire with a face like a slapped arse. Normally Vel was of an easy disposition, a laissez faire attitude to life and was generally willing to let bygones be bygones. However, what he couldn't tolerate was rude behaviour, particularly to someone who had been open and honest and, at the end of the day, was new to the damned legion and needing friends. He knew what it was like, any bloody soldier did, and he knew how lonely it could be to be in something new where reputation would have to be built up again from scratch. What wasn't needed was a fellow senior officer acting like a spoilt child because of a death that occurred nearly three months ago during the height of the siege.

"You mind telling me what that was all about Aleill?" He wasn't one to lose his temper and kept the same levels of concentration in holding it as he did when he went running, breathing in through his nose and exhaling slowly so as to keep his tongue still.

"It was nothing. I was out of order. I'll apologise to him when I next see him," Velawin watched him for a few seconds before finally nodding, deciding that the matter was settled for just now. Again, he knew the source of Aleill and his foul temper, but he was genuinely surprised by it. Aleill had seemed to get over the death of Trent during the course of the siege, and beforehand had never been truly close to the man, but now that he was back in barracks he was suddenly turning into a stroppy teenager again. Perhaps it was like the age old adage, the devil making work for idle hands.

"Do you ever miss Nepriner?" Aleill asked as he waved for another two glasses of wine to be brought over. Vel pondered over the question for a little as the wine was poured into new glasses and brought towards them. He smiled his thanks to the steward and took a quick sip, the bitter taste initially causing him to balk from it before the smooth aftertaste settled on his tongue.

"Sort of. I don't miss the injuries, or the nearly getting killed everyday aspect, but I miss certain bits of it."

"I know what you mean. I'm bored here," Velawin thought as much but allowed his friend to continue, watching him framing the words mentally in his head before speaking them aloud. It would be difficult; Aleill wasn't necessarily the type of man to open up and leave himself in a perceived vulnerable state. "I thought I'd be able to slip into my old habits easily enough, you know? I went to my old haunts and saw my old friends, but it's amazing how much smaller this place seems.

"It sounds daft because I know that Silveroak is a lot bigger than Nepriner was, especially given that Nepriner was little more than rubble when we left. I mean, well…the entire world here just seems smaller and contrite. The people are up themselves, obsessed with their own power politics and bargaining. Life is cheap here, there's little value in friendship, and if you can't afford the latest fashions in the latest streets then you are treated worse than scum. Do you know what I mean or am I just being silly?"

Aleill took a drink, watching Velawin as he did so as he sat in silence. "I'm being stupid. Look, forget it."

"No," Vel replied. "I'm just thinking on what you said. I suppose," he said, placing the glass on the table and crossing his legs out in front of him, "it's the same reason why I like my cabin in the woods. I've always found being in the city is good for short periods of time, seeing new people and places and stuff, but after a little while it becomes tedious and, like you say, contrite. I've never liked Silveroak, I don't think many people do. So no, you aren't being stupid. It's entirely natural."

"But it's not like I'm some green-behind-the-ears new legionary, Vel. I've seen stuff before, I've taken part in small actions and have come out never noticing the difference. Why now?"

"You were exposed to a dangerous environment where you had to survive on your wits and your friends, that's not new to you. It's the usual fare. However, you had to do it over a prolonged period of time. That is new." Vel took a drink and drew on some more of the experience he had garnered from when he was a ranker, trying to remember how he felt after some of the more serious battles and skirmishes he had fought in his time. He knew the feelings well enough that Aleill was suffering from, it was almost like having something niggling at the back of your mind as if you had a job to do. You felt, because you were used to living your life on watches and duty rotation, that time moved more slowly. You felt the need to fill that time and, eventually, you would mentally and physically exhaust yourself in order to fill that time. It was probably why a lot of the legionaries would either end up turning to drink or going to the gym all the time, there was nothing else that could fill the void.

"There's more to it than that surely?"

"Aye, but then that's another story for another time, Aleill. Care for another drink? Tomorrow is a rest day and I fancy getting pissed."

Chapter Six – **Orders**

He looked at Talice and smiled. He watched her breathe deep and slowly, snuggling further into the quilt as a faint breeze came in through the open shutters. The fact she had the majority of it wasn't the point; there was almost a faint smile upon her lips and an enticing leg chucked over his as one side had evidently become too warm. He looked upon it, stroking it with his fingertips so as to not awake her, all the while looking upon the sun rising in the east in the background. He liked the look of a sunrise as much as the next man, but was getting decidedly fed up of them. There was only so many ways, as a romantic and idealist, that one could describe the same colours mentally to oneself over and over again.

Privately he wished he had closed the shutters that separated the early sun from the bedroom. He had been struggling to sleep lately, restless more than anything else, and he was unwilling to take naps during the day time because he felt it was a tremendous waste of time. The trouble, he found, was that he would throw himself into his work every day and tire himself out; only for him to become wide awake during the course of the evening and suddenly find himself having to fight himself to sleep. He wondered if it was something to do with Nepriner, realised it probably was, and that there was nothing he could actually do about it. If it was a phase, then it was one he would probably have to just ride out and let nature take its course.

He mentally thought of everything that he was supposed to do today. The vast majority was the usual humdrum and boring activity that was associated with life in a camp. He was to conduct a joining interview with the new heavy infantry commander, the man Aglon, and give him a rundown on how the legion conducted its business compared to the likes of the Leviathans. He would probably go out for a run afterwards and check up on how the recruiting was going at the old mustering grounds. He also had to visit the Guards barracks where headquarters was located and pick up the official orders that would probably see them marching south to hand over with one of the legions there. It was one of the worst kept secrets in the Wolves, he reckoned, but then it had been exactly the same when it came to the Wolves marching to Nepriner.

He cursed silently as he remembered he was due to give a speech to the new recruits on the parade ground about how the legion was a good place to live and work, but he couldn't think of the right words. He smiled, thinking about just being honest with the assembled recruits. He could picture it now; the assembled senior officers beside him on the podium and the trainees' instructors watching their new charges with eagle eyes having warned the recruits to behave and stand in a line in just so a manner. Beran as commanding officer of the legion would then open his mouth to say that most legionaries had bad drinking habits, were habitual liars to further their own drunken fortunes and stories, had been in more shit than most folk in prison, but were probably the best friends and listening ear that men could hope for and would back you to the hilt and beyond in your time of need. He grinned and stifled a chuckle in order to not wake up Talice; he knew the vast majority of his men would laugh at the honest speech and grin at each other, but he figured that the recruits could find out about life in the legion in their own time. No, he would give them the usual hearts and minds speech, telling them to listen to their senior officers and do what they were told and all the other things he was expected to say.

"What time is it?" He looked away from the open window and down into the face of Talice, her eyes slowly beginning to open and her face framed by her red hair. It didn't matter to him that she had just woken up, to him she looked beautiful regardless of the time of day. He stole a quick kiss on the lips and was finally able to shift his arm and place it under his own head, moving up into a sitting position with his back against the head board.

"Past time I was getting up. You are making me soft."

"That's funny, only last night you said the opposite," she said with a grin, sitting up as well and allowing the quilt to fall slightly. She rubbed some of the sleep from her eye and suddenly swung out her legs, sitting up before standing and padding soft footed across the carpeted floor to where the house coat was hung on a peg on the door.

"You know what I mean," Beran said with a grin of his own, watching the subtle sway of her hips as she walked. "Would you like some breakfast?"

"Be still my beating heart! Are you actually offering to cook?" She threw a smile over her shoulder, brushing her hair back before opening the door. The house itself was warm as he tentatively left the comfort and security of the quilt and he was grateful for it, not wishing to freeze half to death prior to making it to the kitchen.

"I offer all the time, you just complain that I under cook the bacon and the eggs aren't scrambled to your liking. Now, do you want breakfast or not?" She was about to answer, but as if on cue there was a polite knock at the front door. Beran had heard the clocks strike the seventh hour earlier on and gave a soft curse, knowing that the real world was once again demanding his presence instead of mercifully forgetting him for the day. Talice gave a knowing smile, nodding her head downstairs to the entrance of the house, and mouthed silently that she would make the breakfast.

He threw on a pair of woollen trousers and a loose fitting shirt, trying to give the appearance of someone who had been up for some time and hadn't been lazing in bed. He left the bedroom and walked down the hallway and descended the staircase, deciding that he would have to think about sanding down the bannister and finally sorting it out after getting yet another splinter. Walking up to the front door, he could hear Talice moving about the kitchen with the unmistakeable smell of bacon beginning to waft through; his stomach growled with hunger in reply.

He opened his own door having refused to employ a steward or a servant to run about the house and tend to their needs. It stuck in his throat that someone in his position was expected to employ a plethora of staff, and he had argued that he had managed to wipe his own arse for years without a problem and saw no reason to change his habits now. Furthermore, the lack of a steward grounded him in some sort of normality. Yes, they lived in the middle of a barracks in a house that was provided to them courtesy of the legion, but it was still their own house. The only concession he had made was allowing those men under punishment to tend to the garden that was attached to the property at the front and the back, Talice and he not being particularly green fingered.

"What's wrong Erallac?" The tall veteran was looking to his right as the door opened, almost as if he were studying the distant horizon but more than likely seeing an infringement of standards on the parade ground nearby. Beran could just about hear the shouted orders as a group of recruits were taught how to walk in a straight line without "tick-tocking", a phenomenon whereby said recruit would swing their right arm in time with their right leg and so on. It was the bane of every drill instructor everywhere, whilst everybody else thought it was hilarious.

"Nothing. Thought I saw something," he said predictably, "I take it you aren't going to headquarters dressed like that?"

"Well, given that the clock has only struck the seventh hour and we aren't due there until the tenth then I wasn't planning to no. Why are you so early?"

"They've brought forward the briefing," Erallac said, his nostrils flaring slightly as the faint waft of bacon hit him.

"Of course they bloody well have. I take it you've known about this for a while?" He had the decency to look a little sheepish at that. "Aye, well, what time are we due there now at?"

"Not until the ninth. I did send a runner, Ban, but obviously he didn't get the message to you yesterday. We've still got bags of time though." The chances were he had sent a runner and it was a simple mistake, but Beran knew that unless a report was acknowledged then it wasn't a report.

"Well you may as well come in anyway and settle yourself down for a bit. Talice has put bacon on and I'm sure we've got some going spare. You can brief me on the state of recruitment, and the drill." The two men walked through into the large kitchen and saw two slabs of bacon waiting for them on plates with toasted bread and scrambled eggs on the side. Of Talice there was no sign, but then it was hardly likely she would be willing to stand about in her night clothes when there was another person in the house.

"The recruiting is going well, surprisingly. I think the triumph helped a fair wee bit, normally there's not a lot of folk who want to join up in the middle of a war in case the new recruits get involved in it eventually. Given that we're winning then folk are thinking it'll be over soon enough and that they'll get their own triumph soon. We still need another thousand men before we're up to full strength."

Beran placed the bacon on one of the slices of bread and topped it off with a generous portion of scrambled egg. Picking up the other piece of toast, he squeezed down and brought the mixture up to his mouth and ate happily. He liked his bacon damn near raw, kissing the frying pan for long enough to rise slightly before it was flipped around. He couldn't stand it crispy, believing it be to be far too dry and bitty.

"Is this anything to do with the talk that we are heading south to play the role of peacemaker?" Erallac wasn't terribly enamoured with the idea of acting as any sort of intermediary given that it usually meant that both sides hated you for vastly different or strangely similar reasons.

"Something like that. This Ufwalan Queen, Wellisa or something, has pretty much united one of half of the Southern Coalition and just taken Vitrossy. That's her pretty much got the entire border sealed up meaning that, if she runs out of domestic enemies, she could probably come north. Now," he said taking a bite out of his breakfast and mulling over the problem as he chewed, "why headquarters are sending an under strength and under trained legion into the shitstorm that will soon develop is beyond me, but that's why I'm only a legion General and presumably not in the staff."

"Why not send us back to Nepriner?" Erallac wasn't particularly hungry, but he had never been one to turn down food in the past and attacked his meal with a gusto. He would have liked to have seen Talice again, but he figured she was presumably busy.

"There's enough already invested there. Anyway, the Wolves aren't ready to face the Imperials again. Not yet, anyway. How is training going?"

"Well enough I'd say," Erallac said, instinctively looking towards the parade ground, "the men are remaining enthusiastic and the veterans amongst them are trying to show the newer lads how things actually work. Physical standards are abysmal, but so long as they pass their fitness tests for just now I'm happy. Some of them are actually pretty decent swordsman and archers, I know Vel and Aleill have been taking a particular interest in their development."

"I've got to meet this Aglon later on. You managed to meet him yet?" Erallac shook his head to the negative, "I haven't either. I received a letter from his old commanding officer though, someone called Gamin."

"I know him, he's former Guards. Didn't expect him to transfer out, actually. Must have not been able to afford the mess bills." The Guards were notorious for being classist, the elite of society often sending their eldest sons into the legion for the prestige and the ability to say they had done some sort of military service without the added risk of being killed. Though the Guards would sometimes be deployed, they would only do so if a member of the royal line was there at the same time. Royalty, these days at any rate, didn't deploy.

"Would you say he's a good judge of character?"

"He's an old officer of mine, recommended me for promotion, so probably not. He was a decent sort, anyway."

"Well he says good things, which is...well...all to the good, really. Hard worker, good ethics, proven fighter and a bit of an historian as well. Loves the legions."

"Sounds like a bit of a throbber."

"You think anybody who shows up for their duty on time is a bit of a throbber!" Erallac chuckled, finishing off the last of his breakfast as he did so. They spoke at length some more before Talice finally came down and Beran made his apologies saying he needed to get dressed and ready.

He was, in truth, looking forward to get moving again. He liked the fact that he was at home with his wife and was able to take it easy, but there was a restless feeling about the legion these days amongst those that had survived at Nepriner. Silveroak was a city that they had been in prior to marching off to war, it was a city that they had got used to and therefore bored with long before they came back. Many of the men had found that it was damn near impossible to slip back into old habits, at least this soon, and trouble was beginning to rise up. He wondered, briefly, if Dunwal was having the same problems with the Marshal legion.

They weren't marching off to war, of that he was sure, but getting out on the march would allow some of the men to get rid of any pent up frustration. Often, a change of scenery was as good as a rest.

They approached on horseback, Beran having had enough of the city to know that he didn't particularly wish to try and travel through by foot. He was glad he had managed to persuade Erallac of this fact for the city was busy once again. He couldn't remember Silveroak being as busy as this when he had first been stationed here some six months ago, but then history was in the making and people liked to be at the centre of gossip.

Cardavy looked as if she were going to found a political union, of sorts, between themselves and the Artenonian Republic. As well as that, the continued wars in support of Attainia against Rupinian aggression were attracting all manner of merchants and their ilk who sought to peddle their wares and future 'wonder weapons' that would make the war easier for the common Cardavian soldier. As well as that, the new influx of business and trade from the Southern Coalition made Silveroak, and Cardavy as a whole, a new lucrative market that other nations wanted to tap into. Aye, people were getting rich.

He wore his actual armour now that he had used at Nepriner having managed to lose the parade ground uniform that he detested. The armour he wore now felt like a second skin, was soft where it needed to be and didn't chafe, but was weighty enough to be a reassuring presence around his body. The parade uniform wasn't designed to feel nice, he was sure, and nor was it designed to give any sort of protection to the user. As Beran had to concede to Talice on more than one occasion when wearing it, he probably wouldn't be facing a regiment of Rupinian soldiers within the streets of the capital anytime soon.

They approached the granite buildings where the Kings Guard were based. The grounds had been heavily stylised over the years with previous Kings and Queens lavishing great sums on the headquarters buildings in order to secure the loyalty of the soldiers within, even to the point where there was a fountain in the middle of what was once a parade ground. There was a low wall that separated the barracks from the street with iron railings separating them further, and it lent the place a more civilised look than most garrison buildings often would. Outside the main entrance to the base were two circular guard posts capable of holding three men apiece, one of whom would be standing out in front of each post at all times. In between these were the black iron gates that bore the royal crest and, slightly below this, the crest of the legion. They were wide open at the moment and Beran was able to guide his horse through without having to provide too much in the way of identification to the guardsmen at the gates.

For Erallac it was like returning to some sort of holy land. The man had been trained here when he had first joined the legions many years ago and had been effectively raised here. He had joined as a tearaway, as a polite person would say, and had left a respectable man of the legions. Aye, he had served in legions since then, but this would always be home for him. The place still had the same feel and he could see in the men around the same type of people he had once respected and feared. Of course, he was a war hero now several times over and therefore these men looked upon him with something akin to reverence, but there was always going to be a small part of him that felt like a very young man whenever he entered those black gates.

The two horsemen dismounted in front of the entrance to headquarters, helpfully directed along the way by cast iron sign posts that pointed out where buildings were to strangers and visitors. It was the type of luxury that a legion that was permanently based somewhere could afford, and something that the men of the Wolves legion would probably use in evidence to suggest that the Guards weren't fit for purpose if they couldn't find their way about their own billet. A stable boy appeared as if out of nowhere and took their horses to the stables reserved for officers reassuring Beran that they would be treated well.

"You look as if you are lost in memories, Erallac." The big man smiled and nodded his head in the direction to the headquarters building, the great oaken doors wide open but shadow lying beyond.

"I was on the main gate when you were still drinking milk as your only source of food," Erallac said with a grin and a wink, "You have no idea how many memories I have wrapped up in this place."

"Good ones?" There weren't many men that could get away with being so familiar with Beran, but when a man has fought and bled with you for years then it takes the meaning of friendship to a whole new level. As well as that, Erallac was like the uncle of the legion. He would initially appear gruff and unapproachable, but it was an easy mistake for the recruits to make. The man was legion through and through and was just very particular about what type of person should and should not be admitted.

"Aye, quite a few, even the ones where I was marched to the officer commanding's table and given punishment for being drunk or late or something," he grinned and chuckled, the infringements of yesteryear suddenly becoming something like a schoolboy jape. "Aye well, them were days."

The two men walked through the entrance to the building and were directed upstairs to one of the innumerable briefing rooms that the building housed. The interior was similar to every other barracks that Beran had ever been in, though this one he noticed was perhaps a trifle better decorated and certainly seemed richer. There were various coats of armour stretching all the way back to the first style of armour that the Cardavians employed, as well as a selection of different types of weaponry that the legions had experimented with along the way. Within several hallways were portraits of former commanding officers as well as colours that had become discoloured with age or through being used in battle. He had to give it to the Guards, they certainly had style.

They were directed to sit down on a wooden bench by a duty officer who had been assigned to look after them as they had entered the building, providing a running commentary on each and every single thing that they had seen. As a lover of history Beran was enthralled, but it was obvious that Erallac had heard it all before and, no doubt, had probably to learn it by rote when he had originally been with the legion. They sat now and waited, listening to the faint murmur of voices and the clipped tones of reply. There was the sound of footsteps coming from down the hallway and the occasional order of command from the parade ground. The wind had picked up as well rattling against the window panes held in their lead casings, but the rain seemed to be keeping off even as the clouds seemed to gather in. He was beginning to wish he had brought his oilskin cloak in case it did rain.

"The Field Marshal will see you now," the young officer said. Beran was surprised, but took pains to make sure it wasn't noticeable. He had been lost in thought, his mind drifting into space as he examined one of the crests that were mounted on the wall showing the old Kings particular seal. Beran stood and thanked the man, making sure his dress was correct and the helmet was tucked into the crook of his arm in the correct fashion. He walked through the door and stood at attention, throwing a salute that a Guardsman would hopefully be proud of. He had always enjoyed drill when he had to conduct it, but the people here took it to the next level and beyond that. For them it was something that was one step below the will of the Gods, and even then if the Gods didn't fall in three deep with the tallest on the wings and the shortest in the middle then they could standby.

"Take a seat, General Corus. It's a pleasure to finally meet you." The man in front of him had a genial look to his features, not at all the type of staff officer you would normally expect to see. He was tall and of slight build, but had an aristocratic bearing to him. Beran was unsure of who he was, not being one who would normally associate with the higher echelons of command. He had no plans to go any higher in rank than he was, happy to be in charge of a legion for the rest of his time within the army. Right now, though he was subject to the whims of headquarters and all that entailed, he was still at the top of his game. If he were to lose the command then he would probably by expected to teach somewhere or run a job in headquarters, something he didn't particularly wish to do.

"I expect you are wondering who I am," the man said as Beran and Erallac took the offered seat at the opposite end of the small table.

"It had crossed my mind, sir, I don't think we've been introduced properly in the past."

"No, I don't think we have. At any rate, I am Raffin." The man sat back in his seat and watched the two officers. "May I offer you congratulations on your defence of Nepriner? It was a fine piece of work you did, considering the odds that were against you. As an aside, it's because of your words to the King that I am now in charge." Beran quirked an eyebrow, his hands halfway to a glass of water as the man spoke. "You see, the King recognises what you said and knows that the legions will be required to fight more in the future. At any rate, sending in legions 'piecemeal', as you say, is a bad idea and one that I spoke strongly against. Out with the old and in with the new, I'm afraid."

"Well, in which case congratulations are in order for you as well, sir." Beran found himself warming to the man for he seemed to have a degree of common sense that he thought hitherto had gone unsought in Cardavian circles.

"I'll get to the crux of the matter, for I know you two gentlemen are busy. I'm sure you've heard about the rise of Wellisa, this Queen of the South?" The two men nodded and Raffin continued, "Garren, our diplomat attached to the Ufwalan kingdom, has finally managed to send us a note north. He states, and I'm sure your aware, that she has managed to seal the border completely. Now, we're friendly with the Ufwalans for the moment, but it's by no means a warm friendship. Whilst this war in the north continues against Rupinia we can't necessarily do anything about her, at least not totally.

"Now, she's not making any threats. She knows she can't do anything against us, like march north, in case the people of the south end up banding together and taking her in the rear. Ufwala is becoming a victim of its own success, but so long as trade continues to flow north through the border and she continues to fob off the Imperials then parliament is happy for her to continue.

"Basically, we need someone down there who she has heard of. The three legions we have stationed in the passes are well led, don't get me wrong, but none of them has an officer with a fighting reputation that has been recently won. There aren't many people who haven't heard of Beran of the Wolves and the siege of Nepriner."

"So what do you want me doing down there? I'm sure you are aware, sir, but I am not a diplomat. I'm pretty sure I offended half of Parliament when I met the King, and, with the exception of yourself, I'm hardly going to be popular with some in headquarters given that I've somehow managed to get one of their own replaced."

"No, that is true," the field marshal said with a smile playing upon his lips. "You are no diplomat, but then it's not a diplomat we want down there. All we need you to do is to swap around with the men in the western pass, nearest the coast. You'll be in charge of the defences there, liaise with the naval squadron that is at the port city, and generally just be there. It'll be a good opportunity to get some decent rest inside your men as well, and provide them with sufficient training in the region and get used to the weather in case there is any campaigning."

"What about the other passes, sir, will they be getting swapped around?"
"Dunwal already has received his marching orders and will be taking control of the eastern pass," Beran nodded and looked towards the chart that had been pinned to the wall. In the event that the Queen did decide she had pacified her domestic enemies and would march north, then it was likely she would go for only one pass. If she went for either of the two flanks then she would encounter either the Wolves or the Marshal legions, two bodies of men that had already been battle proven and tested under proven commanders. If she were to march for the centre then it was likely that the two Cardavian legions on the flanks could advance and encircle her position, becoming the hammer as the centre pass became the anvil.
"Would you have any objection to me taking my wife, sir?" The man looked at him for a few seconds before nodding.
"It's up to yourself, and by all means speak to her. The coast is lovely at this time of year, I am told, and the effects of winter are felt less harshly there. However, if war does come, do you want her to be in harm's way again?"
Beran nodded, knowing that the man had a point. There were a few more issues that needed to be sorted out, but the main meat of the matter had been discussed. The Wolves would march south in two weeks' time to man the pass, and Cardavy would get another fresh legion to send into the meat grinder that was Attainia and her greater Republic.

Chapter Seven – **The Borders**

He had come away from his meeting with Emperor Rhagan with nothing but questions and recriminations running through his head. No solutions had been offered and promises lay broken and unfulfilled. There would be no pay, there would be no blood money for the widows who had been left behind and there would be a call to arms in the Spring when a new campaign would be launched that would finally see the destruction of the Greater Attainian lands. He hawked and spat onto the ground, the snow having melted to be replaced with fields of fertile grass and soil once more. It was as if the World was waking up again, the bitter winter finally breaking and allowing the people to dream and hope again of better harvests and better times. It was a nice time of year, when the lands would be sown with seed and the animals would be looking to rear young of their own. However, it meant that Spring was coming and the next cull of Clansmen would begin.

He had heard reports and rumours of trouble flaring up when he had been in the capital, the great political circles that surrounded the Emperor often looking upon the clansman as if he were going to pull out a hatchet and have a bid for freedom there and then. He knew then that somebody had been speaking, that there was someone or, possibly, various clan chiefs that viewed his words as treasonous and inciting rebellion. He had to grant them that they were right, but then to throw away any attempt at surprise was surely more treasonous in itself? To betray your people to an overlord who only cared enough to make sure that there was a ready supply of manpower to launch against the walls of yet another city. Where would it end? Would the Empire be happy with the lands that they gained in Greater Attainia, lands they had subsequently lost in the retreat, or would they push on and try and annex the entire Republic?

Would that even stop them; would they not push on into Cardavy given that she was the only power who had the potential to actually stop them? The moon hung high in the sky now, a few clouds flying overhead as strong winds whipped at the tops of the tree. He instinctively burrowed himself deeper into the bough of the great tree he sheltered under, the canvas of his tent billowing with every gust no matter how much he tried to tie it down. The fire he had lit was well sheltered and provided him with a modicum of warmth, the rations that he had with him bubbling in a pot that he had suspended over the flames. He was glad to be alone with his thoughts for just now, the cavalry escort he had assigned to him riding off at the first opportunity to wherever they were billeted.

No, a night like this was the type that was best to have by yourself.

He looked to the east and saw the mountains of his homeland; a land of broken clans and false friendships. He looked to the south, knowing that the border with Greater Attainia and the city of Nepriner with the massed armies of the allied coalition were only miles away. Nepriner, it was true, was a good one hundred miles distant, but it was close enough.

"I suggest you come out of hiding, whoever you are." He knew that someone was watching him, could feel their eyes boring into the back of his skull as he sat and watched the stew boil. He didn't know how to explain it; he just knew it was simply an awareness of how he exposed he was or there was a slight shift of the wind where a scent could reach him or the flight of a bird as it swooped away from a hiding place where someone lay. It was said there were clansmen who were blessed with second sight, albeit it at a very base level, but for him it was a talent that he simply took for granted.

"I've got enough stew for two, if you're hungry. I'd be happier if you were to provide your own rations though," he gave a chuckle showing a sense of mirth that he did not feel at that point, "I'd also prefer it if you brought your own tent rather than expect to share mine."

The sound of silence greeted his hail, the wind still echoing through the trees causing the branches to crash together. He shrugged his shoulders and stood up, ostensibly to stir the stewing mixture in the pot. He loosened the short crossbow he had taken at Nepriner and made a fuss of tightening his cloak even as he slid two bolts into the bow. He crouched onto bended knee and placed the crossbow onto the ground near to where he was sitting and picked up a large stick, cleaning off the dirt and leaves and used it to stir the point. Satisfied, he picked up an earthen mug that he had placed near the side and dipped it into the stew and sat back in his original position. Even if he were wrong, being this close to the Attainian border meant he would have to think about his own personal security.

He allowed the wind to cool the stew, a little unhappy that it was more of a poor soup than anything else, and took a swallow. The meat was gristly and stringy, probably some of the worst rations of beef that he had ever had the misfortune to eat, but it served the purpose in filling a hole. He cast his eyes about the clearing once more, careful to avoid looking into the fire lest his night vision become affected and therefore be temporarily blinded whilst his eyesight adjusted again. He remembered once hearing a veteran talk about different parts of the eyes, something he had heard from a doctor in some camp, and the fact that it often took forty minutes for the eyes to completely adjust to the darkness. He liked knowing things, but some of the things to do with the human body were completely beyond his understanding.

He still couldn't shake off the feeling that he was being watched, so instead of worrying about it he simply drank from the stew instead. Once finished, he would see to his horse and take the scabbard that sheathed the broadsword. He cursed himself inwardly for he knew he should have had it on his person at all times, knowing that somewhere his father was looking down upon him from the heavens and slamming his head against a wall in frustration. It was one of the lessons he tried to drum into his two sons from an early age, telling them again and again that a man who went without his weapon anywhere was as good as naked. He thought he would get away with it with the plethora of knives and the crossbow he held on his person, but there was something about the security that a decent broadsword offered that spoke to him.

He thought of his brother, now the Chief of the Red River clan. The system of inheritance was one of gavelkind, where the possessions of the deceased were split equally among the surviving sons. Quittle had turned his side of the share down, knowing that his career rested in the capital and the Imperial court of Rhagan. His elder brother, Alfdarr, would need all the possessions and farms he could muster anyway if there was ever a bid to oust him from power; at least this way his direct vassals would actually provide him with manpower should some of the nobility of the clan decide they were better suited to rule.

He had seen him last at the meeting of the clan chiefs within the clansmen section of the camp, the night when the siege towers still burned and illuminated the walls with their ghastly shadows. The smell of burning flesh still hung in the air, the charred and smoking ruins of wood lending their own scent making the entire area smell like some perverted version of a campfire feast. There was also the spoiled egg smell that came from the black powder that the Speirakians had used upon the northern walls gatehouse, a smell that was obscene both in the price that it cost the clans and in its peculiar nature. There had been a decidedly sombre mood within the camp, many of the men taking time to clean their own wounds and mourn their dead in their own way.

Alfdarr had been there sat alongside Tortag around the fire pit that had been dug, sharing a flask of something alcoholic that was sure to put hairs on a mans chest. They had all listened as Quittle had spoken, his brother with a look of disbelief etched across his face as he was obviously completely taken aback by the words coming from the mouth of his younger brother. Quittle wasn't sure how to gauge his opinion at the time, and even afterwards when he had asked his elder brother what he thought had been fobbed off with words.

He hadn't seen much of him since the siege ended, but he knew he was alive and back in the homelands. It was where he was going now, working under the belief that if the rebellion was going to start anywhere then it had to be from within his own clan. Had they not been the first ones to fight the

Attainians when they had marched north those centuries ago, planting their colonies as if they were trees in a new forest? Had not they decided the Rupinians could be fought to a standstill, and damn near come close to winning if it hadn't been for the unthinkable happening when Rupinian and Attainian put aside their civil war and fought the clans to a bloody halt? Had not the men of the Red River clan been the only ones with such a streak of belligerence and belief in the people of the north to actually pull this off?

He looked up again, draining the last of his stew, sure this time he heard the crack of a stick as it broke under a heavy footfall. It could be the movement of a wild creature, maybe a badger or something, but he wasn't terribly sure whether they wouldn't be the type to hibernate in the winter. Maybe, given that the winter was slowly starting to end and the days were becoming longer and warmer it was the first of the early risers? Field craft was a science, almost a black art, that he made no claim to be a master of. He picked up a few of the cleaner leaves that still littered the ground, making a show of cleaning out the last vestiges of stew from the mug. Outwardly satisfied to any watcher, he stood up with an audible grunt and brushed himself down before moving over to his horse. He stroked the flanks of the sable coloured mare and whispered reassuring words into her ear, eventually moving to collect the feed bag filled with oats. He brought a few out and held it close to the mouth of the horse and allowed her to nibble at them gently before strapping the feed bag around her muzzle. He stroked her flanks down and placed a large blanket over her to keep her warm during the night, taking care to unstrap the sword that was strapped to the saddle. Satisfied that she had her fill, he unstrapped the feed bag and allowed her to rest before walking back to the fire.

There was still no sign of anybody approaching his fire and he decided that it was just the night playing tricks on him. He was far enough away from the border region to ensure security, and anything that did penetrate this far was going to be part of a much larger force than he would be capable of defending against anyway.

"You never were one to sight your camp in the best manner," Quittle belayed his size and turned about on his heel in a flash, the scabbard flung away in an instant and the sword brandished. He still couldn't see anything and he peered as best he could into the shadows, trying to look for the ones that were darker than most. "Would it help if I said that there were twelve bows trained upon you just now and that your life is forfeit if I should so choose?"

"I don't think a man of your sort would be willing to do that, Tortag," Quittle said, finally recognising the voice.

"No," the voice said, "I wouldn't. Put down the blade and allow me to approach your camp and sit by your fire. I've brought wine."

"Then you're more than welcome," he said in reply, a small smile beginning to form at his lips as he saw the figure of his friend approaching from the gloom. A faint mist had begun to rise from the ground, the heat from the dirt obviously mixing with the coldness of the air. "Your friends are more than welcome to sit by my fire as well."

"I lied about them," he said sitting by the fire. He pulled out a mug from his cloak and dipped it into the stew, allowing it to cool for a few seconds before taking a sip. "Your broth could do with some salt as well, and maybe a little spice. It's a bit bland."

"I haven't had your experience in preparing food in the field."

"I can tell; a man would starve to death on this rubbish." Tortag said with a grin, gratefully finishing off the rest of the contents of his mug. "Anyway, your camp can be seen for miles around. I've been following you about since this afternoon."

"I thought being in the centre of a wood would shield the light from the flames." Tortag nodded before looking about him.

"Ordinarily, but not in a forest of new saplings that are likely to move with the wind. It was like a flashing beacon on a lighthouse. Here," Tor said as he passed the wineskin over, "get some of that down you. It's a red, but it's a decent vintage."

Quittle took a deep drink from the wineskin and was glad of it, enjoying the feeling of being able to talk to a man in his own tongue and close to home. It was almost like a pleasant camping experience, and the two of them were quiet and enjoying the company. Tor added a few more sticks to the fire and watched the flames lick at the dry sticks, eventually taking them and sending fresh spits of cinders into the night sky.

"Where's your horse?"

"In the forest a way back, she's bedded down for the night and probably a lot more comfortable than your one is. She's also well-hidden so any thieves or highwaymen in the area won't find her." He took the offered wine skin back and had a drink, wiping the excess away from his mouth with the flat of his hand. "It's you I came to see anyway."

"Aye; what for?"

"Don't play stupid, Bear, it really doesn't suit you. It's like watching Kiegal playing stupid or weak, neither role suits either of you. You know fine well what I'm on about." Quittle nodded and conceded the point, settling back into the bough of the tree and watched the fire burn for a few seconds.

"What do you want me to say?"

"Nothing, I want you to listen." It was obvious that Tortag was thinking about what he was going to say, that there were things that he needed to get off his chest. The fact that he was, for all intents and purposes, a representative of the Imperial army meant little when Quittle was supposed to be one of the few who spoke with the voice of the Emperor. It occurred to Quittle then that this conversation couldn't take place in any other location, that here and now was probably the safest they'd get. "Do you know what's been happening since we got back?"

"I've heard rumours and such whilst I was at the Imperial court, but I wasn't exactly flavour of the month. It appears someone has been speaking about what was said outside Nepriner."

"Aye well," Tortag began, throwing a few more sticks into the fire. "That much is true. The Imperials have stepped up their patrols within our lands, and I'm talking all clans here and not just those they suspect of being disloyal, and there's rumours of a couple of regiments coming up to the peninsula to enforce the weapons take come the Spring for the army. As well as that," Tortag began before taking another swig of the wine, "I've had some sprog Imperial try and lay down the law on my land from the safety of his fort demanding higher crop yields and more taxes. The land is being bled dry, the people are being bled dry, and all because of a bloody rumour!"

"Then you know what I've been saying is true."

"No, what I know, Bear, is that we are slowly being forced down a path that nobody wanted to go down. I've got young clansmen champing at the bit to get at the Imperial garrison now, there's been at least three fights in the town nearest and one that damn near involved murder. I've even got veterans like Kiegal looking at me as if I'm conspiring to destroy the clan and suddenly throwing myself at the feet of Emperor bloody Rhagan and present myself to him!" He hawked up some phlegm and spat into the fire, hearing the sizzle of the spit as it burnt away. "This is your fucking doing, Quittle. Bastard well forced down a path that's only going to end in misery for everyone concerned, and probably the destruction of any freedoms we enjoy at the moment."

"So what are you going to do?"

"Bugger all I can do really, Bear." Tortag said in a remarkably calm fashion. "I can't and won't act until we've got justifiable reason to go to war, and the way things are going means I'll probably have a justifiable reason sooner rather than later. Until that day comes, and I really hope it bloody doesn't because it's me that is getting shat on, then I'll do everything I can to simmer things down."

"And what if they don't?" Quittle asked softly, his voice barely audible above the gathering storm. The faint patter of raindrops could be heard on the treeline above them now, the lighter columns of grey signalling that rain was falling able to be seen in the distance. Quittle knew that events were gathering momentum, that the men of the Black Moon clan were hardly going to be the only ones feeling the pinch of Rupinian aggression. It was enough to infringe on the liberties of people on a daily basis by introducing new laws and taxes, and it was generally meekly accepted when this was done behind the scenes. However, when that aggression and control was exhibited blatantly in front of all it became something entirely different.

"Then I'll do what is best for the clan, Bear. I don't care what this country used to be called, I don't particularly care for our history because that sort of stuff is in the past for a damn good reason. We didn't have the ability then to defeat any invader and we certainly don't have the manpower now; not after being bled dry over Nepriner and countless other small insurrections or whatever." He gave a dry chuckle, looking at Quittle for perhaps the first time in ages. "Anyway, who are you going to get to help us? The Attainians hate as much as we hate them, the folk from Boarslat are so isolationist I'd be surprised if they knew there was even another country out there, and that only leaves the Cardavians who don't exactly owe us any favours!"

There was a grin on his face as he spoke considering the absurdity of his statement. Tortag realised that Quittle wasn't smiling back, not even a glint of humour in his eyes as he continued to stare at him.

"No…. now I know you've fucking lost! The bloody Cardavians? You'd swap one occupier for another?!"

"It's an option. I doubt they'd occupy anyway, look at what they are doing in Attainia. They've not occupied them even though they could do so with ease." Quittle stretched out his left leg and felt the calf muscle twitch from an earlier cramp he had. "Anyway, like you said, it's a stretch."

"You're nuts." He stifled a yawn and looked up into the night sky, the clouds obscuring the moon now and the land in front of him bathed in darkness. If it weren't for the rain then it would be peaceful. "Look, get your head down and you can come back to my farm tomorrow. Elyn will want to see you anyway."

Chapter Eight – **Torch Bearer**

The sun had risen, but the only thing separating the daytime from the night was the fact it was slightly lighter Tor thought. Tortag considered it for a few seconds and decided it was facetious, especially given that what often separated night and day was the light. It would be, he mused, perhaps more accurate to say that it was a slightly lighter grey.

The fog was everywhere, pervading every nook and cranny of the countryside. There was a fine drizzle in the air, a light rain that would soak through to the skin after prolonged periods of time being in it. The mist rose off the fir trees and other breeds that were littered hereabouts in border country in any fashion, the mist looking as if it were smoke rising from the forest floors itself. Mountains and hills were everywhere giving a sense of being completely closed in and a greater sense of how small the problems of man were. What would the mountains care in a thousand years for the issues that he now faced? They had seen disaster befall people before, they had seen the people hereabouts rise up again, and the cycle would no doubt continue no matter his actions in the here and now. He wasn't fatalistic, he knew that he could affect the outcome to some degree, but time made a mockery of every persons ambition in the long run.

The sounds of birds could be heard chatting to each other in the trees, the steady soft thump of the horses hooves into the forest floor adding to the overall ambience. The smells of the forest as well were powerful, distinct smells of chives and garlic reaching him as the two horsemen continued to skirt the town and the Imperial fort within, and the continued rain only served to enhance the freshness of the air. All in all, he thought to himself, the weather may be depressing but everything else seemed to be going well.

He took a sidelong glance at Quittle, his beard freshly groomed and his clothing changed over as he made an effort to reassure Elyn that he was more than capable of looking after himself. The town of Cafeld was somewhere to their left, but whilst the troubles continued with the Imperials then Tor wanted to avoid it. Quittle had readily agreed to skipping the town and the fort that it housed, not wishing to come across any Imperial entanglements just yet.

In truth, and Tor wouldn't let on to Quittle, he was beginning to see things from the perspective of his friend. His clan were demanding action, the rumours that they had heard or made up during the long retreat from Nepriner almost becoming a self-fulfilling prophecy. He couldn't speak for the rest of the clans within the peninsula, but he did know that there was a lot of ill-feeling being bred. It was becoming even more readily apparent as the Rupinians tried to muster yet another offensive army. They had already lost the greater part of two of their armies outside those bloody walls, and those men were the more experienced of the Rupinian armed forces.

"Do you smell burning?" Quittle asked suddenly. Tortag shook his head to the negative before bringing his horse to a halt, sniffing the air around him. In truth, he had a very poor sense of smell which was both a blessing and a curse at times, and he struggled to smell anything above the smell of decaying flora and leaves. There was something though, a faint hint of wood smoke that came in through the northern breeze.

"Might just be the smithy's at the fort, maybe? Either that or the bakeries." The fort was just to their north west, and to say it was rudimentary would be to give it too much of a compliment. It was placed upon a slight hill and held only one gate in its wall. The lower section of the wall was stone, the upper levels where a rampart would have ordinarily been being made out of turf and stakes of wood. The actual keep itself was a timber construction slowly being rebuilt with stone, a more permanent fixture that seemed to blight the landscape.

Tortag had looked upon it numerous times and wondered, as he was want to do in quieter moments, how he would take it. He felt, and not without reason, that the time where he would have to put the theory into practice was fast approaching. He sniffed the air again and gently nudged the horse to move onwards again, a dark feeling beginning to take form at the bottom of his stomach.

"We're being followed," Quittle said quietly, fingering at the short crossbow and drawing back the wires. Deftly he loaded the bow with two bolts and kept it loose in his left hand even as he held the reins with his right. Tortag nodded, his eyes scanning the trees around him even as he tried to keep a nonchalant look upon his face; as if there was nothing bothering him in the World and that he was simply going for a ride out with his friend. He let his right hand drop and brush gently against the sword hanging from his left hip. Tortag knew fine well the gift that his friend had and had seen him use it when the two went out hunting in happier times. He knew enough that his friend wasn't one to jump at shadows.

"You ready for a fight, just in case?"

"You sure you wouldn't rather just hand me over to the Imperials?" Quittle retorted, a smile playing upon his lips thus taking the sting out of his words. Tor gave a weary sigh, a grin spreading across his own as he shook his head.

"You really are becoming a lot more trouble than your worth. Anyway, you haven't done anything yet. You've just ran your mouth, as usual. It's your job."

"If only the Emperor would see it that way!" He hadn't been declared outlaw, not yet anyway, but he knew that it was coming close. Words and ideas were often more dangerous than swords and actual physical violence. Blows and wounds would eventually heal over time, or people would learn to adapt, but some words would settle on the mind and be allowed to continue to grow. An idea was like a seed, it just needed to find the right type of soil to flourish.

They carried on in silence, the brief moment of humour giving way to tension again as the two clansmen scanned the trees and the undergrowth half in expectation of seeing an Imperial. They were, therefore, surprised when they saw Kiegal with a band of men behind him. They were, all of them, armed to the teeth and wearing armour. Quittle, Tor could see, was smiling faintly whereas he was beginning to curse silently. The smell of smoke was beginning to make sense now, for the overpowering scent of wood smoke was too much for a smithy or a bakery at this time of the morning.

"Well, it looks like you boys have been busy!" Tor said, a grin on his face as he tried to fight down the growing sense of trepidation at the bottom of his stomach. Kiegal didn't return the smile, covered in soot and what looked like splatters of blood. Tor hadn't seen him look like that since Nepriner, and the unpleasant connotations caused his stomach to lurch.

"Where have you been, chief?" Tor quirked an eyebrow, his face, he didn't doubt, reflecting his confusion. He was not one for giving out his movements, particularly when it wasn't campaigning season, but he was sure Kiegal had known he was going across the borders to escort Quittle in. He looked at the men escorting his friend and nodded to a few he knew better than most, seeing each of them having the same grim and determined expressions on their faces.

"Has there been a fight?"

"Of a sort. Look, chief, can we talk?"

"I thought we were just doing that!" Tortag felt the growing sense of unease amongst the gathered men, as if they were waiting for the moment to charge or run away. His poor attempt at a joke as well seemed to have no effect on the gathering.

"I meant privately, chief."

"Kiegal, I've known you for years, since when were you respectful of my rank?" It was, he realised, something that had been niggling at him since Kiegal had first spoken. Often his friend would use it either to wind him up or be official, but this seemed to be different in some way. Quittle, Tor noticed, was remaining silent throughout as if it were a domestic problem that he shouldn't get involved in. "Why are you in the forest anyway, shouldn't you be chasing down outlaws?"

It suddenly struck him there and then, almost as if it were an arrow coming from the bush. Kiegal was, when not fighting with the Imperials in their damned wars, a thief catcher. He was notorious for roaming the hills in pursuit of those who had broken the law, often dragging them back to Cafeld in order to stand trial in front of their peers. He was a woodsman of the old school and, it was said, he could track anything that walked or crawled.

"Are you hunting us?" Tor said, his loyalties suddenly divided in a surprising way. He didn't want to draw swords against Kiegal, for the man was a friend and a member of his clan. However, he didn't want to stand aside and suddenly abandon Quittle who was one of his oldest friends.

"No, chief, look…this is important, can you come with me just over there? What I need to say to you is better spoken in private." Tor finally relented, satisfied that Quittle wouldn't suddenly be dragged from the horse and bound. He nodded his head in the direction of a tree a few paces away and dismounted smoothly, patting the horse gently along the neck before walking away to join Kiegal. The man stood by a tree with his hands on his hips, a look of deep concentration on his face as Tor walked towards him.

"Well, here I am. What's wrong?" Kiegal grimaced and scratched at the empty lid under the eyepatch, struggling to find the words.

"It's about your wife, chief." Tortag knew it would be, he instinctively thought it as soon as the words were uttered urging them to privacy. The smell of the smoke suddenly came back to him and the hollow feeling in his stomach opened up threatening to throw him into a chasm of dark thoughts. He coughed, clearing his throat and trying to gather his thoughts. "Aye, what about her?"

"Look, Tor… this ain't easy," Kiegal was struggling, visibly so, in trying to find the appropriate words. Tortag knew what he was going to say before he even uttered them. "She's dead, Tor, the Imperials killed her."

"Why?" His heart was thumping in his chest, a sudden constriction in his throat making it hard to breathe. He pictured her again when he last saw her; her blonde hair reflecting the sunlight as she spoke of the lambing season coming up, her eyes lighting with excitement when he said that he would never go away again and would be around to annoy her and help with the farm properly. She spoke of her plans for visiting friends whilst he was away, organise a small get together for when he got back to finally celebrate him hanging up his sword. Now she was no more, gone to ash and returned to the dirt. She would never again laugh, or cry, or love.

It took everything within him not to break down at that moment, to suddenly fall onto the dirt and cry. His fist was clenching and unclenching by itself on the pommel of his sword, his blood screaming out for revenge to drown his grief. He could feel an anger beginning to burn deep within him that wouldn't be quenched unless it was through Imperial blood.

"I asked you a bastard question, Kiegal, why was my wife murdered?" He hissed it through clenched teeth.

"When you went last week, that Rupinian, Elenol, started casting about for someone to blame for the recent troubles." Kiegal reached inside a pouch that was housed on the belt that hung around his waist, pulling out a piece of parchment that had become grubby with fingerprints. He handed the paper over and Tortag scanned the contents, his eyes alighting on words that immediately jumped out of him. He was declared outlaw, a vagrant and vagabond, who had been consorting with traitors and was the sole reason to blame for the destruction and loss of life outside Nepriner. His lands were forfeit, his life forfeit, and his chiefdom revoked. All good men were to hunt him down, in the name of the Emperor, and would be rewarded with lands taken from him.

"When was my wife killed?"

"They came to the farm in the night, a detachment of a hundred men from the fort. Nobody was offering information, nor siding with the Imperials. They wanted to make an example, make the clan complicit in their crime." Kiegal looked weary and heartbroken; there wasn't many that hadn't been touched by the gentle spirit of Elyn. She had been like a soothing balm compared to Tortag and his fiery personality.

"One of my men saw the smoke rising from the farm buildings this morning. I think it was just a minor house fire at first and so brought some men together." Kiegal watched his chief as he spoke, more worried at the silence than he would have been had the man raged and tried to lash out. "It wasn't a house fire. Your livestock had either been killed or driven off, the outbuildings torn down or burned."

"And my wife?"

"We found her body in your house. We buried her."

"How did she die?"

"Look, Tor...it's not going to help."

"How the fuck did she die, Kiegal?" He roared, his voice beginning to break as his emotions threatened to engulf him. He cast his eyes around the forest, the magic of the place suddenly lost on him and the happier thoughts of a few moments ago long gone.

"She had been hung from the rafters, we found her body next to a broken beam and the charred remains of a rope around her neck." Tor nodded, the anger suddenly leaving him and giving way to feelings of despair and hopelessness. If he couldn't protect his own wife, then how was he supposed to lead a clan and men? "I tracked them back to the fort, Tor, it was the Empire."

He watched his friend and chief with worry in his eyes. He had never seen the man look so downcast, broken almost, as he thought about the death of his wife. Aye, the two of them had their arguments, but then Kiegal defied anyone to show him a couple that didn't disagree at times. He knew as well that the chief was going to be hanging up his sword, had even joked about it in the tavern a few weeks previously saying that he was going to be a farmer. The man wasn't even forty and had spoken, finally, of having children and starting a family of his own. To have all that snatched away from him, to have his dreams destroyed over a spat with some officious officer, was beyond the pale.

Kiegal placed a hand upon his friends shoulder as he tried to provide a reassuring presence. He was at a loss of what to say, not knowing what was appropriate to say in the circumstances and what wasn't. There were times when gruff was needed and there were times when humour was needed, but this was entirely new for him.

"We'll avenge her, Tor. We'll pay the bastards back in kind." Tortag looked up, nodding dumbly at first before the words struck home. A spark was lit in his eyes, anger once again replacing his grief and his disconsolate appearance becoming steadfast once more.

"Blood for blood."

"Blood for blood, chief."

"Tonight," Tortag said.

Aldin was on duty, again, and staring out over the busy clan town of Cafeld. The sun had set and there were few clouds in the sky, the fog of the earlier morning and the bad weather of yesterday evening disappearing into memory. The air felt fresher, the place cleaner and the people happier. There was a feast planned for later on that night and, as a junior member of the half regiment within the fort, he had been told in no uncertain terms that he would be duty. He cursed his superiors, picturing the great quantities of food and ale he had seen being carted in through the gate during the day.

He stood outside the gate now, his armour becoming chilly and weighing him down. He hadn't been sleeping right for days, the rumours of clansmen beginning to take up arms against the Empire filling him with dread. He had only been in the army for a year, which was enough time to conduct some sort of basic training where you learned how to look after your kit and walk in a straight line, and the rest of the time was coming to the arse end of the Empire where there was always far too much water in the atmosphere.

The weather was always wet he had discovered. It seemed to get into everything, through clothes and boots and even into the buildings. The old fort itself, built presumably when mud huts were still the height of fashion, had spots of black mould within the barracks sections. The ironic thing was, he thought, that the fresh water that was supposed to help the garrison stay alive was generally festooned with dead insects and sheep piss. It even seemed to affect his joints, his lungs feeling heavier, and at the age of twenty-three that worried him. He'd be glad to get out of this place, maybe even get some leave for a bloody change.

He looked to his left at the other guardsman on duty, a veteran of the wars with Attainia but on guard tonight for being drunk and having a fight in the town. He refused to say anything to Aldin, calling him a "sprog" once or twice before he promptly ignored him for the rest of the night. It suited Aldin at any rate, he didn't particularly like the man and considered him one of a dying breed; the type of men who would sooner shit on someone for being junior in experience rather than imparting their own experience and learning onto younger heads.

There was a cart now approaching up the slight rise pulled by two great grey horses, the type bred around these parts and considered the heart of the economy. Aldin liked horses and these great beasts demanded respect, proud looking and unbroken even as they pulled the cart up the hill. He was of the opinion that most animals had personalities, and whenever he looked at those beasts of burden he reckoned that they were only doing what they did because they felt sorry for the stupid creatures that couldn't carry their own burdens.

The cart was covered with a large tarpaulin, the shapes of whatever was underneath causing permeations. It would be another food wagon carrying all manner of goods no doubt, he thought, and would probably end up getting shat out by some over privileged wanker in the morning. He cursed inwardly knowing that a few of the men would leave the fort after the feast and go into the town looking for some sport and more drink with the local women, and then they'd come back in steaming drunk when he was presumably back on the gate and try and offer him food that they had managed to get from the bakery when the sun began to rise again.

The man sat on the cart was an older man with a hooded cloak, the hood pulled over his head to presumably keep out the chill of the early evening air. There was a rut in the road and the cart bounced causing the hood to fall back from the face by a couple of inches revealing a man with one eye, the other covered with a black eyepatch. Aldin presumed the man was a veteran, no longer working in the Imperial army due to his obvious disability.

The man was waved through the gate by the other sentry and the area became quiet once again, the town carrying on with its business as people sought to close up shop for the night. There were people moving about with sacks carrying their daily wares over their shoulders, and the place looked peaceful. He turned to his left and realised there was an absence of sound. The cart had stopped in the middle of the gate and the horses were steady, pawing at the cobbled ground even as the rider dismounted. Aldin presumed the wagon had thrown a wheel and looked forward again, seeing a group of men now beginning to walk up the rise.

There was a sharp intake of breath and the sound of a scream being cut off swiftly. He gripped his spear and turned instantly. Right into the knife of the one eyed man.

"Sorry, laddie." Kiegal said.

The alarm bells broke out instantly and the keep was thrown into disarray as the clansmen swept through the wide open gate, the wagon preventing the gate from shutting. Underneath the tarpaulin men spilled out and all became blood and chaos as they swept on into the courtyard, killing those soldiers they found and doing their best to mitigate casualties for those who didn't wear armour or weapons. Chances were a lot of them were going to be soldiers who hadn't seen fit to wear armour whilst they were attending a feast, but there was a chance that a few were clansfolk from the town and therefore had to be protected. Either way, they were corralled and placed under guard.

Tortag ran through the swirling chaos, sliding on his knees as he went under one Rupinian. He held his sword up fully as he did so, slicing through the man's groin causing him to topple to the ground screaming. Quittle came running in with his axe and smashed it into the side of the man's head silencing him forever.

"What now?"

"The keep, before the bastards shut the door!" Tor roared out, pointing his sword and gathering a group of warriors around him as they formed a fighting wedge and charged towards the open entrance.

Surprise had been complete; no actual formed resistance being found as clansmen flowed in. The smithy and bakery were being ransacked, the sounds of crashing and the occasional scream reaching the ears of Quittle as he looked around. He had never been involved in a fight like this before, let alone the sacking of a military fort. He found it exhilarating and frightening at the same time, the blood rushing through his veins and the adrenaline making his reflexes quicker than he would have believed possible.

Someone shouted out a warning and he spun around, going on bended knee and fired off the short crossbow taking a man in the right eye. He was dead before he crashed into the dirt. Quittle stood up and looked around again for Tortag, seeing him making short work of another Imperial with a riposte across the midriff. Tor disengaged from the falling body and into the keep. A wounded Rupinian tried to stop him with feeble resistance by holding out an outstretched hand whilst his free hand held a bloody knife thrust deep into his stomach. He was barely given a second glance as the thirty or so men pushed on.

Quittle followed on into the gloom of the keeps entrance, stopping for a few seconds to allow his eyes to adjust. Half the town seemed to be trying to push on behind him as they sought to ransack the castle and destroy the occupants whilst there was still time. Quittle had to hand it to Tor. He had originally suggested the raid on the castle and how to go about it, but it was Tor and Kiegal who had brought the men and means to conduct the expedition.

There was a scream from above as a man was presumably disembowelled, the sounds of swords smashing into one another. He pushed on, running up a staircase and past an office where a scribe was sprawled across paperwork that would never be read. He didn't give the man a second glance nor feel any sympathy.

"Put up your damned swords!" He heard Tortag roar out, his voice all the more powerful for echoing throughout the building. Quittle burst onto the scene in the banquet hall and took in the scene, seeing a small circle of Rupinian officers surrounded by the bloodied swords of the Black Moon clan warriors. The rafters were decorated with garlands of flowers and banners depicting the colours of the Rupinian regiment and Imperial family. There was a large fire roaring sending waves of heat into the hall, though Quittle didn't feel it. There were long tables that had once been richly decorated with white satin sheets, but the tables were now overturned and broken whilst the white sheets were covered in a mixture of mud and blood.

He stood alongside Tortag and looked upon the Imperials in front of him. Tor was staring at one man in particular, the look of hate etched on his face causing his lips to peel back in a snarl. He was a man that looked capable or murder, and would carry on killing until the pain of the death of his wife had finally faded.

"Your fort is lost, Elenol. Your men are dead, bar those that you have with you." Quittle was almost startled at how softly spoken the words were, but he realised that was often when Tor was at his most dangerous. It meant the man was thinking, and a thinking man is a deadly thing. "You have called me outlaw. Why?"

"You have sided with rebels. You have broken your oath of loyalty to Emperor Rhagan the First!" Quittle had to hand it to the man for his courage in speaking so, but given the circumstances all that was available to him as a gesture of defiance was words. He must have realised that all that was left to him was the precious few moments of conversation, if he were lucky.

"You killed my wife."

"A casualty of war."

"A casualty of war?" Tor nodded as he approached the man, nodding as if he understood. Quicker than Quittle could even comprehend there was a knife in the hand of his friend, buried up to the hilt in the neck of the Imperial officer. "Aye, and here's another."

"What are you going to do with the rest of us?" A soldier asked, a worried expression upon his face. In fairness to the man, Quittle thought, he'd be pissing himself in fear by about now. There were no guarantees of the conventional rules of warfare, captured men were liable to be fair game if the example of Elenol was anything to go by.

"Do I look like a man with a plan?" Tortag said, staring down at the body of the dead Imperial. He knelt down and removed the knife with a sick flopping sound, a spurt of blood following it. Tortag looked upon the knife with distaste and wiped the blood on the dead man's clothing. "Ask him, ask Quittle. He's the leader here."

It was as if the World suddenly turned to look at him. Quittle realised that this was the moment, that they had gone well past the point of no return. History had been made here, and it would either become a success story or a failed rebellion. It suddenly felt as if a huge burden had fallen upon his shoulders. He realised that, for all his talk, he had never expected any of his to happen. He had expected to go around the various different clans and be rebuffed, maybe eventually raise a small rebellion himself that would be instantly crushed and himself killed. This, everything about this, was beyond what he could have hoped for. His rebellion and bid for independence had been born with an entire clan backing him; more importantly his friend backed him. He wished, though, it could have happened in different circumstances. He knew Elyn and had loved her because she loved his friend and made him smile. No country, no dream or ambition, was worth the life of one good person. He would never forget her, not so long as he was able to draw breath.

"Go to your Emperor and tell him that the clans are on the rise. Tell him what transpired here. Tell him, when he comes, that we shall be ready for him. Tell him that, Imperial. You will have safe conduct to the borders."

The Rupinians looked about them at the faces of the clansmen knowing that the men were only holding themselves back because Quittle had spoken. The first Rupinian dropped his sword onto the floor, clattering onto the wooden and rattling before finally coming still. It was followed by more, the crashing sound of weaponry dropping being the only noise within the banquet hall.

"Kiegal, see them out and take them to the borders. No harm is to come to them." The man nodded and then nodded at a few of his men, beckoning the Imperials to follow on. They trooped out like whipped puppies, eyes downcast as they refused to look about them for fear of causing offence.

"Chief Tortag Mane?"

"Aye?" The man had stood up now and was looking at the departing Imperials, Quittle knowing that he wanted to butcher them where they stood. He couldn't allow that to happen, knowing that when the blood finally cooled and Tor was able to think about it that he would regret his actions and cause him to be even more maudlin.

"Gather your men in the town square. Have a section ready to fire the fort. We cannot stay here, and we cannot allow this building to fall into the hands of the Empire again."

"As you say, sir."

"Get a rider, one of your best, and have him deliver this message for me," Quittle said as he handed over a scroll. "I want him to ride with all haste to Gephy."

"Gephy?"

"If we can get them on side, then we open up another front to this war and we can work in unison. We will cast the Rupinians out of this land and secure our borders, as well as those of the Attainians. Together, and only together, will we win here."

"I'll have the rider sent out within the hour."

Quittle nodded and looked about him, seeing men look to him for guidance and orders. A few were detailed off to collect weaponry and any foodstuffs they could find, whilst others were detailed to begin preparations for firing the keep.

The rebellion was underway, and the war of independence about to begin.

Chapter Nine - **Diplomacy**

Four kingdoms as one under the banner of Ufwala, three others who were allies who pledged their support and five who remained neutral or weren't fully hostile. The Ufwalan capital of Dawold was in the grip of a carnival like atmosphere with the people celebrating the capitulation of Vitrossy. Garren was sat in his study within the embassy, his small area of seclusion and safety where he was able to think away the problems of the World by looking into the fire and drinking wine.

The leather chair he was sat on was comfortable, broken in and worn with age. He stroked the arm rest in an affectionate manner, his legs outstretched with his right leg resting on his left shin. He was not alone, but the Attainian diplomat Roac was decent enough company. The man had grown to become a close friend over the last few months, especially since their first meeting when Garren had believed the man to be a chinless and spineless specimen who would break quicker than wet paper. He too sat in the comfortable silence that can only exist between friends where conversation needn't be forced for the sake of filling the void.

The sun was shining through the stained glass window of his study, the coloured light reflecting on the otherwise plain walls. There was little ornamentation in the room, Garren being firmly of the belief that such things were often little better than ostentatious dust collectors.

"What do you think she'll do now?" Roac asked, breaking the silence with the question that the two men were obviously thinking of. They were due to go to a parade later on, a dull affair where the military liked to show off their better side with flag waving and smart uniforms. Garren had only been in the legions for a year prior to discharge, but he often wondered at the logic of so many parades. The people didn't care for the wars that were fought in far flung lands so long as it didn't affect them, and if Ufwala continued to win glory then all the power to the Queen as far as the populace were concerned. In his mind, so long as there was still hot food available and money coming into the coffers to improve everybody's general lot in life then they didn't so much care. This parade was just grandiose boasting of the sort that Garren had come to despise, the diplomatic and military equivalent of a pissing contest as far as he could make out.

"She can't move any quicker than she already has done, or she threatens to break down everything." There was a time when he had been a little in love with the Queen, and even now he knew he was and his judgement could thus be thought of as impaired, but he was a realist. "She has four Kingdoms she needs to pacify, and garrisons in three others who are allies. She's strong enough politically and militarily to wage war on the other five, but she hasn't secured her recently won territory. If she doesn't then the entire edifice is likely to come crashing down around her and the Coalition will fall back into its usual state of near anarchy."

"Peace in our time?" Roac said with a wry smile. The Attainian had never come close to the Queen, not whilst Nepriner had been under siege and it had looked as if the old Republic were finally going to crumble and wither away. It was only after the regiments, with a great deal of assistance from the Cardavian legions, had finally turned the tide against the onslaught of the Imperials that she had deigned to talk to him. His perception of her had been coloured because of those actions. As far as he was concerned, the Queen was power hungry and was likely using the Cardavians and the Imperials to suit her own ends whilst she faced political problems at home. She could play the two countries off against each other and reap the benefits without necessarily committing to a full alliance. She was canny, he would concede, but outwith diplomatic functions he had no time for the woman.

"Perhaps. Depends on the mob. Depends on the Generals. She has a fairly large standing army now as well, and I don't think her economy can support it. She may have taken new lands and such like, but she needs to get their economy sorted out. Armies tend to deal a massive amount of devastation."

"I know," Roac said with feeling, "I've been getting the reports from Nepriner. The city may not have fallen, but it is a shadow of its former self. The entire province is liberated, right enough, but there is enough devastation there to last a generation or so. There was even a rumour circulating around the Senate, so I'm told by my sources, that they were considering abandoning the city around Nepriner entirely and making the new capital at Gephy."

"Would they keep the citadel?"

"Of course, it would make sense. However, from what I gather, Senator Elgrynn has put a stop to the idea with a few speeches and is actually leading rebuilding efforts himself." He took a sip from the wine and considered Nepriner for a few moments more before carrying on with his previous thought process, "Wellisa will be crowned High Queen today, won't she?"

"I certainly hope so otherwise we shall be the most overdressed men in the city!" Garren said with a grin, "It will be shortly after the parade though, when her Guards regiment is before her so she can guarantee a happy regiment as well as a happy population."

"Have you not heard the rumour then?"

"I have barely been in the city in all honesty, Roac, since I came back from Vitrossy and I haven't heard anything of note." Roac was slightly taken aback, unused to having heard anything before the wily Cardavian diplomat. It was an unspoken fact amongst the pair that the Cardavian usually had his ear to the ground and therefore was one to hear the whispers of the street; to suddenly be the one breaking the gossip was something altogether. It also made Roac a little unsure, wondering whether he had gone for a small detailed fact when there was something bigger afoot distracting his friend.

"We are agreed that Wellisa is playing everybody off against each other by promising everything and nothing?" Garren nodded as he sipped his wine, focussing his attention fully on his friend and away from the crackling logs of the fire. "Good. We both know the Imperials had been backing the rebels in Vitrossy and the other failed states and, therefore, had given them a mass of supplies that the rebels weren't able to dispose of and that, as terms of their surrender, they had to hand over all military and material stores?"

"I know the terms of the treaty with Vitrossy and their King, Roac, I saw the surrender of the Rock." It was said with an easy smile and the venom was taken out of the words. There was a polite chap at the door and Garren shouted for the person to enter.

"My Lord," a soldier entered and stood crisply to attention. Garren still requested his guard to go about fully armoured and carrying weapons ever since he was attacked by the Clansman, an event that seemed as if it had taken place several years ago instead of only a couple of months. He was not by nature a paranoid person, nor was he naturally inclined to give the impression that he didn't trust the security that the Queen of Ufwala provided, but he had resolved since that day the only people he would trust around him were Cardavians and the Attainians. The soldier handed him a scroll which he took with a nod of thanks, beckoning the man to pour himself a glass. The soldier professionally shook his head as he declined the offer and, dismissed, he turned about on his heel and walked out the room.

Roac watched the guardsman disappear and shut the door, counting to five before he continued. If the rumour was correct then everybody would know within three or four hours anyway, however, if he was wrong then he didn't want to look like some gossiping fool in front of soldiers. He knew only too well that a story could go from one end of the Republic to the other just because of how soldiers could gossip.

"You have heard of the black powder?"

"I have heard that it was mined or developed, something like that anyway, by the Speirakians and used during the siege of Nepriner. It was reported they used the stuff to breach the northern and eastern gates, as well as bombard the industrial district." Garren looked at the purple wax seal on the scroll, the velvet ribbon tied around it securing it further. He strained his eyes in the light as he sought to make out the crest, inclining forward to hold it closer to the fire as if the seal would provide him some clue as to the contents. All he could make out, due to the colour of the wax seal and ribbon, was that it was a dispatch from Parliament.

"You're correct, of course. Our sources in the north say that this black powder is a mixture of sulphur, saltpetre and charcoal." He cleared his throat and coughed, taking a sip of wine to wash down his mounting excitement. "The Imperials used it as you say, but they've been developing it further and hadn't the confidence in their new inventions to properly test it out. Beforehand it was simply sacks of the stuff with long fuses that would be lit, causing an explosion and damage but often killing those who were trying to wield it. Now they've created some iron tube, a big one, that can fire huge stones at a decent range directly into a body of men or fortifications."

"So why does this concern Queen Wellisa and Ufwala?"

"Because she's got black powder now and, like it or not, a trade route with the Empire by sea. She has iron in abundance now as well. She also knows that the Cardavian navy won't intercept or board an Ufwalan ship flying its own colours and can therefore potentially bring these weapons in."

"Does she have any of these iron tubes yet?"

"I don't know, to be honest. However, it'll only be a matter of time until she finds a practical use for this powder that won't see her own soldiers being killed whenever they light the stuff. Once she works that out, then the three forts in the mountain passes that the Cardavians set such store by could be breached." Garren nodded, disquieted at the thought of these new wonder weapons that were being developed and the implications that could come with them. He realised, as well, that he hadn't opened the scroll either and so decided to fill the ensuing silence with his own reading whilst he tried to gather his thoughts.

He read through the contents quickly and then read them again, a faint smile beginning to appear on his lips. Satisfied with it, he passed the dispatch to Roac and sat back into his chair, pouring himself a fresh glass of wine. He watched Roac over the rim of his glass as he read the contents of it and nodded with satisfaction as the man's eyes grew wider as he read.

"Beran Corus, of Nepriner fame and General of the Grey Wolves is coming to the western pass?"

"It would appear so, Roac. His brother, Dunwal also of Nepriner fame, is taking the eastern pass. Now, whether the Parliament has caught wind of your rumours as well or this is simply a billet for them to rest and recuperate is up for conjecture, but I do know that the likes of Morro and the Queen will sit up and take notice of the fact that a fighting legion has just landed on their doorstep."

There was another knock at the door and it was answered with a shout for whomever it was to come in. The message simply passed was that their transport awaited to take them to the parade and the ceremony, if they would be so kind as to join them as soon as it was convenient.

"Shall we get this show over with?" Garren asked, finishing off the last of his glass. He was feeling a tad light headed, but nothing more than he could cope with. He would suggest he was feeling a little more relaxed about things now that he knew the Wolves were coming, but equally that could be the half bottle of red he had just drunk with the Attainian.

"Are you feeling up for it?"

"Not particularly, but apparently a diplomat has to be seen to be diplomatic every now and then. You know, I long for the day they finally sending someone else here and I am able to retire to an estate near Silveroak where my only worry will be whether I have another bottle stored away in the cellar or something rather than all this political talk."

"Maybe Beran has come to replace you. Apparently he was very diplomatic with the Imperials!"

He had seen the Royal Castle of Dawold decked out in all its splendour once before, and that had been when the Queen had hosted a ball to welcome in the diplomats of the continent and show off her royal majesty in all its glorious splendour. However, with the better part of half the coalition under her belt, that event seemed to pale into insignificance compared to what could be mounted now.

He always knew that the Queen had been self-confident for, in a World largely dominated by men, the young woman had to seize every opportunity she got to wrong foot her opponents. Whether, Garren suspected, the opponents were perceived or real was immaterial. The Queen would always have to politically or militarily outmanoeuvre people until she had a number of years on the throne under her belt and had well and truly shown the powers that be what type of Queen she was. From what Garren had seen, Wellisa had managed her affairs in an excellent manner. He was a little biased, he was honest enough to admit his own faults, but she had combined the need to win over her population with political and military victories as well as her various charity works. Schooling was now mandatory for all children with free meals provided for the poorest amongst them, and hospitals were being built to nurse the sick and the old. Roads were being resurfaced and new trade routes were being set up. Businesses were given breaks in their tax if they set up in the newly conquered provinces and employed people therein, and the farmers were blessed with decent weather to allow them to sow their fields with new seed for the coming spring and future harvest. The Queen had been blessed, a mixture of fortune and design going a long way to endear her to her population. She was also lucky in the fact that she was naturally beautiful for, though it was often a chauvinistic or demeaning thing to think, people didn't generally associate bad things with naturally good looking people. Little were they to know of her machinations with the garrison commander of Vitrossy that led to the massacre of a disciplined body of men, or the threats to burn the city and the castle on the rock to the ground lest the King surrender. No, the people saw a young and beautiful Queen who was simply winning what was deemed hers by heritage and blood, and helping them along as well.

He sat now in the covered awning slightly behind the tall oak throne where the Queen sat. He noted that unlike other royal thrones that this one was bare of any ornamentation. It was richly varnished and obviously well looked after, had even been well designed with etchings and such like carved into the wood, but there was very little, if any, in the way of jewellery or other displays of wealth. She was, he knew, a woman who used simplicity of design to emphasise her own characteristics.

The military band were marching behind the guard of honour and were giving song to some military tune that presumably resonated with the Ufwalan crowd. They were kept at a respectful distance from the parade itself that was taking place in the courtyard of the castle. The outer walls of the keep had been opened to the public and they were filled with happy and smiling faces, a respectful silence having fallen on them the minute the military band had struck up. Within the awning there was muted conversation, the Queen and Morro locked in a quiet, yet intense looking, conversation. Garren watched them for a few minutes and tried to discern what they were talking about, wondering if they too had received news of the Cardavian movements on their borders. He knew Morro, being formerly of the Ufwalan intelligence gatherers, would see the significance of the action.

Roac was sitting in apparent deep conversation with a clansman, a new arrival since the previous incumbent of the position had been dismissed after the assault on Garren. The two of them were even sharing smiles and gestures, something that confused the Cardavian immensely given that the two peoples were at war. He put it to the back of his mind, but noted that it was something he would have to investigate at a later point in time.

The inspection of the guard was slowly coming to an end and there was another hush descending upon the gathered crowd of civilians and dignitaries, it becoming obvious that the Queen was going to speak. Out of the corner of his eye, Garren could see that the Kings who had sworn alliance to or been conquered by the soldiers of Ufwala were beginning to stir. The Queen was to be crowned today, an official ceremony so that the assumption of power became more civilised rather than one that had been seized by force under the flimsiest of excuses. Everything was quiet as she stood, the eyes of the crowd focussed upon her, and her hold over them was complete.

"My Lords, Ladies, gentlemen and men of the Guards! This is a very special occasion for us. Ufwala rises on the crest of a new wave. Ufwala has never been in a stronger position. Our economy is growing. Our children go to new schools. Our experienced and victorious armies march to battles in soon-to-be-won territories on freshly built roads. None of this would be possible without any of you here.

"You, all of you, should be sharing in these victories. Before you now," she said with an eloquent gesture of her right hand as she drew attention to the conquered heads of state and those who had pledged alliance, "are seven rulers. After a short ceremony, there will be a High Queen. It is my pledge to continue what we have been doing. We will continue to build our country, we will continue to secure our trade and use the money that comes in from that to benefit each and every one of you. We will be strong. We will be a united country under one banner, ready to face all threats both domestic and foreign."

There was applause from the crowd and cheering, the promise of increased wealth and living standards going a long way to win over any population. Garren was a cynic, had been for years after seeing promises being broken upon the rocks of reality. Talk was easy, promises even easier to give. So long as there was still an external threat, as Garren saw it, then Wellisa could quite happily point to them and say that they were the source of the populations threat.

The Queen continued her speech, the talk from her mouth like silk to the ears of the gathered crowd. She sat after a while, not lingering too long on how she would achieve her aims, and allowed Morro to take the stand. The conquered and allies marched in front of her, King Jaca of Vitrossy foremost amongst them. He still cut a splendid figure, not at all broken nor downcast, and the diplomat wondered once more whether something else was being concocted behind closed doors. They went on bended knee and repeated their oaths of loyalty and fealty, pledging homage for lands they once held independently to Wellisa and her descendants.

The South was becoming united, a nightmare scenario for Cardavian politicians and royalty for centuries, and there appeared to be nothing they could do about it.

Chapter Ten – **Grim Journey**

Grim thought again of Katrin when he last seen her as the trio had walked out of the city gates of Silveroak, his kit slung over his shoulder on the end of a yoke and his cloak pulled tight across his shoulders to protect himself from the rain. It was secured with a bronze broach of an eagle, its wings splayed in mid-flight. He could barely remember they conversation they had, but he remembered the last words he had said to her.

"When will you be back?" She had asked, her hands clasped in front of them and a smile no longer on her face. He had grown used to that smile, had come to love seeing it first thing in the morning and last thing at night. It had been three months since the triumph, four since Nepriner, and the days in between had been filled with the lovely woman in front of him. Nek had had even the good graces to leave them be and pretend to tend to the horses they had bought that would carry them north. He had taken her soft hands in his calloused ones, cursing inwardly at the fact they were sodden and cold and he hoped he could provide her with a degree of warmth.

"Soon," he had answered, his voice croaky. When he had received word that he would be returning to Gephy and there to await orders he had seriously considered throwing his chit in.

He hadn't been assigned a new legion and was instead kept in the barracks of the Guards. He had watched his former legion, the Eagles, going from strength to strength but had found himself replaced as their commanding officer as soon as they had found a suitable replacement. He, and Nekstar, had become a buggerance. It was useful to parade them every now and then as the heroes of the hour, the former rankers turned officers and war heroes, but when memories of the triumph began to wane suddenly those in charge were at a loose end what to do with them. He had approached Beran shortly before they marched south to Noriandie and the borders of Ufwala, but he had to apologetically explain that there simply wasn't room for him in the Wolves command structure just yet.

"I'll wait for you, Grim." He had kissed her and thought of asking her to marry him, but decided that if he were to die then it wouldn't be fair to leave her a widow before she had even worn a wedding dress. Equally, and rather fatalistically, he didn't enjoy the idea of him leaving her and having her put her life on hold for him to come back. However, there was a comfort in those words and he smiled the more for it.

"I love you, Katrin." She had kissed him and bade him go, the pair of them not being good at saying goodbye. It was strange, for he had never left for anywhere before whilst having anyone wait for him. It was both a source of joy and weakness, he knew, and it was something he found near impossible to describe to his friend.

It had taken them a significantly shorter period of time to cross the lands of Cardavy and the Inner Republic than they had figured, but then two horsemen riding without any cares were always going to be faster than their previous method of entry which had been in the column of a legion. They had reached Gephy by the second week of their travels, the winter snow having melted and given way to decent weather.

They had seen the hive of activity that was Nepriner, though neither man wanted to go near the city. There was a permanent military encampment around it now with two Cardavian legions supplementing the innumerable Attainian regiments. It appeared to the two veterans that they were preparing for another offensive in the coming weeks from the north. The city itself was a hive of activity, large wooden cranes lifting massive blocks of stone to reinforce and repair sections of the wall that had become damaged or destroyed during the great siege. There were no tall buildings left, the old industrial district having been levelled during the siege, therefore the only significant structure visible at range from within the city was the formidable citadel which Beran and the survivors had held at the last.

There was also the question of the refugees and those who had been displaced during the battle. The city had been torn apart and then smashed into a thousand pieces, virtually no house was untouched from unchecked fires or the rampant bombardment that the Imperials had subjected it to. Nor had they fared much better from the counter fire coming from the cities own artillery. Thousands were homeless and many of those thousands were camped outside the safety of the city walls relying on ration handouts. Those that were lucky enough to still have a home often found that they would have others staying with them, whether they liked the idea or not. It wasn't the only problem. Due to the length and ferocity of the siege a lot of the civic functions had been abandoned, a lot of the necessary maintenance and repairs had been forgotten and, to that end, sewers were still broken and the threat of disease was rampant. Corpses were still being dragged out of rubble as entire streets were cleared, or so they heard from a passing merchant, and thus the job of at least getting the city clean was of paramount importance before the warmer weather brought disease.

They could see the mountain ranges of Gephy in the east and had camped out in the plains amongst the ruins of a wagon train that the Imperials had abandoned, long looted of everything of worth leaving only planks of wood that were useful for a fire. Nek and Grim had spoken that night candidly, each expressing their hope that this wasn't another suicide mission they were embarking on but knowing full well, given the fickle love of the Gods and the inept abilities of everyone and everything in the higher echelons of society, that they would be "launched straight into the shit as usual" according to Nek.

They had ridden out as soon as the sun rose and they could see where they were going, the area still being covered in traps and counter measures that the defenders of the port city of Gephy and Nepriner had laid on for the men of the Empire. They entered the range, darkened by the looming presence of the peaks and the wind howled down the funnel creating an eerie feeling. It was somewhat abated by the fact they weren't the only travellers. Shipping was obviously getting through to Gephy and it was becoming a major port once again, the reconstruction work of the Attainian frontier finally taking precedence over works in the capital and the inner Republic. Merchants rubbed shoulders with workmen as each one sought to take their wares and talents west where they would be sold and money made. Say one thing for war, say it's profitable.

"Remember standing here after the march south?" Nek asked, his voice barely above a whisper as they approached the gatehouse.

"How could I forget?" Grim retorted, remembering how he looked upon the wall with a great deal of nerves. He had, somehow, found himself leading the remnants of his legion and allied Attainians south after the brutal fight at Turgundeon. Along the way they had picked up refugees by the score, starving and lost as they were. Harried all the way south, and one memorable ambush by a lake that was fought off with a great deal of effort, and they had finally found themselves outside the walls. If it hadn't been for the Harbour Master Aarlin admitting them, then they would likely have tried to find succour in Nepriner.

"At least the place looks better than it did then. They've even managed to get rid of the siege lines and the bodies."

"Bodies and discarded weaponry tend to put the tourists off, I found. They tend to put monuments up instead and the weapons go to a museum."

"You've become a bit of an expert on that sort of thing," remarked Nek as they finally pushed their horses through the gatehouse and into the main avenue which led towards the military port and their ultimate destination. Nek hadn't felt at all side lined as his friend continued his romance with Katrin, indeed he had revelled in it. He wasn't taken for himself and nor was he particularly looking, but he enjoyed the change which had come over Grimfar. He had lost a lot of the pessimistic view of life and there was a new vibrancy about him, he stood straighter and generally looked to the long view now. He was more sure of himself as well, more confident, though whether that was because of Katrin or surviving Gephy was up for debate. It was hard to describe, if he was being honest, but there had been a change for the better.

"I'm becoming cultured," Grim replied with a smirk.

"Is that what you call it?" Nek retorted, a grin spreading across his face. "I thought you were finally showing your age and becoming a boring bastard!"

"I've offered before, Nek, if you need help working out what those curious shapes are that are on paper and everywhere you seem to look, then I will quite happily help you learn to read. It'd make you a better person."

"Why read when I can look at pictures? Cheeky sod."

The port did have new life and the two friends had to fight their way through the traffic on the roads. It seemed like half the Republic, and a fair few from foreign lands, had descended on the place after word of the Imperial pushback. There seemed also to be a carefree attitude in the air, something that confused the two veteran soldiers, for weren't the Imperials mustering yet another grand army to come south with a view to taking all these lands? It was something that Grim put at the back of his mind, something he figured would no doubt be brought up when they finally received their orders from Aarlin.

"There's the lighthouse!" Nek said, somewhat more excitedly than Grim had ever come to expect from the cynical and experienced legionary.

"Gods, I was hoping you had forgotten about that bloody naval battle. Why didn't you just transfer over to the Leviathans when we were at Silveroak and bloody stay with the Navy?"

"You'd have missed out on my amazing talents and stories. Anyway, your life would be a lot duller without me."

"Yes, I've often commented to Katrin that spending the majority of my time off trying to drag you out of whatever trouble you've got yourself into is always a highlight of my leave."

There was a new gate where before there had been a simple archway that would permit the two Cardavians into the naval base. There was a marine there whom Nekstar recognised from the siege and the two were happily conversing on bloodier days, comparing scars as veterans were want to do, and commenting on the new lease of life around the port. It was only when they were permitted entry and, therefore, out of earshot that Nek began speaking of what he had learnt.

"The Imps aren't invading, not this year anyway. There's trouble in the north with the clans."

"How do you mean?" They directed the horses down a side street, skirting round a workshop which had its barn doors wide open where the noise of hammering and sawing could be heard. Grim had a look in when they were going past and saw a ship being constructed, the wooden hull being firmly in place and the paint being applied to the bow whilst others were working on the superstructure of the fo'c'sle.

"There's a rebellion. Apparently some clan chief has decided not to pay his taxes or something. Anyway, he's slaughtered the local garrison and proclaimed that the clans are free. Apparently he's overplayed his hand anyway, the Imperials now have an army on his border and another rampaging at will in his lands. He's not terribly popular amongst his people either and some of the clans have taken up against him too."

"Sounds like a complete fucking disaster then, Nek."

"Aye...so you know exactly where we're heading then."

"Of course, straight into the bloody shit once more." Grim said with a grin and a laugh.

"I don't see what they are expecting us to do, Grim. We aren't Generals, not really, and our only experience with glorious last stands and hit and run tactics was limited to a great big bloody retreat. Leading men on the field is something else entirely."

"No idea, my friend, but let's see what Aarlin has to say first before we start thinking how we can carve out a Kingdom for ourselves."

"Who said anything about that? The man who would be king, eh? I can just see you now getting your right royal arse kissed by all and sundry."

"So long as you are there to wipe it beforehand then I can't see how it would be a bad thing in life. Anyway, Katrin would suit a crown on her head."

"You've gone bloody soft!" Nek cried, a grin on his face and his eyes alight with good humour.

"Not at all, I've just learnt that there are better things in life than downing a bucket of wine and seeing how high you can piss against the wall outside the tavern."

"Only because you never won," Grim flashed a grin as they rounded a quarter. This was the smarter part of the port, where they had gone that first night when they had reached Gephy after the long retreat. They had barely been afforded the time to drop their kit off at their quarters before they were summoned to meet with Aarlin on a cold and dreary night. He remembered then that he had no idea whether they were still going to be kicked out of the city, whether they would have to abandon the refugees to their fate and possibly make a move to enter Nepriner. What he didn't realise at the time was that the meeting would begin a firm and fruitful professional friendship.

A page came out and took the horses after they had dismounted, two stewards came to collect their kit from the saddlebags, and all promised to look after their charges before they were hustled politely into the building. They were escorted by a man who looked familiar, but neither of the men could place the face and nor did they wish to ask in case they looked foolish. The steward chapped on the door of the Harbour Masters office and they were admitted in.

The man before them cut a stronger figure than either two men could remember. He was still tall and broad shouldered, but the grey hair seemed to be darker and the beard carried less silver than had it done previously. Grim was also sure the man had been out and about more than he had been before, for the arms were stronger looking and tanned. It was obvious that the Harbour Master was getting fed up sitting behind a desk and had taken himself off to sea on more than one occasion. There was a wide smile across his face, and he approached them with open arms and took each man into an embrace before bidding them to sit down. He ordered the steward to bring three goblets and two bottles of red wine from the cellar. "It's good to see you again, gentlemen! Damned good!" He finally said at last when the wine was brought. He dismissed the steward and did the pouring himself, decent measures of the sort that promised to never run empty.

"And you, Harbour Master. You are looking very well."

"Aye, you've started dying your beard for a start!" Nek said, relishing the easy atmosphere that can often exist between superior and subordinate after they've come through hell and back with each other.

"Trade has its uses, Nekstar." Aarlin replied, taking a sip from his own wine. "The men from Revoy have some uses when it comes to bringing in their product. Anyway, it works well with the ladies."

"Always the sailor then, Aarlin?"

"Always, Grimfar, always. How has life been treating you since you left us months ago?"

"It's being going well. I've met a lovely woman called Katrin. I'm thinking of asking her to marry me once we're done here."

"That's bloody news to me!" Nek said spluttering, nearly spilling his drink in the process. "You've not bothered bloody telling me that!"

"Well you never asked," he replied with a grin and a wink. He turned to Aarlin again, "I've noticed there's a lot of traffic heading west to help in rebuilding Nepriner, but there doesn't seem to be the usual atmosphere of an impending siege that I became used to in these parts."

"Straight to the crux of the matter, as I expect from you." He stood up and wandered over to the far wall, past the model of the port where they had once planned out how to defend the area and the city itself. "I take it you gentlemen have heard of the troubles that the Imperials are having in the north?"

"We've heard rumours, but nothing concrete." Nekstar replied for the pair of them, Grim happy for him to take the running given that he was the one who had heard the story.

"Did you ever hear about the Imperial herald, a man named Quittle?" The

Cardavians shook their heads to the negative, "Quittle is a man of the clans, in particular the Red River clan. He was present during the siege and was often used by the Field Marshal in charge, Neard, I think, to deliver terms to the defenders. Anyway, he saw everything and was involved in the entire debacle. According to our sources in the north, as soon as he got back to Imperial lands he went to the capital and sought an audience with the Emperor. He was, for all intents and purposes, fobbed off.

"Now, I have no idea what their grievance is or what has led up to it, but I do know that the Imperials have lost them and the Black Moon clan." He pointed to the chart where the two clans were located. "The homelands of the two clans are right next to the borders, but they are good lands with fertile ground and ready access to the rivers that run into the sea as well as the south and east. Now, what they are trying to do is rally the rest of clan country and throw off the shackles of Imperial control. This has been met with force, and not a great deal of popularity in some quarters. The vast majority have remained neutral, hedging their bets really, whilst some have decided to back the Empire in the hope that they can secure more lands."

"So why are we here, sir? If this is just an intelligence brief, then someone in the diplomatic could have received it and relayed it to Parliament and command." Grim chipped in, already beginning to see the way things were unfolding.

"We already have, Grim, which is why you boys are here." He walked back to and resumed his seat, pouring himself a fresh glass of wine. "You two are used to irregular warfare, none more so since my nephew Takol was killed. The clansmen are brave men and, from what we've heard, well led by this Quittle and his ally Tortag, however, they don't have your experience of fighting against Imperials. I appreciate this may sound flimsy, but ultimately the Senate and Parliament have decided that you two need to be there.

"We've opened up a dialogue with them, are even sending them some stores and weapons that we can spare. Trouble is, we don't want them going down the same path that Rupinia did by forming their own empire. We do not want the clans to suddenly destroy everything in front of them without remembering that we were there to help them. Essentially, the Senate wants to protects its northern border in the future by investing in the clans now.

"Now you two are popular men," he took a drink and cleared his parched throat after he realised he had spoken at some length, it also allowed him to collect his thoughts. "You've seen it yourself, it's why you aren't with the Eagles at the moment. Like it or not, you two have had a taste of command and won't fit back into a legion or a regiment again without commanding them. No General can deal with that, because there can't be too many leaders. It's why you haven't been assigned a new legion. However," Aarlin added seeing the anger rising on the face of Nek, "It means you are infinitely more important to your country and mine than you realise."

"Sir, Aarlin, look…it's nice having smoke blown up your arse by being told how brilliant I am, but can we get to the point?" Nek said, draining the last of the wine and pouring himself another. Aarlin, normally one who wouldn't appreciate such a burst of insubordination from anyone else, merely smiled.

"Very well, Nek. You two are too useful now to be rankers and line officers, but your faces don't fit. You led the Imperials on a merry chase. You won. You will be going north to advise and placate the clans. You will be going in through a fishing boat and you will receive no support from anyone in Attainia nor Cardavy until the time is right. You will be alone, to a point."

"To a point?" Grim queried. He wasn't angry, the prospect of new adventure fired him in ways that he had forgotten as he felt the adrenaline run through his body. He felt guilty for all of two seconds as he thought of it, picturing Katrin waiting at home, but he knew well enough that she wouldn't want him to become so sedentary that he was to lose sight of who he actually was. He was a soldier and, more to the point, a man who needed to actually be needed for what he trained for.

"I will have a squadron on standby at all times with three regiments of marines ready to disembark and get you out if it all goes wrong. It is the very least I owe you. I would join you, but I've been ordered not to with the strictest punishments in store if I do." He looked at the two men before him, a pang of guilt seizing him for a few moments. He was a man who respected action rather than words and craved adventure. He still longed to go to the fabled eastern continent but knew it would have to wait for a few years yet, at least until he had retired and was in a position to buy a decent ship. "Are there any questions, gentlemen?"

"Oh…none at all, sir. Help ferment a rebellion, take on several thousand clansmen who want you dead, take on several thousand Imps who want you dead, and form a new Kingdom with a view to forging an alliance. Can't imagine anything I'd like to ask." Grim answered with a grin, Nek chuckling into his wine glass as he did so. Aarlin raised his glass in salutation.

"Good! Gentlemen, the boat leaves tomorrow. So tonight we shall get drunk, talk about old times on the wall, and find out why Nek didn't join the fleet like he kept saying he would!"

"This isn't fucking natural, Grim!" Nek was green, wet through and desperately cold. He was stood at the bow, determined to watch the waves crash against the ship and brace himself before they came in. He had tried to stay below but the constant rocking motion of the stormy sea against the hull of the flimsy fishing vessel had caused him sleepless nightmares. It was, to him, like being stuck in the belly of the flimsiest and sensitive of beasts. He hated it. The sea stank and, more to the point, was damned cold and inhospitable.

He looked sidelong at his friend, equally as sodden as he was, and noticed that he had a grin plastered across his face. He felt the boat lurch in the water and the bow drop down suddenly, a wall of white water throwing itself up in front of his worried eyes as he instinctively bent his knees and leant into the bow. The wall of water crashed down upon him with a physical force he would have thought impossible merely hours before, the feeling of being crushed and drowned at the same time becoming almost the norm.

The water cleared for a few merciful seconds and he quickly gasped for breath, realising he would soon have to swallow his fears of drowning and go below to get some warmth into his bones. Initially, he had complained rather humorously, he thought, on the fact that the rain was starting to come down. Now, as he stood like a drowned rat, he realised that the rain was the least of his concerns.

The Captain in the bridge of the fishing boat, and the term "bridge" he considered to be a misnomer given that the thing looked like an outhouse and no doubt smelt like one now, was busy bawling out orders at some of the seamen and demanding that they lash things down on the deck. The men moved deftly to his commands and skipped along the deck, timing their movements with the lurching of the hull as it continued to crash through the waves.

"I thought you wanted to join the Navy!" Grim shouted, forcing Nek to turn back and face the broiling sea once again. He glanced at his friend, seeing the manic grin on his face and the glint in his eye. It was as if the man were excited, actually enjoying something where he wasn't able to control his fate. He hadn't even bothered to try and lash himself against any of the superstructure and was relying on sheer muscle power to keep himself secured to the deck and, therefore, safety. What was worse, perhaps the most galling thing, was that the man had somehow managed to stuff his pipe and light it in between the crashing of the waves. It was now clamped firmly between his teeth, thin tendrils of smoke coming from the pot.

"You've gone off your bloody head!"

"You've got no sense of adventure!" Grim retorted, taking the pipe out of

his mouth and jabbing the nib at him as if to emphasise his point.
"I'd sooner have no sense of adventure and solid ground under my feet than this shitshow! We don't even know where we are!"
"No, but the navigator does."
Another wave crashed over the pair of them and, for a brief and panic stricken moment, Nekstar knew real fear as he felt his feet go out from under him. He scrambled at the railing with flailing fingers which only served to bruise them badly. He instinctively released his grip and felt himself being tossed away, nightmare images of being swept out by the receding waters and forever lost at sea. He briefly wondered, as time slowed, how long he would be able to stay afloat amongst the foaming maelstrom. He felt an iron grip on his forearm haul him upwards and he gratefully dragged himself to the railing again, his nerves shaken and his breath coming out in ragged gasps.
"Nekstar of the Eagles Legion, teller of a thousand dits and complaints, winner of a dozen battles shaken by the sight of a little water." Grim said with a grin spreading across his now bearded face, the use of fresh water on board having been restricted to cooking and drinking only since they had set sail nearly a week ago.
"Fuck yourself!"
"Well there's gratitude, next time I'll let you drown!" Grim grinned and winked before staring out to the horizon again, the white foaming crests of the waves beginning to die down a little as the clouds began to recede. The lurching of the boat was becoming more settled and there seemed to be a general sense of more control over events rather than trusting to the fickle love of the Gods.
"At least it's getting quieter," Nek noted as he scanned the water, distrustful and almost willing it to try and defy him once more and seek to whip him into the abyss. He briefly wondered if any fish had been chucked onto the boat during the numerous waves, but quickly reasoned that they would have taken the sensible decision and dived to a decent depth of water.
The Captain of the trawler must have noticed the weather was becoming more civilised and ordered the sails to be let loose again so that speed could be gained. Sailors came out of whatever boltholes they had found shelter in and began to loosen the small mainsail that was the primary source of propulsion for the boat. Nek watched it with a professional eye, a small amount of awe at the movement of the Republican sailors as they practiced their craft with an unsurpassed ease. He could see the Captain, a commissioned officer in the Attainian navy, handing over to the navigator and jabbing his finger into the distance.
"Do you see the lights in the distance?" Grim asked, wrenching him from

his thoughts and forcing him to stare ahead again.

The moon hung high in the sky now highlighting the clouds like some great silver beasts that flew across the horizon, the faint shimmer of distant stars and even fainter clusters becoming visible as the winds gathered pace. The boat, he felt, was beginning to move faster as the sails found the wind. Nek strained his eyes, squinting them as if to see better in the gloom and dark.

"I can't see sod all, my eyes are burning because of the bloody salt. Why, what do you see?" Nek replied, finally giving up. Truth be told, and he would never say to his friend, but he was beginning to feel his age sometimes. He knew his eyes weren't as good as they used to be, and whenever he was running with kit on his back then he was guaranteed to have a bad back or strange noises coming from his knees the next day. However, whilst his friend needed him then he would utter no real cause for concern.

"Well...lights, for a start, on a distant shore. Could be a beacon of some sorts."

"You reckon it could be the clansmen waiting for us?" Nek asked, beginning to see the bright light of either a beacon or a village on fire.

"Could be, I'm assuming Aarlin had the foresight to contact whomever is his source that we were coming." Grim paused and pulled out a battered, well-loved hip flask from a cloak pocket and took a swig. He passed the flask over to Nek and continued to stare, even as he held the burning liquid in his mouth for a while and then let it slip down his throat.

"I still don't see," Grim said finally, "what they are expecting us to achieve given the very limited manpower available to us."

"Don't know about that, Grim, surely we count for about three or four dozen of the bastards." Nek said, eliciting a wry smile from his friend. "Anyway, we seem to be turning towards the source of the light. I reckon that's our stop."

"Might as well get our kit on then and look the part before we meet the bastards. Wonder what I'll say."

"Just don't spin them a shagging dit and I'm sure we'll be fine!" Nek said with a laugh, downing the rest of the flask and chucking it back to Grim.

Chapter Eleven – **Strange Bedfellows**

The last month had been nothing but fire and sword; death had hung across the land like a dark shadow as the clans went to war with each other. Crops had been fired and livestock slaughtered, their bones left bleaching under the sun. Kiegal hawked and spat over the side of the cliff and into the dark ocean in disgust as he remembered, looking at the thin light from the moon as it cast its silvery light across the rippling tide. It was better weather here, he could see, than it was out in the middle of the sea. The wind picked up as if in answer to his thoughts and pushed his cloak causing it to billow, a sudden draught of cold making him curse and bring the cloak ever tighter amongst him; at least it wasn't raining, he thought.

As soon as Quittle had raised the flag of rebellion, and it was strange to think of him assuming leadership of it when it had been Tortag that it had sparked it off, the clans had turned on each other. Long held animosities that had been buried under allegiance to the Emperor had suddenly surfaced like a whale broaching for air. It had happened suddenly, almost as if it had been planned, and the fighting men of the two rebelling clans had quickly had to take stock and work out what they were going to do. It was like a tremendous hangover after they had sacked the fort by the town. It had seemed like a terrific idea at the time, and the men knew why they had done it, but as to how they were supposed to react afterwards none had a clue. None of them had supposed that they would command loyalty from the entirety of the clans, none of them were naïve enough to believe that, but none had suspected that fellow countrymen would descend upon each other with a rapacity and fervour that had thus far been demonstrated. They also knew that the Empire would not take the slaughter of a garrison lying down, they knew that there would be reprisals and an army launched across the border within days of the survivors making it to the nearest friendly garrison. The response hadn't been long in coming either. Within two weeks all civilian traffic into the area had ceased, all trade had ground to a halt and there was no word from the outside. All eyes had turned to the western borders, and all eyes had widened in surprise when no Imperial armies had come pouring across in response.

Being who he was, and given that he had been second to Tortag for years, he had become part of the inner circle of command in the rebellion. He had raised the matter of invasion during a council of war held a month previous, though such an elaborate term didn't alleviate the fact that they had conducted the entire meeting in a cave that was perfectly hidden behind a waterfall whilst the rest of the 'army' were encamped around the pool and deep into the forest.

"Why haven't we seen any Imperials yet? It's been nigh on a month," he had asked. He had looked to Tortag, his chief and friend, but ever since the death of his wife the man had withdrawn into himself. It had been a cause for concern amongst many in the clan, but Tor had reasoned with a few of the more well-known and respected characters amongst them that he would be back to his old self given enough time. Tortag looked at him and shrugged his shoulders, a flicker of response that was akin to a speech by the veteran these days. It was Quittle who answered.

"From what I gathered when I was at the Emperors court, the Imperials have enough troubles of their own at the moment without expending more manpower on us. They've got enough allies, for a start, to keep us pinned down and held here. Their eyes are still focussed on the south."

"You were at court nearly four months ago; it could have all changed by then."

"Of course," Quittle said as he opened his hands in acknowledgement, "I'm not saying that it has or hasn't. However, they took a beating at Nepriner and Gephy. They need to make sure the Speirakians are still on side and that the men of Boarslat don't suddenly get jumpy and go back to their border raiding ways in the north."

"It would be good if we could get them on side," Tortag said as if waking up from a long sleep. Men who had been quietly chatting amongst themselves looked to the veteran and wondered if he would carry on. "Mind you, they'd get wiped out if they advanced. There has always been an Imperial army on their doorstep; their best bet would be to declare war and hope that there would be an idiot in the Empire willing to try and cross those mountains and their passes."

"Not a bad plan if we could carry it off," Quittle replied, unsure of whether to dismiss the plan outright for the suicidal venture it was or to mollify his friend in order to bring him out of the shell he had created. He knew the tribes of Boarslat and a more barbarous people he didn't want to meet. He had seen them perform their human sacrifices, seen them dance naked in meadows around large stones and such like. He wasn't keen on them. Barbarians they might be, but they had a damned fine fighting spirit. It was rumoured, and as such a rumour it had gained traction, that they were some sort of distant relation to the clansmen.

"So no invasion? Are the Imperials heading south then?"

"Doubt it, Kiegal. They got their arses felt, one army destroyed and another on its last legs, they need the rest to maintain their own borders and security. They've only got another four full strength armies, and one of them is based by the capital for training." Quittle paused, deep in thought as he pictured their dispositions. He was, by no means, a military genius but he did know how the human mind worked. The Emperor couldn't suffer a rebellion, let alone a Kingdom being born out of said rebellion, for too long without losing face. Lose too much face and he was liable to lose the throne. Do that and the whole rotten mess would cave in. "I give us six months before they start sending an army across the borders."

"So what do we do in the meantime?" Alfdarr, the chief of the Red River clan spoke up. He was the brother of Quittle and had made his warriors come over to the cause. He had seen the destruction at Nepriner and, though he wasn't particularly enamoured with the idea of making a bid for independence, he was less keen on going down in the history books as the man who sat back and did nothing. Worse still, he didn't want to abandon familial ties nor be the one who took part in the destruction of his brother. Pragmatically, he realised, if he didn't cast his lot in with Quittle and remain neutral then he would have been likely to either lose his head to an Imperial or a rebel. Now, the way he saw it, he just had to worry about the Imperials.

"We stop calling ourselves Clansmen for a start," Quittle replied. "Gentlemen; we were of one nation once before we were fractured fighting the Attainians. Those divisions bore deep and it was their policy to keep us separated. We gave them a bloody nose in centuries past, we damn well scared them, and we nearly stopped the Republic before it could even get off the ground. In our last rebellion it took the Rupinians, Speirakians and Attainians together to put us down. We had a name once. Kiegal, you're the historian amongst us, you tell them."

"Traemwen was the name of our clan lands." Kiegal said, aware suddenly of all eyes being on him. "Bear has the rights of it. We are a nation of sorts, clan chiefs brought together under the rule of one High Chief or King. The Attainians divided us, bought off some of the clans that we fight today and allowed them to fight us. Together we could have stood a chance, or so the stories go, but as it was, we were divided and fell into the state of being a minor province.

"We face similar problems now. There are only two clans that have declared for rebellion, us in the Black Moon and you, Alfdarr, with the Red River. We know of four others that are awaiting developments but are otherwise friendly. There are three staunchly against us and using pressure on the remaining six to contribute either men or resources. We need to unite under one banner and have one voice. We need a King."

"Then pass a bloody crown to Quittle and get it over with," quipped Alfdarr, getting a laugh from some of the men in the cave and removing any tension that was beginning to develop. Quittle grinned in turn and was about to answer when Tortag stood and opened his mouth to speak.

"If bloody only. We need ceremony of a sort. Show the World that we aren't some backward, arse-scratching barbarian idiots." He said it with a grin, a little sign of the old Tor breaking through. "We need allies in the south. We need them to keep up the pressure on the Imperials and make them think twice about coming at us with all their strength. Whilst they do that, we can start focussing on our neighbours. By the time those Imperial bastards finally come to the borders, we'll be ready for them."

"How do we gain allies in the south?" Eadwald, the second to Alfdarr, asked.

"I've already written to them." Quittle interjected, earning a nod of appreciation from Tortag. It was something they had spoken of, though not in any great depth. "I've stated in my letter our grievances with the Emperor, a little of our history with the help of Kiegal, and what we would like from them. I've also stated, under no uncertain terms, that we will never again as a nation bend the knee to any Overlord ever again."

"I take it you signed it as the King of Traemwen? Alfdarr asked with a smirk.

"I thought it would have a certain flourish." Quittle replied with a grin, more settled that nobody had voiced any objection to his taking the throne. "So how are we to perform this ceremony?"

"We'll need to wait for whomever the Cardavians or Attainians send. We'll need witnesses to take the word back to their homelands. With international support, I'd give us decent odds at getting through this without having our arses kicked."

The meeting had broken up and Kiegal had thought nothing more of it. He had focussed his mind on different things, like trying to survive. It had been with a degree of optimism that they had started out, but a month of few results apart from sleeping in the wild and heading in the general direction to those that wanted to do them violence had done nothing to steady their collective nerves. He did, however, have to concede that the idea of fighting under a united banner and one ruler touched him in a way that he didn't think possible.

"Looks like that fishing vessel is about to beach if the skipper isn't careful," Eadwald said.

"I think that'll be our future guests and allies, though I'll admit to hoping there was going to be slightly more of them than that."

"A fleet of warships with provisions and a couple of Cardavian legions and Attainian marine regiments?" Eadwald quipped.

"Something like that, though right now I'd give my right bollock for a decent bed and a meal that was actually properly cooked for a change."

"Piss poor awful weather to be taking a boat trip, they'll be in a foul temper."

"Aye, well, this hasn't panned out quite the way anyone was expecting. It's probably best if they get used to that fact now before they find out the hard way."

"I'm never getting on a bloody boat again," Nek said as his feet found solid ground on the beach. The term 'solid' was a misnomer for it felt as if the very ground were shaking beneath him. It took a greater deal of strength than he would have thought possible to stay upright. He looked to Grim and saw that his friend was struggling as well, the cloak of the Eagles that he wore not helping matters by occasionally lifting itself with the wind and pulling him in a different direction.

"Sea legs!" The captain of the fishing vessel said, strolling up to them as if navigating his boat through a storm and then beaching it came second nature to him. Nek had to give the man credit, the man had a pair of bollocks that were made out of solid steel.

"How long does this last for normally? I don't want to appear pissed in front of the clansmen," Grim asked, steadying himself a little as he took another dizzy turn.

"He has airs and graces now ever since he was a General, you see." Nek said, unable to contain himself whenever it came to getting a friendly dig in when he could.

"Couple of minutes at most, sir, and you'll be fine." Two sailors brought their luggage with them, their worldly possessions carried on the yoke of a stick apiece that was designed to be carried over the shoulder whilst a legion was on the march. They passed the large sticks over and the two Cardavians took them gratefully, laying them gently down next to their kit bags which contained their essentials that would see them through.

"What will you do now, Captain?" Grim asked even as he watched the cliffs. He could see a group of men descending them using, what he presumed to be, a path that had been chiselled into the rock face. They were carrying torches, the flames from the tips bright oranges and reds contrasting sharply with the darkness around them. The weather was completely overcast, the stars and moon now blotted out by the passing clouds.

"We'll take on fresh water from a river near here, see if we can get any provisions from a village nearby that I've stopped in at before, and then we'll be back to Gephy. Might even do a spot of fishing on the way to double the profit." Grim and Nek nodded, curious to know how much the skipper was actually getting paid for this venture but not having the bad manners to come outright and say it.

"Well," Grim said as he crouched and then hefted up his bergen and slung it over his shoulders, "It's been a pleasure for the majority of the trip, Captain, but I think we're going to be expected in a few minutes or so. Safe voyage home."

"You as well," the man replied as he offered his hand. Grim and Nek shook it in turn and moved off, Nek grumbling a little as the sand squelched under foot and worked its way into the grips of his boots. The skipper watched them for a moment, considering, before he shouted to them to pause. The two men turned and watched as he ran up to them. "Look, I don't know what you're doing here and I've never asked in case things went wrong. I don't want to know either, frankly, because if it's bloody daft then I'd be liable to try and talk you out of it. Now, I don't have a right to do that and I'd never ask military men like yourselves to disobey your orders or break your covenant or whatever it is you call it these days. However, I like you pair. You've given me no trouble and, more importantly, you've kept out the way when you've been asked to and you've dug out with the lads if you've seen them struggling.

"There's a fishing village to the east of here along the coast, maybe a day's march at most. If things do go to the shit, ask for a man called Aefed and tell him Alathil sent you. He'll see you right."

"Appreciate it, Alathil. You take care of yourself. Next time we're in Gephy, we'll get you a drink." The skipper nodded, wondered if he should say any more, and decided that he didn't need to. With a nod, he walked away and left the two men to it. Nek watched him until he was out of earshot before speaking.

"What does he mean if it all goes to shit? There's no 'if' about it, plans always go to shit."

"Aye, but he was well meaning. Still, at least we have a bit of an escape route now. Don't know about you, but I didn't fancy trying to break out to Turgundeon from here."

"Wherever here is." Grim grunted in agreement and turned about, walking towards the clansmen waiting at the base of the cliffs. Nek watched the skipper for a few moments longer, tempted to just up and leave and forgetting bloody stupid orders. He turned about and watched his friend and shook his head, knowing that he didn't have it in him to let him down. He muttered a curse and walked after him.

The two Cardavians approached the group of clansmen and looked at them from a professional view. They were obviously warriors, though whether they were soldiers was up for debate. Each man carried enough weaponry on him to run a small armoury if their minds ever turned to business. The big one with the black cloth around his left eye had the look of a leader, though he also had the look of a doorman outside of a tavern. Nek could see that half his ear was missing on one side, and the man also appeared to have no neck given how broad his shoulders were. He was, in the mind of Nek, the archetypical clansman.

"Friendly looking bunch," quipped Grim as if he were reading his friends thoughts.

"Was just thinking that. They look as if they've been through the wars. Wonder if any of them were at Gephy."

"Or Turgundeon?"

"True. Reckon we should ask?" Nek asked with a grin causing Grim to chuckle.

"That'd be a real score for diplomacy, that would. I could just imagine it." Grim had been thinking about it on the trip over the waves, but still hadn't come up with an idea on how to introduce themselves or how to open up a decent conversation that didn't necessarily involve causing offence.

"Do you want to do the talking?" He offered to Nek, who shook his head to the negative.

"Nope. I'm afraid, brother, that you're on your own with that one. Comes with the rank."

"We're the same rank now."

"Ah, but you were higher than me at one point and I'm pretty sure you were commissioned before me and therefore have seniority. You're used to hob-nobbing and eating funny smelling cheeses."

"I've seen some of the shit you eat, you aren't exactly averse to eating funny smelling stuff either."

"Ah, but, you see, you have training for it." Nek said, getting the last word in with a smile.

They stopped a few paces short from the group and an uneasy silence existed between the two groups. Nek could have sworn he saw a flash of recognition on the faces of a few of them when the cloak billowed in the wind displaying the colours and emblem of the Eagles legion, but they at least had the good grace, or were disciplined enough, not to say anything. In truth, the wearing of the cloaks was probably going to be a contentious issue, Nek realised, but given the weather then it was the only sensible clothing they had to keep them warm. Furthermore, he thought, if he were willing to let bygones be bygones, if not forget nor forgive the recent past, then he expected the other side to extend the same courtesy.

"Do you speak the common tongue?" Grim asked, breaking the strained silence.

"I do," answered the big man with the eye patch and the evil look. "Some of my men do as well. Shall we try for introductions?" The man spoke well, better than Nek or Grim would have given him credit for given his look, with barely the trace of an accent. Whatever he looked like, and that was a murdering thug with a foul temper, he had an education behind him and a keen intelligence it seemed.

"That seems fair," replied Grim. "I am Grimfar, lately the acting commanding officer of the Eagles legion. This is my second, Nekstar, also lately of the Eagles legion."

"I've heard of the Eagles, though I was grateful to never have had to fight them. You held Turgundeon well, and you did even better to get out of it." There was a great deal of respect in the man's voice, the awkwardness of the situation suddenly disappearing like a mist on the breeze. "I am Kiegal, a clansman of the Black Moon clan and a man of the Traemwenian nation. This is Eadwald of the Red River. I'll be honest, gentlemen, I was hoping there'd be more of you."

"So were we," replied Nek, "I see only six of you. That's a pretty piss poor rebellion if you ask me."

Grim kept his mouth shut, though he knew his mouth would have went into a thin line of grimace. He hadn't expected his friend to say anything, though he knew that was perhaps asking for too much. Nek was known, renowned even, for being glib. Fortunately, the clansman, Kiegal, laughed and translated it for their men who laughed in turn.

"I like you, Cardavian! No, you're right. There's more of us. I'm here to take you back to our camp to witness the coronation."

"Coronation?" Grim asked, unaware that this had even been planned. His orders had been brief and succinct; go with the clansmen and forge alliances, help them win their fight.

"Our future King, Quittle, is to be crowned in the morning. It is for him and this land that we fight. I'll explain it more on the way."

"I take it there'll be drink?" Nek asked, seizing on the important matter.

"Of course. Nekstar, wasn't it?"

"My friends call me Nek."

"Then we shall be friends, Nek. Tonight, when we get to camp, we shall get drunk. Tomorrow, when my King is crowned and we can finally start getting things done, we shall get drunk again. How does that sound?"

"It sounds like I should have been born a clansman!"

"Piss on that. You should have been born a Traemwenian!"

Tortag knew he would never get over the death of his wife, Elyn. She had been the soothing balm to the burning rage that daily seemed to consume him. He knew his depth of feeling for her, or at least he thought he had, but now he knew the words he had said to her had simply been mere whispers in the wind. He felt guilty, knowing that most of their married life had been spent at opposite ends of the Empire as he fought in one bloody cause after the other. He would often wake in the middle of the night on the forest floor after dreaming of her, seeing her smiling face as she welcomed him back to the farm that they had shared together. He would picture her nursing a sickly lamb or riding one of the horses, always smiling at him.

He would weep then, silent tears that he would not shed in front of any other men. He was hurting, but he didn't know who to turn to.

The feeling of loss and desperation were like a cancer growing inside him, something that he couldn't ignore nor, he felt, a thing that he should ignore. She made him feel human in a way that he hadn't believed possible. She had made him realise, at a young age when they had first been courting, that there was more to life than just drink and violence. With her death, he felt that that side of him had been ripped away from him. Her death was the tinder that had started the fire of rebellion, started this whole bloody business that set the land of the clans ablaze with rebellion and death. She wouldn't have wanted this, and because of that he felt he had betrayed her further still.

It was dark thoughts that occupied his head, and because of that he had isolated himself from his friends. In truth, it was the last thing he wanted to do and, worst still, would probably demoralise him further. It was these thoughts that led to swings of mood where one minute he would be happy and his normal self, whilst the next would see him trying to extradite himself from a social situation to sit and brood. That, though, had been before the coronation and before he had found a purpose again. He knew that she would always be at the back of his mind, but he knew he couldn't let her down.

The coronation had been conducted in what Kiegal had claimed was the ancient capital of the old Kingdom. Tor had to admit to himself at the time that the place seemed nothing more than a field with the detritus of buildings left to go to wrack and ruin, but he gave credit where it was due to Alfdarr and Eadwald for decorating the area. The fighting men of the two clans, and those women and children who had followed with what amounted to the baggage train, had witnessed the ceremony amongst the granite and sandstone ruins. Numerous colourful tents festooned the area where entertainments could be sought in the shape of drink or song, a plethora of fire pits had boar and other meats roasting over them filling the area with the rich scent of cooking meats. Bunting, and Tor still couldn't work out where Kiegal had managed to find that, was festooned over old pillars to lend even more colour to the proceedings. Jugglers and gymnasts, mainly warriors who ordinarily would not think twice of killing an enemy, made fools of themselves in front of the children just to hear their laughter. It was like a carnival atmosphere. Even better, the spring sun was exceptionally warm and had burnt any clouds and threat of rain into oblivion, the trees showing their first buds and the braver of the flowers beginning to show colour.

The coronation as well had been very solemn, apparently steeped in the history of the country. Tortag was the first to admit he was a cynic and knew that a lot of it was made up on the spot to lend a great deal of authenticity to the proceedings, however, there was something about the entire ceremony that touched something deep within him.

He had never been truly keen on the idea of rebellion, for service to the Emperor had rarely been hard and had always paid well. He had seen parts of the World he didn't know existed, and the wages and loot that he had derived from his military adventures had helped support the farm and his wife. He wondered then what she would have thought of all this, all the pomp and ceremony that came with the crowning of Quittle to become King of Traemwen. He smiled, knowing that she would have thought it a load of nonsense that only silly boys with silly dreams could think up.

He had been the one selected, as the senior military officer in his new capacity as Lord Marshal, to present the sword of state to the new King. In truth, the sword was just the sword that Quittle generally wielded and was about as mystical as any other piece of steel, but from now on it would take on a symbolic value. He had to chuckle at the memory when he passed the sword to the new King. Quittle had been staring at him, a degree of apprehension and nerves upon his face. He suddenly smiled, almost breaking into laughter and spoke the words which would forever cement him in the heart of Tortag:

"Keep looking at me. It keeps my soul from flying off!"

There were other delegates there from the clans, though a few were more notable by their absence. None pledged their allegiance, not outright, and Tor had the impression that they were there to see the thing done and judge the gathering rebels for themselves. The chief from the Iron Mountain clan, however, caught his eye and mentioned that he wanted to speak to him later on in the evening.

The celebrations were well underway by the time that the chief decided to come over. Tortag had been speaking to the Cardavian, Grimfar, and swapping war stories. Tor had been at Turgundeon for a short period of time, but hadn't taken part in the assault on the village. He had a healthy respect for the men of the Eagles legion and, judging by the way the two Cardavians held and conducted themselves, he was glad he had never encountered them either. Any legionary, any man for that matter, that was thrust into a position of leadership and then subsequently was able to salvage a victory from the jaws of defeat was a man to be respected. In turn, Tor felt that the Cardavian had taken a liking to him as each man recognised the leader and the fighter in the other.

Nekstar, he knew, was a man who tried to not take life too seriously or, at the very least, gave the impression of one who tried not to. He was involved in a drinking contest with Kiegal, surrounded by men and women from the clans as each sought to win the honour for their own country. It was good natured, ribald jests flying between the two of them as they downed drink after drink. There were several empty glasses around them, a steady stream of people bringing more drink to the two veterans. They had been that long at the table, so he heard, that several people were wondering if they should bring buckets just in case. Apparently a rule had been developed, mainly by the spectators, that the first person to leave his seat to go for a piss was the loser. Tor had watched, grinning, as the two men squirmed and danced in their seats as each called for a bucket. There would be no give in either of them, he knew.

"Chief Tortag?" The chief of the Iron Mountain clan asked as he approached. Tor looked him up and down, inwardly critiquing the man as he approached. He knew of him, had served together before the walls of Nepriner, but wouldn't claim to anything close to acquaintanceship. The man was shorter than was common amongst the men of the clans, but then the men of the Iron Mountain had a reputation for being quality miners and, by sheer evolution, hadn't felt the need to grow tall. He was broadly built, however, a flat squashed nose over a broad face with a strong jaw. His eyes were dark, intelligent looking, and his hair was a rusty brown colour. As per the apparent custom, the man was unarmed like everyone else who was in proximity to the King.

"Chief Wenrynt of the Iron Mountain, a pleasure to see you. How did you find the ceremony?" Tortag was feeling friendlier than he had a long time and put it down to a mixture of decent company, the festivities around him with good humour that entailed, and the power of a decent pint of ale.

"It was more than I expected, to be honest. One would think that Quittle has already triumphed."

"That would be King Quittle, I presume?" He said, bristling slightly.

"Of course, just like you are his Lord Marshal." It was true, Tortag had to concede. Not only was he the chief of his own clan, but now he was apparently head of the army as well. Admittedly, the army so far consisted of three thousand fit and healthy men who had volunteered between the ages of sixteen and sixty from the two clans, but he had duties to think of now.

"Aye, I suppose. I welcome you to our camp anyway, it's good to see that the country hasn't entirely been given over to the madness which seems to have infected it."

"An infection which the King has brought upon us though, surely?"

"Chief," Tortag began as he felt the blood begin to rush to his face as his anger mounted, "I trust, for your sake, that you haven't come just to poke at me and try to insult?"

"No, far from it. I apologise if it came across that way," the chieftain replied. The man shifted uncomfortably for a few seconds as he sought a way to steer the conversation away from a dangerous course. "What is the King planning now?"

"In all honesty," Tortag had to admit, "I've only just got around to thinking about that. We need allies, a united front before we can face the Imperials. If this country of ours, if this dream of Traemwen is to remain alive, then we can't be constantly looking over our shoulders."

"May I make a suggestion then?"

"By all means, Wenrynt, go ahead."

"We have been playing the neutral for a month now, regardless of the pressure that we have been receiving from the Long Loch clan." He paused, unsure of how to continue.

"Speak your mind, Chief, you're amongst friends here," Tor said as he noticed the man hesitating. In truth, he wasn't a fan of people who danced around a subject with getting to the crux of the matter. It was something he avoided in life and expected others to avoid around him. He would always prefer a blunt speaker over one who used flowery language or tried to protect the feelings of another.

"My thanks," he said as he cleared his throat. "If you were to destroy the army of Long Loch, then the men of the Iron Mountain would come over to you willingly. We aren't strong enough to do it ourselves, not after the last Imperial war. Long Loch is richer than ourselves, they constrict our trade and they have access to the entirety of the clan lands." That much was true, thought Tortag.

The Long Loch clan were one of several clans that had the great loch within its borders, however, it was only they that had the gall and temerity to claim it as their own waters. They had invested their strength and riches into the water-borne trade it was able to provide, and would charge high tolls on traffic passing through the loch which went further to fill their coffers. As a prize, the clan was a rich target and one that gave Quittle access to riches to buy in more weapons. Furthermore, the chance of winning over the men of the Iron Mountain with their rich minerals and metals was almost too tempting to pass up. Two clans, such as these, would give him access to inland and waterborne trade.

"How many men are in their army?" Tortag asked, trying to mentally picture the layout of the land around about those parts.

"Three thousand regulars, maybe double that if they have word that you are coming."

"How many can you provide?"

"One, maybe two thousand. I'd offer more, but, like you and the King, we have to keep some of our men tilling the fields at home. We can't risk all in a single throw of the dice."

"Unfortunately," Tor said before he took a drink from the ale, "I'm afraid it may come to that." He paused and took another drink, noticing that Nek and Kiegal had stood up and were now pissing against a tree before resuming their drinking contest. "Where is their army now?"

"Within our borders, but near enough to their own to claim that they aren't being aggressive."

"I'll have to consult the King," he replied after mulling it over for a few seconds. "How long will you be here?"

"Not long enough I'm afraid, Lord Marshal." It was the first time, outwith Quittle, anyone had used his official rank. It suddenly struck home to him what they were trying to set up and achieve, that the entire idea of a rebellion against the Emperor wasn't merely fantasy war gaming or theoretical battle plans being discussed after a pint or two. In all fairness to himself, he reflected, he had been wrapped up in his grief far too much to even consider the realities of the situation. He realised he needed to consider the several hundred men under his command, the ones who had volunteered to join because they had nothing else to lose, and what, ultimately, the King needed to achieve. It was, to say the least, daunting. He eyes alighted on Grimfar, busily trying to prop up Nek as the man sought to rally and down another flagon, and he realised he would be a man to consult.

"Can you spare me three days?"

"I can spare you two, and then I have to be off to my own lands."

"As I understand it, sire, you'll need light cavalry and archers. Clan infantry is good, but decent infantry will find it hard to fight without support." Grim looked around at the assembled group, the Kings Inner Circle, and Nek who was currently nursing his head in hands. "If the enemy turn your flank, or you remain static for too long, then the likelihood is they will annihilate you."

"Don't you mean us?" Alfdarr asked, his tone dark. There was a degree of mistrust that existed between the clansman and the Cardavian, understandable given that until very recently they had been set to killing each other.

"Not my fight, Chief, as well you know. It's not Nek's either. We're here to observe, offer guidance and friendship, and not a lot else."

"Then what is the point in you being here at all? We're clansmen, we know fine well how to fight other clansmen." There was a palatable tension in there, even Nek looking up. Though the man still looked worse for wear, there existed no doubt for the men gathered that he would leap into defend his friend should the need arise.

"In raiding, brother, not in taking and holding territory." Quittle said trying to placate the situation before it went any further. He was sat at the head of the table and studying the map that was set out before them, rolled out and pinned to the table with various weights of lead. The border region they were in was one of rolling plains and isolated forests, picturesque and easily the best agricultural ground in the area. The territory that they needed to enter, whilst little more than plains and swampy territory, was ringed by hills and wild rivers. It would be challenging enough to get two thousand men across, thought Quittle, never minding the prospect of fighting a battle at the end of it. "What do you suggest, Cardavian?"

"Issue five hundred men bows, sire. Good men with bows will be able to whittle down the defenders."

"Do you have much in the way of cavalry?" Nek asked, sitting up and stretching out his shoulders. He winced visibly as a fresh streak of pain lanced through his head, his stomach lurching in the process. He rubbed the back of his neck, trying to ease out some of the tension with the palm of his hand.

"A hundred, maybe, at a push. Light cavalry though. We've never been one for using horses; too expensive to maintain," explained Tortag. "We tended to leave that to the Speirakians."

"Can't stand the bastards personally," explained Nek, "Speirakians and cavalry actually, come to think of it. You'll need to hold the cavalry back for when the enemy break. Run the routing lot down, grab a fewer of the richer looking ones, and then ransom them back."

"So what are you suggesting then, gentlemen, if we are to try and win this?" Tortag asked.

"We need to destroy them as an effective fighting force, but equally we need to make sure they actually come at us. That means we can't reinforce ourselves with the men from Iron Mountain." Grimfar said, his eyes scanning over the map as he tried to find a way to lay out his plan.

"But that'll mean if they come on with their entire strength then we'll be outnumbered two to one." Quittle said, leaning back into the high backed seat. Kiegal cleared his throat and looked at the map again, his brow knotted as he concentrated. He finally he looked up and looked towards Tor.

"I think I see where the Cardavians are going with this, and it's audacious but it may just work. If I may, sire?" Quittle gestured for the man to continue. "Now, correct me if I'm wrong gentlemen, but are you suggesting we allow them to come to us?"

"In a roundabout fashion, aye." Grim conceded. He still found it amazing that the man before him, one who looked as if he would happily kill someone over a spilt drink, had an educated tongue and a rare intelligence. "We draw them on and make them extend out their supply lines, something that'll hurt them more than it'll hurt us. The chief of the Iron Mountain is still here, so we draw him into our plan. Make him pretend to side with the men of Long Loch, commit his forces to him and form the rearguard. They'll pledge their entire support, but take no active part in the fighting until we've broken them.

"We know the opposition here; we know they fight in the traditional manner with either spear or sword. We'll do the same, but we'll make sure those archers count. Take the high ground, force them to come on, pepper them as they come up and advance with our own pikes."

"There," said Tortag jabbing at the map on a geographical feature. He leant in close and squinted, trying to make out the name of the hill. "Flint Bluff?"

"Must have been named by one of Wenrynt's lot," Alfdarr said with a chuckle, "you know what those men are like with their rocks."

"How do you propose to draw them on?" Eadwald interjected, "What's to stop them from simply skirting around our flank and heading to the border and our towns here?"

"We make sure they bloody well know that I'll be there, they won't be able to resist the prize. I'll even take the centre in our battle line," Quittle said in a manner which suggested he would broker no counter argument. "I'll raise my standard in the centre and make sure the bastards see it. They'll come on like flies to cow shit."

"Risky, Bear." Tortag said, his momentary surprise making him slip into the familiar talk that existed between the two old friends. "If you go down then it'll break the men, and this entire rebellion will fizzle out."

"It's do or die though, my friend. Either we win through here and take two clans with us in one go, or we may as well resign ourselves to facing the Empire alone."

"Oh aye," Tor said. He grinned suddenly, "I understand that, just seems like a huge bloody risk is all. I'll be up for it, so will the boys. How about you Alfdarr, you reckon your lads will be able to keep up with mine?"

"Aye, and mine'll even do it without a skinful to get their courage up!" The chief said with a barking laugh.

Chapter Twelve – **Battle of Flint Bluff**

The clouds were grey and filled the sky, ominously dark in places as the sky seemed to boil. Nek stood uncomfortably in his armour, the sweat rolling down his back as the temperature became even more close and muggy. There was almost a sticky feeling in the air, the type that made a rainstorm necessary to clear the atmosphere and make it feel fresher again. The light breeze that flowed through the serried ranks of the men of Traemwen did nothing to make the situation any more pleasant. What compounded the issue, and what distressed Nek most of all, was the saturation of the ground underneath and the lack of integrity his boots had. He cast a longing look towards the rear where the baggage train would be, or simply where the men had ditched their bergens and spare kit, where he knew his spare dry socks would be. In a war or battle, Nek held firm to the maxim that the most important kit a man could carry was a spare pair of socks.

"Looks like it's going to piss down later on," Grim said in an offhand manner, gazing up at the cloud covered sky and watching a flock of birds fly from north to south. They rose and fell in their own circus act as the warm air took them, barely even feeling the need to flap their wings. He couldn't identify them from this range, and he wasn't one for identifying birds at the best of times anyway, but he always envied them in their ability to fly anywhere at any time that took their fancy.

"Aye," remarked Nek, "and it looks like you were talking a lot of rubbish when you said we were just here to watch. Thought we weren't getting involved in the fighting?"

"We're in the third rank, ain't we?" Grim said, a smile tugging at his lips as he sought to wind up his friend.

"Of the Kings bloody division!" Grim burst out laughing, a sound full of good humour as he felt the tension draining from his shoulders. "Right in the bloody middle of it! Gods, you know what, I'm telling your Katrin what a damn fool you are when we get back."

"Quit whining," Grim said with a smile, "If we were any further back then you'd be complaining that we're missing out on all the action. You'd have nothing to tell the Traemwenian women anyway when we get back to camp."

"I haven't seen any bloody women in the camp!" Nek said affronted.

"No? I would have sworn that because you were complaining like one that there was a small knitting circle there." The retort from Nek was loud and obscene causing Grim's grin to widen even further.

"You reckon they've fallen for it?" Nek asked, nodding his head in direction to the valley floor. Grim looked down towards the formed ranks, just out of range of the archers, where the men of Long Loch had mustered. To the rear of them he could just about make out the men of the Iron Mountain.

"Well, the plan has gone well so far. If our new allies fulfil their part of the deal then it should be relatively easy going…providing we hold, of course."

"Aye, there's that. Mind you," said Nek with a bright smile, "I reckon with one or two legions we'd probably be able to smash this lot and call the place our own."

"Funny you should say that, was talking to that Kiegal bloke yesterday on the march here about such a thing. He must have been thinking the same thing. Anyway…"

"Grim, is this going to be a history lesson?" Nek asked, interrupting with a wry smile. He reached into his cloak and pulled out his pipe and tobacco, judging that they weren't going to be fighting any time soon and that he may as well enjoy the peace and quiet whilst he could.

"Do you have somewhere better be?"

"I can think of a few…"

"Alright, do you have somewhere better to be right now that you can actually reach?" Grim quirked an eyebrow, smiled and nodded his head.

"Aye, thought so. Anyway, there's been plenty of armies to do that before we got here. The Attainians tried it, and the Empire tried it, and then in a rare act of solidarity they both tried it together. Never worked. Know why?"

"No, but I'm guessing you're going to tell me." Nek struck a match, and then a second as the wind blew out the first. He muttered and cursed the wind as he waited for the tobacco to catch.

"Because they don't fight battles they know they can't win," answered Grim as he ignored the glib remark. "Any time anyone comes on with a disciplined force that they think they cannot beat, they'll retreat into hills like this or forests and burn everything as they go backwards. They'll then nip around the sides, harass the supply lines, and cause the other side to eventually withdraw."

"So how'd they get bloody conquered then? Last time I saw at Gephy, this lot were quite good friends with the Empire. In fact, Grim, I'm pretty sure the poor bastards we're expected to fight down there are still pretty good friends with the Emperor."

"Because the Emperor divided them up amongst themselves, played each of the Clan chiefs against each other and then led the survivors on a merry chase for favours. Clever blokes the Emperors of Rupinia."

"Aye, well, let's hope the dozy buggers down there aren't quite as clever, eh?"

Quittle sat on his horse beside his standard bearer, the light breeze making the colours flourish. He was unaccustomed to being in battle, something that was obviously premeditated and not a spur of the moment action of which he had been in plenty. This was altogether different and alien to him. To fight an opponent there and then who wished you dead, or at least seriously injured, was almost natural; to have to wait to fight said opponent and watch him muster his men and go about his own battle plans went against everything he knew. It was a certain type of discipline that he had never before had to muster. The only thing he could liken it to, and he knew that it was a poor example, would be a particularly tense debate. He smiled suddenly as he thought that a man could only die once in a battle but a thousand times in an argument.

"Something amusing, sire?" His Standard Bearer asked him, a young man named Eacwult. He had come recommended from Alfdarr as a stout man, one not given to rash action and useful in a fight. As far as Quittle was concerned, these were especially useful qualities in a man in the middle of a battle. He had yet to see him fight, he had to admit, but he was assured on that by the man's sheer physical size. It was said that the man was the strongest in the army after having worked in the old logging camps that littered the lands of the Red River clan.

"Just a passing thought, that's all. Looking forward to today?"

"Not particularly, though I'll be happy if we win." Quittle had to chuckle at Eacwult's blunt honesty, reminding himself that the men and women of Traemwen weren't given to subservience.

He and Tortag had spoken long into the night over the past two weeks trying to work out how best to achieve their aims. That time had been fraught with worry as well, particularly over the allegiance of Wenrynt and the men of the Iron Mountain. If a man could so easily lie to one series of apparent allies, then what was to stop them from turning traitor a second time? Perhaps, as Quittle feared, they wouldn't turn traitor at all and help the men of Long Loch. It was these questions and these worries that kept Quittle awake at night.

He looked around him now at the assembled men and wondered, briefly, if he had led them to the correct course of action. He thought of the times in the Imperial service and wondered whether it had been so bad as he remembered. It didn't, therefore, take him long to remember the debacle before the walls of Nepriner. It didn't take him long to remember how the Imperials had treated the men of the clans as fodder, nameless drones to do their fighting and dying in the hardest environments whilst they reaped the benefits. Most of all, as a man who normally treated oaths as sacrosanct, he hated the Imperials for forcing him into this situation in the first place. He caught the eyes of the two Cardavians and remembered his conversations with Beran Corus of the Grey Wolves, wondering what the young General was doing now. He had taken to the man, as he had indeed taken to most Cardavians that he had met. He didn't begrudge him his victory, nor the thousands of deaths he had, via his strategies and machinations, inflicted upon the men of the clans. They were on opposing sides, and soldiers were given orders to fight until that order was rescinded. Quittle knew, or liked to think, that there was no malice in the heart of Beran when it came to fighting. He gave a wry smile and wondered whether this battle would be any easier if he had some of the famed legions behind him, or even a few of the Attainian marine regiments. He consoled himself with the thought that should he win the day here, then he would gain the loyalty of Traemwenians who could be counted on to remain by his side.

Tortag and he, when not worrying over things they couldn't control, had also thought about the disposition of the limited manpower they had. They had three thousand men under arms, whilst the men of Long Loch had six thousand. The men that Quittle led understood that the odds were against them, that they needed to fight long and hard against the enemy to even think about carrying the day. The five hundred archers had been split into six different groups, placed on the flanks of the three brigades of infantry and formed into a wedge formation to provide effective cross-fire support. It was an idea of the Cardavian, Grimfar, and something that Quittle nor Tortag had ever seen employed. He was sceptical, he admitted, but if it worked then he would offer no complaints. The cavalry was on the extreme flank and slightly to the rear, ready for the signal to launch themselves down the hill if they found an advantage. In truth, Quittle knew fine well the shortcomings of clan cavalry and highly regretted it at such a time at this. He knew if the Empire had been fighting this battle that they would have had light cavalry on one flank and heavy on the other to charge and counter charge the enemy. Jealousy panged at him for a moment before he reflected on the matter at hand again.

The three divisions of infantry was where the crux of the fighting would take place. It had been decided that Tortag would take the right flank with his clan, whilst Alfdarr would take the left with his. Quittle would take the centre like a prize bull and hope to attract the enemy straight to him, and under him he had a combination of the two clans.

"Looks like they are ready, sire." Quittle looked to where Eacwult was gesturing and saw that the enemy were forming themselves up into three divisions. Their spear tips glinted in the light of the sun, their banners flying, and Quittle was sure he could hear the wailing of their pipes and their drums beginning to pick up a beat. He couldn't make out the details on the banners, but he had a feeling that their chief would be in the centre. With any luck, the man would be a headstrong fool and attack the centre. With even better luck, and Quittle realised he was relying on a lot of it, the chief of the Long Loch would draw in the rest of his men and allow an encirclement. However, Quittle realised that, should his own centre break, then the entire rebellion would collapse and his own life would be forfeit.

"Suppose I better say something," Quittle muttered as he nudged his horse forward. His immediate entourage, fighters and clansmen who had enlisted as his personal bodyguard, gestured to move forward but he waved them off. Instead, he waved for Eacwult to move forward with him. He took his horse to the centre and finally turned it about to face his men. He took a deep breath, feeling the warm air fill his lungs.

"Men of Traemwen!" His voice roared out, louder than the wails of the pipes from Long Loch and the beating of their drums, and louder than he would have thought his nerves would allow. "It has been a month since we sought to win our birth right. Those men down there call us rebels! I call them traitors! We are, each of us, clansmen. More than this, we are Traemwenian! We stand here on the precipice of history.

"If we win here today then there'll be more hard fights to come, more idiots to battle with, but we will be free. If we lose, then we go back to generations of servitude and licking the boots of a distant Emperor. I've nothing more to add than that, lads, we either win as free men or die as slaves. I've brought you here to this party, now let us see if we can dance!"

There was a roar, and a feeling of exultation that swept through Quittle that he didn't think possible. Men cheered his name, called out for him to lead the charge down the hill and sweep away all those that would oppose them. He held his sword aloft, his arm rigid as he held it above his head, and heard the cheering begin anew. If they didn't win the battle now, he thought wryly, then it wasn't due to a lack of enthusiasm.

He turned about his horse and looked upon the men of the Long Loch and watched them as they began to advance up the hill. They were making heavy work of it, the previous night's rain having made the ground sodden. Marshes that would have previously been a minor barrier were a thick morass that sought to swallow the men that dared to tread over them. They hadn't even moved a hundred foot from their starting positions and already their unit cohesion, which as spearmen they depended on, was already falling to pieces. Advancing up the hill in groups, or small units, without even coming into contact with the enemy would spell disaster. With a cautious glance he looked towards the men of Iron Mountain, relieved to see them waiting at the base of the hill. He put them to the back of his mind and focussed on matters at hand.

"Archers!" He roared out, raising a mail covered fist high into the air. It was the signal for the archers to put arrows to their bows, to make ready and prepare to launch their deadly missiles. He waited a few seconds, but for him it lasted a lifetime. He threw down his arm violently and suddenly as he shouted, "Loose!"

Five hundred arrows flew into the air, a dull thrum echoing from behind him. He watched in fascination at their graceful flight through the sky as they arced ever higher before they reached their highest point. They seemed to hang in the air for a few seconds before they dipped, streaking towards the men of Long Loch as they struggled up the hill. There was another thrum as the archers launched their deadly barbs again, the second flight in ten seconds. Suddenly, there was screaming and cries of terror and rage. Quittle looked down and watched as men fell, struggling to lift their shields to protect them from the deadly onslaught.

"Well, at least Alfdarr hasn't charged yet!" Tortag said in passing. Kiegal was acting as his standard bearer, as was his right as the champion of the clan. The man merely nodded in reply and looked towards the King as he backed his horse away from the edge of the hill and into the ranks of his own division. "Aye, and I'll give Bear credit, he could always make a good speech. I suppose it's a pre-requisite of being a King really."

"Suppose so, and don't be so hard on Alfdarr. The man knows what he's doing," Kiegal admonished him gently. In truth, he said it more to reassure himself than anything else. He knew that the success of the battle depended greatly on discipline, something that clansmen often found hard to achieve. More often than not, when not performing some sort of clandestine or guerrilla form of warfare, the primary tactic of a clansman was to charge headlong into the ranks of the enemy and hope to the Gods that he killed more of the enemy than they did of his allies. It never even seemed to enter the mind of a clansman, or Traemwenian in general, that they could become a casualty.

"Oh aye, I know that fine well, and Bear swears by him. But he doesn't like the Cardavians, and he doesn't trust 'em. Man's a fool if he carries a prejudice against them because of Nepriner."

"I was wondering about something actually," Kiegal asked as another flight of arrows flew through the air to disappear beyond the hill. "Are we still officially allowed to call the King, Bear?"

"I suppose as long as we don't do it in front of anybody official then it should be alright, he's not said anything to me yet about it."

Tortag nodded, seeing the logic in it before considering the absurdity of the situation. He was, or so he boasted, a veteran of a thousand battles. In truth the figure was nearer to two dozen, and there wasn't a single time where he hadn't faced a full bladder and a dry mouth as he tried to not piss himself with fear. His stomach would be knotted with tension, his shoulders aching and his mind longing to be anywhere else. This, though, was entirely different.

The Empire had used the clans to be shock soldiers, to charge straight into the enemy and disrupt their formation long enough for the Rupinian elite to close and engage. This battle, or whatever it was they were doing now, was methodical. He looked at Quittle, his friend and King, and saw him in a different light. This fight wasn't how the clansmen typically fought, this was altogether Rupinian. He was wrenched from his thoughts as a warhorn blew, signalling that the second phase of the battle was due to start.

"Right lads! Time to advance!" He shouted out, automatically in unison as his mind operated by default. "Section officers, call out the time. The man who breaks ranks and charges will answer to me, so help me God." He turned to Kiegal and smiled. "Ready?"

"Didn't get dressed up for nothing," the standard bearer said with a grin.

The Kings Division marched to the forefront of the hill where it began to shelve steeply. Nek, not being content with waiting in the third rank because he had nothing to see, had shoved his way to the front rank with a couple of grins and a wink. Grim, shrugging his shoulders and knowing what his friend was like, had simply followed. The sight before them was one that would live with them till their dying day, they knew.

As soldiers of the legions of the kingdom of Cardavy they were used to the sight of death and destruction almost on a mechanical scale. They had seen men of various different nations, idealistic groups or religious beliefs throwing themselves upon the shield wall of the legions like an angry tide breaking against the rock. This was something else entirely.

They watched the men struggle up the hill, plastered and coated in mud as they were. Their condition was further worsened by the light drizzle that had descended upon the battlefield, a feature of life that was ordinarily uncomment worthy in the lands of Traemwen for the natives. Nek watched them group together believing there was safety in numbers, huddling like herd animals, as they sought to shield themselves with the bodies of their friends and comrades. Very few of them, apart from the obviously richer sort, carried shields. The majority were pikemen, used to holding the haft of their weapon with two hands, and a buckler was often seen as an anathema amongst the clansman. Apparently it would encourage weakness and doubt in the person's ability, however, Nek couldn't help think how the men scrambling would regret their vanity and profligacy now.

He watched another volley slam into the flanks and sides, the ten second volleys having a terrific and deadly effect upon those clambering upwards. It was more personal now that he was at the edge of precipice, looking down upon the milling mass of men. He saw one man who had struck out upon his own, obviously hoping to rally men, turn and hold his sword aloft. An arrow slammed into his spine finding a gap in the chainmail he wore causing him to fall to the ground, an animal like wail emanating rising above the din of noise from below signalling that the man was wounded but not yet dead. Nek watched for a few seconds more, seeing the man twist his face in recognition of the fact that he was now crippled for life as he tried to crawl to the Kings line using only his hands. Nek looked at him, could swear the man looked him in the eye, as he realised his life was forfeit and sunk his head into the boggy ground to drown himself. The World was harsh, and, no matter what kind words chiefs or politicians would say, would never support cripples enough.

Nek tore his gaze away and saw the front line finally beginning to gain some semblance. Their pikes were beginning to lower as their officers tried to gain some sort of control over the formation as it continued to march over the marsh and heather. Nek watched them and, for the first time in his life, was able to enjoy it with an almost detached point of view.

"When does a battle become a slaughter?" Grim asked, interrupting his thoughts.

"I've no idea, but if it keeps you and I safe in the middle of this shitstorm then I'm more than happy." Grim looked at him for a few seconds before nodding, obviously content, before he looked back to the mass of men coming up the hill. The archers had worked a deadly toll on the enemy and there was at least a third to a half down if he was any estimate. He squinted, the sun coming out from the sun and blinding his eyes for a few seconds. There was a shout from one of the officers and then the main body of the Kings frontline began to advance down the hill.

"Guess we're for the off then?" Nek asked, a grin spreading across his face. He tipped the rest of the contents of his pipe to the ground and slipped the still warm pipe into his cloak of innumerable pipe. "Tell you what Grim," he shouted as they marched toward the enemy down the slope, "I'm starting to like the countryside around here!"

Grim chuckled but kept his eyes on those on front, trying to keep in step with the pikemen to their front. It was frustrating that they couldn't break formation, there being an incessant belief in himself that a single charge whilst the enemy were in complete disarray would win the day. He wondered, briefly, whether the King was demonstrating the new found discipline of the clans for the benefit of the men of the Iron Mountain. He disregarded the thought, deciding there and then that it was beyond his sphere and influence and, therefore, outwith his area of control. All he could ensure, he believed there and then, was the protection of the man to his left and right.

The two Cardavians had short swords and tower shields, completely out of form with the rest of Traemwenian formation. However, as Nek reflected, they had the ghost of the Eagles behind them. Turgundeon and Gephy may have been the latest of their battle honours, but it certainly wouldn't be their last. As one man had once commented, Nek would have followed the standard of the Eagles up the Gods collective arses in an effort to retrieve it. He wasn't just fighting for Nek and Grim, he was fighting for all those men who didn't return home.

Nek and Grim advanced, their shields presented. They smashed their short swords onto their shields and bellowed out their war cries in their native tongue, alien to the clansmen around about them. The noise was terrific, adding to their terror and adrenaline. Nek felt the blood coursing through his veins, his pulse almost in step with every stride that he took. He tried to focus on those before them, but the faces swamped into the masses and became obscure blurs covered in blood and gore. He presented his shield, stretched out before him with his sword presented at the ready. He flicked his glance only slightly to the left and noticed that Grimfar had done the same and thus had his back. He smiled grimly as he dipped behind the shield, thrusting out his sword as it licked at yielding flesh. He smiled, his training taking over.

"Just remember, this was your sodding idea!" Nek shouted above the din of battle. He couldn't see how the other divisions were doing, nor whether they had even engaged. All was confusion around him and his eyes were for those in front and in his vicinity. He stabbed, withdrew, rebalanced and stabbed again almost like a machine. He could do no less. The clansmen opposite him may have taken a beaten on their advance up the hill, but he didn't have the mental acumen to work out whether the odds finally favoured him or not. Even if he had, Nek reflected as he rammed his sword into the gullet of an enemy as he tried to scramble back, he wouldn't have given a damn.

He stared down his next opponent, watching him as he screamed abuse into his face. Nek stood for a few seconds, semi-crouched into his shield and grateful for the rest as the man spewed his hatred. He wished, above all else right now, that Grim and he had had time to teach the clans on how to properly reforms their lines and recycle their manpower. He hawked and spat into the ground, shouting at an obscenity or two at the direction of the clansman from Long Loch before gesturing for him to come on.

He hawked and spat onto the ground once more, the phlegm building into his mouth as he locked eyes with his opponent. There was no give there.

He couldn't hate the man, he knew, for he had nothing to do with him, however, he had a job in front of him. He watched the pike sway in front of his shield as the man desperately tried to keep in whatever formation the men of Long Loch were subscribing to. Nek didn't even have to move really, the opposition being forced this way and that as more men were forced to form a conglomerate as a protection against the arrows of the Kings men. The pike wove in front of his eyes due more to unsteady hands than an attempt at confusing him. Nek grinned without humour and swore, smashing his sword twice into his shield and launched himself forward when the timing was right.

The man opposite had seen the blade coming, the shining steel lancing for his throat as the Cardavian bypassed his only means of defence. He died with a scream on his lips as Nek forced his way through. He swung his sword instinctively to the right, the sharp bite of steel sending shoot pains up his arms before it became suddenly became numb. He gritted his teeth and roared, launching himself forward with the boss of his shield. He smashed his opponent once and twice in the face as he advanced, not bothering to see whether he died.

He could feel their formation breaking, an imperceptible shift in the battle as the Kings front line launched itself forward in an effort to form a fighting wedge. Nek ducked behind his shield quickly as a clansman aimed a sword blow at his head, a wide sweeping movement that overbalanced the man and ended with his swift death as Nek dispatched him with a sword thrust through the armpit. He smashed out with his shield and pressed onwards, heedless of whether anyone was about him.

"Nek, fucking fall back!" Grim roared out, desperate to try and form line with his friend. He could see that the clansmen were beginning to ditch their spears and bringing out their small daggers, but he could also see that the Traemwenians on their own side weren't moving nearly as fast as Nek or he were used to. "Nek, get your arse back here now you stupid bastard!" Grim sighted one of the clansmen coming at him with a beautifully designed butterfly axe, charging with rage in his eyes. He was able to get his shield up in time, but the ringing blow near numbed his arm and forced him back a few paces. He gritted his teeth and watched as his opponent threw the axe back again for another blow. Placing the ball of his heel firmly into the mossy ground, Grim launched himself forward but misjudged his footing. What was supposed to be a lunge turned into a trip and a fall, terrifying at the best of times but doubly when men were intent on your death. He landed on his stomach, the wind driven out from his lungs, and through sheer luck and self-preservation was able to twist to the right and turn onto his back. The axe head thudded into the dirt where has head had been mere seconds ago.

He lashed out, his sword cutting in a wide sweeping arc and slicing neatly through the man's lower leg causing him to howl and collapse in pain. Grim made to stand but was knocked down again as feet trampled past him. He cursed and cried out, desperation taking over as he saw his death coming ever closer. The only thing he could be thankful for, he absurdly thought, was that the feet were advancing towards him at a steady pace rather than as part of a desperate rout.

"Some fucker help me up!" He shouted, trapped as he was behind his shield in an effort to protect himself. He felt himself stuck to the ground, almost embedded in the mud. A strong hand reached down and wrenched away the shield, and in that moment Grim knew he would either have to kill or be killed. The sunlight blinded him for a few seconds, long enough to prevent him from stabbing upwards with his sword.

"Is that any way to speak to a friend?" Nek asked, his hand outstretched.

"If I see one, I'll bloody speak to one properly." He gripped the mans outstretched forearm and was hauled up.

"Well, your kits in a right bloody state. You'll be up on a charge if the King sees you." Nek said, trying to inject a little humour into conversation. He knew he had done wrong when he broke formation, had found that out when he found himself completely surrounded and cut off. He would have been dead if it had been for the Kings division advancing at a good pace causing the men of the loch to retreat in some disorder. He knew also that there was a large degree of luck involved, something that he wouldn't be able to rely on forever.

"I've a mind to knock you out, I swear." Grim glared at him for a few more seconds, his fear lending strength to tired muscles and his anger. Eventually, in a few heartbeats, he took a breath in through his nose and out through his mouth. "You alright?"

"Couple of scratches, maybe a bruised rib from when of the bastards rushed me, but nothing major somehow. You?"

"Couple of scratches, bit of dented pride, nothing life threatening." He looked around about him and saw the same scene being repeated elsewhere. The three divisions belonging to the King were advancing down the hill at a steady pace as they kept formation, some still carrying the spears and pikes that others had abandoned during the close quarters fighting. The archers that had been placed in between the divisions were continuing to fire deadly volleys down the hillside, their deadly barbs slamming into the backs of men as they sought safety.

"At least the battle is going well," remarked Nek, nodding towards the light cavalry that had been released from their position and thundering across the battlefield. Some were rounding up prisoners and other survivors whilst others were busy riding down those that were too proud or stubborn to lay down their arms. "I can't make out what's happening at the bottom of the hill. Reckon the men of Iron Mountain will hold to their end of the deal?"

"After that display? They'd be bloody daft not to if you ask me." Grim looked about him, trying to differentiate between the two sides casualties but had no such luck. The plaids and colours identifying the clans fallen were awash with mud and gore, utterly indistinguishable to someone who had only just started getting used to the different designs. "If you could give me a year, maybe a legions armoury and a decent parade ground then I reckon we could transform this lot."

"Given that you ended up on your arse, Grim, and I broke formation, I think Quittle and his mob did well enough!"

It was well into the evening and the King and his leading allies were gathered in a village hall, a large and spacious building with a high roof of thatch. Quittle sat on the tallest chair available in the room, placed upon a podium, where he was able to look upon the men gathered in neat rows before him. Some of them carried wounds whilst others, particularly those of the Iron Mountain, looked fresher and more eager. Victory always came easiest to those who hedged their bets and lumped in for the winning side. He mentally shook off the feeling and remembered that the evening was supposed to be about muted celebration, a victory against the Imperials, but one that had been won against other Traemwenians.

Between the two rows of loyalist clans stood the Imperial garrison commander, a Speirakian who hadn't involved himself in the battle, and the chief of the men of Long Loch. He had to give them credit for neither showed any sense of fear or trepidation, though the chief often winced whenever he walked due to a particularly nasty looking wound to his temple. In truth, Quittle would sooner have let the man try and recover from his wounds before going through with this, but he had been persuaded into it by Tortag and his brother.

There was a general rumbling of conversation amongst the men gathered as each spoke with the man on either side, their conversations blurring into a general noise. He wondered what they spoke of, whether they were talking about the glories they had won on the battle or whether they were discussing their views on him as a King. He wondered, briefly, if he was sitting in the chair properly and with a degree of regal authority. This, all of this, was something he never thought he would ever have to actually go through with. He had thought about it, particularly outside the walls of Nepriner, and he had spoken about it, but there was a world of difference between actions and words.

Now, as he considered it, he had beaten an Imperial garrison in a bloody skirmish and now defeated a clan and taken the surrender of another garrison. Events had moved on faster than he could have predicted, or even hoped would happen. He briefly looked at Tortag, resplendent now in breastplate and surcoat displaying his clan colours. Victories would bring riches, Quittle knew, and he was adamant that the Imperial armoury would be put to good use in kitting out his men. They were outnumbered, he knew, and they would need every advantage they could get.

"Sire, shall we get this over with?" Tor said, formally using his title and wrenching him from his thoughts. Quittle nodded his head, the sounds of conversation slowly dying out as men fixed their eyes on either him or the prisoners in the centre of the room. "The prisoners shall advance!"

There was no sound now in the room barring the steady chink of armour as the two men walked across the narrow causeway, each with their eyes fixed to their front and not a hint of apprehension or nerves in their gaze. Quittle could respect pride, as much as he wanted to humble the two men. Neither of the men were restrained either, having surrendered their weapons and being subject to search. There was no point, as Quittle saw it, heaping humiliation on them. He had learned from bitter experience that a man backed into a corner with nothing left to lose was often at his most dangerous; was that not how the clans had got into this situation?

"Speirakian," Quittle began as the two men finally came to a halt, "you have surrendered your garrison in the Iron Mountains capital without bloodshed. Under the terms of the agreement, you and your men will be allowed to march away from the Kingdom of Traemwen and back to the borders with the honours of war. You will be provided with an escort and a warrant from myself providing you with safe passage."

"We do not need your escort," the man hissed. His eyes, his expression and his very being screamed hate at Quittle. Why shouldn't it? The man would forever view him as a rebel and a usurper so long as the Rupinians held sway over Speirak.

"Nevertheless, you shall have it. You will leave this camp forthwith, though your horses will be retained by my men. Further, you will only leave with your personal arms and not the contents of the armoury."

"The usurper turns thief as well as traitor?"

"Speirakian, one more word from you that displeases me will see you hung from the highest tree after I have had you disembowelled. Do you understand?" The man made to say something, his eyes flashing hate, but thought better of it. Eventually he nodded, self-preservation taking over false pride. No doubt, Quittle thought, the man believed there would eventually be a reckoning.

"Good. You may leave." The man turned about smartly on his heel, taken out of the hall by his escort, and leaving the chief isolated. Quittle looked at the man, however, he couldn't stir up any feelings of hatred or anything stronger than a degree of sorrow. He had achieved a startling triumph today, something that had surprised even him, but it had been against men of his country and Kingdom that he was supposed to defend. The man in front of him, technically, was obeying an oath he had made to a distant Emperor and tried to execute his duty. Surely this made him a stronger man, a more loyal man, than Quittle?

"Chief Balda of the Long Loch, it is a sad state of affairs when men of Traemwen fight against each other in the name of a distant despot. I understand why you did it, and I commend you on your loyalty to your former master. However," Quittle continued, "I am King of these lands. Your loyalty, now at least, should be to myself and the people of this country. Have you anything to say?"

The man, though obviously pained due to his wound, looked at him up and down in an appraising manner. It would be considered by some to be forward and impertinent, but Quittle knew he had to win over the chiefs of the major clans to his side if he were to ever call himself King. If he were to fly into a royal rage because somebody looked at him in a funny manner, then he would be no better than the despot he had risen against.

"By what right are you King?" The chief asked, his voice barely above a whisper. There was a collective gasp from the room, men beginning to mutter amongst themselves. There were a few angry shouts, some demanding the man to be strung up post haste. The chief, more coherent than Quittle would have imagined him to be, ploughed on. "You have won your battle, sire, but a battle does not make a King. You have won your crown at the point of a sword, but even you must know that there are other garrisons and other clans that would sooner fight for the Emperor of royal blood than a jumped up peasant?"

There was further angry shouting, men almost jostling to reach the man and tear him down in an effort to prove their own brand of loyalty to their King. Quittle stared at the man and knew how he would have to react and simply laughed. He laughed loud enough for all to hear, tried to inject actual humour into it, for to do anything but laugh would show him to be uncivilised. If he were to throw this man to his men, and he realised that this was very easily within his power and not a word would be said, he'd be no better than the rebel and traitor the Imperials called him. Worse, they'd blacken his name and call him a barbarian.

"You are right, Chief Balda," Quittle said once the noise had quietened down, "I have won my crown at the point of a sword. Even you, though, can see that the Imperials aren't worth fighting for. Look at them now! They have surrendered their garrison without so much as a fight, happy for clansmen to do their fighting and dying for them yet again.

"You were at Nepriner and Gephy, you saw how the Empire and their Field Marshal Neard would throw our men at the walls as if they were nothing more than a child's plaything. Do you remember seeing their broken bodies coming back to the camps, the dead and the wounded and the maimed mixing together into one disgusting mass as they launched us at the walls again and again? Do you remember, Balda, the long march back through territory that was once abundant with life and people that the Empire had forced us to destroy and murder? Do you remember going back to your own capital and lands and explaining to the widows, the fatherless children and others how their menfolk wouldn't be returning?

"What has the Empire ever done for you, Balda? Aye, they've given you pretty baubles and trinkets. They've given you a few titles to mollify a proud man, they've tried to castrate you and use you. You! The man who took the eastern wall and fought in the arena against the Attainian general Takol! You have brought great honour to your clan and your people, you have fought bravely and well. Surely you of all people deserve more? Surely all of us in this Kingdom deserve more than what the Imperials deign to give us.

"We are not dogs to be fed scraps from the table. We are Traemwenians!" He slammed his closed fist onto the arm of his seat, working himself into a fine passion now. He could see the effect it was having on the men about him and before him, but more importantly he could see the effect it was having on Balda. There was a look to the man's face now, questioning one moment and then thoughtful the next. It was obvious the man was thinking, and thinking fast. Now, Quittle knew, was the time to strike.

"I won't offer your clan to you, Balda, nor even your lands. They are not mine to offer you for they are already yours." It was technically a lie, he knew, for he had every right to claim victors' spoils and take the land for himself, but he needed loyal allies. "What I offer you is the chance to be by my side. Fight with me, for a new Traemwen, and for a new page in our history. Bring your men over to us and we shall march, after a day or two of rest whilst we treat our wounded, and together four clans will march into your lands and expel the Imperials that infest it. What say you?"

The man looked at him and then studied those on the podium. His eyes rested on Tortag, a man he knew of old, and also on Alfdarr and Kiegal. He knew each of them well, had bled with them in the streets of Nepriner and drank with them in front of friendlier hearths. He looked upon the two Cardavians, still in their amour that they had worn during the battle. He glanced at Wenrynt of the Iron Mountain and knew that bad blood would exist between them until the day one of them died. Finally, he looked upon Quittle and accepted the inevitable. He bowed his head.

"What do you require of me…sire?"

"Your loyalty, Balda. Nothing more. Fight for me as you once did the Emperor, and I'll gladly break bread and drink with you. Tonight," he said addressing the gathered crowd as well as the chief, "we shall drink to lost friends and, more importantly new found ones. From this day till our last, I declare the men of Long Loch and Iron Mountain to be our firm friends."

Chapter Thirteen – **Threat Brief**

When Beran had first received his orders and relayed them to his men that they were to head south to the ominously named 'western pass', he had been good humouredly ridiculed by the likes of Velawin and Aleill. They had explained that any pass which hadn't even been named was probably twinned with the various depths of Hell and was either subject blistering sunshine or heavy snows. In truth, Beran had begun to regret even raising the subject of bringing Talice with him during their long march, so sure was he of the rumours that the place was the nearest thing to a lingering death this side of the continent. He had broached the subject with her and she had leapt at the chance, obviously keen to be with him and away from the capital with its politics and cliques. She had settled, she argued, but she preferred to be by his side. Furthermore, as she added succinctly, there wasn't much point in being man and wife if he was to be stationed at the arse end of the Kingdom on a diplomatic mission.

The Wolves had gathered their strength on the march south, often passing through towns and villages where Beran would have a few of the more charismatic men hammer the drum in the local squares and promise men a lifetime of adventure. If he were to have got a few of the more honest men to bang said drum then chances were there'd have had a mutiny shortly followed by a revolution of some sort, something that was never looked upon terribly well by anybody. They had, through the judicious use of spinning dits to getting people outright blind drunk, managed to fill their ranks.

The march south as well had also allowed these new recruits to be put through their paces, literally being thrown in at the deep end as they were expected to march alongside the veterans of Nepriner. When they weren't marching, and they weren't exactly setting a blistering pace, they were put to task in basic sword drill and manoeuvre. The sight of hundreds of men trying to learn how to walk, wheeling about on the march and forming line had caused convulsions amongst the experienced members of the legion as they crashed into each other or 'tick-tocked'. Men were filtered out by their talents, some being taken into the depleted heavy infantry whilst others moved into the other wings of the legion. Velawin, who was one for always exclaiming the virtues of the light infantry, had built his particular arm of the Wolves into something akin to legend. It had assumed an elite status in the eyes of the recruits, something that Vel was keen to exploit. In all, morale seemed higher than Beran would have thought achievable and there was no shortage of well-wishers and hangers on; each and every one of them keen to see those that had defended Nepriner. Talice too seemed to be enjoying the journey, and the veterans protected and doted upon her more closely than Beran would have given them credit for. They remembered how the young woman had helped the General during the siege, though he hoped they didn't know quite how she had helped him. More importantly, they remembered how she had organised the bands of women who brought aid and medical treatment to those that were wounded. If anyone got too close, and it was mainly traders who tried as they sought to sell their wares when Beran wasn't around, then there'd be a dozen legionaries asking the merchant politely to whom he thought he was talking and if he wouldn't mind buggering off. It had caused Talice no end of mirth, but Beran sensed she was also deeply touched by the protectiveness of the Wolves.

Beran also took the time to find out about his new leader of heavy infantry, the man Aglon, and was in the process reassured about their newest senior officer. He had watched him march with the men and train with them, often taking the time to pass on his own experiences to the newer recruits whilst also taking the time to listen to the more experienced veterans. It was actually something that pleased Beran no end; he was a great believer in the ability to talk and lead, but he also knew that there was a time and a place to shut up. Most of the time, as he saw it, there was no harm in listening to people who were more experienced than you in order to learn from their mistakes or achievements; failure to do so would either lead to a person becoming arrogant, distant, or incompetent and aloof. When leading men in battle, or leading any group of people in any walk of life, any one or combination of those would lead to disaster.

It was a cool day when he had approached him properly, having only had the briefest of conversations with the bald man beforehand that, upon reflection, were mere formalities of welcome. The sun was high in the sky and they had marched some ten miles, another five to go before they would think about pitching and making camp for the night. There was a small breeze which prevented any sort of stifling heat due to the moderate cloud cover, and the rains of the previous day had dampened down any dust that may have settled on the road they were travelling along. There was even, if Beran strained his ears and listened above the tramping of boots and the songs and ribald jests of his men, the faint sound of bird song.

The man snapped off a professional salute which was duly returned, Beran pulling his horse alongside the man and rode on for a few moments before he decided to dismount. He walked alongside and stroked the flanks of his horse before turning to the heavy infantry leader.

"How you finding the Wolves, Aglon? Meet your expectations?"

"Reputation is well earned, sir, mind you," he said with a wink and a grin, "I don't think these northern barbarians are a patch on the Leviathans!"

There were a few jeers shouted from those in immediate earshot that caused the tall, bald man to grin widely.

"Aye, they are good lads," he said with a chuckle. "How you finding the mess?" Beran had heard from Vel of some disagreement between Aglon and Aleill when the man had first joined, but as far as he was aware nothing had flared up and the two had developed a good working relationship.

"Good mixture of characters in there. Vel is something else though, that man is disgustingly fit!"

"Don't let him hear you say that, it'll cause his head to grow even larger than it already is. Anyway," Beran remarked with a smile, "I think it's natures way of making up for his lack of height."

"He's almost as tall as you," said Aglon as he relaxed into the conversation.

"Ah, but such a word is 'almost', Aglon. One cannot be *almost* alive, nor *almost* correct. You are either dead or wrong, and Vel is therefore short." Aglon grinned and eventually broke into a low rumbling chuckle as he adjusted the grey cloak. The heat of the road was beginning to become stifling as the wind blew some of the clouds away, the high sun having dried the road and begun to reflect the heat from all angles.

"Leviathans are based where we're going, aren't they?"

"Sir?"

"Call me Ban, every other senior officer seems to bloody well do it these days so you may as well." Aglon was about to ask where it came from before Beran held up a hand. "Don't ask where it comes from either, you'll be disappointed by my version of events and Aleill can spin the dit in a much better way."

"I didn't quite catch what you said...Ban?" He wasn't terribly sure which part of his question he was actually framing as a question. It went without saying that the first part was, but using the name, even a nickname, of his commanding officer was something that he had never done before and was almost confusing.

He knew the Wolves were a different breed to his previous legion, but this was something else. The only way he could reason it through, and as a man he liked to think of himself as logical, was that the men of the Wolves didn't actually feel the need to prove themselves by beholding to a rank structure. It was there and in place, he knew, but it wasn't used almost like a weapon. Weaker officers, and even those in the lower ranks, in his experience tended to use their rank almost as a shield and a sword at the same time to both defend themselves and attack those of lower rank. The rank structure of the Wolves seemed to be there simply to avoid confusion when the legion went into battle.

"I asked whether your old legion was based where we are going," Beran asked again. He looked further up the column and could see the hills in the distance, reckoning to himself that they could probably push on and be at their final destination by nightfall if they were to go at a harder pace. He decided against it almost in the same thought, judging rightly that they weren't at war and that there was no need to tire out the men; another night under canvas wouldn't do them any harm.

"How much did the higher ups pass on during their briefing?"

"Well, given that you asked so candidly I'll return it. Remember those wee maps sold by street hawkers you used to get when you were a child near the coast or beach, the ones that claimed they were treasure maps with a large X written on them?" Aglon nodded. "Well it was a bit like that. Brief was simply go here and don't annoy anyone, but if you do then do it diplomatically. Never heard a bloody thing about the place."

"Where do you want me to start then?" Aglon considered himself a jack of all trades, a healthy interest in everything that Cardavy and other nations had done in their history. The land of the south with its intricate political dealings and interminable warfare had become a particular interest of his, especially given that he had spent a significant portion of his career looking into the country.

"What's the history of the place, who is based there, is it decent for a piss up, is my wife likely to try and drag me off to some society ball? A thousand and one questions, Aglon." He grinned suddenly, that sense of humour that Beran possessed suddenly coming to the fore. "Really it's your fault for not telling me beforehand, Commander." He grinned again, finishing with a wink.

"I'll try keep it brief, Ban, but I'm one for wandering about in my thoughts so stop me if you get bored."

"I'm not being funny Aglon, but in the last few weeks all I've been looking at is absolutely bugger all apart from the occasional village and the weather. I've got being bored mastered to a fine art form. You crack on with your story."

"Well, sir, it's like this. There's a massive port city, Noriandie, that's where the Leviathans are based out of. It was taken from a prince of the Southern Coalition nearly a hundred years ago, bit of a sore point as I understand, so we've always maintained a garrison there just in case. It's also where the majority of the southern fleet are based out of, the river running from the mountains through the town eventually breaks into the open sea. It's a good trading port, pulls in most of the custom and taxes from the south but also relies heavily upon local sheep farming and the fishing fleet. Legion and fleet help by bringing in the wages for the tavern owners."

"You said it was taken in a war?"

"It was a very small one, not much actually to say about it. There was a southern prince who decided that he was going to be the saviour of the south and unite the country. To do that he decided that he was going to have a pop at us. He got his arse felt and we told him to behave. Anyway, he decides to have another pop when the legions went north again and we took it completely. It's why the place, and you'll see this when we go past it, still has the red tiles roofs that are common in the Coalition."

"So I take it we're being based outwith the city then?" He already knew they were, but he was keen for the man to share his knowledge as well as break out of any shell that he had. He knew he was rather unorthodox when it came to his approach with his officers and men and, therefore, he wanted to encourage Aglon to come out with his own ideas and opinions.

"Yes, I'm guessing we'll be relieving the Stags."

"Never heard of them."

"You won't have, arseholes for the most part."

"Oh aye?" Beran asked, scenting a dit. "Little bit of inter-legion rivalry?"

"Could say that, sir." He had slipped very slightly back into formality, but it was a casual formality that came naturally to those that had served any sort of time in a legion; it was the type where you'd replace the word 'sir' with 'brother' or 'friend' and nobody would notice.

"Well tell the story then! By the Gods, Aglon, it's like drawing teeth. I'll have you up on a charge, you know, or make Erallac talk to you for more than five minutes about how he invented soldiering." Aglon grinned and shrugged his shoulders, the slight breeze bringing relief as well as the scent of fresh flowers. He could hear some sheep in the distance as they called out to each other, the hillsides dotted with little white balls of fluff as they bounded about the hills. He had heard from a farmer once that the sole reason for a sheep to exist was to find an interesting way to get trapped and inconvenience said farmer, but all he could see were the happy lambs as they bounced after their friends. He was an unreserved animal lover and was more than happy to be back where he felt he belonged.

"We used to host a sports competition between the two legions, the fleet, the city and a few of the outlying villages. It was a mixture of different events. Fleet always did well in the tug of war, whereas we always did better in the wrestling. Anyway, the one everyone really took an interest in was the brawling. Gentlemen's rules, no weapons or low blows. Bastard Stags ruined that in the final, their champion damn near gouged out the eyes of our lad." He chuckled for a moment, "It actually started a huge fight, provosts and civil police got involved and it looked as if it was going to descend into a full scale riot."

"So who won?"

"We did. Buggers pissed off fast enough when they realised we had the fleet behind us." Beran laughed and Aglon found himself chuckling along, remembering the fights in alleyways and streets after the brawling match. He knew that there was always cheating, but as a young junior officer back then he had revelled being part of something that was bigger than himself. Being in that fight with his men at his back, his friends around about him, had reinforced to him what it meant to be in the legions.

"So what's the borders like, is it a hard border with a wall or a soft border?"

"Bit of both, to be honest. I went south a few times when on leave. Where we are going is a massive fort, capable of holding a legion easily plus allied attachments. It's smack back in the middle of the mountain range and the coast, maybe a mile or so away from Noriandie. It's not a bad place, or so I'm given to understand, but most of their lads end up jumping on wagons that are heading to the city for a night. Most trade…well, actually most things, have to pass the fort in order to head further north."

"So there's no other defences around about it?"

"Apart from the city and the mountain range? You've got the fleet."

"Never worked with the Navy, don't know what they are like."

"Decent enough, good lads." Aglon was on stronger ground here. At one point he was chasing a commission in the fleet prior to joining the Legions, but had decided against it at the last minute. It had been a minor act of rebellion against his father and generation of ancestors who had been Navy through and through; he had been the first to ever join the legions.

"Interesting." He reached into his saddlebag and tossed Aglon a flask containing red wine, which was gratefully received. "Keep it. I've got spares. I'm off to the front of the column. You're doing well here, Aglon, I mean that. We'll probably camp under canvas tonight," he raised his voice, "it'll be interesting to see if the infantry can cope with living rough as well as the cavalry do!" Good natured curses were taken up once again and Beran flashed a grin, mounted swiftly and waved as he galloped off.

"Is that smoke?" Erallac asked, squinting into the distance.

The Wolves weren't far from the fort now, a few miles out at most after another night under canvas. Beran was mounted next to him, head of the column with Talice by his side. He looked into the middle distance, seeing a thin tendril of smoke going into the morning sky. It wasn't big enough to signify that the fort was on fire, but it certainly was bigger than a camp fire.

He felt his hand twitching and reaching for the pommel of his blade, the hairs standing on the back of his neck as he watched it. There was a creeping feeling at the base of his spine, working its way slowly up his back as he continued to watch. The steady tramp of boots and hooves onto the stones of the road merged into the background noise, the occasional shout or loud voice coming from the column. He squinted harder, suddenly envious of the birds flying overhead that could see what was happening for miles around. He cursed softly, the ground around far too flat to gain any advantage. He turned about in his saddle trying to find a small hillock or any high ground where he could gain advantage and, seeing none, he cursed once more.

"It might not be anything," suggested Talice hopefully. She was alternately watching Beran and the smoke, seeing another tendril reaching into the sky. She looked hopefully to the west where the sun danced merrily upon the clear water, the glistening light almost blinding as the shadows of fishing boats darted to and fro as they tried to get their catch.

"It might," Beran conceded, "although it might be something worse." Talice looked upon her husband and saw his expression, the look in his eye which signalled that something was afoot. It was like Nepriner, the same shadow crossing his face and the same setting of the brow. She noticed, almost for the first time, that his jaw became clenched and unclenched as he literally chewed over his thoughts. She touched her stomach, almost protectively, as sickness threatened to overtake her. She could feel the cold sweat upon her brow after the initial flush, the rush of saliva to her mouth that needed to be spat out. Her head spun, but she still looked upon Beran. "You need to see," she said between almost gritted teeth. He looked upon her, his expression going from one of consternation to one of worry. "I'll be fine, Ban, but those folk might not be. Go check. Clear your mind." He looked at her and nodded, seeing the concern in her eyes.

"I'll be fine, it's probably nothing," he tried to say as reassuringly as he could.

"You better be, or I'll make sure you suffer for it." He grinned and kissed her on the cheek, looking at her once more before duty settled on his shoulders once more. He spun about in his saddle and shouted a series of orders, having the hundred or so cavalry from the vanguard to move out of position. He turned back to Talice and grinned again.

"I love you."

"I love you too. Don't be too long. Erallac," she said with a smile, "make sure he doesn't do anything stupid."

"Been trying that since I knew him, the bugger still doesn't listen to me!" The big man said with a grin and a laugh, touching his heels to the horse and cantering forward with the cavalry line. Beran was passed a lance by one of the cavalrymen left in the vanguard. He touched heels to his own horse, one last look to Talice, before he swept onwards.

The sun was obscured now by some grey cloud, the threat of rain on the distant horizon as low level cloud hung to across the mountain top like a thick blanket. The air was stuffy and he was glad for the change of pace, leading his horse at a canter as he assumed his position at the head of the cavalry column. He could still make out the tendrils of smoke in the distance, but he couldn't work out whether the smoke was beginning to get thicker or whether it was a trick of his imagination. He also didn't like the fact that this was a spur of the moment decision, something that he didn't expect to make when he was this far into home territory and so close to a legion fort.

He shouted for the men to take their horses to the canter, the pace becoming faster as the familiar drumming of hoofs on road and then dirt began to take over his senses. He began to smile, turning swiftly into a broad grin as they reached a small rise. He turned his head and looked to Erallac, the second heavy infantry leader deciding to forgo his normal roll for a chance of a different experience. The man was smiling broadly, though he rode a horse with all the grace of a sack of potatoes. Beran laughed loudly and was met with a curse.

"This isn't fucking natural!" Erallac roared as he tried to control a horse that had other ideas on how it was to behave.

"Maybe if you didn't spend so long grubbing about in the dirt and actually behaved like a gentleman you'd know how to ride!" Beran retorted. Erallac fixed him with an evil glare, keen obviously to have a retort of his own but more focussed on simply retaining his seat.

Beran turned to his front again and looked beyond the crest. His heart sank as he took in the scene. He could see in the distance, nestled between the mountains and the coast, the small wooden fort; what turned his stomach was the sight of a trade caravan being brutally attacked. Where in the name of the Gods were the Stags, the men who were supposed to be defending this patch of the borders? He cursed, the weight of the lance in his hand suddenly at the forefront of his mind.

"Form line abreast!" He roared, staring at the cavalry raiders as they darted in and out of the wagons. He counted nearly forty of them, maybe a few more chasing runners, and he couldn't make out at this range whether any had spotted them. Two of the wagons belonging to the caravan were on fire, the oxen or horses pulling all ten wagons and carts lying dead in their traces.

"Left squadron is with me! Right squadron with Inalad!" He shouted, judging the distance to be some three hundred yards. Inalad, the officer commanding the squadron simply nodded and nudged his horse to the right and was followed by the other forty-nine men under his command. Line abreast would see them push on and sweep through the area down the two flanks. It was an age old tactic and one that brought maximum power to a charge. Beran signalled for his men to move slightly to the left as he looked towards the raiders again and then back to the fort; something stank here and he was determined to find out.

"Erallac, you don't have to charge with us." He said quietly as he made sure that none of the men around him heard; the man may have been a natural and gifted infantryman but he was not cavalry. The man also had a colossal amount of pride and Beran didn't wish to impinge on that.

"Bugger that, Ban. If you get hurt or worse then your Talice would fucking kill me. I'd sooner take my chance with this bloody horse and a few bloodthirsty bastards." Erallac grinned, but Beran could see the nerves behind his eyes. "What do you think they are doing in that bloody fort anyway?"

"Gods alone knows, but I want to find out after this skirmish." He hefted the lance and tested the balance with a few thrusts in the air, finding an easier and more comfortable grip. If he had known that they were about to go into a skirmish then he would have liked to have had his small and trusty crossbow loaded just in case, the two deadly bolts from that saving his life on many an occasion. "Look, just stay behind me and don't do anything stupid."

"You as well, Ban. Didn't survive Nepriner to get killed on a jolly." Beran nodded and looked at his formation, satisfied that the men were as arranged as properly as possible. He hefted his lance once into the air and gave the order for the men to trot.

The distance began to close and Beran could start to make out a few of the faces amongst the raiders, most of them unbearded and uncaring of their impending doom slowly and calmly approaching them. He watched as one rider calmly rode his horse with lance levelled, spearing a man in the back and launching him forward by sheer force. The lance broke and the man flopped to the ground, unmoving and broken.

"Canter!" Two hundred yards and the horses began to pick up the pace, the dry ground kicking up a cloud of dust behind them. He felt his cloak beginning to billow with the increasing wind, the sweat from his brow cooling swiftly and drying leaving him feeling sticky and dirty. He gripped his lance, feeling the strength of the haft in his fingers as he mentally counted down the time to signal the charge. He could hear the jangling of armour and weapons as the horses picked up speed, champing at the bit to fly off into the gallop and the charge. He turned to his right and saw Erallac, grimly holding onto his reins for dear life but matching his pace. Looking beyond him he saw the men of the right squadron matching them step for step, their discipline and training coming to the fore as the Cardavians bore down on their unsuspecting enemy with a professionalism that was jealously guarded.

"Charge!" The distance had closed and Beran touched his heels to his horse, looking for an enemy and focussing on one that he would take on the first pass. The horses leapt forward as they were finally given free rein to go at their full gait and pace. The hooves hammered onto the ground, his heart beat thundering in time as the hooves smashed again and again. He could feel the wind rushing past his ears, the noise terrific as it combined with his pulse that drowned out all else.

Time seemed to move slowly, the charge seeming to take an inordinate amount of time. He watched his target, his enemy, slowly turnabout in the saddle. He saw the face of the man, the first emotion obviously one of battle lust and joy. It slowly turned into one of his surprise, his mouth forming a perfect O as he realised that there was a new and deadly threat. Then there was horror as he tried to shout out. Finally, there was shock as the lance Beran carried was thrust through his body, throwing him bodily backwards to land in the dirt.

Beran was through, time suddenly catching up with an alacrity that disturbing. The lance Beran had been carrying had turned into little more than a splinter and he threw it away to his left, in the same movement drawing out the long cavalry sabre from his left hip.

He sighted another man and pushed through, careful to avoid hitting any of the civilians who were still running about and trying to find safety. The cavalrymen of the Wolves were everywhere, chasing down the raiders who had dispersed into a bloody chaos. A raider, braver than most, tried charging straight at him and he found himself swiftly having to change target and tack. Beran kicked his heels into his horse and closed the distance as he hurtled headlong towards him on the mans right side. He counted in his head again, trying to breath calmly through his nose and not becoming overly excited. He needed to maintain his discipline.

He noticed the raider was shouting something but it was lost above the rest of the noise, but he knew that it wouldn't be anything other than the usual obscenities. The distance closed and Beran suddenly nudged his horse quickly, shifting his position in the saddle unexpectedly so that he was now attacking the man on his left. The man didn't have time to register the change nor to try and defend himself as Beran stood in the saddle, bring his sword hard down upon his head and cleaving through the helmet and into the skull. There was a gory explosion of brain matter and gore, some of it covering Beran as rushed past.

He held tightly onto his reins and pulled his horse to a stop, the hooves flying into the air as his steed fought him as it tried to maintain speed. He regained control as he maintained his seat, scanning the sight once more. There was no resistance, nothing even closely resembling it, as the Wolves darted in amongst their prey like their namesake did so easily. It was then he became aware that he was alone, that Erallac hadn't managed to keep up with him. Initially he wanted to chuckle thinking that the man had finally lost control of his horse and fallen off. Almost as suddenly as the thought appeared he dismissed it, a cold feeling of dread steeling over him. He quickly scanned the field again, trying to see if the giant man was standing anywhere and bellowing out his hatred at the retreating raiders. He could see nothing.

The feeling of dread now threatened to engulf him, the rare feeling of panic beginning to well in his breast as he looked around desperately. He pushed his horse forward again at the trot, forgetting everything else around him. The battle was win, and in any case Inalad would be able to mop up any surviving raiders and, hopefully, take a few prisoners. These were secondary thoughts though as he desperately sought one of his oldest friends, a man whom he considered like an older brother as well as a mentor.

It was then he saw the chestnut horse chewing at the grass next to a figure slumped on the ground. He kicked his horse into a gallop to close the short distance, fear chewing at him as he looked upon the still figure. He closed the distance, knowing that it took seconds but feeling like it took a lifetime. He was not used to being scared, but terror lapped at him and he felt physically sick.

"Erallac!" He shouted out, his voice angry sounding as he tried to cover his nerves. He jumped off his horse and ran the last few steps, discarding his bloodied sword onto the dry grass as he fell onto his knees. He turned the body over and looked down at his friend, tears suddenly welling into his eyes as he looked upon the wounds. Two bolts had hammered into his chest, something that would have pitched even the best horseman onto the dirt. One had torn through the mail and padded armour that his friend wore, the blood coming from the wound a bright red colour and frothing indicating that a lung had been punctured. Beran tried to apply pressure to the wound causing Erallac to wake up suddenly, eyes wide as he roared out in pain before subsiding into coughing. Blood was welling in his mouth and Beran knew there would be another wound.

"Just you fucking stay away, Erallac. Don't bloody well fall asleep!" Beran desperately shouted for a medic or anyone to come over and help, but his words were falling on deaf ears. "Stay with me Erallac!"

"It hurts like a bastard, Ban."

"I know, brother, but we'll get a doctor and you'll be better. Just need to get you to the fort. You'll be in bed before you know it."

"You always were a shit liar," Erallac said with the ghost of a smile. He tried to laugh but he began coughing again, the blood pouring freely from the chest wound as well as the other by the abdomen. "Never liked cavalry anyway. One of the bastards hit me with a spear on the way down."

"We chased them off. You took part in your first charge." Beran said, trying to desperately make light of the situation. He vainly tried to hold onto the chest, trying to maintain some sort of pressure so that the man didn't choke on his own blood.

"You think there's anything after this?" Erallac asked, his eyes glazing over and focussing on something behind Beran.

"I hope so, brother." Beran replied, but it was too late. Erallac, one of the heroes of Nepriner, was dead.

Chapter Fourteen – **Rough Handover**

The remaining vanguard of the legion had reached the crest of the hill where they could see the aftermath of the skirmish, the grim spectacle of destroyed carts and wagons greeting them. There was a foul reek of filth, smoke and burnt clothing. Death hung in the air and the carrion birds circled greedily overhead. She shuddered, remembering all too well similar scenes of destruction in Nepriner. Memories which she had thought supressed, or at least alleviated, flooded back to her. It was then she had seen Beran kneeling on the ground next to a body.

Her heart had lurched in her chest, remembering when he had been seriously wounded when the north gate had fallen during the siege and his body had been carried into the field hospital she manned. She had nursed him back to health then, but as soon as he had felt better he had went off to carry out his duty. Now he had carried out that duty again and was kneeling on the ground. Her head felt light, a sudden onrush of noise seeming to overwhelm her senses as she had kicked her horse into a gallop. Men of her bodyguard unit had yelled out at her to stop, unsure of whether it was safe or not, and scrambled to catch up with her. The main body of the legion continued to tramp onwards, their professionalism and training taking over.

She was a good rider and dismounted swiftly as she pulled the horse to a stop, running up to Beran and holding onto his shoulders. He looked up at her, tears welling in his eyes before looking once more down at the body on the dirt. It was only then she looked down, gasping as the shock of recognition struck her as she saw Erallac was dead. The man had seemed indomitable, full of life and strong beyond measure. No he was dead, never to know love again or the feel of the wind on his face or the joy of a kiss. His eyes were shut now and his face looked almost peaceful, that half mocking smile he wore on his face still vaguely there.

"Ban…I'm so sorry." She was at a loss as to what to say. She remembered when she had first met the man during the siege. She had been concerned about Beran at the time, knowing that he had been on the wall day after day and night after night exhausting himself. She had gone to the barracks where they had been stationed in the north east corner of the city and came across a man called Trent, another who had been killed eventually during the siege, who had shown her the way into the officers' mess. She had walked past Erallac then, seeing him for the first time as the gruff and brash soldier who was more used to speak to fellow legionaries than women. However, her first judgement of the man had been wrong and she had grown to love the older man in her own way. He was shy and used his height and strength to hide that natural quietness, but it was a front and when she had looked beyond the surface she had realised what a warm and funny character he had been.

"He had a punctured lung, Talice. He didn't need to die. Not over a fucking skirmish. Not after bloody Nepriner." Her cavalry escort raced up and surrounded the kneeling General and his wife, and she realised that the tears that had threatened to overtake her husband before had now disappeared. Appearances must be seen to be kept no matter what hurt a man felt; a leader must not be seen to cry. He stood up and tore off his cloak and covered the fallen body of his friend with as much respect as he could. She watched him, knowing that he was working automatically and not allowing his brain or his heart to think or feel too deeply about the situation.

"You!" He roared at a merchant who had finally come out from underneath a wagon. The man looked startled, fearful almost, as he looked swiftly around for whom the General could be speaking. With a look of horror he realised it was himself and, for a brief moment, Talice thought the man was going to run. Beran must have thought the same for he walked towards the man until he was within arm's reach, close enough to be threatening if need be but not enough to overly domineering. "Who were these men and why the fuck did that Legion not come out?"

The man looked blank, a look of incomprehension across his face as the words were spat out at him. He muttered something and Beran cursed loudly once more and strode away, looking towards the fort with hate in his eyes.

"Trooper," he said pointing to a cavalryman. "Find Commander Aglon and tell him I need him here now."

"What's wrong?" Talice said slowly approaching him. She wanted to take him into her arms there and then and reassure him that everything would be alright, but she knew it would be a lie and that he wouldn't appreciate it.

"What isn't bloody wrong?" He said swiftly, anger flashing briefly. He fixed his eyes on her as recognition struck him, his words hammering into him like body blows as he looked upon her face. He felt regret, his shoulders sagging visibly for a few seconds. "I'm sorry Talice, that wasn't right. This isn't your fault and I shouldn't take it out on you." He took a deep breath and expelled it slowly, collecting his thoughts. "It seems the caravan belongs to the Southern Coalition. No idea what kingdom or princedom, but they don't speak the common tongue anyway."

"This Aglon speaks it?" She asked having never met the man properly.

"Bloody hope so, he was based down here for long enough." Beran looked around and the cavalry officer, Inalad, came up and made a brief report. Casualties were apparently light, a few walking wounded with minor cuts and bruises, but nothing major. Beran nodded, somewhat relieved, and relayed the news of the death of Erallac. He detailed him off to find a cart, preferably one that wasn't fire damaged, and have the contents transferred to another so that his body could be placed in it. The man nodded, saluted, and walked off shouting out orders as he went.

"You are Luca, aren't you?" Beran asked a soldier of the bodyguard that Talice had. The man nodded, blanching slightly at being suddenly addressed by name by his commanding officer. It was a simple fact, Talice had realised swiftly, that the men in the lower ranks somehow thought they were anonymous because there were that many of them.

"I am, sir," the man said saluting swiftly. He dismounted out of respect, feeling it unwise to be sat on a horse whilst his commanding officer was walking.

"Good. I need you to go and find Commander Velawin. Tell him to have the Legion brought up into battle order. I want the baggage train at the rear and the men ready to storm that fort within the next two hours." The man nodded and mounted again, inwardly and silently cursing at having dismounted in the first place and sped off. Beran turned around and stared hard at the fort as if trying to discern answers to his questions just by looking at the walls.

"What are you thinking, Ban?" Talice asked standing alongside him. She had watched it all, seeing Beran go from mourning to commanding the situation again. There couldn't be any sign of weakness, any sign of emotion, and she knew that would be hard for him. There was, however, the faint signs of anger again creeping into his eyes. His brow was becoming more furrowed, the eyebrows becoming lower and the jaw becoming more set.

"I want to know why that bastard never released his cavalry when there was a caravan under attack. I want to know why, more importantly, that there hasn't been any sign of life from that fort since we arrived here."

"Do you think it's empty?" She asked, looking at the wall and trying to make out the tell-tale sign of sentries keeping watching. She could see banners displaying the colours of Cardavy, and she could make out a few others that she presumed were the colours unique to the legion. She liked that about the Cardavian military and knew that her own people in the Republic had adopted similar, the Wolves wore Grey and the Marshal legion under the command of her brother in law, Dunwal, wore blue. It helped to differentiate between bodies of men in battle so that they could be rewarded, or punished, according to their behaviour.

"I wouldn't think so," he said slowly as he considered the point. "The borders have been quiet, to my knowledge, for a generation or so now. Anyway, it'd take a huge army to take a properly fortified position. That fort is made of stone, it's not a temporary one like a marching camp.

Cardavians may lose pitched battles…very rarely…but they never lose fortifications." He finished it with a note of pride, looking upon her as the afternoon sun reflected off her red hair. It shimmered, darker colours blending into lighter as the hair framed her face.

"Then why do you think they didn't come out?"

"No idea, Tal, but I intend to find out. I'll have the raiders corpses examined as well for any papers if I damn well have to, that's if Inalad hasn't already got men doing so."

"But isn't marching against the fort a bit aggressive?"

"Probably, but I've always found the direct approach works best," he said with a grim smile. He looked back and she did likewise, seeing the Wolves deploy from line of column to their battle formation. From a birds' eye view, and she had been lucky to see it during a mass exercise once from the top of a hilltop during the march south, she knew that the formations in front line would overlap those in the second and third only slightly. It was like looking down upon a massive parallelogram of well trained and professional killers.

The commander Aglon came up on a borrowed horse and, to the surprise of Talice for he was an infantryman, managed to ride with some grace. He dismounted and looked upon the body of Erallac being carried as gracefully as possible into a cart. He removed his helmet swiftly out of respect and made the sign of his Gods before putting the headgear back on, carrying out a salute almost in the same movement.

"You wanted me, sir?"

"Aye. Speak to the merchant there," Beran said indicating the merchantman being guarded by two Wolves, "I want you to find out who he is, where he's going, why he was attacked and who is in that bloody fort."

"Anything else?"

"I think that's enough, Aglon, don't you?"

"Sir," the man said. He walked off and began his questioning, speaking in the language that sounded harsh to the ears of the Cardavians gathered. Beran had never been particularly good at foreign languages, Talice knew, and it was a conscience effort on her part to speak the common, otherwise known as the Cardavian tongue, whenever she was near him. She didn't find it hard being proficient in several languages for, as the daughter of a Senator, it was often expected that she would attend official parties of embassies where she would be expected to mingle. She had tried in vain to teach Beran another tongue, but he would always grin in the cheeky way he did and suggest other uses for their respective tongues.

"What are you thinking?" He asked suddenly, noticing the slight reddening of her cheeks.

"Well," she said with a slight smile deciding that some crude honesty would lighten up the situation slightly, "I know their language a little, we've had some of the Coalition princes up in Attainia before. My father entertained them in Nepriner as part of their delegation."

"Aye? I had no idea."

"No, well, you never asked," she said with a smile. "Anyway, I was just thinking we could try and resume your lessons in language if we are to live here for a while. You may as well learn how to speak to the neighbours." He smiled genuinely, one full of warmth as he reached out and put an arm around her slim waist. She knew he considered briefly about pulling her towards him, but covered in gore as he was he probably didn't want to ruin the pale grey dress that she wore.

"Are you okay, Ban?"

"No," he replied simply. "I will be, but I need time. He was a bloody good friend, and I'll drink to his memory, but for just now I need to put it to the back of my mind no matter how much it pains me." She nodded, unsure of what to say and not wishing to intrude any further on his feelings. Beran was a proud man and he couldn't afford to let the façade crumble. There was a silence between them, each wrapped up in their own thoughts that was only broken by the approaching Aglon.

"Sir?" The man asked unsure as to whether he was intruding on a private moment. With a degree of reluctance Beran withdrew the arm from around the waist of Talice and nodded for Aglon to make his report. "Seems sir that you were right, they are from Ufwala and Queen Wellisa. Trade caravan coming out of Vitrossy carrying iron and other materials for the Cardavian armouries in Silveroak. They say that the fort, to their knowledge, is fully manned by a Cardavian legion. They also claim that robbers and highwaymen have been rife on this road since the fall of the northern section of the Southern Coalition, since Wellisa usurped the thrones and started building her own nation."

"Have they suffered any casualties?" Beran asked, looking over the shoulder of Aglon towards the merchant man.

"A few, sir, and their horses are dead. They have no idea how they are going to transport their wares to Silveroak."

"Brilliant," Beran said with an exasperated sigh. "Tell them when I've spoken to the forts commander that they can have draught horses from there, failing that, we'll second some from Noriandie. They will also be compensated for their losses. Tell them as well, in fact promise them, that I'll inform Wellisa what has happened." The man nodded and walked off again to be replaced by Velawin and Aleill, the three of them being the last surviving senior officers of Nepriner. She suddenly missed Dunwal, the brother of Beran, and wondered how he was doing. He was often the voice of reason, the logical one that would help calm Beran and make sure he didn't launch himself into destruction. She could have done with him then. Velawin was the first to speak, his eyes fixed on the fort.

"Erallac?" He asked.

"He died, brother. Two bolts in the chest, one that pierced a lung, and a spear thrust through the abdomen. He wouldn't have survived, and if he did then he'd have been finished as a soldier."

"I'll miss the old bastard," Aleill said quietly. Talice looked at him and knew the words to be true. He was, perhaps, the greatest conundrum amongst the three of them. When Trent had been killed, Aleill, who had previously never had a good word to say about the man publicly, had fallen into a pit of depression that had only been alleviated by the constant battles and skirmishes with the Rupinian and Imperial forces. She also knew that Aleill liked to use cutting remarks, not designed to be harmful, but simply as his way of identifying with others. With Aleill, she found, the more he tried to insult you then the more he liked you and respected you. The battle of wits that often happened between Aleill and Erallac were subject to legend.

"What's the plan then, Ban?" Vel asked, ever the professional. He was very similar to Beran, the two of them could have been carved from the same rock and were brothers in all but blood. Vel was the fitter and could fight for days on end, but Beran was the leader. They both recognised each other's strengths and helped to alleviate any supposed weakness, and because of that they were two of the finest men that Talice knew. If it hadn't been for them, she knew, then Nepriner would have fallen and she'd have been a prisoner of the Emperor by now.

"I'm going to make some new friends," Beran said.

"He's going to lose his temper, he means." Aleill interjected with a grim smile, staring towards the fort.

Talice had only ever seen Beran this angry once or twice and both of those occasions had been during the siege of Nepriner. She knew that her husband had a temper, what soldier didn't? It was something that he struggled to control on a daily basis sometimes, but it was not something she had ever been on the receiving end of. She knew she'd have been able to handle him, for Beran in a rage would never hit a woman nor harm a child. He would rage and bluster, shout probably, but he'd never lay a finger on her. No, when it came to Talice during their rare arguments, she knew Beran would sooner take himself out the room and away before he lost it at her. Now, however, he was not thinking.

The brief and bloody skirmish had cost him the life of one of his dearest friends, a man whom he had shed blood with and loved. A man whom he called brother. The bonds of friendship that the two men had built up over the years had been born in circumstances that few men could ever comprehend. They had shared experiences and shared facets of each other's character that few other people would ever see. They had seen each other at their very best and at their very worst. She was rather envious, in a good way, of the bonds of comradeship that Beran had built up between himself and the men of the legion. Now, though, she knew the price of that love. Beran was hurting.

He was on horseback now before the gatehouse of the stone fort looking upwards, the standard bearer beside him on his right and Velawin on his left. Aleill was beside her with the main body, his archers ready at the forefront ready to pour fire onto the fort if they dared to offer any defiance or resistance. She shuddered, unsure of how to feel. She knew Beran was out for blood, and she was sure that he would get that blood or retribution somehow.

"Open the gates!" He roared, his voice carrying on the wind. The rain that threatened to break earlier came lashing down now, the wind throwing it in such a way that, no matter what way a person turned, they were forever exposed. Aleill had, rather gallantly she thought, offered her the use of his cloak. She had refused, not willing to let the archer freeze to death on her account. He had, in turn, argued the point and claimed that he had another cloak. She finally relented and took up his offer and, a few minutes later, was feeling the benefits. Aleill, true to his word, had managed to get a cloak from the baggage train of a shabbier quality. She felt a little bad, but the warmth and comfort of the rich lining and proper fur put paid to such regrets.

She watched the gatehouse and prayed that somebody would pop their head over the parapet before Beran ordered the men to storm the walls. She had no idea whether the men of the Wolves carried ropes with hooks where they could ascend the walls, or even whether they had ladders that would make their progress even easier. If it was a full legion in there, would the Wolves even be successful? She remembered Beran once telling her that an attacking force besieging a place generally needed a three to one advantage, surely here their numbers were on par.

"Open the bloody gates!" Beran roared again, his voice louder and angrier. He turned and said something to Velawin, lost on the wind, and the man nodded. The wind picked up and the weather continued to become more foul, the rain unceasing as it turned the ground in the surrounding area into a quagmire.

"We'll need to make up our minds soon," Aleill said quietly as he interrupted her thoughts. "This rain, I don't care how good my archers are, they'll struggle with this wind and rain."

"Do you think we will advance, Aleill?" She asked, worried suddenly. She knew the killing powers of the legion, and Beran's talk of three to one odds continued to hammer through her mind.

"Well," he said with a grin suddenly appearing on his face, "I won't be, and neither will you. The lads will though." He said it in a flippant manner, and if it weren't for the fact she knew Aleill well then she would have thought him callous, but she knew different.

She looked to the gatehouse again and was almost relieved to see a head pop out from the parapet; more reassuringly wearing a Cardavian helmet meaning the fort hadn't fallen or been abandoned. Still, she thought, why hadn't they come out to aid the caravan? Beran was shouting something at the man, his back to her now and the wind whipping away his words. Eventually the sentry scurried off, evidently off to get someone higher up the pay scale who could afford to open the fort.

After an interminable wait where the only noise heard was the lashing rain and the howling wind, the gates finally opened. Beran nudged his horse forward swiftly followed by Velawin and the Standard Bearer. Aglon, just to her rear, bellowed out a loud order that sent the men forward. Their weapons were unsheathed and shields were presented as if they were advancing upon an enemy fortification. The archers opened up gaps in their ranks automatically as the heavy infantry, the backbone of any Cardavian legion moved forward. The discipline, she had to concede, was immense. She could hear a few grumbles from the men about the weather, a few more complaining about the mud, and one voice complaining about how he would have to clean his kit once they went to their quarters. She had to smile.

"So what do we do now?" She asked Aleill as she watched the infantry moving into the fort. All that was left on the plain were the cavalry and archers, and on the road was the trade caravan still awaiting its fresh horses so they could get underway again.

"We sit and wait, I suppose, until the infantry is inside. Then I'll take my men and man the parapets."

"What about the cavalry?"

"What about them?"

"Well, won't they advance?"

"Wouldn't be much use in there, Talice." She nodded and considered his words, lightning briefly illuminating the plain. She counted at least ten seconds before the rumble of thunder. The infantry in front of her, in shadow as they were with their armour glistening from the rain, looked like something taken straight from history. It had an almost ethereal feel to it, as if events were being played out on a stage where the actors were ambivalent to what the audience thought or said.

"I've never been one for waiting," she said suddenly. Aleill looked at her and shook his head, knowing exactly what she was thinking.

"You can't go in, Talice, it could be dangerous." There was a real concern in his voice, something mirrored in his eyes as well.

"You forget Aleill," she said gently with a smile, "I'm a daughter of a Senator and I outrank you." She touched heels to her horse and made her way into the camp, determined to be at the side of her husband before he got himself into a fight.

Beran pushed his horse through aware of thousands of eyes upon him. There was no doubt in his mind that the garrison was fully manned, that there were no significant issues preventing them from launching even a small cavalry squadron to try and stop raiders from harassing caravans as they passed through the borders region. There was nothing, in short, that struck him as out of the ordinary. As far as he could tell the fort was in a good state, the accommodation looked sturdy and well maintained and there was even smoke belching out from the armouries despite the rain and the wind. Why had they not done so?

Cardavian forts were of a uniform pattern anywhere, particularly those that had been laid down for a while and he therefore instinctively knew where to go. He was heading straight for headquarters, angered at the deliberate insult of the legions General. The man, unless he was stupid, blatantly knew that his relief was approaching. Furthermore, the sentry that didn't report the fact that a caravan was being attacked wasn't worth his salt. More so, the sentry that didn't report in quick time that a large body of armed men had appeared outside the gates and were preparing themselves for a battle should be hung. No, he thought, this smacked of a deliberate insult.

He looked to the headquarters building and couldn't even see a delegation waiting to receive him, not a single legionary nor officer. He tried to think desperately as to who the General was, whether he had wronged him or annoyed him at a point previous to this. His mind was drawing a blank, not able to picture the man nor what his name was. He may have been informed at some point, but the sheer shock of the lack of discipline and respect being paid to him was clouding his judgement.

There was an angry muttering behind him like a thousand buzzing bees and he knew that the Wolves were entering in their droves.

"What are your thoughts, Ban?" Velawin asked, hideously aware of the fact that his back presented a broad and welcoming target to any loose arrows or bolts. It was an unwelcome feeling to be in the middle of a

Cardavian camp and having to worry about such things, something he never thought would actually occur. He too was curious, however, to know why the Stags were more than happy to allow raiders to cross the border. He didn't care for the loss of material or even the apparent injured pride that Cardavy might suffer, but he did care about the professionalism of the legions. Let one transgression go past and you'd eventually let them all. "I have no idea what to think, but something is wrong here. Could you imagine the likes of Dunwal, or even the likes of old Ironside standing aside whilst civilians were being butchered?" Vel shook his head though he understood that the question was rhetorical. "Do you know who commands here?"

"Can't remember," Vel said after wracking his brain for a few seconds. "I can't say I've heard much about the Stags either."

"New legion, I gather, from what Aglon was telling me. Full of the mad, the bad and the sad as well as any other outcasts from other legions." It was sad fact of life that there were plenty of men that were willing to pull on a uniform and look good in it, but when it came to actual soldiering and deployment they tended to find an injury of some sort. Rather than waste wages, Vel thought, those in the higher echelons had decided to pull them into one legion where the region would be quiet.

"Could be the reason they didn't march out then?"

"Could be, but that's one hell of a ballsy call if that's the case." They reached the headquarters building and Beran dismounted, looking up into the orange lights that were being cast from the glass windows. It may have been mid-afternoon, but with the dark clouds and torrential rain it may as well have been closer to midnight. He hadn't seen a downpour like this in years and put it down to being near the coast and a mountain range. Vel dismounted, dripping wet and sodden as he was, and brushed down his cloak and rearranged his weaponry.

"Ready?" Beran asked.

"I really think we need to think of something to say before we go in there, brother. If we go in shouting and throwing accusations, then they are liable to do something stupid." Beran nodded even as he watched the archers from the Wolves file into the fort and begin taking up positions on the wall. More worryingly, Talice was slowly guiding her horse towards him. He felt a rush of anger for a moment believing that her action would put her life, and his potentially, in danger. He fought it down with a deep breath knowing that she was just wanting to be by his side, potentially proving a soothing balm to his foul mood. At any rate, he thought, he was pleased to see that her bodyguard unit were staying close to her.

"I'll find out who their commanding officer is, find out why they haven't done anything, and probably kick out the legion," Beran said eventually.

"They'll take that as an insult," Velawin said in warning.

"They probably will, but then they can't do anything about it. I'll have a report drawn up afterwards and a fast rider to take the dispatch straight to Silveroak detailing there duplicity in the murder of merchants and the death of Erallac." Velawin looked at his friend for a few moments and knew there would be no persuading him otherwise. What troubled him further was the fact that there appeared no other option. The fort certainly wasn't big enough for two legions and, with the bad blood that existed between them now, fights were liable to break out if they were to wait for the weather to improve. It was a damned unfortunate situation.

"Will you be taking Talice in with you?" He asked eventually as he looked up at her. She had a concerned look upon her face as she surveyed the scene before them. Some of the men wearing green cloaks belonging to the Stags were freely moving and talking happily to the grey cloaked Wolves, but there was an undercurrent feeling of violence and tension hanging in the air. It wouldn't take much for the entire situation to blow up, one false word or one slight gesture and the two legions would be upon each other in a massive brawl.

"It's probably for the best, at least that way she'll be safe." Beran said, almost as if reading the thoughts of Velawin. Talice looked in askance for a few seconds as she wondered whether she should ask if she had a choice, but thought the better of it. In a situation as fraught as this there was no need to question the moral authority of the commanding officer no matter how close they were. Beran nodded once as if resolving his own mind, checked his weapons as he did before every fight and strode inside.

He was immediately struck by a wall of warmth, the fire in the hearth strong and welcoming. There was the fine scent of roasting meats and vegetables coming from the kitchens somewhere and the sound of noisy chatter coming from elsewhere. He looked around bewildered as he saw luxuries beyond what was normally seen in any headquarters, let alone any legion fort. There were rich tapestries on the wall depicting military glories from the past, none of which involved the Stags he noticed. The candelabras were proper gold and not just painted in such a colour. The walls had been painted a rich and deep blue colour, an expense in itself, whilst the staircases had obviously been removed and replaced with rich walnut and inlaid with silver decoration.

"They must have a bloody good quartermaster," remarked Velawin flippantly.

"They've become a glorified gang of bloody highwaymen," Beran whispered. He was disgusted at the display of wealth, the grandeur almost decadent and entirely unsuited to a military garrison. He appreciated that places needed to have their own home comforts, but when the curtains were made out of heavy silk and the rugs were thick and heavy over well varnished wooden floors then there was something going on. He was not ascetic, but nor was he decadent and hedonistic. He believed that a garrison and, more importantly a legion, should behave and look the part. So far, as far as he could make out, the Stags couldn't even look it let alone act it!

"What now? I still don't see any…" Vel stumbled to silence as a steward opened two sets of large swinging doors carrying a large silver dish where several cooked meats were mounted. Beran glared at the man, tempted to reach out and grab him and demand to know what was going on. He decided against it at the last second, fighting to retain his calm.

"Steward?" The man spun in shock and surprise, something the two men of the Wolves found strange.

"Yes, sir?" He asked, his voice quavering slightly through the exertion of carrying so much hot food.

"Where is the officer commanding this legion?" Velawin asked. He watched Beran slowly move over to the kitchen doors and open one slightly, the smells of fresh food escaping as soon as the door was even nudged open. Velawin felt his stomach growl and twist, his hunger suddenly flashing forward and alerting him that he hadn't eaten since the early morning prior to the march.

"They are preparing for their tea, sir."

"Early scran, is it?" Beran asked, watching as another servant brought forth a plate of boiled and roasted potatoes. Beran nodded at the man to stand next to the other steward though he felt his mouth filling with saliva at the displays of food on offer.

"Pardon, sir?" The man asked incredulous.

"Early scran?" The man still looked non-plussed. "Come, you must know what scran means. Everybody knows what scran bloody means! This is the legion, right?"

"I'm afraid, sir, that the gentlemen don't use such parlance." The servant tried not to bring a sneer to his face and nearly succeeded, but he had been unfortunately blessed to have one. Talice saw the look and lightly touched the arm of Beran, emotionally pulling him back. The steward was grateful to the lady even if he couldn't verbalise it.

"Is the officer commanding this legion in that mess hall through there?" Velawin asked finally.

"They are down the hallway to the right, and then one turn to the left sir down another corridor. If you follow me, sir, then I'd be quite happy to show you."

"Amount of bloody noise they were making I could have sworn they were next door," Beran said. As if on cue there was a crash of glass from somewhere, possibly either expensive wine glasses or several bottles of the same, crashing to the ground. There was wild cheering and at least four men shouting in what sounded like triumph. "No, you wait there one second. Velawin, go out and get the bodyguard of Talice and bring them in here. I want them taking up position in this hallway. Find another one hundred men and divide them, I want fifty outside at each of the exits and another fifty with us. We'll find out what's happening in this rats' nest."

General Feron Rinian was drunk and happy, he was starving right enough, but he was happy nonetheless. There was always a cause for celebration in the fort and today was no different, for tomorrow they would be relieved and then he'd finally be on his way back to the capital. It had taken a few favours being called in, but at least he could reassure himself with not being transferred to the Attainian front. The last thing he wanted after managing to save so much money over the last couple of years would be to die in some foreign battlefield for some jumped up foreign bastards. He knew they looked down their noses at Cardavians everywhere. He knew Cardavians looked down their noses on him especially, even his own officers sometimes, because of his Coalition blood. His mood grew darker suddenly as he thought about it, once more blaming his father for sticking his prick in the first damned woman he saw. The man was a bloody fool. He grew quickly to anger and hurled a goblet at a passing servant, a good throw striking the man in the temple and felling him like a tree. The tray full of glasses he was carrying crashed to the ground, the delicate vessels shattering into a thousand pieces. Loud cheering greeted it, sycophantic in the extreme, but he liked it all the same and grinned widely again. He was loved. He knew he was loved. He'd go to Silveroak, begin some proper investments and then go into politics. Fuck the legion, what did he owe them anyway? He'd get rich, get into power and screw himself into oblivion.

"A toast!" His second, Khimin, roared out as he stood. "A toast to our brave commanding officer, who will take us away from this arsehole of a place back to where the Stags belong! To home!" A dozen throaty voices echoed him, their glasses slamming into the air and sending some of the contents spilling into the wooden floorboards again.

Feron stood and soaked in their praised, basking in it like some sort of returning prodigal son after an incredible journey. He was all smiles, a grin splitting his face from ear to ear as he looked upon his officers. He reached down and picked up another goblet that a steward had placed on the table, drinking deeply from the silver vessel. The wine was an expensive red, the scent a heady mixture of berries and plums. He didn't care, really, but it was the type of bullshit he realised he needed to know when he went to

Silveroak. He stood and awaited silence, the cheering and laughter slowly coming to a halt.

"Gentlemen," he was able to say eventually as he held his left palm up for silence. "Gentlemen, we have worked hard over these last few months," laughter greeted this, "but now we go back to Silveroak for our reward. Our reliefs will be here tomorrow morning and then we shall be away by the afternoon..." He stumbled to silence as the doors crashed open, half expecting to see a drunk steward stumbling through the doors carrying yet another dish.

Instead there was a man of medium height wearing a Generals regalia and the new armour of a cavalryman, his face crimson with rage, and a grey cloak around his shoulders. The man was approaching him, the silence in the room total as more legionaries filled in and took up position around the room. There was a dark muttering from the officers' present, but they were caught completely off guard. What could they do anyway even if they did have weapons? Most of them were drunk, and the others had neglected their duties on the training field that much that they would present more of a danger to themselves with steel in their hands rather than some adversary. The man continued walking towards him with his left hand resting on the pommel of his sword. The helmet he wore with the nose guard and metal coif almost gave him a demonic look. The chainmail around his body was made less loose with the addition of a broad brown leather belt around the waist on which a sword hung as well as a curious small crossbow, a bandolier hung around the chest containing a series of deadly looking bolts. The thick cloak he wore around his shoulders were made from wolf pelt, grey in colour, and held in black with a thick silver chain upon two broaches.

A thought struck him and he suddenly felt himself becoming worryingly sober, the happy feeling of the drink leaving his body in an instant and filling him with a sense of vulnerability instead. It appeared almost that the man was the only one in the room, that nobody could affect his path. He felt fear then, real fear that he hadn't felt in years. He tried to muster as much dignity as he could as the man finally came to a stop before him, the eyes cold and loathing as they looked him up and down as if he were on parade. He knew he was being inspected, he felt as if the entirety of his sins from the last few years were being laid open as if in book format. "Just who the fuck do you..." he managed to finally stammer out before being brought to a halt, a single finger being raised that commanded silence. The man shook his head, allowing the rest of his men to file into the room. They had taken up position now throughout, each man with his sword out in his right and shield presented in their left. Had the fort been taken? They looked like Cardavians, and they wore the colours of

Cardavians, but so far none of them had spoken. He didn't even recognise this man in front of him. Another came forward, athletically built and dressed in similar armour but darkened to a dark grey colour. The chainmail looked lighter, more expensive looking, and he carried enough weaponry to open his own armoury if need be. He took up position next to the man who held up his finger who finally spoke.

"Who are you?" It was a Cardavian accent and relief flooded through him instantly, the fear being replaced by a mixture of different emotions. Was this some sort of sick joke, a prank that had gone too far? Had his crimes finally been found out? Was this a mutiny? Ultimately he felt his anger building at the fact that someone had ruined his party, put a pall on an otherwise good night.

"I should be asking you that damned question!" He snarled, his voice stronger than he thought his nerves would allow. He placed his hands on the table to steady the shaking in them, desperate almost to have a drink.

"You probably ought to have done it first. Now, I won't ask my question again. Who are you?" It was simply said, but it was the sheer simplicity of the words that struck terror into him anew. This was not a man who was used to brokering argument. His second, Khimin, looked at him questioningly for a few seconds and slowly, imperceptibly, began reaching for a steak knife.

"I am General Feron Rinian, officer commanding His Cardavian Majesties legion the Stags. Who are you?" The steak knife was now in a firm grip and held and he tried with his eyes to indicate that the man shouldn't do what he was blatantly thinking of doing, but the man was stupid drunk; the type who would sooner carry out an action without thinking it through and try and excuse it the next day by claiming they were under the influence.

"I am General Beran Corus, of the Grey Wolves legion. I am your relief. And General, I am not happy with what I see here." They were like hammer blows, realisation striking at him like fists in a dark alley. He had no defence, he wanted to shout and roar for the officer of the day to be brought before him for not reporting that there a was a legion approaching. He locked eyes with that officer, drunk as he was and asleep where he sat oblivious to the events taking place around him. "General, why is your garrison as rich as it is?"

"What do you mean?" His second jumped up, steak knife raised. Velawin slapped him with the back of his hand sending him sprawling to the table, striking his head as he did so and falling unconscious.

"That's assault," Beran said, almost in the same manner as someone would say 'that's rain'.

"I don't understand what is going on," Feron countered.

"No, I don't think that is true. I put it to you, Feron, that you are a damned traitor. I put it to you that you are working in collusion with the traitors, highwaymen and other vagrants in territories hereabouts that have been attacking caravans. I put it to you, sir, that because of your action one of my men were killed in the defence of a caravan that was being attacked this morning just outside your bloody walls." Beran took a breath for the words had built up a pace of their own as the charges came pouring out, his accent becoming thicker and angrier sounding. "What say you?"

"Prove it," Feron countered as bravely as he could. There was guilt in his eyes, he knew, but all the man opposite had to go on was circumstantial evidence. Feron was honest enough to admit that he had a lot of faults, but he wasn't stupid.

"That's the beauty of it, I can't. You will be sent home in disgrace though for gross incompetence, that I can prove. You willingly allowed a caravan to be attacked outside the fort walls that caused the deaths of several civilians as well as one of my men. A dispatch will be sent to Silveroak where, I believe, your legion will be heading. You will leave now and vacate this fort. Handovers to be complete by early evening whereupon, if you aren't out this damned garrison, I'll have you forcibly removed. Do I make myself clear?"

"But it's close to early evening now, my men…"

"I suggest you stop gawping like a fish a then and get moving." There was no argument, no waiting for a counter argument or suggestion. Beran Corus walked off, the room emptying of men suddenly as they went to their sections to tell them to pack quickly. Suddenly Feron was alone, his dreams of his future greatness and ventures into politics coming to a crashing stop.

But then he had cousins in the south, didn't he? His mother's family were still there. He also had one contact in the south that could help him, one he had never met true, but one high up enough that could give him and his men a hand. Why go into politics when he could have his cake and eat it? If he was going to be disgraced, and by default his men and officers too, then why not throw everything on one toss of the die. This area was ripe for rebellion anyway, he had made sure of that, and the Southern kingdoms longed to regain these lost lands. He began to think quickly, thinking of how to persuade his men and how to sneak over five thousand across the border without attracting the attention of Beran and his. Lightning flashed as the sheets of rain continued to crash against the windows, but he could make out the shape of the mountains.

He began to plan.

Chapter Fifteen – **Stronghold**

There were only two Imperial garrisons left in the country of Traemwen now, one of them on a castle which many considered to be impregnable whilst the other was within sight of Quittle and his four hundred men now. Rupinian soldiers had been pulling back from various positions over the last few weeks as more clans began to come over to the side of Quittle. Their fortunes had changed for the better after the battle with the men of Long Loch, no longer having to rely on purely guerrilla warfare to try and achieve their aims. Now they could fight pitched battles without having to put everything on one throw of the dice, pitched battles were no longer the do or die affairs that they used to be and multiple operations could take place at once. The command of the Long Loch inland fleet had given them a significant advantage over their enemies, allowing them to land with impunity on beaches up and down the area and able to deploy men where necessary. The Imperials, for all that they were immortal in pitched battle, weren't able to cope with this continual whittling down of their forces. Caravans and convoys carrying wages and food were often targeted as they went through hilly terrain and forests, caught between rocks and fallen logs before the clansmen descended upon them from above or below. Nowhere was safe for them. When the local garrison rallied, sometimes aided by pressed men from the clans they were apparently trying to defend, they would be led astray and sent on a wild goose chase. The clansmen of Traemwen would simply fade into the fog or the forests, preventing the Imperials from bringing them to battle. This was a double edged sword for it often led to reprisals against the major towns; men, women and children would often be used as hostages as guarantors of good behaviour. It was an unpopular decision, one that would often see those who had loved ones taken from them suddenly go from a neutral standpoint to one that outright favoured Quittle and his men. Villages were no longer safe havens for the garrisons or Imperial patrols, towns were becoming outright dangerous places given that they were a haven of dark alleys and side streets where Imperial soldiers, be it in bands or singly, could be tempted inside and brutally murdered.

This war of independence, Quittle knew, was not one becoming of a gentleman, but it was so far successful.

Quittle also knew from reports on the borders where Alfdarr had stationed himself that the Imperials were going to be soon on the march, that the Emperor had decided to lead the assault on his rebellious people in person to boost his flagging support. There was a real danger now, according to sympathetic spies and informants, that the Emperor would see his position for the throne challenged before the year was out if he were to lose another campaign. The defeat at Nepriner had shaken the throne, but this rebellion had torn at the very foundations of his Empire. This was not to say that the Emperor still didn't command the loyalty of thousands, and certainly vague hopes of entering into a compact with the Speirakians had come to nothing for the men of Traemwen, but in dark corners of the Imperial court there could now be heard mutterings. Why should one man, no matter how important he was, take counsel from a select group of advisors and not the lords and knights of the realm? What mandate did the Emperor have to order the gathering of so many thousands to fight and die on foreign fields? By what right, or so Quittle heard, did the Emperor have to lose grounds and lands that were rightfully theirs when other, perhaps diplomatic, options lay in front of them?

Quittle had heard it all, perhaps worried for his own position at times as well. It had been a similar argument, or at the very least a friendly debate, that he had once had with Tortag after a gathering of the clan chieftains that were loyal to them. The meeting had gone well, better than any could have hoped, and had been held in a castle that had formerly belonged to the chieftain of Long Loch but had now been turned into a permanent royal residence. It was sighted in the middle of the loch on of its innumerable islands, safely guarded by three dozen longboats and other craft from the clans.

He remembered back to a previous conversation, prior to the coronation and the three-month campaign that they had waged. He had remembered when there were only two clans out of the seventeen of Traemwen that supported him. Now he could count on ten after they had seen that the rebellion simply wasn't a flash in the pan. He didn't begrudge them for waiting back and for jumping on the back of his victories when, arguably, he didn't need their support as much. These men and women had their own people to worry about and think of, not some desperate madman who wanted to create a Kingdom and a crown from nothing. There still was, however, at least three clans that would fight him to the bitter end, and they were holding another four to ransom given their relative positions to each other. If Emperor Rhagan advanced sooner than he would have liked, then chances were he'd have to fight two pitched battles in quick succession to prevent them from linking up.

The discussion between Tor and he had been simple, with Tor suggesting that he should have his own council of followers taken from the clan chiefs. He fully recognised the need for dynamic leadership and taking charge, but he didn't truly believe anyone else in the realm had to have a say. "Too many cooks spoil the broth," was the way the clan chief described it. Quittle had argued differently, suggesting something along the lines of the Cardavian model; a country which had never had a major civil war in centuries. The power of the King was limited and parliament would debate and decide on matters, seeking ratification of their decisions from the crown. It was in this way that everybody had representation and investment in the realm as a whole. The debate had went back and forth before eventually dissolving into friendly talk of hopes and dreams for the future.

Now Quittle lay in pine needles on his stomach, looking out towards one of the last Imperial garrisons in the Traemwen. They had fallen back to a strong castle that was surrounded by a deep moat. The bridge was lowered due to it being daylight, and the tree line was several hundred yards away from the castle itself for the rest had been cleared away. He had only four hundred men with him including the two Cardavians, Grimfar and Nekstar, but he also had with him Tortag and Kiegal. Wenrynt, with his hundred men, were watching the passes and the valleys leading into this area keen to make sure that no supply columns would come through and supply the castle. They had already led one bloody ambush and any foodstuffs or wage chests that they couldn't carry off had been destroyed and scattered. The town next to the castle belonged to the men of the Broken Hill clan, named for a series of hills that had been carved like butter by a glacier during times long ago. It was a prosperous town in the south east, one of the last great ports that belonged to the Imperial forces and their allies. Shipping lay scattered in the bay as they carried their wares to and fro, but there was no trade going out. The Attainian fleet had finally come into play and were helping their erstwhile allies. He hadn't had a chance to meet their Admiral, but messages flowed to and fro so that they were in constant communication. When he had informed Grim and Nek that the man in charge of the fleet was Admiral Aarlin they had simply grinned.

The castle may have been strong, but it was not big. The garrison had swollen to ten times its original size with the regrouping of Imperial forces. There was possibly something close to five thousand men there now and they had to build a two storied barracks just outside the town limits. Quittle, at the suggestion of Kiegal, had sent in a few of the lesser known men to mingle with the locals during the previous day and night to find out what the routine was, keen to make sure that the castle only held a limited number whilst the new barracks, with its paint barely dry on the exterior walls, housed the majority of men. Importantly for the success of the mission was the good wishes of the people in the town itself, for the Broken Hill clan were one of the last neutral clans that could affect properly the conduct of the war. They were also strong well-wishers, he had to grant, but then they were hardly in a position to actually do anything given that they were under occupation. He hoped by destroying the Imperials hereabouts and, affecting an Attainian landing, that the two would declare for him and Traemwen.

He was lost in his thoughts, watching the castle and the movements of the sentries upon the parapets. He could make out the flag of the Empire at this distance as well as carts moving through the gate. He had a good idea of what he needed to achieve and a fair idea of how to actually do that, but what he needed were the scouts to come back. By his reckoning they'd been gone for two days now and he was becoming paranoid. If they had been captured and made to talk then the entire operation was at risk, particularly given that he only had four hundred men with him. They wouldn't stand a chance against five thousand Imperials, particularly if they had Speirakian cavalry with them. He had seen a few of their patrols that added further fuel to his paranoia, his nerves beginning to fray as they made a beeline for the trees where his men and he hid before pulling away towards the coast.

Kiegal crawled up to him on his stomach, low to the ground so as to not attract the attention of anyone by movement. He too viewed the castle for a few minutes and his eyes danced along the parapet and then down to the town before going back to the King.

"Any word of the scouts?" Quittle asked, his voice barely above a whisper. There was no chance of anyone hearing them at this distance, not with the constant braying of seagulls in the town and the movement of so many people going about their daily lives, but Quittle had learnt over the past three months of ambushes and cloak and dagger warfare that quietness was a virtue.

"Nothing yet, sire, and I don't think we'll hear anything from them until this evening when the sun finally sets." He paused as he looked towards the sun and judged it to be some hours away yet. "They are good lads, Bear," he said slipping back to the familiar nickname that Quittle had before he was King. "They know what they are doing."

"I hope so," Quittle said with a smile, "otherwise this will get far too interesting far too bloody quickly. What's Tor doing anyway?"

"He's sent a few of the lads out to hunt some game, says there's no point sitting in the forest starving when there's plenty of deer kicking about. Can't say I blame him." Quittle nodded and his stomach growled at the idea of roasting meat. They had been living off hard tack and rations since they arrived in the area, none of them keen to light fires when they were so close to an Imperial army. Nobody wanted to be interrupted at their dinner when they were least prepared.

"And the Cardavians?"

"Went for a wee look down the coast at the Republican fleet. Nek has a bit of thing for ships apparently, though Grim maintains he's as sick as a dog whenever he gets on one." Kiegal grinned suddenly at the image and

Quittle couldn't help but give a silent chuckle. The two Cardavians had done well over the last two months since they had arrived on their shores. They had become good allies, arguably the reason for their victory at the battle against the Long Loch men. They were also good friends, Kiegal and Nek becoming extremely close since their drinking competition after the coronation. Grim, by far the quieter of the two men, had grown close to Tortag in the meantime; both men recognising the soldier in each other and the professional.

"They aren't going to like my plan, Kiegal," Quittle whispered. He had only one option, as far as he saw it. He had put it to the Attainians that they try and force a landing at the town, but they quite honestly turned around and said that they wouldn't be willing to do it. It was one thing to land men on a beach when there was not opposition, it was entirely different to do that when they were going to be facing a concentrated resistance. They'd be cut to pieces as soon as they grounded their craft, providing they were shot to pieces by archers on their approach.

"What is your plan?" Kiegal asked as he raised the eyepatch, scratching at the eyelid. Quittle had come to recognise that this was a sure sign of the man thinking, possibly mulling over his own plans. He also knew that if Kiegal did have another plan that he would be a man to listen to. He was a champion of his clan, picked to carry the clans' standard for that very reason, but he was also a brilliant tactician. When this war was over and, the Gods willing he was victorious, he would award Kiegal lands of his own from one of the clan chiefs who refused to bend the knee. It was the least he could do for the man.

"It isn't honourable," Quittle began.

"Burn them out." Kiegal finished for him. "I'm not being funny, Bear, but none of us have conducted this war honourably or according to the conventional rules. If we did that then we'd have been buggered from the get go."

"You agree with the plan then?"

"I was going to suggest it if you didn't, to be honest." Kiegal said with a grin

---

Aarlin was happy to be at sea again. He missed Gephy, but he didn't miss the paperwork and the constant administration that came with it. He didn't miss the city burghers making demands of his time or complaining about groups of sailors getting drunk, as sailors were want to do, and he certainly didn't miss having to refer questions and demands back to Nepriner and the city council there. Senator Elgrynn may have been an erstwhile ally at the time of the siege, but the man was still a Senator of the Republic and was liable to look after the public purse and the needs of Nepriner. He couldn't blame the man for that for Nepriner had suffered tremendously and the city was still being rebuilt and repopulated, but Gephy had also been under siege and, arguably, if it hadn't been for Gephy holding out against the blockade and siege then Nepriner wouldn't have been relieved as effectively as it had done.

Now, however, with a wooden deck under his feet, the wind in his hair and a fleet behind him he felt like he had come home. He knew within a month or two he would long for boredom again, for he was the first to admit he was not a young man anymore, but for now he could dream about his youth and spin dits to the younger officers and sailors about life back in his day. He took an almost perverse joy in hearing nautical terms being bandied about by men who actually knew what they were talking about. He enjoyed watching the bollards being polished and the decks being washed. He enjoyed hearing the complaints of sailors as they were made to scrub out, remembering his own time having to wash down the decks or painting the sides. Complaints, or drips as they were known, never changed. Every sailor everywhere believed that they were the most seen off person in the fleet, regardless of the actual truth of the matter, and every old salt believed that the newest generation to come through were an indictment of how far the country had fallen; which was also wrong.

"I'm surprised the Imperials haven't sent a squadron to try and break the blockade," remarked Dex with Aarlin nodding in turn. Dex had been the man who had ran and broken the Imperial fleet outside the harbour mouth of Gephy. He had been dispatched from Port Marmeen with a strong fleet and, with the aid of the smaller ships from the Gephy squadron, the two Attainian fleets had managed to drive off or destroy the entire Imperial force. It had been a tremendous victory and one that had raised the morale of the defenders to new heights. Practically it also allowed the Republic to bring in supplies as well as men and equipment meaning that Aarlin, in his role of Harbour Master at the time, could choose when and the manner of their break out.

"I think you did a good enough job on them a few months ago. It'll take their eastern fleet at least a year to repair and build its strength up again." He paused and looked towards the town for a brief moment. "Chances are that most of their eastern fleet were based here anyway, they've lost a significant portion of their eastern coast now."

"Especially with the regiments finally beginning to advance," Dex added. Aarlin nodded knowing that the fleet being here wasn't just a happy coincidence with the efforts of Quittle and his men. A few regiments of the Republic, as well as one of the Cardavian legions from Nepriner, had begun marching north. They were there to reclaim the rest of the eastern coastline, the thin strip of land that remained to the Empire outwith clan lands. It wasn't a grand operation, but it was a bold one. It was, to the recollection of Aarlin, the first time that the Attainians had actually advanced into Imperial territory with any chance of success. Moreover, and perhaps more importantly, they hadn't decided to go for any grand objective or sweeping movement. Instead they would take pieces of the Empire and seek to hold and consolidate them before, and if they judged it wise, to advance further.

"It's about bloody time the army did something rather than relying on the Cardavians all the time to drag them out of the shit," Dex added emphatically. Aarlin smiled and appreciated the usual inter-service rivalry that existed between the two arms of the Attainian forces.

"Talking of Cardavians, I wonder if our two friends are out there watching us just now?" Aarlin asked. He picked up his seeing glass and looked towards the castle looking straight into the face of a Rupinian sentry. The man was heavily bearded, his helmet fixed upon his head and spear in his hand as he looked down upon the town. Aarlin scanned further to the west where he knew that Quittle and his men were hiding in the forest as they waited to strike at the castle. He could see no signs of movement, but then he didn't expect to find any anyway. He continued sweeping towards the coast line and the dramatic looking cliff tops, white crested waves crashing into the sharp grey rocks. He grinned suddenly as he saw two figures sitting on the cliffs, their legs dangling over the sides with one emphatically pointing.

"I think I see them," he said as he passed the glass towards Dex. The man grinned as well knowing the reputation of the two men. He had only met them once or twice after the fleet had broken the blockade, but he had taken to them in an instant. He was glad and relieved to see them, believing initially that the task they were given had been nothing short of a suicide mission. He still believed it was, but if anybody could pull off the impossible then it would be them. Had they not been the ones that brought back the Eagles from Turgundeon?

"Looks like they are on the move anyway, Admiral. They must be heading back to their camp in the forest." Aarlin nodded, taking the glass back, and watched the two friends disappear eventually from view. He was reassured himself having spent many a sleepless night worrying about the two of them. It was he who had sent them to this land in the first place, and it was he who had recommended their names to the allied coalition commanders when they were looking about for volunteers. If they had died during the operation then he would have taken their deaths personally, for he liked them.

"I think King Quittle will make his move tonight," Aarlin said in an offhand manner. "I bloody hope they are anyway. How is the supply situation?"

"We'll be fine for maybe another week, but we'll have to go on quarter rations if they don't make a move by the end of tonight. We've got naval superiority so it wouldn't take much to send a few of the bigger craft back to Attainian lands to resupply."

"True enough, but our eastern coast is a warzone and barren at the moment. The farmers, or at least those that survived the Empire, thereabouts are too busy trying to feed themselves and plant seed for the coming months. We'd need to send them back to Gephy, and we both know that journey could take a month there and back again."

"So what do we do then, Admiral?" Dex asked.

"If push comes to shove, and as much as I don't want to do it, we'll have to start making beach landings with the marines that we have. That's if the Traemwenians don't make a move though."

Night had fallen and the clouds hung over the land as they obscured the moon and the stars. There was a faint breeze, which was something that Grim was thankful for as it kept the midges away. The council of war, and it was a grand title for what was effectively a gathering of friends who happened to hold senior positions, had been summoned and were not sitting deep in the forest watching a stag being slowly roasted over a fire. The dripping fat sizzled as it dropped down onto the burning logs, the fire low and the wood bone dry so it did not cough out smoke or a huge amount of line. Though they were a mile away from the castle and its environs none of the men wanted to attract any unwanted attention.

"You've done well here, Tor." Grim said with a smile, relishing the prospect of having some cooked meat. A man could live on raw vegetables and dried meat for a while, but such fare became stale and boring.

"I can't take all the credit. I've always been a shit archer," Tor replied with a grin. "How long till it cooks, Nek?"

"Buggered if I know, I've never been one for cooking. Anyway, I thought you were that hungry you'd eat the thing raw?" Nek said with a smile and a wink. He sprinkled some of the last of his salt rations on the meat and turned the spit over slowly once more. He knew enough to know that the meat could be served rare if need be, but he wasn't keen on killing off a King and his senior officials if he could help it.

"It'll be a good meal before we make a move tonight," Quittle said as he appeared out of the shadows with Kiegal. The men stood up out of respect before they were beckoned to sit down. Quittle wasn't one for old friends standing on ceremony.

"So we're making a move then?" Tortag asked as he resumed sharpening his swords. The man had finally managed to shake off his grief, but there was a slight change in him. He was still swift to laughter and the witty remark, but there was forever a dark shadow over his spirit now. Nobody mentioned the murder of his wife for nobody wished to pry, but, surprisingly, the one whom he had confided in the most had been Grimfar. "Now or never," said Kiegal sitting upon a fallen tree. "The scouts came back basically saying what we already know. The town of Kaernarvas is apparently ready to support if we need it. Their chief, Britherg, is being held in the castle though. Chances are if we make a move then he'll be killed."

"We can't put a stop to the entire thing because of that though," said Quittle. "I don't like it any more than the rest of you, but if we don't take this city then we are likely to lose the Attainian fleet. They can't remain here indefinitely."

"He's right," Nek said as he carved off a piece of the roasting venison. He had stripped a tree previously of some of its bark and had managed to create makeshift plates from it. Spearing a decent cut with his knife, he placed it on the plate and passed it to Quittle. "The fleet has been here for a week or two now, and that's not including their time trying to get here. We don't know the lay of the land in the Empire or whether the legions and regiments are marching north."

"Agreed," added Tortag. He thought about it for a few seconds as a piece of roasted meat was passed to him, his mind suddenly focussed on his hunger. "I suggest we wait until night is at its darkest and the sentries are liable to be distracted. I don't know how it is for you boys," he said indicating to Grim and Nek, "but Imperial sentries tend to get sloppy when they think they are safe. If we go in under cover of dark, then we can take the castle."

"What about the four and a half thousand men on the outside in the barracks?" Grim asked.

"We're going to have to burn them out," Quittle interjected. He was, by principle, unwilling for anyone of those gathered to make the hard decisions that needed to be taken. This act, he knew, would haunt these men for the rest of their lives and he didn't want any one of them to suffer the additional burden of having suggested it in the first place. He looked at their faces in the silence and knew that they had all been thinking along the same lines. "We've got enough wood hereabouts to take with us into the town, and there's a ready supply of peat and other combustibles that we've been gathering for this very task."

"If I can make a suggestion, Bear?" Tortag asked to which Quittle nodded his assent. "I recommend that we cover ourselves in ash, blacken ourselves up so that we blend more easily into the night. The good thing is that we're only going up against Imperial soldiers so there shouldn't be any confusion. I'd recommend that everyone only take what is absolutely necessary as well, no loose armour or weaponry to give us away."

"Sound idea, Lord Marshal," Quittle said using his formal title, as if using a formal title would somehow make the bloody work in front of them slightly more honourable. He looked at Grim and saw that he didn't particularly look enamoured with the idea. Cardavians liked to fight honestly, he knew, and this would be a sore point. Men like him didn't expect to be murdered in their beds and generally reciprocated that. "Any other suggestions?"

"We split the force. We send in a small force under myself to kill the sentries. Nek will, with half our force when the all clear is sounded, begin piling up combustibles on the outside. They'll fire the building and kill anyone who tries to make a break for it. In the meantime, Kiegal and Grim will be waiting for the castle drawbridge to come down. When it does and a decent amount of have come out of the gates, they'll ambush the bastards and push on into the castle." He paused for thought before striking forward again, "Is there a chance we can get the Attainians to effect a landing tonight?"

"Too late for messages, this is all we'll have." Quittle answered. It wasn't ideal, but then greater numbers could lead to blunders.

"Then it'll have to do, but it's a damn close thing. The trickiest bit will be taking the castle. If we don't time it right, or they have particularly alert sentries, then this entire plan will go to the dogs."

Silence greeted that as each man thought of the possible consequences of failure; if they were to win then they'd probably secure themselves the entire kingdom barring those rebel chiefs still holding out in the north east. If they were to lose then they'd be captured, the entire campaign would collapse and the idea of Traemwen would die.

Chapter Sixteen – **Fire and Sword**

"I don't like this Nek," Grim said before they had split up. They were both smeared now in black ash, any exposed skin now blending into the shadows of the night. Nek had even ingeniously managed to make a green and brown paste by crushing leaves and some mud together that went further to camouflage them. Even so, Nek knew well where his friend was coming from. They were former members of the Eagles legion and they fought the enemies in front of them, they didn't go skulking about in the middle of the night to slaughter men as they slept in their beds. Yes, there was justification, but that sort of backhanded warfare was generally left to those in the light infantry who were better suited to this line of work. Nek and Grim had been used to fighting as part of a shield wall, commands being shouted out and the line moving forward as one body. Their career had taken a different turn recently, they both recognised, but this was new. "We'll get through it, don't worry about it Grim." Nek replied, though he could see the doubt in the man's eye. He had spoken earlier whilst they had sat on the cliffs about Katrin and how much he missed her, how he had plans and what he thought she was doing there and then. It was something that Nek had heard before from countless men down the years, for men on campaign like nothing more than to talk about things that were otherwise unobtainable there and then. Nek let him talk anyway, for it did Grim good as well as him. He, for all his pride in being a legionary, liked to be reminded that there was a life outwith soldiering.

"I'm not worried about that, Nek, I'm worried about us. This is going to be a massacre," Nek nodded and couldn't think of much to say. He knew his friend had a conscience, and was often one to wear his heart on his sleeve, but he also knew that now was not the time to debate the whys and wherefores of the immortal soul.

"The castle will be more like honest soldiers' work, Grim, don't worry about it. I'll worry about the consequences when I come across the Gods," he said it with a grin as he tried to make light of the situation. It raised a smile from Grim and Nek punched him lightly on the shoulder in turn. "There, that's better. I'll see you when we finish this business, you owe me a pint anyway."

Grim nodded, matching the look of his friend and looking him in the eye. Kiegal approached them and stood silently while the two old comrades had their moment, unwilling to interrupt it. Eventually They gripped hands and Nek nodded once, unsure of whether he should hug his old friend or let it be. Instead he went into his cloak and brought out his old battered hip flask, the contents half full with red wine.

"You'll need this waiting about whilst we're doing the lifting and shifting.

Good luck, brother." His old friend nodded and took a deep swallow of the drink, feeling the smooth wine slip down his throat. He offered it back, but was waved off, and Nek was quietly called away by Tortag.

"You ready, Grim?" Kiegal asked as he watched the departing form of Nek, eventually fading into the gloom of the night to become no more than an obscure shape.

"Is anybody ever ready for something like this?" The Cardavian veteran responded with a half-smile.

"Probably not, but it'll be worth it. You'll see," replied Kiegal, though he was unsure of who he was trying to persuade.

"I didn't expect to see you here, sire," Nek said. He approached the one hundred men that were going to be firing the barracks. It was obvious that there had been some heated discussion between Quittle and Tortag as well, and Nek could easily imagine what it had concerned. It wasn't long either when Tortag decided to try and drag him into the argument.

"The King damn well shouldn't be here. This is going to be bloody work. Dangerous bloody work. To risk his person in one throw of the dice is madness," Nek could see where he was coming from and nodded slowly, but looked to Quittle to hear his side of things.

"The King has a right to say what is good for him or not, Lord Marshal," answered Quittle sharply. The formal use of the title was surprising, though Nek wondered whether it was because he had heard it for the second time that night. Was this a sign of strain in the hierarchy? He doubted it, knowing fine well how nerves would be fraught tonight and on edge given the task at hand. His next words reassured him somewhat, "Tor, I know you're concerned for me. But I'm not going to ask people to do a job I wouldn't be willing to do myself."

"What a damn fool notion and you bloody know it! Who taught you shite like that?"

"You did, actually." Tortag opened his mouth as if about to say something, shut it again, and opened it before settling into a dirty look. Quittle grinned, his teeth white compared to the dark ash and paste that he had smeared over his face. His face was bearded now and he looked nothing like the King he made himself out to be, instead he looked like some nightmare from eons passed that a child would be told about in an effort to get them to behave.

"Well what do you make of this, Nek? Do you think he should be risking himself in such a manner?" Tortag asked, looking desperately for one last ally. Nek considered his words carefully, a diplomatic and mature move he very rarely conducted.

"I agree with Bear, sorry Tor. I've always said that the better leaders I've ever had were the ones who were willing to muck in with the lads. Mind you," he said with a grin as he tried to bring a little humour to the conversation, "the best ones get the drinks in when we win."

"Well I know when I'm beaten," Tortag said as he mustered a smile, "I'll be keeping my eye on you, Bear. There's no need to be a bloody hero here, understand?"

"Yes, Lord Marshal, sorry Lord Marshal." Tortag grinned and let out a long chuckle.

"Let's get moving then, before the castle group get too far ahead."

There was almost an eerie silence that existed within the town and no lights were lit in the houses or on the streets. It felt like there was no-one else here with even the barracks being dead quiet. The only sound that could be heard was the occasional cough coming from a sentry, or the odd stamp of a horse waking up in the stables within the courtyard. The gulls that normally cried out at all hours were even quiet, the faint sounds of small waves lapping against the jetties and dockyards reminding the group of one hundred men that there was still life out there of a sort. Tortag strained his eyes and could make out the lights on the Attainian fleet that were used for navigation and sighting purposes. They had the bay completely sealed up at any rate, there was no danger of the Imperials trying to send a relief force and therefore he could, if he strained his ears to the utmost, just about hear the ringing of bells as the duty watches changed over.

The atmosphere was close and tense with the cloud cover, the type of weather that needed rain or a decent lightning storm to clear it. He was sweating heavily, though whether it was through the heart or nerves he didn't wish to know. He had to give his lads credit as they moved silently through the sleeping streets, hugging the walls and shadows as they leapt from building to building. They were silent and sure of foot, no unnecessary cries or shouting out for orders. But then, he always knew how this was going to play out. The Traemwenians, or at least that followed Quittle, didn't have the capabilities to lead or conduct sieges. They needed to rely on the element of surprise and subterfuge, and because of that he picked out the best officers he had and then had them choose their best men. So far, and he wished he could touch wood to safeguard himself, so good.

He looked towards the castle and saw Quittle doing the same. The man had changed significantly since Nepriner seven months ago. He was more sure of himself, and any fat the man had carried had long disappeared. Instead he looked as if he had been fighting for clan and country his entire life and he now carried enough scars to prove his fighting capability. In the early days of the rebellion, or what was now being called the war of independence, many of Tor's own clan had approached him and asked why he followed such a man as Quittle. The man had, to the best of his men's knowledge, never raised a sword in anger. Now there was no questioning of his ability, now Quittle held the moniker of 'Battle King' and command the loyalty of thousands.

Almost as if reading his thoughts, Quittle turned to look at him and pointed towards the large barrack blocks. They easily towered above most other buildings, with the exception of the castle and its walls, and therefore wasn't hard to spot. What the scouts also reported was the fact that it was two blocks rather than just the one they had seen. Thankfully the two were side by side and therefore the plan wouldn't need to be changed by much, but it had led to a fraught moment or two when they were trying to come up with numbers for each front of the ambush. If they were to strip too many men away from the force lying in wait at the castle gates then they wouldn't be effective, whereas if they were to strip away too many from the barrack force then they could miss something and end up being overwhelmed.

Nek approached him, running silently forward on the balls of his feet. He was a good soldier and, if he wanted to, then Tor would have happily made him an honorary clansman on the spot. He was sure of his actions, or at least appeared to be, and that was half the battle to winning folk over. More than that, he had a rare sense of humour and was able to empathise with the men. He was no great thinker, that was true, and would sooner conduct a battle over drink than a battle over knowledge and wit, but he was honest about that. Tor held up a closed fist for everyone to stop, and then signalled for everyone to crouch low.

"I'll take my half now and circle around to the second barrack block. I've already picked out twenty men that'll help me clear out the sentries, the rest of the lads will start setting up the combustibles once you give the all clear." It was hissed out in a whisper, the information short and sharp. It was also information that had previously been agreed on and conformed to the plan so that questions became unnecessary.

"Luck, Nek," Tor said as quietly. The man nodded and waved for his men to follow him. They would take a side street slightly to their right so that they didn't arrive en masse as one formation. Tor watched them bound off and turned around again, signalling for his men to move forward down the street. They could see the barracks now, probably the only well-lit series of buildings in the area. He could also see one of the sentries, a man who looked as if he was beginning to doze off standing up and unaware of his surroundings. It was a hanging offence to be on trot and asleep for a good reason; he may have become a mortal liability for his comrades but he was sent from the Gods for the men of Traemwen.

The thirty men hung back in the shadows of the street as the twenty men, including Tortag and Quittle, half-crouched and half-ran towards the barrack block. The twenty warriors hugged against the wall where the sleeping sentry was happily dreaming of better times. Tor held his finger to his lips signifying silence as he approached the Imperial. He withdrew his knife and saw the gleam of the blade as it reflected the light of a brazier. He almost felt sorry for the man as he quickly clamped his hand around the man's mouth to prevent him from crying out, sliding the knife across his throat and feeling the body jerk automatically in its death throes. He could feel the blood sliding down his wrist and had to steel his stomach. Finally, the body went limp in his arms and he lowered it gently to the ground. The eyes stared up at him, wide open in uncomprehending terror, and he knelt down and gently shut them.

The rest of the sentries were dispatched in a similar manner with even Quittle partaking in the bloody business. One man nearly gave the game away, struggling to cover the mouth of the man and bring his knife up at the same time, until Tor stepped in and stabbed the man through his throat. He had looked the soldier in the eyes as he died, saw the small imperfections on his face where he had picked at a scab as a child or caught himself shaving later on in life. His uniform stated he was a junior officer, obviously one that had won the duty for the night and was doing the rounds to check on his lads. He was probably one of the better ones, but would now be meat for the carrion birds.

Tor knelt down and wiped the blood from his hands on the man's purple cape, drying the sticky and disgusting mess. He could see the colour of them because of the lights from the torches and braziers that ringed the building and saw they were a horrific blood red and black colour from the ash. He felt like retching for a few seconds when he saw them, more so when he had to put them to his lips and blew the signal. He waited with bated breath for the repeat signal, muttering prayers to whatever Gods were watching over them. There was silence from his men, and then what sounded like a wood pigeon dying. Two seconds later it was repeated more authentically and stronger, a sure sign that the second group had achieved their aims and were now building up their stockpile of fire material.

The rest of his squad came rushing forward and laid their peat and wooden faggots against the walls of the wooden building and in the doorway. There was more wood brought in, and the whole mixture was doused with oil. Quittle approached him with two lit torches. Tor nodded and blew the signal again to indicate they were ready to fire. He waited again, men moving in the shadows as they put on the last of the material they had brought with them. Several of the men had also picked up their own torches and were lighting them in some of the braziers that lay scattered around the area. It may have only been a few seconds, but the sense of wait seemed to stretch out for a life time before the return signal was given. They walked methodically around the building poking their torches into the wood and letting the peat and oil catch, igniting the wood they had brought with them. The weather had been good over the last week and the wood that the building was made out of was very dry, easy to catch. It was untreated as well and the wood caught far too easily. Within minutes the lower levels were filling with smoke and fire, screams of terror audible from the inside. Some of the Traemwenians threw their torches in through the windows, relying on the ground to be made out of straw and the beds to be made out of even more wood. Others, like Tor and Quittle, threw their torches higher and onto the thatched roofs. The weather once again came to their aid, a strong wind sweeping the area causing the thatch to catch instantly.

Tortag signalled for his men to fall back and take up positions at the exits. So far nobody had tried to escape from the conflagration. A bright flame leapt up the side of the building, swiftly followed by another as the one blackened and began to crackle. The yelling inside was becoming desperate, the sounds of screaming and scrabbling almost too much to take as men fought their way to the door. He didn't even want to picture it in his mind's eye, knowing that four and a half thousand men tried to fight for their lives amidst horrible circumstances.

The muffled shrieks, cries and cursing from within the barracks was reaching new levels and even drowning out the sound of the roaring fire. Suddenly the doorway collapsed in sheets of flame and men, some of them wearing only their bed clothes and on fire, came spilling out to be met by the cold steel of the waiting clansmen. More fuel was added to the fire, anything that came close to hand now that the element of surprise had been sprung. Soon it wasn't necessary, the great fire hungrily eating at the wood. Men who managed to escape the flames came streaming out of the building, many with cuts and bruises on their face where they had fought previous friends in their efforts to escape. More came spilling out like burning braziers, their hair smouldering or well-lit as they blindly tried to escape. None, though, who escaped the flames managed to escape cold steel.

Tortag felt sick, not proud, even though the moment of triumph was well within their grasp. He knew that if he survived the coming battles that this would haunt him for the rest of his life. He looked at Quittle and saw his face, knowing that his friend felt exactly the same way.

Grim and Kiegal lay with three hundred main in a large drainage ditch that had been dug in front of the castle moat. The weather along the south eastern coast was liable to become stormy at the best of times and it had been deemed wise to build one so as to prevent disease and the rats that came with stagnant water. What was supposed to save the castle was now going to be its downfall.

Grim had watched the barracks for an age and wondered if the trap had been sprung or whether the attacking force had been discovered whilst they were advancing. He hadn't heard anybody crying out from the direction of the barracks or the castle so he had to assume that it was still all clear, that the plan was going correctly for a change, and that this entire thing would actually work. He was lying on his stomach and watching a sentry pace about on his rounds. It was then he saw the figure, almost as black as shadow, approach him from behind and wrap his arm around his head. A few seconds later the sentry was on the ground.

He watched as more shadows came filtering through carrying bundles that he took to be fire raising material. He was not a man for believing in the Gods, for quite often the Gods weren't the type to listen to such as he, but now he muttered a prayer for those inside the barracks block. No matter what way he tried to justify it, he didn't like the idea of killing sleeping men. He wondered if they would do the same to him if they had been given half the chance, and he decided that they probably would, but it still didn't make the action morally right.

Was he getting too old for this, he wondered. It hadn't been the first time he had thought it recently, and once again his thoughts turned to Katrin and the possible home they could build together. He didn't know what he'd do outwith the legion for it had been his life. He didn't join up with a trade and he had never taken the chance to learn a trade whilst he'd been in; he'd always been a fighting soldier, always at the forefront of any campaign if the legion was necessary. He had thought about joining the civil defence force, used primarily for law and order in Silveroak.

He watched the bright sheets of orange flame leap into the sky from the two barracks and whispered another prayer, hoping that Nek was alright and hadn't been injured. He could see men milling about as they waited for those within the blocks to come running out. He saw one door burst open in sheets of flames, oil pots being chucked in straight away afterwards, as men came streaming out with their hair and clothes on fire. Some brandished weapons, determined to take down as many of the clansmen as they could even as they were dying.

He could hear the neighing of terror from horses in the stables nearby, the scent of wood smoke and blood strong on the wind. The bells within the castle began peeling out adding to the hellish crescendo, trumpets and drums combining their own accompaniment. It sounded and looked like a living nightmare. He turned towards the castle now, trying to put the fight in the barracks block to the back of his mind.

"Looks like we're up," said Kiegal. The man wasn't smiling or grinning, something that made the situation seem worse. He often had a smile on his face, and the good humoured clansman was often the first with a witty remark. He was very much the Traemwenian version of Nek, though perhaps the clansman had a greater intellect. Tonight the man looked ghostly white beneath the blackened ash and brown and green paste.

"We wait until the drawbridge is down and two hundred or so of them are across," answered Grim. Kiegal nodded, unsheathing his sword and gripping the pommel with an unusual ferocity.

"Wonder if the fleet will move in and deploy their men," Kiegal said thinking aloud.

"Even if they did, we wouldn't bloody hear them. A thousand or so marines would be welcome about now." Grim turned to look at the barrack blocks, the long buildings now ablaze like some ghastly funeral pyre. A most unpleasant smell was coming from the buildings now; the smell of roasting flesh and burning hair. The sounds of the fire were drowning out any sounds of the slaughter taking place. He tried to look further beyond and into the bay, trying to discern any sign of the transport ships and the fleet, but the bright lights of the castle and the burning buildings had ruined his night vision. He tore his gaze away when he heard the chains of the drawbridge running loose, the bridge coming down a few seconds after to crash onto the dirt. The ground shuddered violently and men began spilling out from the castle in great numbers.

"You ready for this, Grim?" Kiegal said, the ghost of a smile playing on his lips. This was more like a normal ambush, the cloak and dagger that they had become used to over the last few months.

"Am I fuck! I'd sooner have some Cardavians with me rather than these hairy arsed barbarians," Grim chucked back with a smile, trying to inject some much needed humour into the conversation. "How about you?"

"I'd sooner be tucked up in bed." They waited for as long as they felt they could before Kiegal sprang up, brandishing his long sword into the air. "At them Traemwen! At them!"

Three hundred men sprang from the dirt causing confusion amongst the Imperial soldiers. They were in disarray, unable to form any sort of defence against the sudden on rush of clansmen. Worse, some of the men who had been attacking the barracks were charging towards them. Grim stood in a half crouching position as he wished that he still had his shield;

he felt almost naked without it. He rushed forward, seeing one man and charged. The man made a wide sweeping arc with his sword, easily parried as Grim brought his blade forward and down make his opponent stumble forward. His momentum carried him forward and Grim shoulder charged him, sending the man sprawling to the dirt. He was dispatched with a sword thrust through his open mouth.

Sword withdrawn he looked for his next target, seeing more men from the local town now come streaming forward to add their own numbers to the fray. Another Imperial came running at him and aimed a swift thrust to his neck. He had to dodge backwards, nearly stumbling into the drainage ditch from where they had emerged. He regained his balance in time and deflected another thrust with his sword with a downward sweep. He was on the back foot. He jumped forward and bore the man to the ground, the two wrestling on the ground as the battle raged around about them.

The man was stronger and younger and was able, with a deal of effort, to turn Grim onto his own back. He straddled him and began raining blows upon his face with Grim trying to desperately defend himself and reach for his sword at the same time. He kicked upwards as he threw the man off balance, allowing him to twist in the dirt and reach out for his sword. His fingertips brushed the hilt and he scrambled for it. The man must have regained his composure for he saw the threat and leapt for the blade at the same time.

Grim reached it in time but found his sword arm pinned. He punched out with his left smashing into the man's face, feeling the strength of the other beginning to ebb as he relentlessly smashed. It was primal, survival screaming at him to use everything as a weapon. He rolled the man over onto his back and smashed his head against the man's nose again and again until his grip finally gave out. Sword in hand, Grim stabbed him through the side of his neck and ripped the blade away.

He felt exultant, triumphant at still being alive.

There was a sharp pain in his side from a minor stab wound he hadn't realised he had picked up. He made to stand up and felt dizzy, blood loss causing his pressure to drop a little. At any rate, he believed he had done enough for just now that allowed him to get his breath back and he looked around, feeling a little faint, and tried to make out details. By the sounds of things, he thought, the battle was going their way anyway. He could see men fighting in the gateway as the Traemwenians sought to push further in, though, through the groggy details, he could make out that resistance was light.

He spun around as some sixth sense warned him of a threat, throwing his blade up at the same time as he stopped an Imperial from removing his head. He charged forward, missing his shield intensely, and slid his own blade in between the mans ribs. He twisted the blade twice and pulled out, letting his fallen opponent collapse to the ground. He stepped forward, feeling dizzy again, and moved towards the gateway. Another man came running up to him and he took a deep breath, fumbling for the short crossbow he used to carry on him. He cursed silently as he vaguely remembered losing it a month ago. He turned so that his left side was facing forward, his sword held loosely in his right fist as he gritted his teeth and fought through waves of pain.

"Whoa, Grim, it's me." He recognised the voice from memory, the face still just a shadowy blur. "You look like shit, brother."

"I can't see you at all," he said to the vague shape. He knew he had taken a knock or two, but he was beginning to worry now. His only reassurance was that the person in front of him didn't want to kill him.

"How about we take you back to the fleet, eh?" The shape asked.

"They've landed?"

"They've landed, brother, those beautiful bastard sailors have landed." Nek said with a grin. "We'll get you seen to and then you can quit malingering, eh?"

Chapter Seventeen – **A Royal Invitation**

"You're popular," Vel said with a grin. Beran looked up from the letter in his hand, horror etched across his face at the contents.

"You're bloody well going," he said. "You can consider it a duty."

"Ah, unfortunately, sir, it's one of those things. The Queen of Ufwala outranks me by quite some margin, and she's requested you and your good wife to attend."

"I take it Talice already knows?" Beran asked, hope springing eternal.

"She was the one that told me, brother, so you've shit out of luck there." Vel said with a grin and a laugh. "Look, you'll probably enjoy it. Nice wee carriage ride down there and then you'll be hobnobbing with the best and brightest of the Ufwalan realm. You could consider it a honeymoon."

"Could this not count as a honeymoon?" He was grasping for any excuse, trying to think of any exercises or any other prior engagements that he had coming up. The trouble he had was that he had efficient staff officers who took care of things; his diary was bereft of things that he needed to take care of and the Imps weren't likely to try and invade this far south at any point.

"I don't think following orders to your next area of command is a honeymoon," Vel said in way of a counter argument.

"Could be if you use your imagination," Beran muttered. He hated these types of functions, either everybody was on age or trying to curry favour with the person hosting the event. It was a pain, soul destroying, and something he tried to avoid at all costs. The trouble, he knew, was that Talice was a daughter of a Senator who had grown up with official balls and dances. She thrived on this sort of things, at home with politics as much as he was at home with researching history or conducting exercises.

"I don't speak the language."

"Get lessons from Talice on the way. Anyway, I'm sure our diplomat down there will be able to translate for you."

"What in the name of the Gods did I ever do to offend you?" Beran asked with a grin, pouring himself and Vel a glass of red.

"Nothing at all, Ban, you're my best friend and you know that well. I'd trust you with my life. However, Talice has a vicious tongue in her head when she gets a mind to. I still remember her lashing us at Nepriner when she thought you weren't getting enough rest." Beran nodded as he passed the glass over and conceded the point. Talice could be very persuasive. He stood up and looked outside the large oval window that overlooked the southern plains. The main road looked like an armoured snake as it stretched away south broad and distinct against the green fields of grass.

"Have we had any messages from Silveroak yet about the Stags?" He asked, realising that the question had been bothering him. It had been nearly a week now since he had evicted the Stags during the rough handover, a process he was sure would have devolved into fists and blood. He would have quite happily allowed it to happen and entertained General Rinian had Talice not been there. He had wanted nothing than to hurt the man that day, physically or emotionally, and instead had to settle for wounding the pride of the man.

"Nothing yet," answered Vel. "I wouldn't have expected an answer so soon anyway. All they'll do is investigate the matter and slap him on the wrists, probably give him a desk job for the rest of his life. You know how it is, Ban."

"I know, don't remind me." He answered looking back and walking to his seat once more. He sat down and took a sip from the red. "It's the same bloody story though. You do your job well and you'll get shafted, balls it up completely on the other hand and you're liable to get promoted. I'll probably end up saluting him some day."

"Maybe if you were better at your job, Ban. Just saying," Vel said with a grin.

"I'm seriously going to have to find a better second one day. I think Aleill would be better suited than you."

"Talking of him, where is he?"

"He's coming up in a few minutes. He was complaining about the archery butts earlier on. He's really throwing himself into his work." Beran spoke with a degree of concern, something that was picked up on by Velawin. Aleill had never been the same since Nepriner and the death of Trent, and now with Erallac dead as well, the two senior officers dreaded to think how the master of archers would be able to cope. "He gave a good speech at the funeral."

"Aye, but it was no less than the big man deserved. I'll miss him." The funeral had been conducted as soon as it was proper, a solemn ceremony with full military rights. Beran was sure that Erallac, if he was looking down from wherever the Gods drafted soldiers when they shuffled off the mortal plain, would have been decrying the drill of those carrying the coffin. He felt the pang of loss still, but at least now he could smile about him.

"So what else needs doing about the fort?" Beran asked. There was a chap at the door before Vel could answer and Beran shouted for Aleill to enter. The archer looked tired, the black rings under his eyes which had become a distinguishable feature during the siege coming back. It was evident the man had not been sleeping, that and possibly pushing himself too hard. "Glass of wine, Aleill?"

"As long as it's not the usual bucket of piss that you serve everyone," the archer said with a smile as he sat down upon a spare seat. He took the proffered glass and took a sip, holding the contents up to the light coming from the window looking at the clarity. He finally swallowed. "Tastes like vinegar. Southern foreign pig swill?"

"Your palate is still as sharp as ever," said Vel. "If only the creases in your tunic sleeves were as well."

"I'll have my batsman re-briefed. You really can't get the staff these days." He watched the two men and got the inevitable reaction of them both shaking their heads, the look of disbelief on their faces whenever he uttered something.

"You don't press your own uniform?" Beran asked, who, as a soldier, didn't even trust his wife to put the correct creases in where they needed to be. He loved Talice dearly, but he wasn't willing to risk their entire marriage on the state of his uniform.

"No. Why would I? I'm not one of these 'I wish I was a common man' people like you two. Anyway, I have more important things to do like getting this fort into a decent state of repair. You know those archery butts hadn't been properly serviced in ages? They were more mildew and mould than proper targets. The fletchers hut was a wood store and the tools had become rusted."

"I know; I've seen your request forms littering my table. I thought most of them had been actioned now?" Beran replied, pouring a fresh glass for Vel and himself. "Two seconds, gentlemen," he said standing up and walking to the door. He popped his head through and asked his assistant to go to the cellar and bring another two bottles up. Walking back into the room he sat down on his seat and took a sip. "I'll say one thing for the previous incumbent, he left behind a decent wine selection."

"Well that's up for a debate," Aleill said in retort. "Anyway, as to your original question, yes, it has been sorted. Vel will tell you, or even that bald buffoon Aglon, they let this place go to rack and ruin. The parapet has enough plants growing on it that your good wife, Ban, was tempted to convert some of it into gardens."

"Sounds like you need some leave," Vel said with a smile. He didn't disagree with him on any of his points, Aglon and he had conducted a tour of the defences and the outworks the day after they had arrived and the pair had been disgusted with what they had found. The ditch outside had become waterlogged and was in danger of becoming a serious health hazard. The stakes driven into the ground just outside had either rotted to pieces or fallen over, no sign of maintenance whatsoever had seemed to take place on the parapets. The barrack blocks had been the only decent thing about the place, that and the headquarters which also formed the rooms of the General and his wife, but then that was hardly a surprise when the Stags stayed within their rooms when even a caravan could be attacked outside their walls with impunity.

"Well, if Ban would ever give us some leave then I'd happily take it!"

"In that case, you can have it by taking a small trip south."

"I'm not conducting your diplomatic visit for you, Ban." Vel burst out laughing, a sound full of good humour and genuine mirth. Beran looked on, mock horror upon his face before sipping the glass of wine again.

"I had no idea that my officers had such little loyalty. I take it Talice has got to you?" Aleill nodded with a smile, holding up his glass in mock salute before reaching for the bottle. Beran took it away with a smile, but, almost as if on cue, his assistant walked in with a fresh bottle and passed it to the open hand of Aleill. Another minor triumph. "Either way, you're right. You aren't going to replace me; you're coming with me."

It was now the time for Aleill to be stunned to silence, something that very rarely happened when the man took great pleasure in ordinarily having a battle of words with anyone. He opened his mouth to say something before shutting it again causing Velawin to chuckle.

"If you're worried about being an imposition Aleill," Beran begun as he put the proverbial boot in, "then I wouldn't worry about it. I'll speak to Talice. I'm sure she'd love for you to be there. Anyway, I'll need another set of eyes when I'm down there."

"I don't speak the language," Aleill replied feebly. Velawin chuckled again and reached for the bottle and poured himself another glass, enjoying his friends discomfort.

"Nonsense, you're nobility. You tell us all the time anyway! You'll fit right in. Might even have a shot at the Queen if you play your cards right."

"Well, I..." he begun.

"I'm taking it you accept?" Beran asked, the image of concern.

"Is this an order?" Aleill asked as he used his last line of defence.

"Not at all, just a friendly request between two old comrades."

"You're a bastard, Ban." Aleill replied, grinning into his wine glass.

Beran wasn't drunk, but he wasn't sober. He was in that magical between period where he felt merry and that all was right in the world. He wore civilian clothes, a white tunic with blue edging over red trousers. A brown belt with gold decoration went around his waist whereupon his scabbard sat and his small crossbow. Around his chest he still wore the single leather belt where his bolts sat and a grey cloak was sat upon his shoulders signifying his legion. It was possibly because of this that he felt more relaxed, for there was no better feeling in the world than not being in uniform.

He was still sat in his office having seen off Vel and Aleill earlier on, the two of them happily berating each other the length of the hallway until they were out of earshot. He smiled at the memory of it, knowing that he was lucky to have such strong friends as them. He looked at the wine glass, wondering for a few seconds whether the drink had finally got to him before he decided that it hadn't and it was the way he genuinely felt. He had been tempted when they had left to go to his rooms and relax there, but he was enjoying the peace and quiet and actually spending time by himself. It allowed him time to think and process events, something that he felt he hadn't done in months. It wasn't that he didn't enjoy being in the company of his friends or his wife, for he loved them more than life itself, it was just that a man needed to have time by himself every now and then.

A convoy had come into the camp shortly before evening carrying the new issue of armour. An explanatory letter had been attached to his own new issue from Field Marshal Raffin explaining that the new armour was designed around the needs of the legions fighting in Attainia. It had made him smile when he looked over the new kit, glad that someone in the higher ups were actually beginning to listen to those on the field.

The new armour was better in many regards, but he was a traditionalist and still viewed it with a degree of suspicion. The new helmet was similar to the makeshift one he had had crafted for himself at Nepriner with a solid nose guard and flexible cheek guards; but he was somewhat saddened to see that the traditional horse hair crest had been removed to be replaced with a metal one instead that ran along the natural ridge. There was now a large padded jacket that formed an underlay to a chest armour that looked like a combination of laminar and chainmail, however, there was also added protection with the reinforced mail on the shoulders running down the arms. For the legs there was very loose mail, almost a skirt, that was attached to the upper armour. The lower legs were protected with leg greaves. He had tried it on, utilising his assistant, and tested out the flexibility and the weight finding it surprising that it was better than his old kit. It was now placed on a crucifix and stood near the open window.

He was lucky with the sighting of his office and the building in general. His quarters that he shared with Talice were on the upper floor of a three storied building, but his actual office occupied something akin to a tower. It loomed above all other buildings within the fort and afforded him perfect views in any direction bar the west towards the mountain range. It was night time now and the orange lights of the candles within the room flickered with the breeze casting dark silhouettes making him aware of how cold it had gotten since the sun had set. He stood up and felt his right knee click in protest, his back giving a little spasm from sitting for far too long. He smiled for a few seconds as he remembered his father's words of warning when he was younger about watching his back, something he dismissed at the time, but now could appreciate with an alarming alacrity. He may have been only thirty-four, and soon to be thirty-five, but he could already feel his back straining at times when he spent too long on horseback.

He moved over to the southern facing window and looked out onto the dark plains, seeing the occasional orange light where a farmstead was sighted. He took a deep breath of the fresh air, smelling the faint scent of sea salt coming in from the coast on the eastern breeze. He had never been to the lands of the south, but he had heard many interesting stories about it. Prior to Nepriner he had believed that the Wolves would have been posted south and a possible war with one of the princedoms or kingdoms of the coalition had been a viable possibility. Now, with the rise of Wellisa, this apparent Queen of the South he thought, the entire picture had changed. Would she be a friend or would she be a future threat? He shook his head as he physically tried to clear his thoughts knowing that, if he went south with any sort of prejudice, then he was likely to ruin any diplomatic effort. It would, in effect, become a self-fulfilling prophecy.

He took a last lingering look south at a distant building and wondered about the nature of the people inside, wondering if they cared a fig for whoever was in charge or what country was talking to whom. He decided, rightly or wrongly, that they probably didn't. They would care about planting their seed for harvest, making sure that any animals were properly fed and cared for, and that there was enough food in the larder and money in the chest to pay the taxman whenever he came round. They'd care for their own issues; issues to them that would be their entire world. He smiled, thinking that he was beginning to become maudlin in his cups and too philosophical.

"Sir?" The door was chapped twice and then creaked open as his assistant, a young man named Fortin, nudged his way in. He was an able assistant, more like a secretary than anything else, but he lacked a little confidence. It was something that Beran resolved he would have to rectify at some point if only to bring the lad out his shell. He would find military life a lot easier if he was able to appear a little more confident no matter how nervous he actually was.

"I didn't even realise you were still here, Fortin. I thought you'd be down the mess with the boys by now?"

"No, sir, I needed to finish off a dispatch to General Gamin."

"Who?" Beran was the first to admit that, unless he had known someone for a particular length of time, he was generally rubbish with names. He was able to recognise faces, and that often helped him avoid embarrassing incidents through a judicious use of bluffing and tact, but names of people continued to elude him.

"He's the officer commanding the Leviathans, sir. Commander Aglon has asked me to write to him requesting information for the next tournament," Beran nodded and chuckled knowing how much that Aglon had spoken of the tournament.

"Well, finish up for the night and get yourself down the mess, young man. I'm about to retire anyway."

"Yes, sir. Goodnight sir," Fortin said as he was shutting the door.

"Fortin!" Beran called out, the door opening again within a second. "Sir?"

"I mean, get yourself down the mess and have a drink. Here," he said passing him a silver coin, "that'll probably pay for a few drinks. Get to know the boys, they are a good bunch." The man nodded, but Beran could see he was reluctant. Still, he knew enough about his secretary to know that he would probably take it as an order and go down. He also knew that young men, when they got the taste of beer, found they quite enjoyed it. He was just glad that there wasn't a village attached to the fort yet otherwise he'd be reading medical reports at some point saying how some of the men in the garrison had come down with the lovers pox.

Yawning, he walked over to the hearth and started building a fire with coal and small logs. Finding some paper from his table he quickly scanned the contents so as to make sure that nothing important was on them; the vast majority of the paper littering his desk these days being requisition orders and request forms. Satisfied, he scrunched the bundle up and placed them between the logs. Finally, he struck a match and began lighting. He stood up from his haunches and watched the fire take, the changing colours of the wood as it began to blacken and burn.

"I always thought I was more entertaining than fire," Talice said as she slipped her arms around his waist. He hadn't even heard her enter so enthralled he was with building the fire. He twisted slowly in her arms so that he was facing her and leant down, kissing her deeply. She smiled and pulled away, her arms still around his waist.

"You taste like cheap wine, Ban," she said in admonishment, an eyebrow raised in mock severity.

"I had a few with Aleill and Vel earlier on, been catching up some paperwork ever since." He said, pulling away gently and moving to his comfortable chair once more. She came with him and sat on his lap, finding the opened bottle of wine and pouring herself a glass. She took a sip and winced once before holding it out towards him.

"This tastes like vinegar. Is this what you were giving them?" She said with a ghost of a smile playing upon her lips. He chuckled and kissed her cheek, caressing the small of her back and her long red hair.

"Well they weren't complaining."

"Aleill would have been, at least he has taste."

"I'm sorry madam," he began sarcastically, "not all of us were born to one of the wealthiest Senators in a Republic. I'm of the working classes." She chuckled and poured him a glass when she realised he was without. Passing it to him she began to admonish him further, her eyes alight with good humour and a smile on her face.

"Well that's rubbish. You've already told me your father owns a large amount of land. It's not his fault that you are a boor," he chuckled and kissed her on the mouth. She broke away with a little reluctance and broke into another smile. "See, I knew you were a boor."

"I was thinking of growing my beard again," he said.

"If you do that then I'll divorce you."

"Does that mean I'd finally be free?" He said chuckling as she lightly tapped him on the shoulder. "I'd be quite the catch you know, Talice, you really are quite lucky to have me."

"Yes," she said with a small smile, "I remind myself of that every day."

"Anyway, I prefer to think of myself as an educated thug. I remember someone, I can't remember who, describing me that way once."

"Thug, maybe, educated though?" She was the only person he had ever met that completely disarmed him at every turn, and now was no exception. He eyes lingered on hers for a few seconds and he realised just how deeply in love with this woman he was. With her he could truly be himself and he counted his blessings for every day since they had been reunited.

"I'm getting a little tired," he said suddenly. Her slightly wiggling as he sat on his lap was beginning to turn his thoughts elsewhere, her body warm and soft next to his. She nodded over towards the fire, still burning brightly behind the metal grate.

"And what about that, General Corus?"

"A good point, Talice, though there is a perfectly good couch over there." He said with a nod of his head.

"I'm feeling a little tired too," she said as she pretended to yawn. She stretched afterwards, letting out a small moan as she did so.

"Aye, I thought you might be."

Chapter Eighteen – **Parliament**

Quittle was beyond surprised. He had always known that to win this revolution, this entire war, that he would need to destroy his domestic enemies. He sat now within the castle of Kaernarvas surrounded by those that had been in his cause from the very start or had joined when his chances had significantly improved. Importantly, perhaps the most important factor of all to his mind, was the inclusion of the Attainian Admiral and the two Cardavians. This international recognition of his position legitimised, put paid to the rumours that nobody outwith the realm recognised his cause or his claim. He knew there were some, particularly in the enclave of resistance in the north east, that still called him usurper and traitor. He also knew that Emperor Rhagan had promised to hang, draw and quarter him for treason if he was captured. He had also been flattered to learn that there was a significant bounty on his head. Tortag had joked that the amount was so high that he was tempted to hand him over personally.

They were within the main hall of the keep, the atmosphere dark and foreboding regardless of the light streaming in through the windows. It was a similar affair to when he had formally received the surrender and homage of the men of Long Loch, a parliament of sorts with him sat on a dais overseeing it all. Voices were arguing at the moment, a hundred men all jostling for position as they tried to put their views and opinions across. It was swiftly turning into a free for all argument with nobody listening to those who they were apparently talking with. The common rule of thumb, or so it appeared to Quittle, was that the louder a man shouted the more legitimate his cause or concern seemed to be.

He rubbed at his weary brow wondering when he had last managed to get some proper rest. It had been a week since they had taken the castle on that dark night. The slaughter of the men sleeping in the barracks still hung heavily on him, a stain on his soul and conscience that would stay with him for the rest of the days. What perhaps made matters worse was that he felt he couldn't speak to anyone about it, certainly not those within his close circle anyway who, at any rate, had all been involved in the same action.

"What do you say, sire?" A chief asked. He was torn from his thoughts and oblivious to what had previously been spoken about. He hadn't expected this, none of this was supposed to have happened the way it did. When they had started it had been on the back of a murder, and now people who were far more qualified than him to lead were looking upon him in askance.

"I think we need to gather more information," he replied in a bluff manner. Men around him nodded at his sage wisdom whilst he desperately tried to focus on the matter at hand.

He had summoned them as a parliament, the first held in Traemwen for far too many years. Many of the leading chiefs had turned up in reply to his summons, some sending their heirs if they were otherwise occupied. Religious figures from the major cults and temples had also appeared thus lending the support of theocracy.

He was, barring one man, the only one sitting upon the dais with the rest of his entourage standing. He looked to his left and saw Grim sitting in his chair, the bruises and swelling beginning to dissipate. The man had looked half dead when Nek had half-dragged him towards a tavern where they had set up a temporary sick bay. When Quittle had received word, and he remembered vividly that he had been in the castle courtyard at that point having just fought off a skilled Speirakian officer, he had made his exit in as calm and dignified manner as possible. Kiegal had managed to avert a potential catastrophe by pressing the men to make another charge towards the keep itself, thus avoiding people thinking that the King was fleeing the battle. If any man had earned the right to a seat, Quittle believed, then it was Grim.

The other man upon the dais was a comparative stranger, the Attainian Admiral Aarlin. He hadn't spoken much to the man but he was within his debt already. The naval blockade hadn't really begun to pinch on the Imperials that had once infested these parts, but it had proved a welcome distraction. Moreover, when the barracks had gone up in flames and lit the sky for miles around, Aarlin had immediately ordered his launches and transports to make for the quays. Arguably, and he knew it could become a bone of contention in the future, the Attainians had helped to carry the day. The clansmen, for all their impetuosity and natural ability with weapons, had simply been a raiding force. They had not been equipped or armoured anywhere near enough to take on a fully fortified position. They had utilised the element of surprise, but when the castle garrison had seen the few numbers and their state of dress, he was damn near able to marshal his men and led his men in a fighting retreat to the keep. It had been touch and go, the entire operation possibly having to be called off. They had achieved their major aim and that was to destroy the vast majority of the Imperial garrison, but if the castle remained in the hands of the Imps then it would have cast questions on his ability to lead; no matter how justified those questions were.

The naval party had landed without any sign of resistance, most of the townsfolk already trying their best to aid Quittle and his men by doing what they could. The local tavern owner had turned his premises into a mock sickbay where the worst cases could be seen to and operated on if necessary. Bakers would go up to men and pass them fresh or stale bread depending on their level of sympathy knowing that the attackers would be famished. The local women had been lifesavers, quite literally, by taking their self-appointed roles as either water providers or providing medical assistance. The naval party had then come on, their bands playing and banners flying as if they had just been out on a pleasant exercise.

Some of the more powerful ships also came within range of the castles and there was a thought that they would start providing fire support, something some of the clansmen remembered fine well from their time at Gephy. People initially, Quittle included, thought the idea to be a good one until Tortag reminded him that artillery, though well meaning, could very well drop short of their target sometimes and he didn't enjoy the idea of being killed by the enemy let alone his own side. The very brief discussion was concluded and a hasty message dispatched to the catapult ships to not fire, though the threat of bombardment kept the Imperials from manning the parapets.

"Sire," spoke another chieftain. Quittle desperately tried to think of the man's name, a talent he was normally good at having been an ambassador in what seemed like a previous life, but failed completely. He put it down to being far too tired that his abilities to remember the smallest bits of information were starting to fail him. He did, however, recognise the plaid cloak and the colours signifying that the man was one of those that came from the north east neutral clans; the Iron Dragons. Quittle nodded his assent for the man to speak.

"Sire, we in the Iron Dragons were wondering when you would begin your march north and liberate us from the chokehold that has been established. As you are aware, sire, we are loyal to your cause but cannot do anything whilst we are ringed by traitors and the last Imperial army in this land." The man stopped for a few seconds as he tried to collect his thoughts, enough time for murmurs to turn into shouts again as people tried to either decry him or support him in turn. Quittle held up a hand for silence, his patience beginning to fray as the leading men of his country acted like bickering children and motioned for the Chief to carry on.

"You have achieved something, sire, that none of us thought possible. A lot of us here have come to this gathering far too late in the day and face accusations because of it. I cannot blame those who have been in this war from the start thinking we are glory seeking, or tacking our name to a winning horse. However, I was there before the walls of Nepriner. I was there when you spoke your words when you gathered the chieftains and spoke of your dream. I supported you then in my own way, now let me support you again."

"Chief Gudri," he said as he suddenly remembered the man's name and he could have leapt for joy when the man inclined his head. "We will be marching north east, but it won't just be this small raiding party that you see before you now that will go. We have three clans pitched against us, three of the strongest no less, with strong support from the Empire. We need to approach this cautiously, for if we rush in to this then we are likely to lose our struggle. Even now the Emperor his massing his men on the border and, gentlemen, I can guarantee you that the idea of Traemwen would be trampled into the dirt should he win."

"So when do you march, sire, my people cry out for relief! The taxes being extorted from us are killing us, our fields and livestock have been turned over to the rebellious clans." Quittle had to stifle a chuckle as the thought about how quickly terms changed, just over three months ago he had been considered a rebel who was simply exploiting the grievances and ill-feeling that the Nepriner campaign had produced. Now the shoe was on the other foot and he was seen as the legitimate power in the country.

"We march, Gudri, when I say we are ready to march. I trust you know the Lord Marshal?" Quittle looked over his shoulder and nodded to Tortag. Gudri nodded even as he looked at the man, Tor with his face impassive and his posture foursquare with his arms behind his back. He looked relaxed, but resolute and ready should the need arise.

"Then you will know," Quittle continued, "that the man doesn't give bad advice unless it comes to what drinks we should have." That garnered a much needed laugh, some of it sycophantic, but the majority genuine. He looked over his shoulder and saw a flicker of a smile playing on the bearded lips of his friend.

"Then, when you decide to march, sire, the Iron Dragons will be ready." Quittle nodded and looked to the Attainian admiral, the man deep in conversation with Nek and Grim. He knew that there was still ill feeling that existed between the Attainians and the people of Traemwen. Every child was told the stories of how the Attainians had tried to subjugate them in centuries past whilst they used terms like 'civilising' and 'trading opportunities'. They were taught how the Traemwenians had cast them out, uniting for the first time under one banner and became a people again. They also knew that that freedom had been short-lived, that Rupinia with her Speirakian allies had come. The ultimate betrayal had been when the Rupinians and the Attainians had finally resolved their differences, for a short time, and actually united to crush them. Now the Attainians were back and apparently helping them, but none here deluded themselves by thinking that they were doing it out of the kindness of their hearts.

Quittle liked to think he knew about politics and the machinations of government. He knew he was being used by the two allied powers, Attainia and Cardavy, in an effort to bloody the nose of the Empire. The two allies would never be able to take a territory or country the size of Traemwen by themselves, not without significant investment that would see other fronts and other concerns stripped of their manpower. A rebellion, however, needed no significant investment on their part when the people native to that country were already fighting against their former masters. Quittle was a realist though, he knew he liked the likes of Grim and Nek. He remembered Beran Corus and how the man had been. They were, individually, not bad people; he had even grown to like them. However, if or when the day came that they tried to impose their own standards and beliefs on his people then they would remember why the clansmen were the best natural fighters this side of the world.

For now, he would do nothing that he wouldn't do anyway. He was planning on marching north, for that was where the threat lay. He had also received only limited support from the Attainians and Cardavians. Yes, the Cardavians had sent two advisors, but they hadn't sent their legions. The Attainians may have provided a fleet and a few marine regiments, but they hadn't supplied the majority of his manpower. This was for the good, he didn't want to be seen winning his war by using foreigners to kill his own people.

His only real reassurance about the Attainian was that Grim and Nek had personally vouched for him. He had been a harbour master, apparently, at Gephy and had been a stalwart figure then. He was to be judged an honourable man, more concerned with the welfare of his men than furthering the aims of government. He was also older, which, in light of the disasters that the Attainians had faced over the last century, meant that he wasn't likely to recommend that the old Republic overstretch herself again and establish permanent military garrisons on foreign soil.

He realised his thought process had drifted off again and that he had missed some of the discussions taking place, but he could see that Tortag was addressing some questions. The topic at hand was about a general mobilisation, or the closest that a Kingdom such as Traemwen could organise. There was muted discussion in the hall as neighbouring chieftains spoke to each other, another indictment on the success and speed of his successful campaigning so far. Not long ago, the Chiefs in this hall would have sooner killed each other than speak a civil war. Slightly before that, the only thing that held the chiefs together had been the threat of Imperial retribution against an unruly clan.

"Lord Marshal, a quiet word?" The man nodded and made to move over to the throne but Quittle waved him off and pointed to a small ante chamber. Tor nodded and moved off, Quittle standing at the same time.

Conversation in the hall came to a crashing halt as men stood and watched, Kiegal telling them that the parliament would resume after a short break before following his King.

"What's wrong, Bear?" Tortag asked when they were out of earshot and away from the crowd. The antechamber was a decent size and possibly would have been a room used for the lady of the castle whilst she was entertaining guests. Quittle was about to speak before the door was opened again, Kiegal entering the room shortly followed by Grim and Nek. Aarlin was nowhere to be seen, possibly himself aware that he wasn't part of the trusted inner circle yet.

"Nothing, but Gudri raised a good point," Quittle answered.

"Gudri is a blowhard who believes his men can win battles by themselves," answered Kiegal with an unusual amount of venom. "Do you remember the mess they made of the northern wall when they were assigned to take it? I wouldn't trust them to run a piss up in a brewery let alone back an offensive."

"I must admit, I'm with Kiegal on this one. The Iron Dragons might sound like the type of people you want backing you in a fight, but they are hopeless. If they are being subjugated, then it can only be because they haven't actually done anything to improve their lot."

"They still have a point though," Grim interjected. The three Traemwenians turned to look at the man, each noticing, as if for the first time in decent light, how pale the man looked. He had taken a battering when he had fought for his life with the Imperial outside the castle and, though he was able to walk unaided and had a healthier complexion, he still looked as if he had just been brought back from the dead. Quittle remembered thinking how he himself should have a rest, but Grim looked as if he needed one.

"Say what you're thinking, Grim, you've earned the right." Tortag said in a friendly manner. If Quittle had been the first one in to make sure that the Cardavian was alright, then Grim was the second. Now, a week after the battle, he still took a great concern in the wellbeing of his friend.

"If Bear wants to win the throne, and I mean kick the arse out of the Emperor whilst he's at it, then we need to order the clans to gather their regiments now. That's what, close to eleven thousand men? You've got another three thousand from the Attainians. Take the north east, drive the bastards into the sea."

"There's still the issue of the borders though," Kiegal stated bluntly. "Alfdarr is there with a thousand men monitoring the progress of the Emperor and his army. We don't know how many men he is likely to bring with him, though I don't think it'll be anywhere near as big as the army that went to Nepriner. Have we actually heard anything from your brother?"

"No, he's been quiet," Quittle answered. It was something that bothered him a little, but as far as he was concerned with that front was the less news then the better the circumstances.

"Well that's some good news. My scouts haven't reported anything either," Tortag added. "So what's the plan then, Bear? Do we march north east now or do we wait and see what happens?"

"I think we need to muster as many men as we can and march north east, prior to the Emperor crossing the border. If he does that and we turn to face him, with our rear exposed, then we will be down and out before we can affect a different outcome. Worse, if they end up uniting their two forces then we'll be forced to conduct this war of attrition again. Do that and we might lose the ground and support we've already gathered."

"Well," said Nek, "at least it's becoming traditional that we risk everything on one throw of the dice!"

"My Lords and Chieftains!" Quittle shouted as he entered the main hall once again. He was resolved in his mind now, the lack of counter argument from Tortag securing him in his judgement. He needed to resolve the situation in the north east if he had any hope of holding back the Empire when they finally came on. The hubbub of noise in the room dwindled until there was complete silence, all eyes on the King as he made his way to the makeshift throne. He sat down, feeling the weight of responsibility upon his shoulders.

"My Lords. My friends. It is time to unite this country once and for all. If we do not unite then we face destruction. We will see our entire way of life destroyed, our culture assimilated into the Empire and besmirched. We will no longer be the masters of our own destiny. Our sons and daughters in years to come will have to bend the knee to a foreign despot who simply views them as providers of tax and food. Our sons and grandsons, even ourselves, will have to carry out wars that we care little for. In order to avoid this, we need to destroy the rebels.

"To that end, it is my royal command that the regiments of every clan muster again. I require from each of you one thousand men, fully armed and equipped. You will receive monetary compensation for their time away, and your men will be fed from my own pocket and the lands I intend to seize from the rebellious chieftains." There was some muttering, but Quittle was of the opinion that nobody in the room had expected any less. It reassured him that he was taking the right course of action, their silence being taken as a sign of acquiescence.

"When will we muster, sire, and where?" That was Balda of the Long Loch clan, one who formerly stood against him yet was now a staunch ally.

"We will muster here in two weeks and then march directly north. Chief Gudri," he said almost as if summons.

"Sire?"

"You will stay behind after this parliament is over. You will tell my council and I the lay of the land in those parts. Then I want you to go back and be friendly to those that rebel against the crown."

"Friendly, my lord?" There was some more mutterings of discussion and Quittle was put in mind of some of the shows he had seen when he used to be in the diplomatic service of the Emperor. Often the audience were invited to participate in the shows and, it seemed, parliament was the same sort of thing. He turned to Tortag and noted the look of confusion upon his face, his lips framing the words 'friendly' as if in question.

"Aye, friendly. Everything will be explained after the meeting." He was growing tired and a little excited now as he considered the next movements. He wondered, briefly, if he would grow bored of the crown when there were no new challenges to surmount. He reasoned, quickly, that the problems would change but doubtless the odds wouldn't improve. "Is there any other business?"

"My King, there is an issue with the mines in my count..." Wenrynt of the Iron Mountain stumbled to silence as the doors of the main hall were thrown open. A man walked through, a fresh bandage wrapped around his forehead and a wound on his arm that had burst its stitching. The silence was absolute as the assembled men opened a path allowing the man to come through. He still carried his weaponry, though his mailshirt was covered in mud and what looked to be blood. If anything, the man looked to be a survivor from the previous weeks' engagement who had suddenly woken up. Quittle squinted and recognised the man as Eadwald, his brothers second. He stood up, unable to keep the look of worry from his face.

"Sire," Eadwald began. He sounded tired, bone tired, as if he had been riding for dear life for the past week. His features were gaunt and there were dark rings under his eyes from lack of sleep, there was also the unmistakable smell of smoke upon his clothing.

"Sire, the Emperor has invaded." Nobody spoke and nobody moved except to allow the man to pass through. It was evident that Eadwald also had a limp, a thick and bloody bandage bulging out from underneath his trousers. "Chief Alfdarr sent me away to tell you that he is falling back, burning farms and crops as he goes conducting scorched earth tactics. He estimates that the enemy has some twenty-five thousand men with him."

"How far have they penetrated into our borders?" Tortag, in his capacity as Lord Marshal, asked. He was nervous, knowing that his lands were right upon the borders and therefore the likeliest target for retribution and vengeance.

"Not far, Lord Marshal, and their progress is slow. Their main force is engaged to the south with the Cardavians and the Attainians. They've taken Cafeld," Tortag felt his heart sink at the loss of his town and all that it had suffered. It had become a symbol of Traemwen, for the taking and sack of the castle had been the first action they had successfully undertaken.

"Has Cafeld been sacked?" Quittle asked, aware of the significance of the town.

"I don't know, sire, I was sent away by the Chief just before it had happened."

"How did you come by your wounds?" It was as if there was no one else in the room apart from this man and his interrogators, thought Quittle. The moment that they had been preparing for, indeed fearing, had finally come to pass. Emperor Rhagan may not be a battle proven General, but he was highly educated. His Generals and advisors, if he listened to them and they weren't fighting against the allied advance to the south, would be in a good place to advise him on what to do. All Quittle, and by extension the Kingdom of Traemwen, could hope was that the Emperor was by himself and surrounded by courtly toadies and sycophants.

"There was a sharp skirmish with Speirakian outriders. Their horse archers and skirmishers were the first ones to cross the borders. We had no word of their approach, the bastards had hid their advance well. We were ambushed and we paid a heavy price, maybe leave two hundred of our one thousand men dead in the forests."

"And my brother, is he okay?"

"He took a wound, sire, an arrow in the leg but otherwise fine. He's directing the scorched earth personally, as well as the evacuation of settlements to the hills. The Emperor hasn't any interest in going into the hills yet."

"So we can assume he doesn't know where our main strength is yet," Kiegal muttered. Quittle rounded on him, his temper flaring as the stress of the situation got the better of him.

"With respect, Kiegal, we don't even know where our main strength is just now!" He hissed before raising his voice to address the assembled crowd knowing that this was the final crisis point of his reign.

"Gentlemen, because of the situation, it is imperative that you muster here within two weeks. I have gone over enough what is on the line and it doesn't need repeating. This parliament is over." The men filed out the room with doubts and misgivings hanging over their heads, but each man knew that they had already pinned their colours to the mast. Some of them, Quittle knew, would leave the parliament and muster their men out of

223

loyalty. Others would do it out of fear of retribution from either side.

Chapter Nineteen – **Council of War**

The room was filled with the blue tinged smoke that Nek's pipe produced, a rich and aromatic flavour to it. Grim was sat in a corner nursing his own drink and pipe, puffing occasionally as he looked at a highly detailed map of the north eastern area. Tortag and Kiegal were in deep discussion as the pointed at random features here and there, often attracting more comment and details on where they could fall back from. Quittle stood silently next to Aarlin, the Attainian Admiral, keen to bring him into the conversation knowing that naval support could become key in the fast transfer of forces around the country.

Gudri looked disconsolate sitting in the corner with his head in his hands. Quittle knew exactly what the man was thinking and feeling for he had often thought it himself. The man was wondering how to extradite himself from the trouble he now found himself in. He knew that the Imperials, and by extension their clan allies, viewed him with suspicion. However, the man was in the proverbial lion's den. He knew, also, that if Quittle and his men won the day and he was found wanting then he would be hung for a traitor if he was lucky. Had he not already pledged homage to Quittle for the lands that he held? Quittle couldn't help but feel for the man.

The north east of Traemwen was generally a law unto itself and fiercely loyal to their own chiefs. It was virtually cut off with a river that ran from sea to sea, and those areas that weren't submerged in water tended to be covered in hills and swamp. There were only a few key points where a host would be able to cross in decent order, and only one where it would be able to cross and threaten the rest of the country immediately. It was this bridge crossing that was focussing the mind of Quittle, Tortag and Kiegal.

The trouble that now presented itself to them was somehow to persuade the enemy to make that crossing their only one. If they were sensible or confident in their own abilities, then they would likely split their forces and have them rendezvous with the main Imperial host as it continued to march east. Once the conjunction of the two armies was complete then they'd be able to trap the Traemwenian fighters into the south eastern corner, where they were now based, and thus end the war and any chance of freedom.

"How well do you know this area?" Tor asked as he continued to stare at the map. Gudri stood up slowly and walked towards the table where the chart lay as he scanned the details, almost as if he was trying to familiarise himself with it for the first time.

"I know it well enough, Lord Marshal. I grew up around those parts," he said as he finally answered. Quittle watched him for a few seconds wondering if the man was going to volunteer any more information, but it was becoming evident that it was going to be like drawing teeth. The trouble that Quittle and the rest of his men had was that they needed Gudri to stay onside. He was, whether they liked it or not, an integral part of their plan.

"Good, that is good." Grim said, almost innately picking up on the tense atmosphere and what was perhaps riding on it. Grim decided to try and ease the man into the conversation, see if he could get complicated answers out of him eventually by asking him simpler questions at first. "Would you say it's good territory for movement?"

"In smaller raiding groups, Cardavian, yes. But a full body of men? They'd have to cross at one of the few bridges." He was confirming what they already knew, but they needed to cajole the man and appeal to any vanity he had.

"Why is that?" Grim didn't normally play the fool nor someone who was ignorant, however, he was used to dealing with officers or officials who had ideas far above their station in life. As far as he was concerned, it was better for the likes of him, who ultimately had nothing to lose, to appear a fool rather than the King or Tor.

"The swamps and the hills, Cardavian," Gudri said as if explaining to an idiot. "The swamps are huge and run the length of the river bed. Where there aren't any swamps there are hills, and those clans won't go over them without ending up coming to blows with each other. They are used to raiding each other, and if one man has his livestock out then there's no telling what they'd do. No, their best approach would be to use this bridge." He pointed at the chart indicating the bridge that Tor and Kiegal had already decided where a battle would be fought.

"What's the bridge made out of?"

"You ask a lot of questions, Cardavian."

"I am a seeker of knowledge," Grim answered as calmly as he could. In truth, he wasn't terribly sure of his own abilities to fight right now. He still felt as weak as a two-day old kitten and he found himself becoming tired rather more quickly than he was used to.

"It is made out of wood, if you must know." Nek was beginning to glare at the man, the tension in the room rising as he continued to dismiss the Cardavian questions. Grim, remarkably, was staying calm throughout. Quittle was beginning to have enough, however, not wishing to cause a schism between his allies and his subjects.

"Then it shall become an integral part of our plans, Gudri, and you will be a major player," Quittle interjected before Grim could ask another question. Gudri turned and bowed graciously and became servile again, his condescending attitude disappearing like mist on the breeze. Quittle flashed a glance at Nek and saw the disgusted look upon his face and shook his head slowly and almost imperceptibly.

"I am at your service, sire."

"Good," Quittle stated as if the question was never in any doubt. "The Clans in that part of the land will be advancing as soon as they receive word that the Emperor is here in strength. I think that will leave us three weeks. With our limited numbers of horsemen, we can keep a barrier throughout most of the countries to prevent their messengers getting through, but we can't stop them all. It is imperative that we do not allow the two forces to combine, otherwise we will be facing great odds. You will make the difference here, Gudri."

"What would you require me to do, sire? My clan is small and, even if we did unite with the others, we couldn't possibly put down those three clans by ourselves. They outnumber us by some margin." Quittle nodded along, his face that of reason and compassion no matter what his truly feelings were.

"Lord Marshal, I believe you know the way I'm thinking on this one."

"I think I do, sire, but it's going to be bloody tricky to pull off."

"It always generally is with us," he said with a smile. He waved at the map in indication for Tor to lead on.

"Like the King has said, we need to control the movement over this bridge. We need you to go back to your clan and offer your services, though no doubt you will be pressed anyway. If you come across as willing then they'll trust you to an extent, why should they not? It is important that you direct them to this bridge in three weeks' time. You will take up position in the rear with the other men from the neutral clans. If they are as willing to come over to our side as much as you say they are then the next part shouldn't be a problem."

"And what is the next part, Lord Marshal?"

"A battle that will decide whether we live as free men or die as slaves," Kiegal answered for him. The men looked at him and noticed the intensity on the man's face, the passion that was lying under the scarred surface. They turned back to the chart as if finalising the plan within their heads before Quittle decided to bring this side of the proceedings to an end.

"Chief Gudri, allow me to thank you in advance for your service. If there are any problems, then I need you to get in touch by the fastest messenger you have. I don't want to stress it too much, but the entire fate of the war effort now lies upon your shoulders."

"I won't let you down, sire."

"I know. Now go and enjoy some food before your journey, the weather may be improving with summer around the corner, but it can still get foul out there." The man nodded knowing when he was dismissed, though Quittle noted that he walked with his chest held out and a swagger. No sooner were the great oak doors shut than Nek opened his mouth.

"Well he's an insufferable arse," Nek began before he was silenced with a finger from Quittle. He waited another minute to make sure that their conference could be held in as much secrecy as possible.

"He may be an arse of the highest order, Nek, but we need him now." That was Tortag as he sank into a leather chair. "I don't like it anymore than you do, and I can't stand that man. Given any other circumstance I wouldn't trust him to organise a piss up in a brewery let alone a critical part of our plans."

"Alright, but let's be honest. What if he does bollocks it up?" Nek asked, Grim was silent but nodded along holding his own misgivings. "Let's face it, plans are only well and good up until they are actually put in motion. What happens if these rebel clan chiefs start asking where he's been over the last few weeks? That weak willed moron would fold and tell them our whole plan."

"Nek has a good point," Grim interjected adding his own weight to the argument. "You've said it yourselves, gentlemen, there's plenty of areas for groups to pass the natural obstacles. If he can't get them into the area that we're wanting when we want it then it'll be tricky."

"Tricky is putting it lightly," Kiegal said with a chuckle. "It's true though, and you're right of course. There are no guarantees. Tell me, what would you do?" Grim rubbed at the back of his neck and looked down upon the chart again, but could come up with no different answers. The only place, it seemed, where they could make a stand with a degree of advantage on their side was that one site. It didn't sit well with him.

"I was never a high ranking officer, not for a long period of time anyway. I didn't go on the courses or anything like that," he said by way of explanation. "I can't see any other way to bring them to battle on favourable terms."

"Maybe you just don't like the man?" Tor said with a grin, "I thought at one point you were going to smack him." The men around the table grinned and Grim smiled along.

"I was tempted, though I think Nek would have beaten me to the punch."

"Wouldn't have been the first time either," Nek said with a wink.

"What is this, a game of pick on the wounded man?" Grim cried with mock outrage. "I thought you lot were my friends."

Quittle grinned along, enjoy their easy talk and banter. It was surprising that these two were Cardavians, a nation that was supposed to be his enemy less than a year ago. Nek and Grim, as far as he was concerned, were as good as Traemwenians in his eyes. They were loyal, dependable and steadfast. He turned to look at the Attainian admiral who, surprisingly, had remained silent throughout the meeting.

"How do you feel about this, Aarlin?" He asked by way of bringing him into the conversation.

"I'm not a soldier, sir, but I recognise where Grimfar is coming from. It is a risky and audacious plan, but then," he said with a faint smile, "you aren't exactly the sort to think about the odds if your career to date is anything to go by."

"Is there anything you can give us in the way of naval support?" Tor asked, naturally distrustful of Attainians in general. He hadn't gotten to know Aarlin either, something that Quittle had found strange. Kiegal was, if not openly hostile, certainly guarded around the man whenever he announced his presence. Long held prejudices, Quittle could see, would be something they'd have to eventually overcome if they were to progress as a nation.

"There's not a lot, sir. I can provide transports for when you and your men are victorious to take you to another area. I could, potentially, help you launch a naval invasion of our sorts on the area. However, there is limited transport availability." He rubbed at his black and silver beard and concentrated for a few seconds, before finally snapping his fingers. He looked up, genuine excitement in his eyes.

"I can provide you with my marines though. They are a strong, disciplined force with good armour."

"I can testify to that," Nek said as he stuffed tobacco into his pipe. "Hardy buggers when they want to be, and they are good at following orders."

"Unfortunately, or fortunately depending on your viewpoint, I can testify to that as well," Kiegal said as he scratched at the void where his eye used to be. Quittle nodded, suddenly understanding where his antipathy came from.

"You have three thousand marines with you, Admiral?" Tortag said, willing to allow bygones to be bygones. He was too old in the tooth now to hold grudges over a prolonged period of time. If anything, recent events had proven that the Imperials were his real enemy. He thought again of his wife, feeling the mixed feelings of anger and sorrow gnawing at him again.

"I do, Lord Marshal. I'll be leading them as well." Grim and Nek stared at the man for a few seconds and it was Nek that broke the silence.

"I'm not being funny, Admiral, but I've never seen you fight. You're too important to lose in a battle on land when you're needed at sea."

"And whilst I appreciate the concern, Nek," he said with a smile, "I'm big enough and ugly enough to look after myself. Anyway, do I not have two weeks to prepare?" Nek nodded, conceding the point. Two weeks may be a significant period of time, but was it enough to make someone a swordsman and less of a danger to himself and those around? At the end of the day, the way Nek saw it, you were either a good swordsman or a dead one; there could be no in between. History was littered with mediocre or average swordsman.

"I take it your men will be fighting with spear and shield?" Kiegal asked, casting his mind back to Gephy and Nepriner. The Attainians tended to fight with a large oval shield, working in a hedgehog like formation where the shield overlapped their neighbour. It was a good formation, incredibly useful on open and unbroken country, but should something disrupt the formation then chaos was likely to ensue. It's why, also, the Attainians were trained to be proficient sword fighters.

"That's right, and we'll be wherever you need us. How many men, sir, do you think will come to the muster?" Aarlin asked as he addressed Quittle. "I'll be honest, if we're asking for eleven thousand then we'll be lucky to receive that many. I'd say we'll get nine, and that includes the thousand already with my brother. So eight thousand here in two weeks, plus your three thousand." He chuckled suddenly as it occurred to him. "It takes us to eleven thousand actually."

"Hardly ideal, especially when we go up against the Empire," Grim stated as he filled his own pipe. There was a haze of blue smoke in the room now from the pipe of Nek and Grim added his own contribution. He pointed to the chart with the nib of his pipe. "Is there any chance of getting any more marines, Aarlin?"

"I'm afraid not, the Senate weren't exactly happy sending a force this far up with our own operations ongoing in our former lands." Quittle noticed a flash of irritation on the face of Kiegal, a noted historian who knew the old lands that used to belong to Traemwen in years gone by. The chances were that Aarlin was talking about former lands that, by rights, belonged to his kingdom. It was a matter that could be argued about in future years, but now was not the time.

"How about any Cardavian legions?" Quittle asked knowing that it would be an impossibility, but enough to detract any attention from the Attainian. He wondered briefly whether he should pull Kiegal aside, but decided to let matters be. If he drew attention to it then it could exacerbate the situation.

"I doubt it. In all honesty, Bear, I have no idea what the legions are doing. It's been nearly four months since we were in Cardavy."

"Chances are," interjected Nek, "that they are either supporting the Attainians or watching over the folk from the Coalition in the south. They are pretty stretched now, Bear."

"I thought as much, but chance would be a fine thing." Quittle had a sudden thought, something that hadn't occurred to him when he had originally thought of his strategy. He turned to Tortag, worry etched across his face. "How do we get them across the bridge?"

"Well, Bear, I'm hoping there's a bloody great big wood nearby in accordance with that chart."

"And if there isn't?" Tortag puffed out his cheeks in reply and looked at the chart.
"Could always lie down for a bit, I suppose."

Chapter Twenty – **Packing**

Beran had been involved in several campaigns, at least four major battles, and one drawn out siege. He had seen men at their very worst and their very best. He had seen professional soldiers run when a young peasant girl, armed with a stick, stood her ground and shamed them all into action. He had seen men remain stoic in front of overwhelming odds, and suddenly cry and breakdown when they saw a bird being shot from the air by a hungry archer. He had seen plenty of things in his life, but the spectacle in front of him now was, perhaps, the most disturbing thing he had ever seen. He had tried calling upon his powers of reason and logic, even using prior experience to get him through the situation, but nothing had worked. He had to finally admit defeat, recognise that he had been completely outmatched: a woman who needed to pack for a three-week trip was not be trifled nor argued with.

He watched her from his seat in their quarters and, though some would consider it cowering and hiding, he had always found the best position for a seat was to be in the corner of a room. He was grateful that he had shifted the seat long before he needed to, for one false movement from himself just now was liable to end up in his death. Talice had a list of things that she felt needed to be taken with her, and a list was something that apparently no person, no matter how high up in the command chain of the legions, could argue with. He had volunteered to help once and had never done so again for he valued his life.

"I swear I've got more clothes than I had when we moved here," she said from the bedroom. He rolled his eyes knowing when a question was rhetorical, and he had greater self-preservation than pointing out that she had visited the nearby port city more than a couple of times with the maid that they had hired.

He tried to busy himself with reading papers and parchments that held reports from his senior officers. The fort was now in a better state, more of a military garrison now than it had been in ages. The blacksmiths were belching out smoke and had a decent surplus store of swords and horse shoes. They were looking now into crafting and building the new types of armour, a process that the legionary blacksmiths had had cause to write to Silveroak about. Apparently the process was similar but the metallurgy was subtly different, so much so that they needed someone to come down and train them. Beran didn't mind supplying the cost, knowing that a decent blacksmith who knew his craft was greater than his weight in salt. Velawin was also busy looking into the records of those officers who had put themselves forward to try and fill the post that Erallac had once fulfilled. So far there were one or two stand out candidates, by all accounts, and one or two who thoroughly deserved promotion. However, Beran was thinking about looking outside the legion and had already written a letter to Field Marshal Raffin requesting that Grimfar and Nekstar be attached to his legion. He couldn't think of a better place for them knowing that they already got on with the senior officers. It would also allow him to trial using three leaders of the heavy infantry, something he felt needed to be added to the legion for flexibility in the battle line.

He hadn't received a reply from that letter, nor did he expect one just yet, but one that did disturb him was a letter he had received from the Field Marshal about the Stags. It appeared that the Stags hadn't marched north, or at least not to Silveroak, and their whereabouts were currently unknown. It made an already delicate situation altogether more dangerous, for Beran had no doubts that he had made an enemy out of the man. Whatever his dreams or ambitions or hopes the man had been entertaining upon arriving at Silveroak must surely have been dashed, and a man backed into a corner with no hope was liable to do stupid things. Upon receiving the letter he had written to the commanding officer of the Leviathans asking if he had seen them march north. The reply had come back to the negative, and, more worrying still, another invitation to a function.

"Have you been listening to a word I've been saying?" Talice asked, staring at him from the doorway. The light from the open windows danced delicately upon her red hair, and she wore a light tunic to fight the effects of heat from over exerting herself on the packing. Mercifully the maid was nowhere to be seen, presumably still trying to go through her mistress wardrobe and wondering which would suit her tastes better.

"Sorry, Tal, I was miles away and going over some work." He mentally took a deep breath before he plunged into the next line of conversation. "Do you need a hand with anything?"

She glared at him with eyes like daggers before she turned about with military precision and stalked back into their bedroom. He heard her footsteps padding down the hallway and some shouting about him not being much help before a door was promptly slammed. He waited a few seconds, nodded once and stood up to look around the room.

"Well, bugger it, I fancy a drink," he said aloud to himself. He walked over to the small mahogany drinks cabinet they had bought and brought out a bottle of red. Looking at the label, he made sure the name was sufficiently steely sounding and the picture on the front was nice. He was not a sophisticated drinker, believing generally that those bottles which had a sufficient amount of dust on them were obviously well aged and therefore decent enough to drink. He poured himself a small glass and retreated to the corner again, stopping to turn and retrieve the bottle before returning to his seat. He placed them on a small table next to his seat and walked over to the fire, wondering whether he should build it up for firing upon their return. Deciding that he didn't have anything better to do with his time, particularly given that he had already packed his very limited number of clothes, he decided it was for the best.

He finally sat back down again and watched the natural world going past his window. This area of the world was excellent for birds of prey, and often at night he could hear the hooting of owls in the distance where they resided in the woods. He had been out riding and seen plenty of wild game, both fowl and venison, and had vowed that when we he came back from the south that he would go hunting with Aleill or Velawin; possibly both if time permitted.

It led him again to think of the invitation to the southern lands. He couldn't recall ever being invited to an official function by a foreign power before, at least not one where he had been based on their border to make sure they didn't suddenly get ambitious notions in their head. Intelligence was also short of coming having received no official brief of the young Queen. The Cardavian diplomat, Garren, had been extremely quiet of late. His last report stated that Queen Wellisa had managed to procure some of the black powder which had wreaked havoc upon the defences of Nepriner. He still remembered the continual night bombardments, the buildings exploding around them, as they lobbed the black powder bags into the inferno. He gave and brief and involuntary shudder at the memory, seeing again the desperate last stands that took place as foe and friend alike tried to defend themselves from the flames.

"Have you actually packed?" He heard Talice shout from the bedroom. He chuckled and considered suggesting that she should pack more lightly but decided against it.

"I don't actually have much in the way of civvies. I'll be in uniform for most of it," uniform consisting primarily of his battle dress. He was damned if he was going to dress up like some popinjay to a dance at a foreign Queens tune. He heard a derisive snort and some muttered cursing and this time did chuckle, considering that his wife could behave like a lady when she wanted to and have the mouth of a tavern landlady on other occasions.

There was a chap at the door and he stood and walked over, opening it and seeing Aleill standing there. He could have embraced him, welcoming the distraction and beckoned him inside. The man was well turned out, almost to a parade standard, and Beran commented as such.

"It wasn't my doing," Aleill admitted when he sat down and was offered a glass of wine, "Vel made me do it."

"He made you, as in you didn't use your batsman?" Beran asked somewhat shocked.

"He made me. He really has no class that man. I have no idea how he ever became an officer," he said it with a wry smile taking any sting out of his words. "When are we getting moving?"

"Talice is just packing the last of her things. I swear there's more organisation here than there ever was in Nepriner, or any other military adventure I've been part of."

"Yes, well, that's because you're an idiot and she's intelligent," he said grinning and sipping at the wine.

"Do you know anything about the south?" Beran asked out of hope.

"Not a lot, bunch of savages really. Did Aglon not have anything to add to the official brief?"

"How long have you been in the legions?"

"Must be close to ten years now, why?"

"Then you'll know well enough that official briefs on this sort of thing is generally 'go there and don't get too drunk!'" Aleill laughed out loud and looked around, his eyes alighting on the small library of books.

"I didn't know you could read."

"I don't, I get Talice to read them to me instead." He finished his glass and considered having another but decided against it. One would be enough, especially if he were to be travelling for the rest of the day.

"Well that explains a few things," he said before pausing as if for thought. "Do you think I should go and offer some help?"

"I wouldn't, Aleill. Talice may appear all sweetness and light when she wants to, but she'll lash you out that room with her tongue. Anyway, I'm under the impression she'll try and set you up with someone when we get there."

"Does she know someone?" Beran shook his head to the negative.

"No, but then you know what socialites are like. Talice will no doubt be best friends with the Queen by the end of the evening and this will become a monthly occurrence."

"Maybe I might be in with a chance with the Queen?" Beran laughed and shook his head.

"Of all the things you are, Aleill, of which you are many, I have never pictured you as a King."

"Yes, well, you lack imagination that's why." Aleill stood up and examined the spines of some of the books and was surprised to see a few of the Cardavian literary classics. He scanned the shelf further and wasn't surprised to find a series of books on the formation of the Kingdom, nor some of the more intricate military histories about the formation of the legions. "I take it the better half of your library belongs to Talice?"

"You take it right. I tried reading one of her books once during a stormy night. Anyway, it was all the usual guff about love, depression and isolation. By the end of the book I wanted to kill myself. I often wondered whether that's what the author was getting to."

"I've tried writing a book," Aleill stated. Beran wasn't surprised and motioned for him to continue. "It was during Nepriner, more of a diary really that I was thinking of getting published."

"What was the content like 'scran is shit, company is worse and I'm better than this'?"

"Ah, you've read it then," Aleill said with a grin. "Looks like the weather is closing in," he said as he indicated the window.

"I know; we're going to have to get a move on. Oh," Beran said as he remembered, "I've given orders for a bodyguard unit to come with us."

"Because of the Stags?" Aleill queried to which Beran nodded.

"The very same. If they haven't gone north, and there's the sea to the west of us and mountains to the right, then the only possibility is that they've gone south."

"I wonder why he's done that. I mean, surely the entire legion couldn't have just gone and mutinied."

"I've no idea, but he must know people down…" He heard the creek of the bedroom door and stumbled to silence as Talice finally emerged. From the look of her as she emerged he wouldn't have guessed that she had been wrestling with her clothing for the past several hours. Instead she looked almost serene, a smile on her face, as she indicated her chest. Beran didn't know what surprised him more, the fact there was only one chest or the fact she hadn't emerged covered in the blood of their young maid.

"Are we ready to go?" She asked as if she had been waiting for them to finally conduct their business.

"Aye, Tal," Beran said quickly as he cut off the remark that Aleill was obviously about to make, "I'll have a couple of the lads up to take your chest to the carriage."

The chest was mounted on the back of the carriage on top of his own and covered with a sheet of tarpaulin to prevent rain from damaging the contents. He carried out a quick inspection of the guard and made sure that they were looking good for he knew that the Cardavians would be watched by everyone; he didn't want to be the commanding officer that brought a rabble of vagrants into a foreign country. Each of the men had obviously been well briefed by their officers and their immediate superiors for their armour shone in the sun, their weapons were well oiled and honed to a perfect edge, and the horses had been brushed down and any fraying leather straps had been replaced. In all, he was pleased with the turn out. His own weaponry was close to hand with his sword hanging on his left hip. He was determined that he would carry it regardless of how that was perceived. He was going down there as a guest, that was true, but he couldn't shake the feeling that something was off. It may have been a well-meaning invitation with absolutely no ill will attached to it, but he had learnt enough in his life to know that nothing ever came for free. He would have preferred it if Garren the diplomat had sent a letter or something to brief him on the situation.

The storm clouds passing over head were still threatening rain but mercifully holding off for the moment, however, the atmosphere was muggy and close. He felt himself beginning to sweat a little under the armour, and the padding between the chest armour and his tunic was beginning to radiate heat. He both considered it a blessing and a curse that he was a naturally warm person in circumstances like this. He was half-tempted to remove his headgear and allow the fresh air to get amongst his hair but decided against it until he was in the carriage.

"Looks like rain," Vel said as he approached him whilst he checking out the horses that were to pull the carriage. Beran looked up and nodded.

"Aye, hopefully it won't affect the journey too much. I'm guessing the Coalition have roads."

"Isn't it just Ufwala now?" Vel asked in mild admonishment.

"There's still princedoms in the south, five of them if rumour is anything to go by. They are broken and ready for the taking, but Wellisa hasn't won it all quite yet."

"I wonder what she'll do when she wins. She's built her reputation up, she doesn't sound the like sort of woman who would then sit back and do nothing."

"She'll need an heir, Vel, otherwise all this will be for naught. Ufwala and the coalition, if she were to die, would fall into chaos again." Velawin nodded and felt the first splash of rain, a light haze beginning to descend upon the fort. Beran felt it as well and looked slightly beyond him to see where Talice was. "What's your plans for when we're away anyway?"

"I don't know, the power might go to my head and I might march on Silveroak. I could become King Velawin."

"You know, Aleill was on about trying to woo Queen Wellisa. I had no idea my officers aspired so highly in life." He chuckled, picturing the image of the two men sending barbed comments to each other via their respect diplomats. It would, possibly, be the first time a war had been conducted using wits rather than swords.

"Could you imagine such a country? Anyway, you better be for the off. Where is Talice anyway?" Beran shook his head unknowing and glanced around the fort again as he tried to spot his wife. Eventually his eyes alighted upon her walking towards them from one of the blacksmiths. She seemed to be carrying something wrapped in sheets and canvas. He quirked his eyebrow and gestured towards it.

"Is that a present for me?" He asked hopefully, she shook her head with a light smile.

"It's for the Queen. If she is allowing us to stay in her castle, then it's only right we provide a gift. Anything else wouldn't be proper." Vel nodded in agreement and turned to Beran, shaking his head with a slight smile playing upon his lips.

"You're a barbarian, Ban, I swear. Imagine not knowing that."

"I know, imagine eh?" He grunted, he looked towards Talice again. "We need to get moving, Tal. The weather is starting to come in from the north and I'd like to be off before it really starts pissing down."

"You better make sure you don't use such language in front of the Queen," Aleill said as he appeared from behind and clambered into the carriage. "Otherwise she'll think you really are a barbarian, regardless of the best efforts of your wife and I."

"Well this will be fun," he said with an almost resigned air. "Vel, I mean it, if there's anything that comes up then send a messenger south as soon as you can."

"I'm sure everything will be fine, Ban. Go off and enjoy yourself, get some rest and come back. I'm thinking we can go on some exercises when we get back," Beran shook his head with a smile and clasped the forearm of his friend.

"Well, I leave the legion and fort in your capable hands then Commander. There's a set of handover notes in my office, but you know what's going on as well as I do. My assistant, Fortin, will be able to help you if you encounter any difficulties." Velawin brought himself to attention and saluted, duly returned by Beran, and the formal handover was complete.

"Have fun," Vel said as Beran opened the carriage door to allow Talice to slip in. He turned smiling and nodded.

"Don't worry about me, it's the Ufwalans who won't know what hit them!"

Chapter Twenty-One – **The Battle of Cairn Bridge**

They had mustered some ten thousand men within the two-week period he had commanded at the parliament, one thousand short of what Quittle and Tortag had been hoping for. He remembered seeing them all mustered, the banners and different plaids symbolising the unity of Traemwen. He had felt a surge of pride seeing the mixture of men moving amongst each other when they had initially mustered at the town, the easy banter between different clans as they tried to distinguish which one had the better fighters. Thankfully it had only been words rather than actions, very little trouble between former enemies being reported to the King. He had grown concerned with the Attainian forces, however, often left in isolation by the Traemwenian soldiers. It was understandable, bad blood had existed between the two nations for centuries and weren't likely to get any better in the immediate future.

They had marched off with their pipes and drums playing, the banners flying in the early summer breeze. Amongst the men there had been an almost carnival like atmosphere, morale high as different units tried to play their instruments the loudest. The townsfolk had also come out in great numbers pushing food, drink and anything else into the grateful hands of the marching clansman. Quittle had felt a great deal of trepidation and nerves then knowing that the campaign was coming to a conclusion, that everything he had been fighting for was going to culminate in the next two battles. Once he had defeated his domestic opponents he would need to turn swiftly and deal with the Emperor, a man who was still waging a war of destruction upon the borders.

Alfdarr had continued to send messengers reporting the situation. It appeared that the Emperor, Rhagan, was in sole command. His Field Marshal, Neard, had been tasked with trying to delay the Attainian and Cardavian advance in the south; something that Aarlin reported was going well. It meant, or so Tor had briefed him, that the main strength had been focussed where it was primarily need it. Once again, it seemed, the Rupinians had completely under estimated their opponents. Quittle could only pray that they continued to do so.

Quittle had ridden up and down the line numerous times during their easy march, speaking to groups of men and individual chiefs. He kept hearing the same thing; how the men believed in the strength of their cause and how the chiefs believed that the end was in sight. All Quittle wanted to do was bring peace to a country which had known little of it since the Imperials had first taken the land. He wanted to usher in a new era that would benefit the whole of his populace, and if that meant discussing things with the Attainians and the Cardavians then so be it. He was determined that clan politics wouldn't get in the way, that those who would prove unwilling to conform to the new system of law and rule would find themselves ostracized. He knew though that to achieve all of these ambitions that he needed to win this one battle first.

It was night time now and they had encamped in a forest within sight of the bridge. He had reconnoitred the area with Tortag upon arriving and both men gave silent prayers of thanks that the forest, a mile away from the bridge, was still standing. It was one of a number of things that were completely outwith their control on this battle, but it was a good omen and would form a significant part of their deployment plans. The river which the bridge spanned was swollen with the recent heavy rains and the run off from the hills, the water muddy looking and dangerous. He hadn't ventured far onto the banking before he felt the ground beginning to shake a little. He stepped off with a jump onto safer ground, unwilling to die in such a manner.

The forest they were within now was full of the noise of men preparing themselves for battle. Some were keen to drink as much as they had brought with them, worrying that there wouldn't be an opportunity tomorrow morning. Others turned to religion and turned to Gods that they had previously neglected, making pledges and promises they had no intention of keeping in the long term. Others tried to write letters to loved ones that would never be delivered. More, however, prepared their kit and were honing their blades knowing that the difference between a sharp blade and a blunt one could be their life.

Quittle sat with his inner circle, the men who had been with him since the start. The forest canopy allowed the smoke from their fire to clear the area and kept away the fine drizzle of rain that permeated the area. There was a boar being roasted on the spit having been brought down by one of the archers and given to the King as a gift, skinned and gutted by Kiegal. The smell of roasting meat filled the air and he felt his mouth filling with saliva at the thought of finally eating. There was also a smaller fire where soup was being brought to the boil having been prepared by Grim in case anybody wanted extra; he knew it was better to go to sleep on a full stomach prior to a fight so that the body was more ready in the morning. There was a silence in the group just now, each man happy to have his own thoughts and not fill the air with inane chatter. They had been through enough battles to know what it was like, and they also knew there was no point in empty boasting. They knew the strengths and limitations that each other had and knew there was no point in discussing them further.

"Everybody happy with the plan tomorrow?" Quittle asked finally breaking the silence.

"Let them cross the bridge in numbers, take them in front and rear. Simple really," remarked Nek in an off-hand manner.

"That's if Gudri hasn't bollocksed it up," interjected Tortag. "If he does then tomorrow will be touch and go, no happy endings."

"Well that's a nice thought to eventually go to sleep on. You should write children stories when we're done here," Nek said as he stood to begin carving the meat. Grim looked up from the boiling pot of soup and added a little more salt, cautiously taking a sip from it. Happy that it was finally ready, he dipped his mug in.

"Wish we had bread. I'd kill for a fresh loaf."

"Never know, the rebels might bring some!" Quittle said with a laugh.

With daylight came the sound of bugles waking everybody up. Men performed their ablutions knowing that it may very well be their last day. Food that hadn't been eaten the night before was now eaten with a will, other pots were over smaller fires with porridge being made ready. Quittle was restless not having slept for most of the night, his mind constantly going over things that could or would go wrong. He kept thinking of the warning that Tortag had said, no matter how off hand it was. The possibility of Gudri not having fulfilled his part of the deal would cause complications. The strategy of using, effectively, a fifth column in the enemy party had worked well during the battle against Long Loch, but would it work again?

"Porridge, Bear?" Tor said as he sat down next to him, passing him an earthenware bowl with a wooden spoon. Quittle thanked him and added a little salt from a pouch in his cloak much to the disgust of Tortag.

"You aren't one of those traditionalists are you? I always preferred a little sugar with mine."

"Sugar is a little light on the ground here, we haven't been on the best of speaking terms with the Speirakians if you hadn't noticed?" He grinned and mixed the porridge and salt together and eventually spooned some into his mouth.

"You look like shit, by the way. Didn't you sleep last night?" Tor asked with genuine concern on his face.

"No," Quittle admitted, "I was thinking of what you said. What if Gudri hasn't managed to convince them to come?"

"They'll come in anyway. The danger is what if Gudri has been killed off and his clan absorbed? That'll give them parity in numbers meaning that, even if we do win here, we'll take serious losses. It'll worsen our chances when we go to fight the Emperor."

241

"Well thank you for that comforting thought, Tor. I'll go into battle today with a lightness in my step now."

"You did ask, Bear." He said with a shrug and a smile. Quittle nodded and began attacking his porridge again, the queasy feeling in his stomach from nerves not aiding him in the process.

"All the Chiefs been briefed?" The plan was relatively simple. Four thousand men, including the three thousand Attainians, would be waiting a few hundred yards from the bridge. In front of them would be a thousand archers who would pepper the enemy as they advanced. Once the enemy was committed and coming across the bridge in greater numbers, the archers would begin to fall back to stand behind the front line where they would resume their bombardment. Once a sufficient number were on the Traemwenian side of the bank, the front line would advance to contact. With any luck, it would create congestion and lack of movement on the bridge. If Gudri fulfilled his side of the plan, then the rebels would be attacked from the rear.

"They've been briefed by both Kiegal and myself. They'll hold. The five thousand in the rear know as well not to engage until they are ordered."

"Good, give it an hour and then we'll start to make a move."

"Mind if we fight with your boys today, Admiral?" Grim asked as he approached him. They could see the bridge in the middle distance, the morning sun shining down upon them. The river was in full spate still because of the rains, fallen tree trunks and other debris from further up the river beginning to settle on the bridge supports. The enemy were within sight on the other side of the bank, chanting their war cries as they sought to make themselves brave through song and numbers. Grim looked across to them again and saw their numbers, estimating with a professional gaze that there were some ten thousand of them.

"I'd be honoured if you and Nek joined us," Aarlin said with a smile. "It'll be a good opportunity for us to teach you Cardavians how to fight."

"That'll be a first," Nek said with a grin. "Talking of firsts, I barely recognised you in that armour and helmet. You look like my grandfather after a trip to a museum." The older man grinned and chuckled, stretching out the bronze seeing stick and examining the enemy line.

"I thought we were friends, Nek, so why would you lie to me?" He queried as he focussed on the sight of an enemy standard bearer.

"Of course we're friends, when did I lie to you?" Nek asked bewildered.

"When you said you've been to a museum. I don't think you've ever been to a place of education in your life!" Nek grinned and Grim laughed, the two Cardavians feeling better than they had in weeks now they were part of a firm battle line.

They enjoyed being with people who they knew, people they had fought beside in the past and understood their culture and civilisation. The two men had spoken about it quietly the previous night after they had finished their meal. Both had concluded that they had enjoyed their time with the clansman, but they were different somehow. Individually they were good men, but there was something alien about their culture. They gloried in war, they actively sought confrontation when words could be exchanged instead. Grim had argued that their entire purpose for centuries had been to be frontline fighters, shock soldiers to be thrown at the enemy line. Their entire country and economy was geared towards providing for war.

They had spoken at length about their hopes after this was concluded, knowing that the campaign was nearly over and their involvement with it. They wouldn't be required to stay on should Quittle be successful as military advisors, not unless they were ordered to anyway, and if Quittle lost then they had already decided long ago that they would head to the fishing village. Now with Aarlin here they were somewhat reassured that a fleet was waiting to take them home. Home was something that Grim was thinking more of, his time with Katrin always to the forefront of his mind. He may have only spent a month with her but he knew he was in love.

"That's not good," Aarlin said ominously as he continued to stare through the seeing glass at the enemy line.

"What is it?" Grim asked, seeing the enemy line begin to part slightly revealing four dark shapes. He felt a sinking feeling in his stomach knowing that his day was going to get worse.

"Here, take this and see for yourself." Aarlin passed him the seeing glass and Grim looked through it to the dark shapes. What he saw made his stomach turn even more, his nerves beginning to grow as he saw men being dragged to what looked like pyres. One of them was battered and bruised, blood seeping from several wounds. His head was wrenched back violently, almost as if the man holding him wanted him to see the Traemwenians on this side of the bank. The shock of recognition struck him a blow that was almost physical.

"That's Gudri. That's the chief that was supposed to be on our side," he muttered. Nek reached for the seeing stick and was passed it, eventually looking through and fixing his stare upon the condemned man.

"Well, he's not happy about what's happening anyway. We should tell the King what's happened. I knew a plan would bollocks up eventually." He continued staring as Aarlin detailed a man to run and find the King to tell him of the recent development. Gudri was dragged to the pyre kicking and screaming, his voice drowned out at this distance by the booming of drums and the skirl of pipes from either side. He was forcibly held as men began looping a rope around his waist and, when Nek thought things couldn't get any worse for the man, his arms were raised and nailed to the wooden staff. "Poor bastards," he murmured quietly as he saw the same being repeated on the other three chieftains. One of them looked resigned to his fate and his head was slumped as the rebel clansmen continued to shout jeers and taunts at the condemned. Another, braver than most, was spewing hate at them and presumably cursing at them. Gudri looked to be in tears and had soiled himself in fear, his dignity long gone as blood seeped from the nails in his forearms.

"Bunch of barbarian bloody bastards. Here, Grim, I can't watch this anymore. You take it," Nek said as he pulled the seeing glass away from his eye. He offered it to Grim but the man shook his head, his face pale and his fists clenched and tense. "Well somebody bloody take it; I am not watching this. It's cold blooded murder."

Aarlin took the seeing stick back and watched the assembled crowd on the far bank chant at the condemned men, every second passing making his blood run colder. Quittle rode up on his horseback, the crown circlet shining as it caught the light for a few seconds. Aarlin passed him the instrument and simply pointed with his speak towards the black shapes. He was grateful that he didn't have to see anymore either, the last thing he did see being the fire brought to them on torches that would send them screaming in paint to the afterlife. He continued to watch as the thin tendrils of smoke became thicker, eventually thick black smoke spewing out over the land.

"Tortag," Quittle asked as the man rode up to him. "Our plans have changed. Is there any way across this river without having to use the bridge?"

"There is a caul to the east, maybe a mile away from what the scouts have said, but with the river this high I don't know how easily passable it will be." Tor watched the other embankment and saw the black smoke, even as Quittle continued to watch. The men were now writhing in pain, almost trying to beat the flames back with their feet in desperation; all it seemed to do was fan the flames ever closer. The chanting from the enemy was also beginning to lessen, presumably under orders, so the thin and wailing cries of the condemned chiefs could be heard by the Traemwenians.

"The plan may still work, Bear," he said quietly. Quittle shook his head and passed the seeing glass back to Aarlin.

"I'm not willing to take that chance. Anyway, if they've been found out then the chances are that those who were loyal to our cause in those clans have been wiped out or forced to renounce us. They will, however, still come at us."

"Perhaps sending my lads across this caul would do the trick?" Aarlin asked, determined not to be a bystander to events. Tor thought for a few seconds before shaking his head.

"No, they've already seen you and you are in plain sight. Chances are if you were to move east that they'd contest the caul. It'll have to be some of the reserves we're holding back in the forest, at least the woods stretch up to the bank over the way."

"Good. See to it, Tor. Kiegal and I will command here, along with Aarlin," he said with a nod. Tortag looked once more towards the enemy who were beginning to mass a little out of bowshot near the bridge before clapping his heels to his horse and making for the forest.

"Well, this is going to be tight," Nek remarked as he watched Tor speed off.

"Tight doesn't even cover it, brother, this is going to be bloody Hellish," Grim said with a smile.

Quittle watched the enemy as they began to muster properly, their clan chiefs extoling them to greater heights of bravery now that they had the blessings of the Gods on their side. He found it funny that everyone believed the Gods would protect them, as if the they could actually be bothered with the affairs of humanity. Surely they were immortal, he would often ask, and surely, therefore, they wouldn't care for the fleeting mortality of the human race? He looked across the bridge again and directed his horse to stand beside the archers, Kiegal amongst them. Kiegal was already preparing to give the order to notch their bows and Quittle allowed him to carry on, maintaining a respectful silence. He watched the first of them begin to tentatively step across, wondering whether he should have tried to sabotage the bridge or even prep the ground with caltrops and others traps for when they began their approach. It was too late now.

"Archers, nock!" There was only a thousand, but a decent archer could get an arrow off every thirteen seconds. With death raining down from above those thirteen seconds would be a lifetime for some of the shield less men as they ran towards the Traemwenians. He almost felt sorry for them, knowing that his war wasn't with the people that made up the clan, but rather those who led them. He wondered if there was anybody on the other side who thought the same. He cursed his philosophical and wandering mind knowing that now was not the time to begin to feel pity for anyone.

"Draw!" The thousand men pulled back their bows, their muscles straining as the sheer force of power drew extensively on their upper body strength. It wouldn't be a neat volley, but it would be enough to slow down the charge. Quittle watched, his eyes focussed on one man in particular. He was well armoured, better than most, and his livery and surcoat was of a better design and richer in colour. He wore a tartan plaid around the top of his helmet and, he wondered, whether the man was a chief or just a well-equipped follower.

"Loose!" A thousand barbed arrows flew into the air, some coming down within an instant as men misjudged their shot or hadn't drawn back far enough. More, though, arced gracefully into the air. They reached their peak and began to dip, men on the bridge and the northern end beginning to look up into the sky and working out their chances. Some of the more pragmatic began to duck down whilst others struggled to raise their shields, constricted as they were by the mass of men on either side of them. Some others were forced into the surging torrent of the water by sheer force as stronger men pushed them out of the way, desperate to get some space to raise their shields or duck. Time seemed to slow, Quittle hearing the words "nock, draw, loose," being repeated again as a second volley took to the air.

The first crashed down, time speeding within an instant as men collapsed to the bridge stopping others from progressing further. Others crashed through the wooden balustrades in their death throes, sweeping others off their feet with their flailing. The second volley added further to their misery, though a few of the arrows were taken by the window with some falling harmlessly into the water. Now there began a desperate rush to get over to the other side, men slipping because of the wet nature of the planks through either rain or blood. A third volley crashed amongst them and then a fourth, every time the bodies piling up or falling into the water.

There was now an almost frantic pace being set by those in the front rank, those lucky enough not to have to run through the maelstrom of falling bodies and trip hazards. A few fell, so keen in their own headlong charge that they lost their own footing adding to the misery of those behind. Many, Quittle knew, would be trampled to death.

He looked to Kiegal even as another volley flew through the air, trying to recount how many had now been launched. There would be spare supplies of arrows in the forest with the rest of the supply wagons, but they were still a finite resource. He also found it impossible to work out how many of the enemy would be dead or wounded, but, as he briefly glanced at those bodies that were now banging against the bridge supports in the water along with the other detritus washed from the hills, he knew the number to be high.

"Archers will prepare to fall back!" There was man who made to move back too suddenly and break ranks, "Do not pre-empt the fucking order! You go when I say you bloody go! Archers! Nock, draw, loose!" The volley did much the same as the last one, Kiegal giving the order when the arrows were still in the air to fall back to their prepared positions where stakes had been driven into the ground just to the rear of the four blocks of spearmen.

Quittle sat atop his horse and watched the men as they crossed the bridge, some champing at the bit to be at the fleeing figures of the archers and, even more so, to be at the defiant figure of the King sitting atop his horse. He watched them for a few seconds longer, their senior clansman trying to get them into some semblance of order before they began the advance. Quittle watched them for a few seconds longer before contemptuously turning his horse, doing it slowly so as to show he was not afraid of those men. He touched his heels lightly to the flank and set off at the trot towards the spearmen to take his position there.

"Have you ever thought about retiring here?" Nek asked Aarlin as they watched the mass of men begin to form some semblance of order. Another volley was sent into their ranks, thinning them a little as it caused men to fall to the muddy dirt.

"I don't think so," Aarlin replied. "I have an eye on an estate to the south within the Inner Republic. How about you?"

"I'd sooner shit in my hands and clap personally," Nek said with a grin. He flicked his glance around and looked at the faces of the men around him, each of them showing a range of emotions that he knew only too well. Some had the look of courage and bravery as they faced the odds with a stoic indifference. Others were openly fearful, perhaps wondering if today was going to be their last day as they fought and died in a foreign war that they cared little for and understood even less. Others were just simply confused, wondering why the order hadn't been given to advance or wondering whether the enemy would charge.

"We can't allow too many of them to cross that bridge," remarked Grim, or we'll be done for regardless of the reinforcements. It's bloody typical that we'll take the brunt of it as well."

"You did choose to come into the centre with me, Grim, I didn't ask you to." Aarlin replied with a grin. From a birds' eye perspective, the three Attainian marine regiments and the one Traemwenian appeared to be a crescent moon. When they were given the order to advance they would converge on all sides against the enemy, constricting their movement further and prevent any semblance of order. That, Aarlin thought with a rueful smile, was the plan.

"I've never been one to sit it out really, I end up getting bored and this one," he said indicating to Nek, "would get bored and complain as always."

"When you two have stopped flirting with each other," Nek interjected, "I think we're supposed to advance now." There had been a lull in the screeching of the pipes and now a flag was being waved frantically from side to side beside the King as the four bodies of spearmen were ordered to advance. Aarlin nodded emphatically and filled his lungs with the air. "The Attainian regiments shall advance!" Shields were presented to their front, spears sliding into place as men adopted the close order formation that had once won them an empire in all but name. Nek and Grim did the same, feeling more at home in months now that they were part of a proper formation. Grim couldn't help but notice the small smile of satisfaction on the face of Aarlin. "By the left! Quick! March!"

The infantry stepped off as one, the dressing immaculate even in circumstances such as these. They were heading straight for the enemy, another volley flying over their heads as Kiegal and his archers sought to disrupt their formation for as long as possible. It wouldn't be too long either before the Attainians and the Traemwenian regiments were too far advanced for the archers to be able to effectively fire; once that stage had been reached they would need to advance once more and begin peppering those on the other side of the bridge and bank.

"Remember Nek, don't get too far ahead this time. We've got to show the Attainians how actual soldiers fight," Grim said with a grin as he kept his eyes focussed to the front. Another volley hammered into those on the bridge, but this time it was further to the rear as the archers tried to desperately avoid hitting their own men.

"Aye, and just remember what I've been saying this whole bloody time, no getting killed doing stupid heroic shit or I'll tell Katrin. Deal?"

"Deal."

Tortag had decided to only take two thousand men from the reserves, a figure he still thought was too high given the odds facing those defending the bridge. They were well motivated defenders, it was true, but the men from the north east were known to be brave fighters. He could only hope that the words of Quittle were false, that the clansmen still loyal to the Traemwenian cause would ultimately defect to them when it became obvious that the battle was going to come down to them to be decided. He hoped that this flanking movement wouldn't end up in the annihilation of two thousand men as well, knowing that as soon as they crossed the caul and advanced to contact that they would have to fight their way across the bridge if they had any hope of getting away.

He watched the caul now and was filled with trepidation for the water was muddy and there was no visibility to the bottom. There was simply no way of knowing how well built the caul was, if the causeway was even still functional, or even how deep it was. What added to his fears was the fact that he wasn't a particularly strong swimmer and, thus, one false step or movement would likely mean his death by drowning. It was not a way he wanted to go.

He looked about him at his men and saw that they too felt a degree of fear. Nobody liked stepping into water, particularly water that was able to carry trees as if they were no weight at all. It also became readily apparent to all that battle had been joined with the amount of bodies that were beginning to float past, along with pieces of wood and splinters that looked as if they had once belonged to the bridge. He looked back from his men to the water and took a deep and shuddering breath, knowing that if anybody was expected to take the plunge first then it would be him.

He stepped down the bank and was tempted to use the spear he carried for leverage, to test out the water to see if there was a stable platform underneath. He knew that this could be mistaken for fear, however, even hesitation. What man would follow a leader who hesitates?

He stepped out, his eyes squeezed shut as his mind shut down through fear. And found himself on stable footing.

The current was exceptionally strong and he was having to fight against it to retain his footing, but he made sure his pace was slow and sure and that his steps were always tested first before committal. The ground underneath was a mixture of flat stone and pebbles, devoid of any plant growth or silt. He gave a very quiet prayer to the Gods, thanking them for looking over him once more before he turned to face his men once again.

"Well what are you waiting for, lads? The water is a little chilly, but dry land is just over that way! Watch your footing, don't go too fast, and I'll see you on the other side!"

It seemed like hours to make that crossing and he wasn't particularly sure that he breathed at all whilst doing it. At one point his chest was completely under and he struggled to retain his footing, slipping slightly with a large shout of fear and rage. His head went under before he could take a breath but he managed to slam his foot into a fixed stone, enough for him to wedge himself for a moment so he could resume standing. He stood up, his vision blurring with the water cascading down his face, and his eyes only focussed when he saw a man with a slit throat go past. Contact, he knew then, had been made and actual fighting was taking place.

He reached the far bank and felt mentally and physically exhausted, his nerves fraught and on a knife edge. He watched his men work their way across and, one by one or even in groups, many managed to do so. Some were less lucky. He watched one man approach the halfway point, his face grim with determination, as a body slammed into him. He couldn't recover, the dead weight pushing him away from the caul and out into the murky depths of the river. He wasn't seen again, his armour and weaponry dragging him to the bottom. He saw another man slip and then suddenly stand up again, cracking a joke to the men about him as he thanked the Gods for his luck, before the man beside him suddenly lost his footing and accidentally pushed him away from the safe path.

It was possibly only a short time before the rest of his men, at least those that survived, finally made it across. He formed them as best they could, noticing that the vast majority were shivering with cold due to their wet clothing and skin. Most had lost their spears and were only armed with swords and their small shields now, but there was enough weaponry amongst the surviving eighteen hundred men to make them a serious threat.

"Right, boys, we're marching towards the bridge," he shouted out to them. "I ain't going to lie to you, this won't be easy. If we win then we've won the battle, if we lose then we are dead. Do or die, lads, there can be no half measures. Now let's go and get this bloody business over with."

Spear thrust followed spear thrust as Grim tried to avoid being killed. Twice now he had been involved in the front line before being recycled to the rear again. He was tired, mentally and physically so, as he thrust his spear between the thin gap of shields in front of him. He felt the sickening thud as his weapon touched a man's chest before piercing through. He felt the spear being dragged backwards as his opponent fell to the ground and he wrenched it free before he lost it. There was no tactical finesse here, no brilliant strategy that would win the day or prevent either side from carrying the field, this was just simply butchery.

He looked to his right and saw Nek had the same grim expression on his face, a mirror of his own. His friend had a cut to the brow where a lucky sword cut had managed to break his guard for a few seconds, the assailant being cut down by Aarlin before he could deliver a killing thrust. Blood was seeping freely from the wound now, occasionally having to be wiped from the brow before it obscured his vision.

Grim tried to look beyond the battle line to the main body of the enemy and tried to discern whether there was many more left. He could see the bridge was rammed with men, though some were still falling from the broken balustrades to drown into the murky waters below. The bridge itself looked less stable than it had at the start of the battle, learning over alarmingly to one side now as men continued to pile on.

He was almost caught out as a man launched himself at him, using both hands to tear at his shield and force it from his grip. He was too close to use the spear effectively so he dropped it, drawing out his short sword in one fluid motion and thrusting downwards. With the man dispatched, Grim found himself suddenly being forced backwards as another enemy came at him. His shield was torn from his grip, the dying man still clinging onto the shield like a drowning man does to a raft. The enemy clansman before him grinned with little humour, his face pale as he thrust his sword towards him several times. Grim had to move backwards, parrying desperately.

A thin wedge was beginning to open, a bulge in the formation that would prove disastrous to the Attainian marine regiment unless it was swiftly filled. Grim steadied himself, before thrusting desperately with his sword as his opponent over balanced and tripped on the corpse of a dead marine. Grim had been aiming at the man's chest but completely mistimed it, taking the man through the throat instead. He dropped down dead all the same. The wedge began to collapse but Grim pushed his way through to the rear of the line, shaken and in need of another shield.

"Rough fight this," said Nek as the order was given for the front line to change over once more. It was a complex manoeuvre to change rank and tact whilst in the middle of the battle, no doubt something that the Attainians had picked up from the Cardavians. A shrill whistle would be sounded and the front rank would throw out their shields and charge into the enemy line, long enough for the enemy to fall back and the surviving front rank to fall back.

"It's not going to get any easier. They've still got their cavalry on the far bank. They look too heavily armed to be natives as well," Grim said pointing with his sword. Nek looked and nodded, muttering a small curse. "Reckon that's the Imperial garrison?" He queried.

"Makes sense. If the country over there is that wild, then there wouldn't be any point in having too much infantry. My guess is that it's Speirakians or Rupinians who look like them."

"So how do we get them across?"

"That's above my pay grade, brother. Quittle needs to sort something out. We may have reserves, but if we break here then the cavalry will be deployed before the reserves could do anything."

"Sire," Wenrynt began, "if we pull back one of the infantry formations then the cavalry will cross the bridge in numbers."

"They might," Quittle conceded, "but they won't make any ground quickly. The bridge is crammed with men at the moment." Quittle had watched the battle develop into a slogging match between the two opposing sides, neither gaining any sort of advantage. What interested him now was the shape and structure of the bridge, something that looked precarious at best.

"What are your orders then, sire?"

"Pull back the regiments and open up the gap between the bridge and our line. Have a new battle line drawn up and allow more of the clansmen across. With luck the enemy will begin to think we are withdrawing and start sending their cavalry across in readiness." Wenrynt nodded and clapped heels to his horse to take the orders to the Attainian admiral and the other officers.

Quittle looked to the east and wondered where Tortag was, knowing that the only way this battle could be concluded successfully without using his entire force would be the flanking force under his friend and Lord Marshal. "Come on, Tor, we need you now." He flicked his glance back to the bridge and was desperate to get involved in the battle, something that he had been warned against by the likes of Tor and Kiegal before the battle. It went against his natural instinct to get involved, but their final words on the matter still rung around his head. If he were to fall, they argued, then all this would be for naught. He needed to remain alive and, without any disrespect intended towards him, he would be a natural target for every enemy soldier there and he would only endanger those around about him. The slight psychological advantage given to the Traemwenians would be outweighed by the negatives. He stayed his hand, but looked on with a degree of consternation.

The Attainian and single Traemwenian regiment were beginning to form a fighting retreat as they followed his orders. He knew it was the right decision, seeing the cavalry beginning to muster and move towards the bridge. Volleys of arrows continued to fly overhead from the archers of Kiegal, a few horsemen beginning to tumble to the ground as they advanced.

"Come on, Tor." He whispered.

"Form line for battle!" Tortag could see the battle raging on the southern bank of the bridge, watching the Attainians begin to fall back. At this range he couldn't tell whether it was by design or being forced back by sheer weight of numbers. The Imperial cavalry were beginning to muster now, making their way across the bridge and adding their significant weight to the failing structure. Even he could see that the bridge was beginning to buckle, perhaps even collapse, and he wondered why the rebellious clan chiefs continued to send men across it.

His men positioned themselves around him, the men in front carrying their pikes and spears whilst those without formed themselves in the rear line. Mercifully, as far as he could make out, the enemy hadn't noticed his force mustering and deploying themselves on their exposed right flank. Long may it continue, he thought.

"Forward!" He cried out to his eighteen hundred men, their spears levelled as they advanced towards the bridge. He marched in the front rank, his sword in his right hand as he continued to watch the southern bank. The Attainians had ceased falling back and now formed a new line, but by doing so allowed more of the enemy to cross the bridge. More still were desperate to capitalize on this perceived success, jostling for position as they tried to get to the enemy before they presumably fell back and descended into rout. He turned to face the enemy again, the cavalry completely committed now to the bridge and crossing it. It was then that the first head turned to look at the approaching Traemwenian formation, followed by several dozen more.

"Standby to receive!" He bellowed, now one hundred yards distant. He was tempted to order his men to charge, to cast aside their spears and rush headlong into the enemy with whatever weaponry they had to hand. Momentum was with them, their formation strong, but the surprise to the enemy would be complete. There was still a sizeable force of the enemy on this side of the bank, but eighteen hundred men would do them a significant amount of damage and force a decent amount back onto the bridge.

"Fuck it," he muttered as he resolved himself. "Traemwenians, ditch your spears and pikes. Ready swords!" He counted to five in his head before carrying on. "Charge!"

The men let out a collective war cry, shouting out the name of their two respective clans as they rushed to get into contact with the enemy. Men jostled with other men in a playful manner as they raced headlong, treating it more like a village game rather than a prelude to battle. Others threw comments at each other calling into question their manhood with wide grins.

Tor readied his sword and launched himself into the first opponent that he could, kicking out with his right leg into the man's chest sending him sprawling backwards into the churned mud. He dispatched him with a swift sword thrust through the chest and moved onto his next, ducking underneath a sweeping blade and stabbing upwards through the ribs and out the back. He withdrew his sword, looking left and parried quickly as another man came at him shouting his rage and insults. He died with an arrow through the back of his neck before Tor could even bring his sword up to defend himself and he cursed both in shock and rage, knowing that Kiegal was still using his archers to pepper the area.

He withdrew from the battle to gain a decent look at how the line was holding, noting that the Traemwenians had completely enveloped the enemy on the northern bank. The rebels were being forced backwards by sheer momentum, and someone, possibly Quittle or even Aarlin, had noticed Tor and his men. The arrow storm ceased, but the Attainians were beginning to press their advantage and pushed the rebels backwards. There was a loud crack like an explosion, reminding Tor of either thunder or the black powder that the Speirakians were so fond of using. Fighting died down in an instant as men began to look to the bridge, more cracks and the creaking of wood emanating from the failing structure. The bridge began to subside, men moving desperately as they tried to avoid a watery death as they scrambled towards either bank. The Traemwenians and their allies were relentlessly, forcing more of them onto the bridge to accelerate the destruction.

Suddenly and swiftly the bridge subsided completely as the supporting struts gave way, men and horses disappearing in an instant as they plunged into the cold water that swirled beneath. Heads popped up in the water as they scrambled for air and desperate to make their way to the banks. Tor, no matter how he felt about the enemy normally, felt sorry for those men who were drowning now and dying for the beliefs of a few rebel chiefs. Kiegal, he could see from here, held no pity. He released his archers and they ran to their side of the bank, shooting without mercy those that tried to escape drowning by crawling to either side of the bank. The reserves that had been hidden in the forest came bounding out, lining the southern bank and dispatching those who managed to escape the arrows and the water. The fight had gone completely out of the enemy, the survivors who hadn't fallen out the water surrendering en masse as they realised that all was lost. "Traemwenians, put up your swords!" He bellowed, shouting the order again and again until his men eventually did. "This battle is over."

Chapter Twenty-Two – **Aftermath**

"A hard fought victory, sire," remarked Kiegal. Quittle nodded as he looked upon the broken bridge and the scene of destruction. Bodies littered the southern and northern ends of the bridge, dead Traemwenians mixing with fallen Attainians and Imperials. Death, he concluded, was the only time the three nations would ever find peace and be at rest with each other. His thoughts were dark, feeling morose, as he saw bodies continuing to slowly glide past on the water. He was grateful that he couldn't see their faces, knowing full well that each of the dead would be looking upon him and his vanity. Was it not because of his ideals, his ambition ultimately, that they had paid the ultimate price? If it weren't for him these men would be tilling their fields, or crafting their products of metal and wood, raising children even and loving life. Instead they would now be fertilising some river bank somewhere, their body to be looted of any possessions so they could rot away forgotten by everyone bar the carrion birds.

"Our losses?" He asked, his voice stronger than he thought was possible. He felt the need for a drink, now thinking it socially acceptable that the sun had begun to set. His men, he could hear, were drinking and making merry in the camp in the forest where they had slept the previous night. He knew that many would be telling tall tales of their exploits, boasting of their martial prowess and the weakness of the enemy. He envied them knowing that they were guiltless, following the orders of their clan chiefs and their King. They had fought an enemy that wanted to kill them in open battle, something they were more than willing to accommodate. The collapse of the bridge, and he had heard men comment on this, was surely a sign of divine favour.

"Light, comparatively. Three hundred and fifty-two of our men are dead, double that with wounds. Three quarters of those wounded have only light wounds and will be able to march west with us to fight the Emperor, the last quarter will need to return home."

"And the prisoners?" He asked knowing that a large number of men had surrendered on either side of the bank. He had ordered those on the southern side to be disarmed and corralled together in the open field under armed guard. He had yet to do decide what to do with them, but he had resolved that he wouldn't cut them down. It was one thing to kill a man in the heat of battle, but to kill a man who was at the mercy of the victor in cold blood would sully his name. Not only that, but it went against everything he stood for. He thought then of those who had burned to death in the two barracks and wondered if that course of action hadn't been murder.

"We took one of the chiefs. I've no idea of those on the northern side,

Bear. Tor is only now managing to bring them." Quittle nodded, knowing well that the main force of the enemy had been committed to crossing the bridge at the time of its collapse. The charge by Tor had ultimately saved the death, and countless hundreds on the Traemwenian side as well. He had seriously considered sending in his own reserves prior to his appearance. "I'll speak to them when the rest of the prisoners get here," he finally said. Kiegal looked at him, concern in his eyes as he tried to read him.

"Are you alright, Bear? You look lost in thought. I thought you'd be happy. You've achieved something that was completely unthinkable a few months ago. You've broken your domestic enemies and now are in a good place to face the Emperor."

"I'll just be glad when this is all over, Kiegal," he said with a weary smile in response. He felt bone tired, every fibre of his being crying out for rest. He may not have been involved physically today, but mentally it had been a large drain. He had watched the battle unfold and had subsequently thought that victory was close or the day had been lost every other moment. It had taken an enormous strength of will not to charge headlong into the battlefield, to lose himself in the oblivion of it all so that he didn't have to think about things.

"Once we defeat the Emperor it'll be alright, you can get your rest then and enjoy some time off. You might even have a chance to court a lady and beget yourself an heir," he said with a grin. Quittle chuckled and looked towards the forest, seeing a thousand fires lit as the forest sparkled with life. He looked upwards to the cloudless sky, feeling the first chill of the early evening as the sun began to set. The sky was a dozen different hues of red and purple as the sun slowly dropped behind the hills and the tree lines of the east.

"I haven't had a woman in I don't know how long. I doubt I'd even know what to do with one!" It was truly said, for he had not allowed any distractions in his life since he had embarked upon this quest of his. Kiegal grinned and slapped his shoulder, a sign of familiarity that meant a lot to him at that point. It showed that he was still human, that he wasn't the monster that he sometimes accused himself of being during the dark of night when he couldn't sleep.

"Well, I can't promise any women tonight, Bear, but I can promise you a few drinks."

"Sounds like a plan, chief." He remarked casually, finally resolved to one course of action at least. Kiegal grinned and began to walk off to the tree line again before stopping and slowly turning around. "Chief?"

"Why not? You've bloody earned it if anyone has," remarked Quittle as he slowly caught up with him. "There were at least three chiefs that stood against me today, and you've said that we've only managed to capture one.

Assuming the other two are dead, you can have their lands and their clans. Wield them together into a strong force and control the north east for me."

"I don't know what to say, sire," Kiegal said as he slipped into formalities. He had never thought of himself becoming a chief, never thinking it possible. He had been born the son of a farmer, nowhere near the hierarchy of the clan. Yes, he had fought for Tortag and his family for years, but he had never once thought about counting himself amongst their ranks.

"Then say nothing at all," Quittle said as he gestured for the man to continue walking. "None of this would have been possible without the support of the likes of you and Tor. The nation…I…owe you a debt of gratitude that can never be repaid."

"How did you like your first battle, Aarlin?" Grim asked as he stoked the fire with some more wood. The admiral looked tired and physically exhausted, the beard seeming greyer than it had done earlier that morning. He had washed himself, though, using the small burn that ran through the forest before it joined onto the river and had managed to get most of the blood off his armour and cloak.

"I think I'll keep to ships next time, Grim. I'll leave this hand to hand stuff to you lot. Still, it's something I can say I've done." He reached down and brought out a clay pipe and began stuffing it with some tobacco. He looked up and noticed that Grim was looking at him, his eyebrow quirked. "Nek had a spare and gave me one. I decided that I'd give it a try after today."

"Where is he anyway? I haven't seen him for a while."

"He said he was going to get some drink and food," Aarlin said in reply. Grim nodded and added a few more twigs to the fire before he finally sat down.

Realising that he was still wearing his armour he stood up again and began loosening the leather tongs, feeling relief hit him immediately as the mail and plate slid off his shoulders and chest. He unfastened his scabbard and placed it down as well before finally sitting down, removing the leg greaves and stretching out. He felt cold for a few seconds, a faint breeze moving through the forest and hitting his exposed skin.

"So what's the plan now?" Grim asked as he began filling his own pipe with tobacco. Aarlin shrugged his shoulders as he chewed on the nib of the pipe, striking a match and inhaling. He coughed violently as the smoke went down his throat for the first time causing Grim to laugh loudly. "Take it gently first, Admiral, it's strong stuff that Nek and I smoke. Try rest it on your tongue before inhaling."

"I'll take that advice, I think." Aarlin paused as he considered the question. He knew his orders was to support the fledgling Traemwenian kingdom and her King, but, in his eyes at least, that aim had been achieved. He had solidified his position beyond all doubt by defeating the last of his homegrown enemies, his domestic opponents either dead or converted to friendship. The only enemy left, as far as Aarlin could see, was the Emperor.

"I think our next course of action will be determined by Quittle. If he has need of us, then we will support him. If he doesn't then I will return home with the fleet. You?"

"You know our orders as well as I do, it'll be up to the King. Will he really want foreigners from two old hostile nations looking in on his future campaign?" Aarlin nodded, unsurprised that the Cardavian was thinking along the same lines that he was.

"What are we talking about?" Nek asked as he appeared out of the gloom with a gutted lamb tossed over his shoulders. He moved over to the log where Grim sat and placed the meat onto the dead log. He then moved over to the fire and began building up a rudimentary spit out of broken spear shafts.

"We were discussing our next moves," Aarlin replied as he watched Nek go about his task.

"Aye? What did you two manage to come up with?" He placed the lamb carefully onto the split and built the fire up a little more to allowed the meat to cook quicker. He was famished and the wound on his scalp, now carefully bandaged, was beginning to throb. What he needed, he realised, was a stiff drink and a decent meal.

"That we await the pleasure of the King, basically," answered Grim. "He may decide he doesn't want us to go with him."

"Well that'd be bloody gratitude for you, particularly after all we've done for him. Here," he said he reached into a canvas sack that he had left beside his bedroll, "I manage to requisition some supplies." He brought out three bottles of red wine that he had managed to take in the previous battle.

"I think we deserve a drink with our meal don't you, gentlemen?" He asked with a smile. Aarlin nodded and puffed gently at the pipe as Grim produced three clay mugs, allowing Nek to pour a decent measure of wine in each.

"What should we drink to?" Grim asked as a cup was handed to him.

"I don't know," replied Nek. "What do you think, admiral?"

"Home, and to those that won't be going back." Nek and Grim nodded, raising their cups in unison and downed their drinks. Casualties for the Attainians hadn't been high for they had never went into rout, and a rout was where most of the dead would have come from. They had lost some three hundred men, and another four hundred wounded. It was a small price to pay for a victory, but it was a victory for a foreign King in a foreign war. It left Aarlin with an uneasy feeling, and the only thought he could console him with was the fact that it benefitted the Republic.

"Do you really think the King will send us home, after all we've done?" Nek asked, realising that the thought irked him. Grim shrugged his shoulders in ignorance as he refilled their cups.

"He could, there's nothing stopping him. Our orders were only to establish him as King, not to fight the rest of his wars for him. We've achieved our purpose. If he wants us to stay on then it'll be up to interpret our orders," he paused as he took a drink and watched the fire for a few seconds. "What do you want to do?"

Nek blew out his cheeks, unsure. There hadn't been many times in his adult life that he had been ever given the choice of what he wanted to do. He had been in the legions for as long as he could remember, and prior to that he had to do what his mother had told him to do or the blacksmith he had been apprenticed to for a short time. The choice of independent action was not something that came naturally, at least not if it didn't involve going to the nearest tavern. This was different though and Nek knew well enough that his friend would lay great store by his advice.

He looked at Grim and saw how tired he was, not just physically but behind the eyes as well. This campaign had come off the back of the slaughter at Turgundeon, the retreat from that same place with refugees and the remnants of the Eagles, and the mad and desperate defence of Gephy. They had only had one month to get over it and recuperate, a month that had sped past and had seemed as short as a few days.

"If he wants us to go, then I'm not going to argue with him." Grim nodded and raised his cup in silent salute.

"Gentlemen, the King would like to see you." Wenrynt said as he approached their small clearing. Grim placed his hands on his thighs as he stood up with an audible grunt, feeling his back click into place and his knees scream at him. In truth all he wanted was more of the wine and some food before retiring to bed and merciful sleep.

"Tell him we will be there in a moment, Chief," Aarlin answered for them as he drained the last of his wine. He waited until the man was out of earshot before he carried on. "Well, at least now we'll found out what business lies ahead."

"You are absolutely sure about this, Bear?" Tortag asked prior to the three men arriving. He didn't feel that he was in a position to advise at the moment, his thoughts and nerves shattered after having to traverse the caul again. His progress hadn't been made any easier by the amount of bodies that he, his men and his prisoners had come across on their march east along the northern bank. It had seemed like the river had spat the bodies onto the banks, the carnage of broken weaponry and broken bodies testament to the destruction that had been wrought upon the enemy army. He had given up counting the number of bodies, closing his mind off to their suffering in order to safeguard himself. He regretted it, but he knew well enough that those who now lay on the dirt with the water lapping at their still forms would have delivered an even greater retribution upon himself and his men.

"We have to. With the number of prisoners that we have there will be plenty that join us, including those in the Dragons and the other three neutral clans that survived. I won't press any men to join our cause, we'll release the rest."

"If you release the rest," pointed out Kiegal pragmatically, "then you potentially allow them to regroup and become a threat again."

"I won't have them murdered, Kiegal," he said somewhat harshly. "I know where you are coming from, but we won't win over anyone if we conduct ourselves like the Imperials used to. Anyway, these are your men now. You need them just as much as I." Kiegal nodded in understanding, not having thought about it in that way.

"There's no guarantee they'll join us even if I order them to fight for us," he replied in counter argument.

"No," conceded Quittle, "there isn't. However, if you let them return home then you'll win over some of them, perhaps most of them. If there's one thing I've learnt recently is the ability to be magnanimous in victory, because you'll never know when you need them to return the favour."

"How long do we need to rest for, Tor?" Quittle asked.

"A lifetime?" He answered with a wry smile. "I'd say a couple of days, no more. We need to make our way west and come up with a way of fighting the Emperor, linking up with Alfdarr and finally pushing the Empire from our lands."

Quittle nodded and was about to respond when the three allies were announced by Wenrynt, appearing inside the tent with a flourish. There was no disputing the belief that Wenrynt was enjoying the fact that he was the first to acknowledge Quittle as King. It gave him a privileged position, one that he was keen to use to his benefit.

Quittle stood as the three men entered and beckoned for them to take refreshment, gratefully received by the trio. He wondered, briefly, how he was going to approach the situation and decided that it was best to speak from the heart and be honest. He owed these men, particularly Grim and Nek, more than he wished to acknowledge. If he treated them with any sign of disrespect or dishonesty then it wouldn't sit right with him, for he liked to think of them as friends.

"Gentlemen," he said once they had settled and look on him expectantly, "I suspect you already know why you are here." Nek, he could see, was nodding slowly whilst the other two looked on quietly. He felt as if he were on trial and his emotions were taught.

"I'll be honest with you. You three have done more for Traemwen than I had any right to ask. You have laid your bodies on the line for the kingdom time and time again. You have fought battles with us, broken bread with us and drank with us. You have become friends, and I mean that truly. You may not have come here expecting to become friends, believing this to be just another duty or series of orders to follow, but I hope you think of us as friends as well." He paused, drawing breath as launched into the meat of the matter.

"However, it is time for you to return home. We go now to fight the Emperor, to finally drive him from our lands and forever regain our independence. I intend no disrespect to you gentlemen, but if you were to support me in this then the Empire will put out that we couldn't regain our independence by ourselves. They will say we relied upon foreign support. I cannot allow that, no matter how much it pains me to do this.

"Your support has been invaluable, and I don't think we would have won today without you." He saw they were still silent, studying him almost, and he felt an awkwardness that he hadn't felt in a long time. "Ask of me what you will gentlemen, and, if it's within my power, then I'll grant it to you." There was silence within the tent as they continued to look at him. Grim looked at Tortag and saw that the man was obviously in two minds about it, knowing that Attainian support had proven vital in this battle. Grim could also see the logic of Quittle's argument and, though he tried not to show it, his heart soared at the prospect of finally going home after so many months away.

"Well, we've had a bit of an adventure," said Nek as he broke the uncomfortable silence with a quip and an easy smile. He too, he knew, was split in two minds. On the one hand he felt anger at being dismissed in so easy a fashion after all they had done, but on the other he was glad to be away. The butchery and barbarity that the Traemwenians had displayed over the course of the last two battles had shook him to the core; knowing what they could inflict upon one another had not endeared them to him. It saddened him slightly for he had grown genuinely close to some of them, finding within those he considered friends kindred spirits. There was a roguish quality to them, a never-say-die attitude that he shared and a thirst for life.

"Are you completely sure about this, sir?" Aarlin asked. His orders had been simple; support the Traemwenians until they no longer required it. He hadn't spent much time with them and, ultimately, felt no great attachment to them. There also existed old prejudices between the two nations and he could clearly see the logic within the argument that Quittle made; the Emperor would claim, if he were beaten by a combined force, that Quittle only held the throne as long as the Attainians allowed it. No King could sit on so precarious a position.

"I am, Admiral, though you and your men will always be welcome here," he paused as he took a drink of water before carrying on. "The Attainians and Traemwen may not have enjoyed the best of the relations in the past, but that is the past. Today has marked a new beginning in our relations. If you will, I would ask you to return to your Senate and tell them that they have a friend in me. I will continue to support their war against the Emperor and his men until they have been driven from our lands."

Aarlin nodded satisfied that he had achieved his ultimate aim. Nek looked on feeling a mixture of emotions, more conflicted that he thought he would feel.

"What are your plans now, Bear?" Nek asked, somewhat ill at ease with being dismissed so easily.

"We march west in three days' time," he answered honestly. "I'll be appearing in front of the prisoners tomorrow morning after you depart south and I will attempt to persuade most of them to fight for the independence of this Kingdom."

Nek nodded but didn't feel any less awkward. Grim stood up and looked the King in the eye, eventually moving to him with a hand outstretched. Quittle took it with a firm grasp and a smile on his face.

"Well, Quittle, I'm not going to say it was easy and I'm not going to say it was fun, but you've made a friend in me. If anybody wants to listen to me in Cardavy or Silveroak, I'll tell them you're alright." Quittle grinned in reply and felt himself relax a little as Grim moved onto Tortag to make his goodbyes. Nek followed on and did the same, still a little unsure of what had happened, but happy enough to be going home.

Chapter Twenty-Three – **Honeymoon**

They had been royally received within the capital, crowds turning out to look upon the newcomers. There had not been a Cardavian presence in Ufwala before and the cavalry escort protecting the General and his wife attracted a lot of attention, most of it positive. The journey south had been without incident contrary to what Beran had expected. He had been constantly on the lookout, half expecting renegade legionaries to come bursting from the undergrowth or the forests they passed through. Messages from the Wolves had also confirmed the quietness of the frontier, that no trouble had been seen or was expected. Indeed, the only news that Velawin thought he ought to know was that there would be a tournament arranged by Aglon a week after they arrived home between the Leviathans and the Wolves, something that had generated a huge amount of excitement.

They had been staying in the embassy, the best rooms assigned to them by the diplomat Garren who was more than happy to finally speak to people from his own country. It appeared the man was a complete master on the topic of Ufwala and their young Queen. He described her as a rare beauty, commanding an intellect and foresight that many elder statesmen could only dream of possessing. He had struck Beran as someone who had fallen irrevocably in love with her, almost to the point of hero worship. He had described in great detail her command of the battle, or slaughter depending whom you listened to, outside the city walls of Vitrossy. However, the point that struck him as particularly sinister was the finding of large amounts of black powder.

"Is the Queen in league with the Imps then?" He asked with a hint of suspicion. Garren looked aghast at such a prospect, though he was enough to admit that he had once entertained such a thought.

"No, General. The Queen seized the powder when she took Vitrossy from Jaca. He was the one who was being supplied by the Rupinians in order to carry out their proxy war."

"I can understand that, but surely he could have used this black powder to defend his city from being taken?"

"Maybe he didn't know how to use it," Garren said with a slight chuckle. Beran remained unconvinced but allowed the man to continue his lecture on the lay of the land within the Kingdom. It appeared that the Queen had been true to her word and promise, that she would use her trade power and newly one position of High Queen to bestow benefits upon the nation as a whole. New roads were apparently being built to speed up internal trade and communication, new hospitals and schools were being built to care for the physical and mental needs of the people. In all, Beran concluded, the

Queen was proving herself to be a wise and capable ruler.

"You mentioned something about a man named Morro?" He had asked. Garren nodded with a smile and looked into the fire as he pictured the stocky, grey haired statesman.

"He's a good man, a confidant of the Queen and a wise counsel. He used to be in the army and has been instrumental in solidifying the position of Wellisa."

"A man to be trusted?" Garren looked aghast at the accusation.

"General Corus, in fact, may I call you Beran?" Beran nodded in his head in acquiescence. "Beran, you are a first rate officer and a war hero, but please don't look upon everyone as a potential enemy." He smiled as he tried to take the sting out of his words, not wishing them to come across as an admonishment.

"That is true, Garren, but my question stands. How does Morro feel about Cardavy?" Beran was not a man to be detracted from his questions, nor was he one to take something at face value. Although he respected the position that Garren held, he had learned long ago not to trust someone until he had spent a small amount of time with them. He had seen in Nepriner how people who spoke with silver tongues could quickly turn, remembering with alacrity the fight he had in an alleyway with a merchant who wanted to give the city over to the Empire through treachery.

"He once spied upon us when he was in the army," Garren admitted, "but I've always found him to be a staunch ally and a tempering force when it comes to the Queen."

"How do you mean?" Beran asked, "I thought you said the Queen was wise beyond her years?"

"She is in a lot of matters, but she can sometimes let her heart rule over her head." It was becoming obvious to Beran that Garren was beginning to feel slightly uncomfortable with the line of questioning and thus he changed tack, moving onto less controversial topics. The conversation was the sort of inane topics that people spoke of in order to avoid things that could lead to argument, and Garren had no wish to purposefully annoy the diplomat.

"You will, of course, be attending the ball being held by the Queen?" Garren had asked hopefully. Beran smiled but expected it came out as more of a grimace as he nodded.

"Yes, my wife has been talking about nothing else. I think she is more excited about it than I am. Will there be a certain order to the proceedings?" He couldn't think of anything worse, knowing fine well that he would be expected to talk to all and sundry, doubtless reciting tales of the defence of Nepriner and how he found the country and its people.

"No, Beran, it's a fairly standard affair. There will be a small reception held for the guests as they arrive and then everyone will be invited into the main hall, the Queen will arrive and everyone will be seated to eat. No doubt afterwards there will be a short speech followed by some dancing and socialising." He paused, smiling, remembering the last such occasion held in the grand hall.

"I take it by your expression you aren't looking forward to it?" Beran hadn't realised his face was quite as honest and mentally cursed before flashing a smile.

"Not all, my friend, I'm just wondering if I can learn how to dance before I'm expected to perform!"

"I can't believe you persuaded me to not come in armour," Beran complained with a slight smile as he watched the servers move amongst the tables with a practiced ease. Talice smiled at him and lightly patted his hand as if chiding, the candle light sparkling off the fine array of diamonds and other precious stones she wore around her slim neck.

"It wouldn't have been politic if you did, darling. You are probably the first Cardavian officer that has ever been entertained here. Make the most of it," she smiled in thanks as a light salad was served as an appetiser. Another server brought a fresh bottle of white wine and poured her a small glass. Beran looked at her, noting the joy light up her eyes and face and knew that she was right. Who was he to complain about wearing a tunic and formal wear when it brought Talice a degree of happiness and joy?

"Well," interjected Aleill who was sitting at the same round table, "not quite the first. I daresay when they tell stories of today that I was the first. I am the better looking after all, and quite the wit."

"I'd say you were a twit rather than a wit," Beran responded with a smile. They were seated close to the royal table, close enough for Beran to see the Queen and her close confidants. It said a lot that Garren wasn't seated with them, instead sitting behind the royal table and exchanging pleasantries with another man.

"That's Roac, he's the Attainian ambassador," remarked Talice as she saw him looking. Beran nodded and turned back to look upon her, aware that several people were watching them in turn. It was, he decided, an odd situation and one that he didn't feel comfortable with.

"I take it you know him?" He asked as he finished off the last of the starter. Talice nodded as servants began to take away empty plates.

"He is a Senator, I knew of him in the capital long ago and I was very young. My father probably knows him better though. It's strange how he is still down here though, I would have thought he'd have been recalled now to re-join the senate."

Beran nodded and noticed Aleill was about to make a comment, but he shook his head in warning. They weren't the only people sitting at their table and he didn't know the other three that well, though the fact that they were apparently well connected Cardavian merchants apparently meant they were ideal dinner companions.

The main course of light meats and vegetables followed along with the talk and chatter that Beran had been dreading. The merchants were only too keen to interrogate him at great length about the siege of Nepriner and the exploits that happened during the battle. He had tried to deflect their talk, asking them about their own lives and what they traded in, but all the time the conversation turned back to the military operations of the Wolves.

Aleill picked up on it and studied the man to his right between mouthfuls of food, a questioning look upon his face.

"Have I met you before, sir?" He asked after a while, his brow furrowed in confusion. The man shook his head, unsure, before chuckling.

"I don't believe so, sir, unless we have passed each other in the capital?" Aleill was about to question the man further, believing the occasion to be far more recent, but the merchant launched into a speech of great length about how he missed Silveroak and all the delights it could offer. Beran looked to Aleill whilst the man was talking and noted the suspicion on his friends face, knowing that if Aleill was ill at ease that something was wrong.

Once the dessert had been taken away, conversation was allowed to flow freely between the various occupants of all the tables. The main hall filled with noise rather than the clinking of a hundred or so knives and forks on fine plates. The candles were replaced when they needed to be replaced and drink was constantly refilled. The fires were built up when they appeared to be burning low, and Beran found himself beginning to enjoy the occasion. Talice was relaxed as she spoke quietly with a few of the merchants, talking about Attainia and her family with an understated pride. She was in her element and looking more beautiful than ever, Beran thought.

Eventually there was a tinkling of glass as a stocky man with grey beard and hair stood up. Conversation slowly came to a halt as men looked to the royal table. He was unassuming looking, but obviously commanded a great deal of respect.

"I take it that is Morro?" Aleill asked.

"I assume so," Beran answered in reply. The man looked around the room, comfortable in addressing so many people and accustomed to making speeches.

"My Lords, ladies and gentlemen. Honoured guests," he said with a nod towards the Cardavians sitting together, "I wish to thank you all for attending. It brings me great pleasure to introduce to the realm our new allies and friends. I am sure these honoured guests require no introduction, however. General Beran Corus of the Grey Wolves legion is a welcome guest of Queen Wellisa and, along with his lieutenant and his wife, are more than welcome to consider Ufwala and the south their second home. "The Queen has laid on a band to play music for our entertainment and, after her own dance with a guest of her choosing, she invites you all to join in and enjoy yourselves. Tonight, the drink will flow and the food will be plentiful." The band began to play quietly, though Beran wasn't sure whether they were tuning and warming up their instruments or launching into full song. The Queen stood to polite applause, looking resplendent in a shimmering grey dress. He felt his stomach tighten, almost seeing the ambush happen in his mind's eye before it did. She looked upon their table and met his eye, smiling slightly.

"General Corus," she said in the common tongue with the merest hint of an accent, "would you do me the honour of a dance?" He smiled as gallantly as he could, standing as he did so at something halfway between attention and at ease. Even after the triumphal procession through Silveroak he wasn't sure how one was supposed to speak to royalty. Mistaking his hesitation for nerves, she smiled and chuckled. "That is, of course, if the Lady Talice doesn't mind?"

Beran looked down to his wife, noticing her acquiesce with the slightest nod of her head. Talice may not have been a Queen, but she had the dignity of one. As a young woman from a Republic she also had pride and the idea of a Queen seeking to dance with her husband had touched upon an innate nerve.

"Good," said the Queen with a smile showing off her pearly white teeth. Beran, outmanoeuvred once again when it came to affairs of diplomatic state, made a perfunctory bow and moved to the centre of the floor. The Queen seemed to glide towards him, her eyes fixed upon his, as her smile grew. She outstretched her hand and he bowed once again and brushed her hand with his lips, something that Aleill had reassured him was something that was expected. He reached out and lightly clasped her hand and they led off in dance, the band taking up a soft tune that didn't demand too much in the way of physical exertion.

"It is a pleasure to finally meet you, General Corus," she said with a smile as they danced. He had the feeling as he led that she was only allowing him to do so. It occurred to him that the Queen was not one to play second to anyone. Perhaps she thought she was bestowing an honour upon him by allowing him to lead in a dance?

"My friends have taken to calling me Ban, ma'am." He said without trying to sound gruff or on edge. She smiled in an effort to put him at ease. "And you must call me Wellisa. Ma'am makes me sound like someone significantly older than I am!" She chuckled softly, a lilting sound and one full of humour. He had to concede that she was a beauty, perhaps not in the same way he thought that Talice was beautiful, but there was a quality to her that enabled him to feel at ease.

"Wellisa it is then."

"How are you and your wife finding the city?" He noticed that she was imperceptibly beginning to lead, an almost natural state of affairs that he welcomed. He was not the most natural of dancers and had never really taken to it, preferring to enjoy music from the side-lines rather than make a fool of himself upon the floor. He noticed too that other dancers were beginning to take to the floor, Talice being escorted up by Morro.

"We are enjoying it; the people have been extraordinarily friendly." He said it with real feeling. He had enjoyed seeing the different architecture and the different customs that the country, and city, offered. It was a foreign land and therefore a new experience for him, something that he enjoyed finding out about. He fully intended to find out more about the history of the city and Ufwala by going to one or two of the museums the next morning.

"Good, though I suspect your escort ensured they remained friendly," she said with a chuckle. He felt himself redden a little and was about to excuse it, but she shook her head causing a blond lock of hair to fall upon her shoulder. "I tease, Ban, don't worry. You are more than entitled to bring your own men with you. I trust they have found decent quarters?"

"Our ambassador, Garren, was able to find them space within our embassy."

"He is a resourceful man, and a good friend. I remember when I first met him; we were discussing the coming siege of Nepriner and the Imperial invasion. I liked him then. He fought your corner well," she said as she cast a look towards the table where he sat. Beran noticed that the man was staring intently at them with, perhaps, a spark of jealousy showing upon his features.

"You have done well since then, if you don't mind me saying. You have made Ufwala into the greatest power within the old coalition. I commend you on that," he said watching Garren a little more. The chances were he was right in his first assessment, he thought, the diplomat was a little in love with the Queen.

"Thank you, Ban, it is kind of you to say so." The dance was slowly coming to an end, the music beginning to drift slightly as the band began to finish. "I trust you and your wife will join me at my table at some point in the evening?"

"We would be honoured," he said finding himself with a genuine smile on his face. He found himself at ease in the presence of the Queen, though no doubt the drink he had consumed and the natural beauty of the lady had worked its own magic upon him. She looked back to his own table and noticed Aleill sitting by himself, the merchants having disappeared.

"Who is that man?" She asked, a hint of curiosity in her voice.

"Aleill. He is a commander of the archers within my legion. A good man, but no toady or sycophant I'm afraid. He's well-mannered and house trained though," he said with a grin. Wellisa laughed, a rich sound full of joy as the song came to an end.

"Well, I must meet this man. Is he, perhaps, a bit of a rogue?" It was the turn of Beran to grin as he imagined how Aleill would take such a title.

"Perhaps a little, Wellisa, perhaps a little. Should I invite him up?"

"No…no," she said with a little smile, "if he is a proper rogue then he shall come and ask me. But, and consider this a royal command, General," she said with mock severity, "do not let on that I am interested."

"As you command, I obey," he said with a flourish. He had obviously drunk more than he had cared to realise, or perhaps the food hadn't been enough to line his stomach. She smiled and let go of his hands and he withdrew his arm from around her waist as they politely clapped the band. They were about to depart the floor when Aleill strode up, brazen as anything, and snapped to attention in front of the Queen with a slight bow. Beran raised an eyebrow and suppressed a chuckle.

"Would you like a dance, your highness?" Aleill asked with a smile playing upon his lips.

"Why, Ban, you were right. He is a rogue," she said chuckling. The band were beginning to play another tune and Beran made his escape, thanking the Queen for the dance as he sought out Talice within the dancing crowd. He found her eventually making her way back to the table and made to join her.

He felt a rumbling in the ground, dust shaking from the rafters above. He felt a chill run down his spine as another rumble rattled through the hall. The ground erupted in a tremendous explosion, the sheer force of it blowing him from his feet causing him to strike his head on a pillar. Dazed, he looked around and saw the podium where the Queen had been sitting completely destroyed. A second explosion ripped through the hall followed quickly by a third and fourth, sheets of glass falling from the broken windows.

The rafters began to collapse, parts of the roof falling onto the dance floor spearing some of the couples as they scrambled for cover. A chandelier carrying candles came crashing to the ground destroying the band who had been sitting beneath. Screams punctuated the explosions, a small fire beginning to take effect on a fine tapestry. The smoke added to the chaos and Beran felt blood trickling from his head wound.

269

He reached up and felt his skull, wincing as his hand found the gash. Suddenly he froze, real and unmistakable terror taking hold of him as he remembered Talice. He stood up and nearly fainted, the blood rushing to his head. He steadied himself as another explosion ripped through the hall, the smoke and the noise of screaming and dying people threatening to overwhelm his senses. He sniffed the air as he tried to draw in air and smelt the unmistakable scent of black powder.

"Talice!" He shouted, frantically moving and pushing people out of the way as he made his way to where he had last seen her. "Talice!"

"Ban!" He heard her voice, weaker than normal, and panic welled in his breast. She shouted his name again and he went in the direction praying to anybody who was listening that she was safe, hiding underneath a table and protecting herself.

He found her buried under masonry and the remnant of a rafter, blood seeping from a cut on her temple.

"It hurts, Ban, and I can't feel my legs." Panic gave him strength as he wrenched the rafter off her, launching it away from them.

"It'll be fine, Tal, you'll be fine." He didn't know who he was trying to reassure, her or himself, but all she could do was look up at him with a faint smile.

"Is Aleill okay?" She asked, her voice growing fainter. He removed the rubble from her and saw that her right leg was broken. He was about to move her when he saw a large shard of glass sticking through her side.

"I don't know. Talice, hold on, I'm going to remove this glass." He began to slowly pull the glass away from her side but she cried out in pain, her tears welling with the hurt as she looked up at him. She coughed and winced horribly, her face mirroring the pain that she obviously felt. More worryingly, when she coughed some blood appeared on her cheek. "Talice, I'm going to have to open your dress to check your wounds."

"That is the worst line you've ever said to see my breasts, Ban," she said with a faint smile. She shut her eyes and didn't open them for a few seconds.

"Just stay awake, Tal, stay bloody awake and that's an order!" He couldn't think of what to say, slowly unbuttoning the right side of her dress. He exposed her midriff and saw the dark bruising where fallen masonry had broken her ribs, one of which had pierced her lungs. He looked down upon her and knew that she was dying and he felt his eyes welling up with tears.

"Don't cry, Ban," she said as she reached up and stroked his cheek. He couldn't help it, large tears falling from his eyes as he looked down upon the love of his life slowly slipping away from him. "You made the happiest woman in the world when I found you in that tavern."

"Don't you dare speak like that, Tal! Don't you bloody dare! I'm going to get you out of here, and we're going to go home, and..."

"Your eyes always tell the truth, Ban," she said sadly. "I love you. I always have ever since we first met. The months and years we've had together have been the best of my life." She winced as another wave of pain swept through her and gritted her eyes against the pain.

"I love you, Talice." She didn't respond and he reached for her hand, limp to the touch and unresponsive. He turned over her wrist and felt for a pulse, but felt none. She was gone. He knelt over her body and hugged her close, deep sobs wracking through his body as he held his wife close to him for one last time.

He didn't notice the soldiers running into the hall, nor did he notice the Queen being carried off bodily by her guard as they rushed her to a physician. For him, the world had come to a crashing and sudden halt that night.

He felt a hand touch his shoulder and he looked up into the bloodied face of Aleill, his eye swollen shut and blood seeping from a wound on his scalp and another on his leg. He didn't say anything, words failing him as he looked down upon a woman who had once been full of life and dreams. He knelt down and felt her neck for a pulse, hoping that Beran was over reacting. But she was truly gone, ripped away from the world.

"Ban, I'm so sorry," he whispered. He couldn't know the pain his friend felt, but he mourned with him. He loved Talice in his own way, picturing again the tongue lashing that he had received from her on numerous occasions. She had been one of the few people that he had truly allowed to see his true self, feeling safe and secure with her knowing that she wouldn't mock.

"Ban, you need to see a doctor."

"I'm not leaving her," he answered. "You go, but I'm staying with her. When you can, find out what is happening. I want to make sure some bastard suffers for this."

Epilogue

Thirty-six men and women, some of the greatest of the Ufwalan realm, died in the hall during the explosions. Word quickly spread that the Queen had been mortally wounded, close to death, an accusation which Morro quickly tried to debunk lest it throw the realm into chaos. Just as suddenly as that rumour disappeared, others began questioning who could have carried out such an assassination attempt. Suspicions initially fell upon those in the south, those who hadn't sworn loyalty to Wellisa and her new Kingdom, whilst others rightly pointed out that several Cardavians had been seen leaving the hall prior to the explosion. Had not the two Cardavian officers survived, one of whom had danced with the Queen whilst the other kept her on the floor dancing just prior to the explosions? Yes, the senior one's wife had died as well as the Cardavian and Attainian diplomats, but were they acceptable collateral damage?

Beran and Aleill were put in chains, arrested under the charge of attempted regicide under the order of King Jaca of Molenbeek, and were taken to the city of Vitrossy.

In the north, Quittle and Tortag began their march west. Quittle had managed to persuade a large number of the prisoners to join his banners, his army growing to fifteen thousand men. More continued to flood to the flags, sure now in declaring loyalty to his cause now that nobody was left to oppose or topple him within the realm. They would link with Alfdarr and face the Emperor in open battle, once and for all expelling them from the land.

In Gephy, Grim and Nek were happy to be making preparations to go home whilst Aarlin prepared to finally retire and embark upon his long planned for expedition to the fabled eastern continent.

The War of the Broken Crowns was about to begin.

THE END

Printed in Great Britain
by Amazon

17479616R00157